WHERE DARKNESS DWELLS

Glen R. Krisch

DEDICATION

For Owen, my time lost reflection.

PROLOGUE

Knowing he wouldn't comprehend the weight of her words, Greta spoke to her son. "People I love are going to suffer."

Kneeling near the kitchen table, Arlen worked a mound of clay against the wooden floor. His face taut with concentration, he rolled the gray slab into thin bands. He pulled off smaller pieces and worked these as well, setting aside finished pieces to a larger whole.

She wanted him to do more than just hear her voice; she wanted him to understand. She was desperate to share her burden. But it was her burden and hers alone to bear. Involving others would ruin any prospect of ending decades of pain and the degradation of human life. If people had to die to reach this end, it had to play out through its natural course. Otherwise, nothing would change.

So she voiced her worries to the only person she could.

"Mama, we still gonna be together?" Arlen asked. He looked up from the floor where his claywork took shape. Her son was no longer a boy. He hadn't been a boy in so long, yet he still had a child's mind. His tangled beard was graying, his scraggly pate thinning. While he lived with childlike exuberance, time weighed on her heavily, slowing her movements and shrinking her bones. She was an old woman, near her end.

Innocence shined in Arlen's eyes. He minded adults and would never purposely cause anyone grief. He had such a kind soul. Given the choice, she wouldn't want him to change. She wouldn't risk losing who he was for anything.

"We'll always be together," she answered him. "I will always be in your heart."

Soothed by her words, his mind flitted to other matters. He picked up a small gray blob and rolled it in his palm. "I miss picking with the others. I don't mind my gopher hole, but it ain't the same as the old mine."

Arlen had worked for years as a pile sorter for the Grendal Coal Company. Picking coal was a job fit for a child, sitting atop a tipple pile all day, sorting valuable ore from the waste rock. When the company left Coal Hollow seven years ago, Arlen was twenty years older than the other pile sorters. They'd given him the job, aware he could never advance beyond it.

"You're doing a good thing for your mom, digging that gopher hole."

Arlen grinned. The best part of his smile was an aged, yellow ivory. The rest, empty gaps and decay

It had been Arlen's idea to open the gopher hole at their property's edge overlooking Tipple Road. Townsfolk stopped off the main north-south road through Coal Hollow to buy coal Arlen had dug from the shallow mine. High-grade ore ran in thin, twisting veins just below the topsoil--all he had to do was scratch the surface. People would procure enough fuel to warm their homes, allowing Arlen to help support his mom. There were other places to buy fuel--stores and other gopher holes aplenty--but people went out of their way to buy from Arlen.

He pieced together the finished pieces of clay, realizing the image from his muse.

She could tell his thoughts were skittering off to the starry skyscape of his mind. She continued: "I could point to certain people on the streets of Coal Hollow, say, 'You will be dead by the first frost.'"

Arlen looked up from his claywork, staring out the window as the moon rose above the trees, a beacon cutting softly through the nighttime sky.

"But it has to be. Has to be, or nothing will change."

Arlen smiled. Her voice had always soothed him.

"Sometimes death leads to life. Sometimes there's a greater good." She thought back to the visit from the two boys earlier today. They'd come to her, as all the town's children did at one point or another, to hear her stories. Looking those boys in the eye, she told her tales, setting them on the path to their end. "Until the day I die, I will damn my ancestors for cursing me with this supposed gift."

Arlen scooped up his artwork, offering it to her.

She held the gift in shaking hands. A gray flower more delicate than the clay of its origin. Finely articulated petals, a thin, twisting stem. Beauty rendered from a slab of shapeless gray earth.

She smiled. It was all the thanks Arlen needed, all the approval he so desperately sought. He looked away, staring again at the rising moon.

No, she would never wish her son to be different, to be normal. To be whole. He was more than the sum of his parts, more than whole. And he was a better person than her. Better than those who came before her.

PART ONE

ONE

July 8, 1934

George Banyon climbed into bed, shucking his blanket to the floor. He was exhausted from rising at dawn and hastily working through his chores around the farm, from meeting up with his friends later on, and as the sun set, attempting to impress Betty Harris by swinging from a tattered rope into the Illinois River's murky water. Just one day in what seemed like an endless string, but regrettably, it would soon end. Soon he would have to behave like a man. After all, a month shy of seventeen, he would be graduating the following spring.

On the cusp of sleep moments after hitting the pillow, a tapping at the window nudged him fully awake.

He sat up, sluggish sweat dripping from his sunburned skin. He looked across the darkened one-room farmhouse to Ellie's bed. His younger sister hadn't stirred. It amazed George that she could sleep so soundly with a blanket tucked over her shoulder. Their father, sitting in his handmade rocker, had passed out hours ago.

George swung his legs to the floor and stood, hoping the floorboards wouldn't reveal his late night creeping. He knew who was tapping and so he took his time. Jimmy Fowler, his best friend since either boy could walk. Whenever anything caught Jimmy's interest long enough that he couldn't keep it to himself until morning, he would come tapping on George's window. But right now all George wanted was to stop sweating, and to fall into a deep and welcomed sleep. He went to the open window, not a hint of breeze to bring a moment's relief, and saw Jimmy's scruffy blond head. His blue eyes caught the moonlight and revealed his excitement, which he gave off like a pig's stinking breath.

"Get your fishing tackle," Jimmy whispered.

"Are you nuts? I got to get up at five a.m."

"Forget your chores. Won't matter after tonight."

"You still thinking about old Greta's story?"

"I say we find out if it's true or not. If it's all made up, all we lose is some sleep, but if we *do* track down the beast…"

"Come on, Jimmy. I'm tired."

"Just think what Betty Harris will think when we catch 'em."

George's heart fluttered. He tried not to show it. He'd had trouble speaking to Betty ever since the sixth grade, when he discovered she was the most beautiful girl he'd ever seen. But something had changed since school let out this summer. Her friends became friendly with his, mostly because Jimmy's girl, Louise Bradshaw, was friends with Betty.

"You really think Betty would be impressed?"

"Sure she would. Maybe she'd even let you take her to a movie."

George started planning a first date with Betty. Borrowing a car, getting gas to drive to Peoria, ticking off a list of stuff to talk about during the drive. He pushed it all aside, not wanting the dizzying possibility of being alone with Betty to muddle his thoughts.

He would sneak out with Jimmy. He knew it as soon as Jimmy mentioned her name. George sighed in defeat. "Let me get my things." He looked at Ellie to make sure she was still asleep.

Then, as quietly as possible, George gathered a lantern, his fishing pole and tackle, and a stale hunk of bread for bait. He lowered everything down through the window to Jimmy.

"You won't regret this."

"Even if we *do* catch it, I bet we'll wish we hadn't." He looked in on his meager house. His little sister, who was for the most part more joy than trouble, and then his dad, who would be out for a good while yet and wouldn't notice a thing. George's stomach soured as he headed out the window.

Jimmy stopped him with a raised hand. "I got an idea."

"I hate when you say that."

"How about we bring along your dad's gun?"

"You really want me to get a whooping, don't you?"

"I see him over there in his rocker. He won't miss it a second."

George was about to ask why he thought it necessary to haul around such a weapon on a late night fishing trip. But he already knew the answer.

"Shit." His dad's cherished over/under was a true killing machine, twin shotgun barrels mounted over a still-deadly .30 chamber. "Fine.

But he'll notice it's gone before he sees my bed's empty."

Hearing multiple meanings in his own words, he grabbed the gun from the rack on the nearby wall.

Of all their possessions, only the gun seemed to shine. Everything else was worn and tired. The years since The Crash had been rough on everyone, but around the Banyon place, it'd been a sorry sight long before '29, since their mom died giving birth to Ellie, and their father's heavy drinking became commonplace. Yeah, things had been rough, much worse than he let on, even to his best friend, Jimmy Fowler. George held the gun protectively as he climbed out the window.

Despite the lantern, George couldn't see his feet let alone anything up ahead. Greta Hildaberg had said they'd find the cavern's hidden entryway after passing the untended acreage a mile outside Coal Hollow. Just over the last ripple of the last hillock, George could remember her saying. Before the land turned rocky and no longer tillable, through dense brambles and tangled cockleburs. While all of Coal Hollow's children listened to Greta's stories, most everyone thought that was all they were. Stories. But Jimmy, crazy Jimmy Fowler--if they weren't best friends and he didn't look up to him so much, George'd still be in bed.

Jimmy gained some ground on him, snapping twigs and cussing at the tearing undergrowth. As George's mind drifted to his morning chores--making Ellie's breakfast, making sure she brushed her teeth, and the cord of wood needing splitting--the sounds ahead disappeared. George suddenly felt alone, as if a rift in the earth had opened up and swallowed Jimmy, leaving him in the middle of God knows, not knowing the way home from his own elbow. He quickened his pace, still mindful of the grasping branches, the twisting roots.

When he broke through an opening in the undergrowth, he found Jimmy's legs kicking out behind him, his top half buried in the ground. If George weren't so scared, he would've found the discovery quite comical, but right now humor was the last thing on his mind. He ran to Jimmy, grabbed his thrashing feet, and pulled hard.

"What the hell are you doing?" Jimmy cried out as he tumbled free from the hole.

George let go, embarrassed. "Your legs were shaking. I thought you were in some kind of trouble." *Thought something dragged you off*, George wanted to say, but held his tongue.

Field grass filled the entryway as Jimmy stood. If George hadn't watched Jimmy pull free from the hole, he wouldn't have given the grassy berm a second look.

"I think this is it." Even in the dark, George could see his beaming smile.

"That hole there?"

"It opens up after a few feet. I tossed a rock down a ways, and it just kept going. Sounds pretty deep."

"Are we going in?" George asked, his confidence fleeting with the passing seconds. He hoped Jimmy would change his mind. Not even thinking about impressing Betty Harris lent him any courage.

"Of course we are. We've got a legend to slay. We'll be heroes."

"Right. Heroes. The two of us."

White Bane. The words prickled George's spine. A two hundred pound albino catfish trolling a vast underground lake. The lake was real enough. It had given the local miners constant fits before the Grendal Coal Company pulled stakes. Decades ago, George's distant cousin died in a flooded shaft. A handful of miners drowned when an ill-placed TNT bundle breached the wall of the underground lake. The men died a half mile down, no one near enough to hear their all-too-brief screams.

Greta would speak about White Bane in her quiet, raspy voice, warning about a beast that ate children who went wandering where they shouldn't. As old as the hills, the catfish had long white whiskers and pink, unwavering eyes. White Bane could smell fear, would be brought to frenzy by it, leaping ashore to snatch at children with its jaws, or whip them with its powerful tail. Either way, the result was the same. You weren't going home.

George was about to put his foot down by suggesting they wait until it was light out to take on this particular adventure. But crazy Jimmy Fowler had already thrown his tackle inside and was shimmying into the mouth of the hole. His torso disappeared, then his legs. With a grunt, Jimmy kicked off with his heel against a jutting rock, then was gone.

"Hand me your tackle." Jimmy's filthy hand snaked from the hole, his fingers grasping for George's tackle box.

"Sure, hold on." George lowered his fishing tackle to Jimmy's waiting hand.

"How about the gun?"

"I think I'll hold on to it." They both owned .22 rifles, having hunted small game since they could remember. But the over/under was a special weapon. It could do a heck of a lot more damage than any old .22. If he was going to get a whooping for taking the gun, then he was sure as hell going to carry it the whole time. His dad had been drinking for a week straight and wouldn't even notice he had snuck out, but if he did wake up to see his precious gun missing...

"Fine." Jimmy's hand disappeared, mild disappointment in his voice. "Coming?"

"Right behind you." George strained getting inside while carrying the gun and the lantern. Crawling through the opening, he left behind the night's gloaming, entering an entirely different darkness. As his legs entered the hole, the damp, earthen walls felt like they were closing in to crush his body. He hurried forward, hand over hand, struggling with the gun in the narrow tunnel. Losing his balance, he fell over a ledge, tumbling down a short slope. After coming to an abrupt halt, he braced himself to stand, his hand pressing against Jimmy's shoe.

"That sure was graceful. You oughta be a ballerina."

"Shut up." George looked back through the tunnel to the nighttime sky. He couldn't see much when he was outside, but inside the cave, he was as near to blind as he'd ever want to be.

Their voices were different. As was the air. It was impenetrable, consuming quiet sounds, while amplifying anything louder than their hushed voices. Their breathing disappeared; their footsteps sounded like a Roman legion. George, certain he would soon scream draped in the darkness of the cave, turned the lantern's breathe valve until its glow washed over the far-reaching limestone walls. He took it as a good sign that the lantern survived the fall.

The lamp pushed back the darkness, but didn't reveal the entire cave. He swung the light in a small arc near his knees. Water had dripped away pockets in the yellowish rock, eating limestone layers one drip at a time. Everything was damp, seeping with wetness, shining with cave slime and mud.

They were quiet, shuffling their feet, trying to figure out what to do next. There seemed to be a zigzagging trail, just wide enough to walk down, winding away from the opening.

"We'll be out of fuel in no time with that lamp turned up." While Jimmy sounded angry, his face showed his relief.

"You want me to turn it down again?"

"I suppose not. Not since you got it lit and all."

Jimmy, hesitant for one of the few times George could remember, tentatively headed down the trail. "Smells wet. I bet the lake's not far away." Jimmy made sure George was close by and following.

Spider webs as broad as bed sheets blocked a niche off to the right. After seeing a spider's measured movements, George swung the lantern in front of him again. A chill swept over him as he hurried next to Jimmy.

"Looks like the walls are crying." Jimmy trailed a finger along the porous wall. Mineral deposits stained the trickling water a reddish hue. To George, it looked more like blood than tears.

"Dead end," George said after they had walked for a time. The area seemed to have suffered a cave in. Boulders and rubble sealed the shaft.

"Can't be." Jimmy, not willing to give up the adventure when it had only begun, hunted the shadows for another way. George stood right where he was without moving, not wanting to touch or see anything unsavory. At this point, he'd be happy enough just to turn around and go home.

"Hey, swing the light this way," Jimmy said.

On his knees at the apparent dead end, Jimmy craned his head under a teetering rock. Near the floor, concealed by tumbled-over debris, the cavern picked up again under the rubble, sloping at an even steeper grade into the earth.

"That doesn't look right." *Doesn't look one bit safe*, he thought.

"The shaft gets bigger." Jimmy's earlier reluctance had vanished. He once again bustled with excitement. "Listen... that water is louder. Sounds like a falls to me."

Jimmy had a point. It might not be a waterfall, but it sounded like a heavier flow than the trickle they'd seen so far. "All right. You first."

George crouched low, holding the lantern inside the opening, lighting the way as Jimmy crawled ahead. "Kinda slick. The floor's covered in moss. And it stinks like cowshit." Jimmy didn't seem fazed at all.

"Great. Can't wait." George followed his friend, followed him when he had a feeling he shouldn't. It was the story of their friendship.

The damp moss soaked their clothes. With the steepness of the shaft, it was a minor miracle they reached a plateau without slipping the whole way down. Once again on level ground, the limestone ceiling was high enough to stand without hunching. The shaft opened into an extensive alcove. The twisting path led them to a body of water with a surface so smooth and dark it could've been a pane of cobalt glass.

"Shit," George whispered, his breath stolen by the sight.

Water fell from high up near the ceiling--so high the lantern only hinted at the source--to a limestone spillway. The slab, as big as a church altar, dispersed the falling water. When it dribbled into the lake, it barely dimpled the surface.

"This has got to be it. Shit is right. Let's drop our lines." Jimmy approached the water and set down his tackle. He yanked the barbed hook from the pole's cork handle, and with the line already carrying a tied-off bobber, flipped his wrist and the bobber went flying.

"You haven't baited your hook." George approached the water with caution. While he didn't truly believe Greta's stories, it was better to be safe than sorry.

"I know. Just want to see how deep it is. You can tell by the sound when it hits the water." The hook and bobber had made a thick, thoomping splash. The water was deep. Cranking the reel to pull in the line, the metal gears sounded incredibly loud. "Get me some bread. I guess that'll have to do. Wish we'd had time to dig night crawlers."

George took the hunk of bread from his tackle box and broke off two pieces. They baited their hooks and cast their lines in opposite directions, not wanting to tangle in the near-dark.

They sat side by side, the lantern lit and warm between them. They had no luck for quite a while, and the more time went by without any sign of White Bane, the more George felt at ease. It was a foolish story, anyway. A catfish lunging from the water in order to prey on kids? Just an old story to make sure kids didn't explore the abandoned coalmines marring the Illinois prairie. He imagined every coal town had a similar tale.

"Don't matter if we catch him, I'm going to ask out Betty Harris regardless." George didn't take his eyes from his line. He dipped the pole, dancing the bobber on the cold black surface. His voice softened, becoming sheepish, "Then I'm going to marry her. Well, some day."

"Good for you. She's a nice girl. Tits are a little big, more like a cow's than a girl's, but hey, whatever you like you like, right?"

"Jackass."

"I'm just kidding. I'm happy for you. Just think about what you're doing before you do it," Jimmy said. The humor had left his voice. "That's all I gotta say."

"What's that supposed to mean?"

"Means I'm thinking about enlisting in the Army. My mom might have to sign something, but I'm strong for my size. They should take me, even though I ain't eighteen."

"What the hell're you getting at?" George was shocked, unable to figure out why someone would enlist. Especially someone whose dad had died not long after coming home from the European trenches, his lungs just about liquefied from mustard gas.

"I gotta be a man. Make a living for myself."

"That's not what we planned." Their plans went back many years. George would take over the farm from his dad and buy the vacant land next to their fallow plot. Jimmy would work his acreage with his brother, Jacob; together, with their mom, they'd make a go of it.

"Yeah. Things change." Jimmy stared at his fishing line. George hadn't bothered casting again after pulling in his line. This was serious news. What about picnics with their future wives and future kids? Sitting on the porch as old men, sipping hard cider and swapping familiar stories?

"What about Louise?"

Jimmy opened his mouth like he was about to say something, but then clamped it shut.

"Jimmy?"

"That's the problem. I think I might be a father soon."

"Christ... really?"

"Yeah," Jimmy said, staring at the water. Eyes widening, he pointed to something cutting through the water. "Shit, what's that?"

George jumped to his feet and reached for his tackle box, ready to tear tail out of there. Then the fish changed directions and he realized just how small it was. It might've been a bluegill, a crappie at most. Nothing dangerous. Neither fantastic nor mythical. "That's a pan fish, dingy."

"I knew that. Really I did." Jimmy sighed with relief. Both seemed to want the adventure of searching for White Bane, but nothing of the actual confrontation. "I thought you were going to push me in front of you, let that big, scary pan fish get me instead of you."

"I would have, too. Don't you doubt it for a second." They laughed.

George swung his tackle box around as he reached to pick up his pole again. In the process, he knocked the lantern over, sending it cracked and broken into the underground lake.

Instantly, they stood in utter darkness. Their breath hitched in their throats, otherwise, all they took in from their senses was the cold air.

"Damn, George, now what are we supposed to do? We're damn near a mile underground."

"It ain't near that far."

"Might as well be. We're blind."

Not knowing what else to say, but needing to hear his own voice, George said, "Maybe our eyes'll adjust."

"You got your matches, right?"

"Yeah, I think I've got a couple left. Let me check." George patted his pockets and found the smashed box. He slid it open, felt inside.

"Okay, don't panic," Jimmy said.

"I'm not. I still got three matches."

"I wasn't talking to you, just thinking out loud."

"Hell, just find something to burn. We can make a torch."

They hunted around on the floor, their hands encountering mud and flaked rock. Anything flammable would've quickly rotted and disintegrated in the damp atmosphere.

"How about in your tackle box?" Jimmy asked, his voice sounding far away.

"Didn't think of that. Let me check. How about you? Don't you have a comic with you when you fish?"

"Let me see... If I can find my box... Here we go. Tarzan might have to burn to get us out of here." Jimmy tore open his tackle box. Spoons and hooks rattled as he removed the top tray. Turning toward Jimmy's racket, George saw something, a glimmer, a phantom movement, *something*, in the distance hovering by the lake.

"Jimmy," George whispered.

"Damn. Nothing. I bet Jacob stole my last Tarzan. I'm gonna whip his ass when I get home."

"Jimmy!"

"What the hell are you yapping about?"

"I see something. At least, I think I do." George *did* see movement. A flickering light, maybe a reflection off the water, on the far side of the lake.

"Where?"

"Just the other side of the water."

"Can't see nothing... Wait... I think I know what you mean. A wavery light. It's dim."

They both edged to the shore, standing shoulder to shoulder, trying to pick up the slightest detail. It was so quiet the blood throbbed in George's ears as he strained to hear.

They nearly leapt from their skins as heavy chains rattled from somewhere near the phantom light.

Chains? George thought. "Shit. Let's get out of here."

"Wait, that could be someone. Give me a second." He stepped into the water. "Damn cold."

"What are you doing? You crazy?"

"Yeah, I think I just might be." Jimmy waded deeper. "There it is, found the drop off. It's maybe eight, ten feet in. Then it's deep as hell." His splashing increased as he dog-paddled away from shore. "It *is* a light, George. There's an overhang. Might be a tunnel or something. The light's down the other side."

"Come on now, Jimmy. We should find our way back the way we came."

"What fun is that? Someone must've lit that fire, so there must be someone to help us get the hell out'a here."

"Shit, Jimmy," George said, mostly to himself. Even trapped in darkness and without a light to guide their way, George couldn't stop thinking: *Jimmy Fowler's gonna be a dad. Who would've thought?* His friend risked everything swimming in water as cold as a witch's tit, and with White Bane possibly nipping just under his feet. "Jimmy?"

"Huh?"

"You all right?" Feeling abandoned, George wanted to leave Jimmy and find his way back out. But he couldn't leave his friend behind. And White Bane? Nothing but an old lady's story that no one believed in the first place. Or so he hoped.

"Sure. Little cold's all."

"Hold up, will you? I'm coming with."

"That's just what I wanted to hear."

George took the matchbox from his pocket and placed it atop his tackle box. His dad's gun leaned against a boulder nearby. He wanted to take it with him--there was no way he wanted to discover the firelight's source without it--but it would be useless if it got wet. He wasn't as good a swimmer as Jimmy. He'd never be able to swim with the gun held overhead. He left it behind, noting the location as he stepped into the water.

Jimmy treaded water, waiting. As George swam out to meet him, he noticed he could actually make out his face. The firelight from down the tunnel was brighter, but the ceiling was only foot above the water.

"See what I mean? There has to be people over there. Even if it's just hoboes."

"If we're going to go, let's go. I can't swim as good as you." George struggled to keep his head above water. His soaked clothes pulled at him as if he had rocks in his pockets. "Just be careful."

"Careful? I'm always careful." Jimmy's tone was full of glee, happy to continue the adventure. He reached overhead as he entered the tunnel. "Not much room to spare. There's no tide in an underground lake is there?"

"You're joking, right?"

"Do I ever joke around? I'm as serious as the Spanish flu." Jimmy laughed, venturing farther. "Hey, once inside you can stand. On tip-toes, I can reach the bottom."

"Thank God." With the water lapping at George's ears, he was relieved when his toes finally touched the tunnel bottom.

"Come on, hurry up," Jimmy called out as he pulled away from

George, unable to contain his excitement.

The icy water pressed against George's sternum as he trudged through the tunnel. Jimmy's wet head bobbed some twenty feet ahead. He reached the far end and cut a sharp right, out of sight.

It was just like Jimmy to leave him behind even though he was struggling. Sometimes he had no consideration at all. "Jimmy, wait up. I'm almost there." Violent shivers wracked his body. The ceiling pulled closer to the water, forcing George to weave around low points where rock and water touched.

Jimmy didn't answer. The light brightened, and George could see torches hanging from the far wall. He was panicking now. He couldn't turn around, but in no way wanted to know what was in that alcove. Why hadn't Jimmy said a word?

"*Jimmy?*"

He's gonna leap out and try to scare me. That jackass. George hoped that was the case. He could forgive Jimmy if his silence was a measly attempt to scare him.

The tunnel widened. Jimmy stood on the shore twenty feet away. His friend was scaring him, but not in the typical Jimmy Fowler kind of way. A man with long blond hair held a blade to his friend's throat. Others stepped from the shadows, brandishing weapons of their own. Five men, ten. A score. A couple faces seemed familiar. Coal Hollow people. Behind the gathering, a Negro man stood chained to a wall. A whip cracked, followed by an agonized cry that dissipated into weakening echoes.

"You be quiet, boy," a slurred voice called from the crowd. "Take what's yours."

The blade at Jimmy's throat gleamed with candlelight. Jimmy's eyes were desperate, wide, more scared than George had ever seen.

"Run, George, run!" Jimmy screamed. The man silenced him by smashing the butt of his knife against his temple.

George's heart rollicked. Ever-fading candlelight reflected off the tunnel's cobalt water.

"Get'em boys. Bring'em back alive. If you can."

Something splashed nearby, three men taking up his pursuit. Crazed men. Swinging machetes. Their faces rough with beard growth, stained with tobacco juice. They all looked the same. They could have been brothers, triplets, even.

Still groggy, Jimmy was shoved aside, swallowed by shadows. The whip cracked the air, and again. The chained man no longer screamed; he slumped over, unconscious, the chains tight against his wrists. The firecracker snap cleared George's senses, stripping the numbing coldness from his limbs.

He made a break for the tunnel.

He didn't attempt to walk on his tiptoes as he had on the way in. He took up a full swimming motion, his arms and legs awkwardly cutting through the cold water. He naturally swam faster underwater, so he dove, pushing off the tunnel floor with his feet. He kicked hard, madly, too fast to be efficient. His lungs burned seconds after his dive, and his mind flooded with half-formed thoughts:

Jimmy's dead. They're gonna kill 'im…

Louise, what do I tell Louise?

Who's gonna take care of Ellie when I'm gone?

He broke the surface when his lungs couldn't take any more. Behind him, the splashing was deafening, as if a cavalry were fording a river. Leaving the light behind, his thoughts centered on getting to his dad's gun. Getting to the gun and buying some time.

He kicked down the tunnel, breaking through to the lake where they'd been peacefully fishing not more than twenty minutes ago. One man grunted, lunged for George's heels, and snared his pant cuff. The man laughed, but the sound was cut off when he pulled George under. Water bilged into his open mouth, his nose. Fighting frantically, he grasped above as if his fingers could take in air for his straining lungs. He kicked back, connecting with the man's face. Then again, and still the water invaded his mouth. He kicked a third time and broke free. Remaining underwater, he swam harder than he thought possible. He resurfaced when his palms slapped the rock shelf near the shore.

"Shitheel! Get back here, boy."

As soon as he pulled free from the lake, he convulsed, vomiting silt water. He still couldn't see anything, not without taking time to let his eyes readjust. He had no time. No time at all. One man reached the shelf. George crawled like mad, slipping across the muddy shore, mere feet ahead of his pursuer. George's shoulder crashed into his tackle box, but he welcomed the impact. It meant his dad's gun was close. If he could only remember which direction. Fumbling forward, he somehow found the wooden gunstock. He grasped the gun and rolled to his back, bracing the stock against his shoulder.

Water slid down his cheekbones, and even though it hurt his chest, he tried to conceal his breathing.

He waited for any hint of movement.

A shadowy figure loomed above him. As the machete slit the air, he switched the latch on the gun and pulled the trigger. The shotgun jerked in his hands, blasting a hole in the man's chest, sending him head over heel to the water's edge. For a split second, the explosion lit the cavern as the others closed in. They could've been farmers. They all wore bib overalls, denim work shirts. Their faces revealed a grizzled sameness that left them indistinguishable in age, but they all had a farmer's strength, a corn-fed thickness to their arms and torsos.

As the echo tapered off, George heard the man's liquid-wheezing breath. His dying breaths. He'd killed someone.

How in the world did the night turn so crazy?

George cradled the over/under and rolled to his feet. He ran as fast as possible through the winding trail, knocking his limbs against jagged outcroppings. He couldn't hear the other men, not with his ears ringing from the shotgun blast, but after killing one of their kind, he had no doubt they'd only redouble their efforts.

Who are you? George wanted to shout. He saved his breath. *What did I ever do to you?*

He reached the steep incline and scurried through the slick moss. When he reached the cave-in, he scrabbled into the low opening.

Once on the other side, he took a moment to catch his breath. Wheezing with his hands on his knees, a single thought pushed all others aside:

If I hadn't broken the lantern, none of this would've happened. I wouldn't have noticed the candlelight through the tunnel. Jimmy wouldn't have left me.

When he was ready to take off again, a face appeared in the low tunnel. Just the outline of a forehead, a curve of chin. Shadows for eyes. Nothing else. The man grunted, blindly swinging the machete as he crawled through the narrow opening. George switched to the other barrel and fired the shotgun into the man's skull. Something splattered George's face, but he hardly noticed. He turned and fled, desperately feeling for the next turn in the tunnel.

When he reached the last uphill leading to the cave's opening, he threw himself up the incline, the limestone floor transitioning to mud as he hit top soil. He shoved through the grass veil shielding the world from the unholy hell he had encountered below. Not knowing his location in relation to his house, he simply ran. The fog had burned off and the sky was warm with the rising sun. Before he lost sight of the cavern, he glanced back.

The unwounded third man appeared. Once clear of the small opening, another man's arm emerged from inside. Another man pulled free. The man had no face. Blood and clots of brain matter soaked his denim shirt. Once on his feet, the third man reached the opening, and he too climbed out, the mortal wound in his chest exposing his insides to the morning air.

The over/under had its .30 caliber round, but these men still chased him after being shot point-blank with a shotgun. There was no point in using the last round. George tossed the deadweight aside. He'd go back later for it. If he lived through this.

"You're never gonna see another sunset, shitheel!" said the unwounded man. "Don't worry, we'll make it go right-quick!"

The man's shrill voice didn't create an echo. The air was alive with birdsong, buzzing insects, a lush breeze. It was maddening after the cavern's compressed, blunted air. George ran, his adrenaline fighting the mounting fatigue from a sleepless and a seemingly endless night of fear.

In no time, the clamor of pursuit intensified. Glancing back, he couldn't believe his eyes. Loping through clumsy strides, they were still somehow lightning-quick. But their skin... it had begun to sag, having turned to pulp. All three had started to disintegrate, even the man he hadn't shot. Lesions rioted across their exposed skin, gravity pulling the wounds wide. George turned away and crested a small hill, heading toward wetter terrain. The swamps. At least now he knew where he was. He darted down the trail, through wispy trees and rutted ground, unsure of his sanity after seeing such sights.

Behind him, the men kicked through the underbrush, picking up their pace, gaining on him with every stride.

TWO

Heat waves danced above the rail ties, blurring anything more than twenty feet down the center. Road dust stained his dungarees a permanent earthen color. His threadbare knees and frayed cuffs looked like diseased wounds trying to heal and not quite succeeding. Cooper's face was leathery brown with sunburn gathered under each eye. He walked the center rail with little fear of oncoming trains, having not seen or heard a locomotive in over a day.

For the better part of a year he had been riding the rails, starting off from Chicago, tramping down to Dallas, and then out west, for an extended stay in California. He was now heading back toward Chicago, to home and family and his journey's end. Other people--typically traveling alone or in pairs--populated the rails along the way. Most tramps were men looking for work. Cooper had seen a few runaway children along the way as well. Judging the other tramps' haggard yet wary expressions, they were running from their past more than searching for their future.

Cooper tramped for other reasons, reasons he still didn't fully understand. He had little need for money, and even at thirty-eight, didn't have a family to support. When he set out his lone reason for traveling was simply because he could. Long after quenching his desire for travel, a greater motive compelled him to continue. His grandmother's dying words. He'd known her for such a short while, yet she'd used her dying words to placate him at a time when he felt his world becoming unhinged. With the end of his travels in sight, he wondered if he'd failed her.

He adjusted his canvas pack higher on his gaunt shoulders. It would take an extended stay of eating steaming stews and gravy-dipped breads before he felt human again. In the next town he would check around, see if someone needed an extra hand. Chicago wasn't going anywhere. Besides, he didn't enjoy the prospect of arriving on his parents' doorstep looking emaciated and lacking the answers he had been so desperately seeking.

Not long into his journey he learned he needed to find a job upon entering a new town. If he needed to rest a few nights in a real bed and eat food cooked in a kitchen instead of over a campfire, he would take on an odd job. People didn't understand or respect a man traveling alone without the need or desire for employment. Sweeping a storeroom or some other trifling job would get the stares off his back for the duration of his stay.

Signs of settlement started filtering through a canopy of two hundred year-old oak trees. Some fields looked tended, some long fallow and overgrown. Many homesteads had boundary marker tree stands that doubled as windbreaks during the winter months. To Cooper, they looked like bony fifty-foot fingers bursting from the earth.

He contemplated such a boundary between two farms. Without question one property was worked and occupied, while the other hadn't seen a plow's heavy blade in a generation or longer. Weedy trees taller than a grown man grew sporadically throughout the property. Thick wheat grass grew waist-high, heavy with ripe seed.

The untended property was nearly clear from view when something caught his attention--the only unnatural color for as far as the eye could see. Everything was earthy brown or lush green, but a small red splash lurked within a copse of green growth. Cooper left the relative safety of the rails to investigate, cutting through the thinner undergrowth along a narrow animal trail. The land cleared, revealing a brightly painted water pump.

The pump stood near an abandoned farmhouse hidden away by trees and thorny brambles. He eased his pack from his shoulders and stretched his aching back.

With the home appearing abandoned, Cooper thought it wouldn't hurt anyone to see if the pump still worked. He grabbed the long arm and worked it for a good minute or two before the pump started to sputter and wheeze. Soon enough, water trickled from the wide spout, becoming a short-lived flow. He alternated pumping the arm and splashing his face with the cold water. He then filled his two canteens.

Cooper removed his straight razor from his pack and began to shave off his facial hair. He'd receive a warmer reception in town if he could mirror more the townsfolk's appearance than a man who had been on the road for a year. As he shaved, he surveyed the homestead. It was a nice scrap of land. The farmhouse looked as old as the surrounding trees, and in its neglected state, seemed to sulk like a kicked dog. The former farm patch was hairy with sapling oak and dark green bushes drooping with succulent wild berries.

Checking the sun's declination, he noted he had an hour or so before he needed to start worrying about getting camp ready. This property was as good a place as any to stay the night, he figured. Now that he'd shaved and washed, a good night's sleep would have him rested and presentable come morning.

After serving up bland corn mush for supper, Cooper set up his bedding near the front porch. Sleeping under the overhang would keep him dry, but for some reason, the vacant windows and large brass-hoop knocker made him uneasy. Instead, he situated his blankets on a slight rise twenty feet away. He faced the house, his back to the untended fields.

As the sun arched behind the trees, he wondered why the house was abandoned. Did the economic collapse bankrupt these people? He figured not. The land had grown wild for some time, long before the tenuous times they were currently facing. No, some other reason caused the farmers to shirk their land. Which was odd. People just didn't up and leave rich cropland. No, it had to be something else, some other reasonable explanation.

As was often the case after a day without catching a freighter, Cooper was bushed. His mind drifted from increasingly improbable theories about the people who once farmed this land, to thoughts of his family, before eventually settling on the certainty that he would soon be home. Before his eyes closed for the night, his last cogent thought concerned the library. He wondered if they had held his position as they had promised. He missed the library. Things would be different when he returned, no doubt. After all, he was a different man than when he started his trek. Still, he missed the musty aisles and retreating into the stacks and into the written word, where the world seemed so much more cut and dry than reality. His eyes fluttered, easing shut with the pull of sleep.

Night darkened the house's interior, as if a long ago fire had left behind a charred, empty shell. In the quiet upper hallway, where no living person had ventured in eighty years, a gauzy spark snicked alive, shimmered and expanded under a glass globe, igniting a frayed wick. The lamp glowed golden, banishing the night beyond its ethereal reach. The lamp floated silently from room to room, pausing for a minute or more in each, plaintively pacing the house, as if the flame's bearer was searching for something long lost.

THREE

It was a noise straight from one of Greta's stories. Metal striking stone. The tolling clang of a pickaxe methodically chipping away. At least that's what Betty Harris figured it sounded like. She had no practical knowledge, being sixteen and not nearly old enough to remember the clattering of the former mines. No, she didn't know what could be making such a racket, but what else could it be?

"Junior?"

Her little brother didn't stir. Normally, she hated sharing a room with an obnoxious, always filthy, six-year-old. She looked forward to winter nights when she could escape by sleeping on a mat by the cook stove. Warmed by the dying embers from supper, she would enjoy her quiet nights alone. Snug under blankets, wedged between the stove and the short distance to the back wall, it felt like having a room all to herself. But now she was grateful for his presence, even if he was sleeping like the dead.

"*Junior?*" she whispered, sitting up in bed. "Wake up."

"Hmm?"

"You hear that?"

More chipping sounds. Loud enough now to create an echo.

Junior buried his face under his pillow, began snoring.

For an instant, she wished George Banyon were here. The sudden thought surprised her. With his lanky goofiness, his good-hearted nature--if he could only be here to put his arm around her, tell her nothing bad was going to happen.

Why did she think of him, of all people? Even though she wanted him to actually court her instead of acting like a fool, they'd rarely spoken in any depth. No, George Banyon wasn't here, and Junior was off sawing logs. Betty was on her own.

She stood, slipping on her house shoes. She padded over to the bedroom door, pressing her ear against it to listen.

She couldn't hear her parents stirring. But the sound. Digging. Grating metal on stone. Why weren't they awake?

She stepped out into the hall. Then, beneath the chipping sounds, there was something else. A whimper, full of sadness. She followed her ear, tracking it down the hall, the whimper becoming wracking sobs.

Mom.

Betty entered the kitchen. Her mom sat at the table. Her dad was standing, holding her teary-eyed face against his paunchy stomach. His chest heaved as he tried to hold back the spasms brought on by blacklung.

"You shouldn't be here."

He looked so old. They had been late parents, but even so, his wrinkles seemed too deep for his age. His lip quivered for a moment, then calmed. Along with the rest of his skin, his lips were cadaverous gray.

"But I heard--"

"Go to bed, and don't come back out again. Go on."

"Daddy...? Mom, what's going on? What's that sound?"

"Betty! Do what I say, girl!" he said, then seethed through a coughing fit.

Her mother's eyes brimmed with pain and the weight of an unexplained misery. She didn't say a word.

"Please, Betty-Mae." The intensity drained from him. He looked wasted away, the final snow melting in springtime.

Reluctantly, she turned away.

Digging, chipping, shoveling. The sounds were malicious, cold. She looked at the closed door across from her bedroom. The cellar. She could no longer deny it. There was no other place it could be coming from.

But why?

She shut the bedroom door, and of course, that lunkhead Junior was snoring even louder, oblivious to the night's bizarre events.

The digging quieted, and was, after a short silence, replaced by heavy-footed strides. Multiple people, from the sound. She tried to distinguish how many, but did it really matter? Who were these people?

Maybe Greta's stories were true, after all.

She opened her bedroom door a crack, just as wide as her pupil, waiting to see whatever had entered their house.

Why did she think that? That word. *Whatever.* Didn't she mean *whoever?*

She wished she would've made sure the cellar door was locked. But it was too late now. The doorknob turned, the tumblers rasping with rust. The door creaked opened. Her heart skipped a beat. She waited for her dad to cast out these invaders. No sound came.

All she heard was her mother's continued sobs.

A vile odor swept over her, reminiscent of days Junior spent in the swamps chasing tadpoles. The rank odor of pond muck and rotting vegetation. But this stench was ten times worse.

Someone stepped into the hall. There he lingered, as if considering his surroundings.

Is he looking at me? she cried out inside, frozen in place. All she could do was blink, her heart racing, aching.

She couldn't see anything in the hall's inky blackness. The strangers filled the space, their bodies consuming the pale moonlight creeping through the kitchen windows. Immobilized by fear, she didn't want to move to draw their attention. She also didn't want to see what was out there, but found it impossible to look away.

Then the floorboards sighed as they walked toward the kitchen, toward her parents.

She could tell now, as they moved single file with measured, cautious strides, there were three men. Featureless; as dark as shadows gathering in a well at midnight.

She expected a struggle or cries of outrage.

Their shuffling steps and her mom's cries were the only sounds. One final heart-breaking sob from her mom punctured the night. Then the steady footfalls returned, heading toward her room again.

One shadow-shrouded figure headed down the cellar steps. Followed by another. Seeing her dad's pale blue shirt was a shock after such darkness. His left shoulder came into view, then as he turned, she glimpsed his forearm with his sun-weathered skin looking like dried blood in the gloom. Then briefly, his profile. Two day's stubble, more gray than black. His crooked nose, twice broken in his youth.

His eyes. She needed to see his eyes.

Please Daddy. Let me see you!

But he didn't look her way.

He followed the men into the cellar. The last stranger stepped into view, blotting out the final image of her dad.

She began to cry. Greta hadn't lied. Betty had never believed her stories, not until this very second. But what else could they be besides the Collectors? She blinked away her tears when she heard a noise coming from the cellar. Before she could figure out what it was, a new coughing fit covered the sound.

I just knew he wouldn't go so willingly!

But she was mistaken. She placed the sound as the fit subsided. It was rocks grating on one another. Being stacked in to piles. Replaced to their rightful position. Covering up the tunnel dug into their home. Sealing her dad into the earth.

FOUR

The sun lit the horizon when Cooper woke from a fitful night's sleep, his clothes damp with dew. He gathered up his gear and headed back down the game trail. He took the slight hill to the rails at a solid clip, trying to warm his muscles. He felt compelled to watch the farm house until it disappeared from view. Something there was peculiar. He felt it when he was near the house, a pulling at his consciousness, an inexplicable yearning, and now, as he was leaving it behind, the feeling receded like floodwater.

About a half mile off, Cooper came across what the townsfolk would have considered downtown. He left the rails since they curved away from town and into the hills, as if to avoid the town proper. There was a quaint main street, packed dirt like the other branching roads leading from town. Many of the shops had scavenged boards covering the windows. A bakery and a bar sandwiched a law office side by side by side, all three vacant and quiet.

A few tired-looking cars were angle-parked curbside. Most people living in this stretch of country still relied on horses, as their fathers and father's fathers once had. Others would get by like Cooper, walking to and fro, from here to there, and getting to their intended destination a lot slower than desired.

He stepped up to a plank walkway and considered the first business that wasn't boarded up. A hand-painted sign hung askew from the porch's overhang, touting the place as Calder's Mart. The window front displayed a handsome handmade rocking chair draped with a quilted tan blanket. A sign advertised flour, eggs and ice. Cooper peered through the window and could see a few rows of dusty shelves. Campbells's Soup and sweet potatoes sat alongside glass jars packed with a variety of homegrown preserves. Tilted bins held fresh produce. Lettuce, tomatoes, chickpeas and beets. The stock was thin and the whole place looked sleepy.

Across an intersecting alley, Cooper looked in on a barbershop. An old man reclined in a barber chair, his straw hat pulled over his eyes. He gripped a half-empty bottle of hooch in his sprawled grasp, and though asleep, it didn't look like he would let it fall to the floor anytime soon. Another man was sitting on a wooden bench near the window, flipping through a yellowed newspaper.

"Good afternoon." Cooper said as he walked inside.

"Um, oh, hello." The man folded the newspaper he'd probably read front to back more times than he had fingers. He had short limbs on a stocky frame. His toes barely brushed the floor from his sitting position.

"Are you open?" Cooper's throat felt scratchy, his voice thicker than normal. He hadn't spoken to anyone in almost a week, since well south of Champaign.

"We sure are, come on in." The man slapped his palm against the open barber chair, raising a dust cloud. The man occupying the other seat didn't move. "You don't look familiar."

"I was just passing through, but with such an inviting town, I had to stop." Cooper sat in the offered chair. "Anyways, I need my ears lowered." It felt good to get off his feet and let his weight ease into an actual chair. His bones were feeling fragile lately.

"You sure do. Good thing you stopped in. At least your shave is civilized."

"What's this town called?"

"Coal Hollow. We been 'corporated since before the Civil War. I'm Bo Tingsley," he said and started snipping around Cooper's neck with his sheers. "Dad was in the war, pushed them Rebs right back to hell, he and a bunch of boys from Illinois. Moved down the road from Peoria after his service to the Union, then married Ma not long after," Bo Tingsley spoke as if he had chewed the ears off everyone in town and was happy to see an unmarred pair sitting in his barber chair.

"That so?"

"Sure is." Bo wetted a comb and swiped it dry through Cooper's shoulder-length black hair. "You planning on staying for a stretch?"

"I'm thinking about it. Coal Hollow looks like a good place to take root. By the way, my name's Cooper. Theodore Jameson Cooper. Most people just call me Cooper."

"Nice meeting you, Cooper. What's your trade if I might ask? I know just about everybody within fifty miles. Jobs are tough to come by this far off from anything you might call a city. Still, I might could steer you right."

"Oh, I suppose you can say I've done a little of everything along the way. Farming, ranching, stabling, shopclerking. I worked at a drug store jerking sodas all day. I'm sure I'm leaving something out, but I can do just about anything to earn an honest day's pay." He didn't bother mentioning his true profession as a librarian. Most folk didn't understand an educated man voluntarily taking to the roads and rails.

"Quite a laundry list. I'll have to take a time or two to think on it," Bo said, fighting a nasty cowlick at the top of Cooper's head.

A gurgle rumbled from the liquored lips of the man in the other chair. He rattled off a couple wet snores, then settled back into his murky respite.

"That's Magee over there. This is his barbering place, but as you can see, he's disposed of for the moment, if you catch my drift."

"Bo, I don't know Magee at all, but I do believe you'd give a better barbering than old Magee any day."

Bo laughed with comfortable acceptance.

Cooper observed Bo's handiwork in a cloudy mirror. "That's a nice cut, Bo. I'm glad I stopped in. I feel halfway human again. How much do I owe?"

"Two bits."

Cooper reached into his pocket and pulled out two quarters. If he judged Bo correctly, a big tip would pay off down the line.

"Thanks, Coop. That's mighty kind of you."

"It's just nice to be off the road is all I can say."

Cooper was about out the door when the chatterbox barber called out. "Say, Coop, you know where you're gonna lodge?"

"Magee's is the first place I stopped. Haven't had the time to look around. Is there a place you can recommend with a warm bed and warmer food?" He ran his hand through his close-cropped hair, again checking the mirror. He wasn't used to the short cut, but he looked more presentable than before meeting Bo.

"The Calder Mart up the block has rooms above the store. You get a bed and three squares for a fair price. Thea, she's Henry Calder's daughter. She runs the place, for the most part. When you see her, you'll know it's her. She's a real looker. She went off to California to make movies, and actually made a few, but now she come home. She does the cooking, but it ain't even close to her ma's, God rest her soul." Bo paused and crossed himself before continuing. "Eating her mom's cooking felt like a sin of indulgence. She's gone now, a good four years or so. Pneumonia took her away."

"That's too bad." From the pain on Bo's face, the man still harbored feelings for his neighbor's wife. The barber's eyes darkened and became distant.

"Sounds like she was a fine woman." Cooper felt uncomfortable and wanted to leave Magee's more than anything.

"Oh, she was. A fine woman. A fine cook, but she had a finer heart. The kindliest woman you'd ever meet. Too bad Thea only got her looks. She inherited her Pa's mean streak. He's German, you know." Bo sat in the empty barber chair. He turned on its swivel and continued to speak to the inebriated Magee. Cooper supposed the two old barbers held one-sided conversations like this quite often.

"Thanks for the advice, Bo."

"Oh, sure," Bo said distantly, his face turned away.

Cooper let the door close behind him.

A bell rattled above the entryway when he opened the door to Calder's Mart. Two wide aisles housed fresh produce bins, sacks of flour, jars of molasses and other assorted dry goods. Beyond, a hodgepodge of basic hardware hung on pegs against the back wall. Cooper walked to the far corner where the cash till stood on a high wooden countertop. Perfume bottles and cheap-looking jewelry boxes filled a display behind the counter. A black curtain blocked the view to a backroom. A scarred wooden counter formed an L-shape with the register counter. A few rickety stools stood in front for customers. The place had little stock and seemed deserted. Cooper waited at the counter, not sure if he should look around for anyone working the place.

A hand-painted placard hung next to the jewelry boxes and dusty perfume bottles.

Your business means the world to us. Let us know if you have any suggestions!

"Good afternoon," a harried voice called from a stairwell tucked away between a grimy pickle barrel and a display of Henderson brand pitchforks.

Cooper caught some of his breath before all of it rushed from his lungs. Bo hadn't lied. Thea Calder *was* a looker. She stood at the bottom of the steps, her hands on her hips, a damp apron around her thin waist.

"Can I help you, or are you just going to gawp-about like a doe-eyed simpleton?" Her cheeks were flushed and dark brown curls drifted from a haphazard bun.

Cooper's chest tightened. He realized he wasn't breathing. It had been a long while since he'd seen such an attractive woman. Eyes like smoky-brown coals, full lips painted a shade most respectable women avoided. She wore a simple flower-print dress, but Cooper figured Thea Calder could wear a housecoat in a seminary and still command, at least momentarily, all the men's attention away from God.

"I heard you have lodging. Food, too." He'd regained his breath and a partial amount of his ability to speak. Feeling childish, his face crept with color.

"You heard right. Is that all you wanted to know, or do you want to rent a room in this Godforsaken place?" She seemed downright offended he would consider taking a room at Calder's.

"A night or two is all. I'm passing through from all I can tell." He could look her in the eye now. Bo mentioned she'd been in California making movies. That's where she belonged, away from this small town, her face plastered on billboards and handbills announcing her latest film. She would be a cinch for a coquettish role. She could own the part of a shrew.

Thea nodded and Cooper could just about pluck the words from her head and place them on her tongue: *So you're one of those. A transient? A vagabond?*

He glanced at his clothes, at his threadbare knees and shineless shoes. His pack was by his feet, all his worldly possessions in one small, dingy pile. Thea's glare made Cooper feel about as small as a full-grown man could get. She stormed past and pulled a pad of paper from behind the counter.

"Can you sign your name?"

The question stymied Cooper. No one had asked him that since childhood. Of course he could read and write. He had read a library's worth of books.

"Do you have the ability to read? Can you even speak, or has the cat got your tongue?"

"I... sure I can read." He stepped up to the counter. Thea slapped the pad down in front of him to read.

She decided to paraphrase anyway, in case he'd been lying. "Basically, we have three meals a day. One at seven, one at noon, the last at five-thirty. Five minutes late, you're out of luck. I'd rather serve the food to the dog than to a man late for a meal I slaved over. Also, lights out at ten. A minute after, you'll be out on the street. It'd be a shame considering no one else rents rooms for miles around. You pay for the following night's occupancy during the morning meal. If you aren't going to eat at the morning meal, you'll bring your payment to the morning meal anyways. Are we clear on all that?"

He nodded then signed the bottom and slid the pad back to Thea.

Thea inspected Cooper's signature before setting it aside. "I'll show you the room now. And another thing, for God's sake clean up after yourself. I'm too young to be someone's momma, and I'm not going to start acting like one for you."

"Sure thing, Thea. Uh, Miss Calder. I wouldn't want to be a burden on anyone." He followed her around the grimy pickle barrel and up the stairway.

"I don't repeat myself. If you can't act like a human being, you can move on to somewhere else that tolerates such behavior. And another thing, how'd you know my name?"

"I just had my hair cut. Bo Tingsley recommended your place."

"Don't get me started talking about Bo Tingsley." She didn't need prompting; she started on her own just fine. "That sonofabitch tried to break up my family. He had an unnatural attraction to my momma. He pined for her openly, brought her little trinkets. In some ways I'm glad for the pneumonia. She'd started to bend to the beady-eyed dwarf after awhile."

Cooper had lost the ability to speak again. He had a feeling he risked losing his room if he said the wrong thing. He also had an idea there was never a right thing to say to Thea Calder.

"Here's your damn room," Thea said, reaching the top.

She threw the door open. Cooper looked inside, but when he turned around to thank her, she was gone. All that remained was a haunting hint of perfume.

FIVE

Shocked and confused, Betty had climbed into bed after those men had taken her dad. Pulling the covers to her chin, it felt like a one hundred pound weight sat against her sternum. She watched the bedroom door, waiting for it to open, terrified the strangers would return to take her away.

Exhausted, she fell asleep with the sun's rising.

By the time she woke and pried herself from bed, she'd missed breakfast. She left her bedroom, keeping an eye on the cellar door as she made her way to the kitchen. It all seemed unreal; everything she'd seen last night, everything she didn't see.

Junior was already off doing whatever he did during his lazy summertime days. Probably causing some mindless ruckus somewhere. Obviously, he didn't know their dad was gone, didn't know that three featureless strangers had broken in during the night, had *dug* their way in to steal him away. Or that he had gone along without a fight.

Her mom had left her a breakfast plate at the kitchen table. A hollowed-out baked apple, filled with chopped dates and brown sugar. It was congealed and cold. Betty had no appetite.

She went to the back door, and despite wearing house shoes and a summer nightgown, she stepped outside. Her mom was in the garden next to the house. Her dad's garden. She never ventured into the extensive vegetable patch, claiming she had a black thumb compared to the emerald brilliance of her dad's.

"Mom?" She stopped at the chicken wire fence used to keep out the rabbits.

Her mom was on her hands and knees, crawling through rows of lettuce, working her hands under the wide outer leaves. Holding a long paring knife between her teeth, she looked up at Betty. She took the blade and cut a head from the ground. She then held it up to the sunlight, appraising it.

"Have to take out these heads before they get soft. Can't risk ruining your dad's reputation because I didn't get his lettuce to Calder's on time. I won't stand for it. He doesn't deserve it." She gently placed the head in a basket beside a half dozen others. She crawled a few feet down, found the next ripe head, and went at it with her knife.

"Mom? What's going on?"

"You gone deaf? I'm getting the lettuce ready for market. It'd be nice if you changed into some work clothes and lent me a hand. There's plenty of work to do." She hacked the knife through the lettuce root, held it up, found it to be an exemplary specimen, and placed it in the basket. "This garden... I didn't realize all the work he did," she said through panting breath, pulling the basket along with her to the next row. "Just think, he grows the best lettuce in all of Summerset County. People come from miles wide, because it's the crispest, and stays that way the longest."

"Mom, what the hell is going on?" Betty shouted, surprised by both her force and open vulgarity. "Where's Daddy? Who were those men who came in through the cellar?"

Her mother sighed, ignoring her obscenity. She placed the paring knife inside the basket and groaned as she stood. "Oh, my knees. I don't know how he managed this. I'm gonna be broke in half by winter." She blew an errant strand of hair from her eyes, walking stiffly to the chicken wire gate.

Her mother placed a hand on Betty's shoulder, guiding her away from the garden and empty house.

"You shouldn't go outside dressed like that anymore. You're no longer a girl. You don't know who could be watching you." Her mom squeezed her shoulder, but it wasn't a mean-spirited gesture meant to punctuate a scolding. There seemed to be a smile in her voice. An acceptance that her little girl was a grown woman.

They walked in silence through the apple orchard at the back of their property. A grown-over path through thick grass abutted the property boundary with two other farms. Her mom's cousins, the Newsteins, lived on one. Her dad's sister, Paulette, lived on the other. At the grassy corner was their family graveyard.

At first Betty thought they were walking to her Aunt Paulette's house. Such an even-keeled woman, Paulette would shed light on what was going on. A widow, she worked her one hundred-twenty acres side by side with a dour, quiet man, named Nelson. They had lived together for almost twenty years. Betty called Nelson her uncle, when she knew he wasn't; but he was a nice enough man. Hard working. Honest.

Betty's Uncle Craig was buried here. Aunt Paulette's husband. She came out every Sunday morning at sunrise and sat by the headstone, staring at the ground covering him. She sometimes cried, sometimes she smiled. Sometimes both at once. But she never forgot her Sunday visits, even though she'd been with Nelson twice as long as her first love.

Betty realized they weren't heading to her Aunt Paulette's when she saw the dark brown dirt of a freshly dug plot next to her Uncle Craig's.

"Mom."

A new headstone, with sharp-edged letters untouched by the elements, sat behind a blanket of recently turned loam.

With disbelief, she read the headstone's inscription:

Gerald Lincoln Harris

Born: March 19th, 1875

Died: July 8th, 1934

"No, Momma. NO!"

"Let me explain," her mom said, touching Betty's elbow. Betty shrugged her away. "Betty-Mae."

Betty turned from the grave and stared at their house without really taking in any detail. Her mind was a cluttered muddle. What in the world was happening to her life?

"That's not what happened," Betty said softly. She faced her mom, said resolutely, "He's not dead. I saw him. Those men took him away. You can't tell me different. He was alive. He *is* alive. Momma, tell me, tell me Daddy's alive!"

"He is, Betty-Mae, your daddy's alive."

"Then why, Momma? Tell me what's going on." Betty knelt by the new grave, the moist soil dirtying her nightgown. "Tell me everything is going to be all right." She touched the soil, ran her hand over the cool surface. She cried as if he really were dead. Her tears fell, soaking into the soil. She began to tremble uncontrollably, and she didn't try to fight it.

"Junior mustn't hear a word of this."

Her mom let her tears come and fall, let her purge her pain. Then she told her everything.

SIX

In his room above Calder's Mart, Cooper broke open his pack and pulled out his cleanest and least threadbare clothes. With a haircut and wearing a clean set of clothes, he felt like a new man. Now, if only his bones would stop aching.

The room was sparse, but he thought FDR himself would like it just fine. A porcelain washbasin sat atop a short bureau. A coat rack was in one corner, while the other corner had windows on either side overlooking the main street below.

Before he took to the road, he'd lived in a first floor bedroom of his parents' row house in Chicago's Alta Vista neighborhood. His family had moved to the exclusive town home in '05, and he had little memory of the time before, the years when his parents had to worry about their next meal. After advancing from stockyarder to foreman, his father secured a bank loan and branched out to form his own company. He had refined a method for the further processing of the waste at the slaughterhouse. The Cooper Meat Company now shipped all across the forty-eight states, touting to be "The purveyors of the finest processed meats in Chicago." The quick ascent through class and wealth brought his family relative comfort, but Theodore never had the drive or passion that his father possessed--at least that's what his father told him. He would often rile on about Theodore's lack of understanding for how far they'd come, for just how hard he had worked to afford their home, their furnishings, the damn books in which Theodore always had his nose buried.

Once he finished buttoning his fresh shirt, Cooper reclined on the bed. Nothing had felt softer or more soothing since he'd devoured cotton candy at the county fair when he was a kid. He reached over to his pack and pulled out a battered copy of Dostoyevsky's *The Idiot.* He found the dog-ear where he'd left off and read a few pages until his eyelids became heavy. Starting to doze, his rumbling stomach reminded him how long it had been since breakfast.

When sleep overtook his hunger, Cooper dreamed.

The dew-heavy grass slapped his thighs as he ran. His heart pounded a staccato rhythm, adrenaline seared his veins. Feeling alive, alert and full of fear, he had no idea where he was, just that it was nighttime and gray clouds shrouded the nearly full moon. The sensation of being followed was an interminable focal point. With single-minded clarity, his every thought centered on this feeling--a slathering wolf keening in on a staggered prey. He ran, his eyes prying every shadow, behind every hiding spot.

For reasons Cooper didn't understand, the relief at reaching the top of a sloping field made him feel like he had just been born again.

The roof's A-shaped peak looked like an opened book resting on the August-high cornstalks, as if set aside by a giant for later reading. Closing on the building, its beacon-like windows washed the bursting corn a warmer shade of gold. Someone played a pipe organ inside the home: a lulling dirge sweeping the field like a collapsing sigh of sadness. It was a sign--one he didn't know he was listening for until he heard the organ's lofty bellow. His fear dissipated into the misty air.

He had made it. He would find a new life; any life would be better than the one he had left behind.

He crashed through the last row of corn, his arms stinging from the whipping cornstalks. He felt no pain, only an overwhelming happiness that turned his stomach and slowed his stride. Walking more cautiously as he neared the house, he mounted the steps to the wrap-around porch and paused when he reached the door. A rusted bucket was near the doorframe, a water-dipper resting in the dark water. Another sign. The water dipper. The big dipper. The north star. Follow the north star.

This had to be the house. A brass-hoop knocker hung on the door, but for some reason he knew not to use it. He took one more look around to make sure no one had followed him, then rapped his knuckles on the oak door. Three knocks. Pause. Two knocks.

The organ's final note deflated to silence.

His heart beat more swiftly as he waited. Before long, his fear began to resurface. Maybe he had given the wrong entry knock. Maybe he was at the wrong house. He was unsure if he should try knocking again or if he should run back to the cover of the field. He stepped away from the door and was ready to start running, when the door creaked open a few inches. It was dark inside. Cooper saw little more than an old woman's wrinkled forehead and two dry, rheumy eyes backlit by an oil lamp's tempered glow.

When the door opened further, the woman beckoning him to enter, Cooper did not hesitate entering the darkness therein...

Cooper shook awake from his dream, the last moments as clear as day, yet fleetingly vague.

Looming cornstalks.

An old woman opening a creaky door.

An overpowering sense of security walking into the stranger's darkened house.

Escape.

He checked his pocket watch. It was shortly after five. He better get going or he'd miss his first meal prepared by Miss Thea Calder. No way he would miss this meal. Even if he weren't so hungry, he wouldn't miss it for anything.

His dream faded, but the nearly overwhelming feeling of security and happiness lingered on. Holding onto the feeling, finding comfort in its strength, he made his way down to the dining room. The first to arrive, he sat at the middle of the table facing the door he entered. The large oak table could seat twelve, but only five placements had been set. He took a folded napkin and spread it across his lap.

He hadn't eaten in an actual dining room since leaving Chicago. Since then, he usually prepared his meals over an open fire pit. Occasionally, he would venture into an inviting mom and pop diner and take refuge for an hour or two.

Just when Cooper was starting to think he'd found the wrong dining room, an old man entered. He limped through the entryway and sat across from Cooper without acknowledging him. He took his napkin, wiped his sallow lips, then set it aside.

"Hello?"

"Oh, I'm sorry, but I don't see so well lately. Actually, to be honest, I see closer to not at all more than anything."

"It's all right, really. It sure is dark with the curtains pulled."

"It's not all right by any means. I consider myself a gentleman, and not acknowledging someone you're going to break bread with is just downright rude, regardless of the situation. I'm Jasper Cartwright." His hair was soft, shaggy over the ears and gleaming white. He kept his mustache trimmed in impeccably tidy angles. Cooper wondered if the old man could still see enough to maintain his mustache to such standards, or if he had help, from possibly Magee or Bo.

"I'm Theodore Cooper. Most people call me Cooper."

"Nice to meet you, Cooper. Are you staying under the roof of our benevolent hostess, Thea Calder?"

"I'm staying at least for the night."

"I myself have been a perpetual guest for several years now. Oh, are you in for a treat. Her hospitality is unrivalled!"

"I don't know Jasper, but your voice seems to have a slice of sarcasm to it."

"Certainly it does. Since you noticed, that must mean you've met Thea Calder." Jasper said, his voice as dry as autumn hay.

So far, Cooper was enjoying his visit to Coal Hollow. Even the tension Thea Calder carried with her like a storm cloud was somehow comforting. Cooper had just met Jasper, but he was starting to think the old man could only add to the town's charm.

"I've met our hostess. She doesn't seem all that bad."

"It must be one of her good days."

Cooper and Jasper shared a bonding laughter.

Two men entered the dining hall, talking avidly. Cooper recognized one of the men. It was Magee from Magee's barbershop. He looked none the worse for wear despite having earlier been in a drunken stupor.

"Well, Jasper, good evening," said the man Cooper didn't recognize.

"Evening Doc. Magee. Gentlemen, this is Cooper. He's new to town."

Cooper stood and shook hands with the new arrivals.

"Cooper, if you're ever feeling poorly, Dr. Thompson is the man to see. He can cure a mule of its stubbornness. Sure, he'll make you feel better, but in the same sense, make you feel even more poorly... in the wallet!" The three townsfolk all broke out in laughter, Dr. Thompson the most red faced and teary-eyed. Cooper hesitated to join in. Having spent so long on the road had eroded his social skills to a certain extent.

Dr. Thompson cut off their laughter. "Magee here runs a barber shop. He and his friend, Bo Tingsley," the graying doctor said as he dabbed at his eyes with a napkin.

"Oh, I met Bo already," Cooper added.

"I thought so." Thompson nodded to acknowledge Cooper's fresh haircut. "Turns out half the town gets a Magee haircut, the other gets a professional one. Looks like you got the latter," the doctor said, barely choking back his laughter before finishing the last of his sentence.

Magee scrunched his face like he'd eaten something tart, but his expression softened to a wrinkled smile.

Cooper looked at each man, noting the similarities in their appearance. They had probably known each other so long that they'd begun to look alike. All gray or graying, all with the same laugh lines at the corners of their mouths. All sported Bo Tingsley haircuts.

"I like my haircut fine, but I'll have to try out Magee the next go-around," Cooper said.

A man, who looked like he hadn't sat in a barber's chair for quite a while, entered the room. He wore a stained apron and no smile whatsoever. "Thea isn't feeling well. I'll bring some beef dumplings in a couple minutes."

"Henry, do you want me to look in on her?" Dr. Thompson said, halfway up from his chair.

Henry Calder waved the doctor to sit back down. "No, Doc, I don't think it's anything you can help with. It's a malady of a womanly nature. She just needs her rest."

"If anything changes, you let me know."

"The dumplings will be right out."

When Cooper was sure he was out of earshot, he said, "He's an abrupt fellow."

"Sure is. He wears on you after awhile," Jasper said.

"Wears like a shoe with a rock in it," Magee said, keeping his voice from drifting past the table. "At least supper will be somewhat palatable." Even though Henry Calder would soon serve a more desirable meal, the mood in the dining room had changed. Moments before the room was full of laughter. Now it seemed a heavy cloud of disappointment hung about like a stray animal.

They were silent and Cooper couldn't think of a thing to say to make it otherwise. The bells above the general store's door jangled as the door flew wide. A child's light, sandaled feet slapped the floor as someone ran through the store.

"Doc! Doc Thompson!"

The curtain flew open, and in rushed a dirty-faced girl with loose blonde braids. Salty tears streaked her face. A thin trail of blood flowed from her left nostril.

"Georgie's gone! Daddy's gone, too!" the little girl said between panting breaths. Drenched with sweat, her fair complexion was turning rosier by the second.

Dr. Thompson stood and went to the girl. He moved faster than Cooper thought possible. His knees popped like damp firewood as he squatted to the girl's eye level.

"Slow down, Ellie. You're going to scare yourself into a fainting spell." The doctor took out his kerchief and daubed the blood from her nose.

The girl took a deep, hitching breath. "G-georgie's gone. Daddy went looking for him." With her next breath the hitching in her chest brought along fresh tears. They streamed freer down her cheeks. The doctor dried these, also. "Daddy said to stay put. But I got scared when he didn't come back." It seemed her fresh tears loosened her voice, and now her voice was both smooth and heartbreaking.

"Where'd your brother go? How long's he been gone?" Magee asked. Dr. Thompson shot him a look as he continued to console the girl.

"Last night. He snuck out after Daddy... after Daddy went to sleep. I waited awhile, until morning, just in case he came home on his own. Then I woke Daddy."

Dr. Thompson pushed some hair from her forehead. "Ellie, couldn't George just be fishing?"

"Georgie doesn't fish with guns. I woke up when he took the over/under from the rack. Georgie doesn't touch Daddy's gun for nothing. He took the gun and snuck out the window."

Cooper sat back and took in the whirling conversation.

"Why'd he leave like that?" Magee asked.

"Dunno, but he sure was in a hurry." The girl's tears had stopped for the moment. She put an arm around Dr. Thompson's neck, and she looked like she didn't want to let go.

"Does Sheriff Bergman know about this?"

"No. I knew you eat here, so I came to tell you."

"Well, we should probably let the sheriff know." The doctor stood, his movements much slower now.

"Don't go!"

"I'm not going anywhere alone. You're coming with me."

"Find Georgie for me, Doc. Find my Georgie."

"I'm sure he'll turn up in no time at all. Don't you worry." Thompson and the little girl walked back through the store.

The bells above the door were still jingling when Henry Calder entered, a heaping pot of beef dumplings steaming in his hands. His expression wasn't especially pleasant when he counted heads and came up one short. He slammed the food down then left without saying a word.

SEVEN

Wandering waist-high fields with a group of strangers, Cooper wondered why he decided to tag along at all. He didn't know George Banyon, and he didn't know these people, either. Maybe it was Ellie's desperation to find her brother, or perhaps he had been on the road too long and he had his own desperation eating away at him--desperation for human contact. In the end, he decided he might as well help a little girl along the way if for no other reason.

Not long after Ellie and Dr. Thompson bolted from Calder's dining room, they returned with the sheriff. Everyone but Jasper Cartwright and his failing vision volunteered to look for Ellie's brother. After leaving the dining room, the search party nearly trampled a man sitting on the plank walkway outside the market. Magee introduced the new man to Cooper as Arlen Polk. After a brief conversation with Sheriff Bergman, he joined their ranks.

Polk was dimwitted, Cooper could tell by his always-questioning eyes and slack jaw, but he seemed genuinely concerned about George's whereabouts. He was a shade over five foot tall, and his longish black hair and beard were greasy and unkempt. His eyes had a twitchy quality, and Cooper had a tough time deciding if Polk was closer to twenty years old or forty.

Sheriff Bergman's tan bowler cap seemed out of place sitting atop his pear-shaped head. He was no more than about thirty, and his excitability made him appear younger. Bergman led the way, pushing aside the dry, razor-sharp grass with a long tree branch he scavenged as they began their search. He looked like a scythe-wielding reaper intent on clearing all the land as they went. They would make good time with Bergman in the lead.

Cooper remained at the rear, matching strides with Magee, letting the others determine the direction of their search. He kept his eyes peeled for a boy of unspecified height and features, a boy everyone seemed terribly worried about. They were a good distance from town when they realized Polk carried their only oil lamp to fend off the coming dark. Luckily, the moon cut a bright yellow streak through the cloudless sky.

"Where we gonna look?" Polk asked to no one in particular. After leaving the town behind, they had fanned out and most of their conversation died off. It was a while before anyone responded.

Bergman broke the silence. "George Banyon didn't take food or other provisions. He wasn't going farther than he could walk from his home. This stretch of field covers between town and the Banyon place. We'll cover the ground surrounding their property first. Also, something scared George enough to carry a gun. Something scared him enough to take his Pa's gun without waking him. Even though George has his own gun, it was important enough to take the over/under without permission."

Cooper was impressed with Bergman's logic. He'd been on the road long enough to know that you don't go off on a long journey without first figuring out what supplies you needed. It also made him question beginning their search with night descending and Bergman's Colt revolver the group's only weapon. If George needed his father's gun for protection, and the boy was somewhere nearby, maybe Bergman was walking them straight into trouble.

A thought crossed Cooper's mind. "What about the boy's dad? Shouldn't we consider where he went?" With the commotion of Ellie running into the Calder's dining room, he'd forgotten the boy's dad was also gone.

"Oh, that's easy. Probably passed out somewhere, as usual," Magee said with a snobbish laugh.

Cooper recalled seeing Magee just this morning snoozing in his barber's chair, a half-bottle of whiskey in his hand. He guessed a drunk would naturally know another's inclination, even while looking down his nose at his peer in vice.

"How old is this boy, anyhow?" Cooper asked.

"What, sixteen-seventeen now?" Polk asked, his dull eyes peering at Magee. In the light of the oil lamp, Polk's eyes gleamed yellow, and his beard stubble seemed as prickly as the thorny undergrowth at their feet.

"Sounds about right. Ellie's no more than about eight. Their parents spread them out pretty good."

"Mr. Banyon's a surly sonofa-bee." As Polk walked, he turned the valve to brighten his lamp.

"Sure is. Makes Hank Calder look like a choirboy," Magee said as he watched Polk. "You just don't know what you're doing at all. Give me that." Magee took charge of holding the lamp.

Cooper noticed movement at the top of the slight rise they were cresting. Judging his abrupt halt, Bergman also took note. The field they'd been crossing for the last half hour was transitioning to forest. A green wall of trees provided a backdrop for the movement; two people in the distance, steadily approaching.

For the moment, Magee and Polk seemed more concerned about the oil lamp than finding the boy. Magee played with the lamp's valve as Polk held its handle.

Cooper surged past them, moving toward the others. "Bergman," Cooper whispered. "*Sheriff Bergman.*"

Bergman held a hand up, "Yeah, I see it, Coop," the sheriff said, then blurted in a louder voice, "Everyone get down!" He motioned to the others. The doctor took Ellie's hand and they both kneeled in the grass. Having not heard Bergman's order, Polk and Magee continued walking toward the front of the group. Polk looked like a scolded child as they walked. Magee held the lamp, his chest puffed out like the victor of a great battle.

"Who is it?" Cooper asked, keeping his voice low.

"Don't know, but if something happened to George, I don't want to take a chance."

As Polk and Magee approached, they finally noticed the sheriff motioning for them to get down. They ducked down, continuing to bicker in quieter voices.

The approaching people disappeared into a gully. Cooper was beginning to question his reasoning for joining this search party. If he didn't know this boy at all, why was he putting himself in possible danger?

Ellie's tears were Cooper's answer. Seeing the little girl crouched in the damp grass, the unsettling pain etched into her face, he'd do whatever he could to help find her brother.

Bergman inched over to a mass of bushes, never letting his eyes stray from the approaching people. He pulled his Colt from his belt holster and raised it to firing height. He cocked the weapon, holding his position.

Someone rustled through the underbrush, silencing the chirruping crickets. Someone stumbled, followed by a raspy whisper, "You should've stayed home. I didn't want you out here like this."

While not familiar, the voice carried an unexpected quality. It was feminine.

"Don't move! Stay right where you are!"

After a shocked silence, the woman replied, "It's okay, sheriff, it's just us." She was still not visible behind a blanket of brambles.

"Just do as I say, and I'll say when you can move," Bergman's voice wavered as he approached the newcomers.

The tension eased from Cooper's limbs. He stood slowly, and the others followed suit.

"Larry, you better stop pointing that gun at me and my son!" As the woman's voice rose, its raspy quality smoothed to a light, almost lilting tone.

"Jane Fowler, what in the world are you doing out here in the middle of the night, and with Jacob, too?" Bergman looked exasperated. His face seemed to sag, and the yellow moon made his skin appear pasty and unwashed.

"Larry, the gun?" Jane Fowler said, the frustration in her voice evident.

"I'm sorry, Jane." Bergman lowered his gun.

Jane pushed aside the undergrowth and stood with her son in a small clearing. Mud caked her clothes. A ripped leaf clung to her hair. They both looked wrung through.

Cooper made his way toward Bergman, seeing Jacob at a better angle. He looked like a broomstick with limbs, no more than thirteen or so. His eyes were dark and would probably appear equally dark in the daylight or at night. Without knowing the boy, Cooper figured Jacob's sad expression was nothing new, as if he wore layers of sadness like winter clothing.

"I've known you since I looked after you and your sisters. How dare you point a gun at me and Jacob!"

"Jane, I... well, how was I supposed to know it was you? We got a situation out here and we got to be ready for anything."

"Situation? What situation? You mean you're actually playing policeman! You always loved that game when you were a little one. Or are you playing cowboys and Indians?"

"Come on now, Jane. I'm serious."

"Georgie's missing," Ellie interrupted as she walked to the center of this impromptu gathering.

"Since when?" Jacob asked. His voice was somewhere between being a boy's and being a man's--scratchy and warbled in an effort to find a balance.

"Last night. Real late," Ellie said. The two youngest people in the group had taken over the conversation.

"That makes sense now." Jacob nodded slowly.

"What makes sense, Jacob?" Bergman cut in.

"Well, for starters, Jimmy's gone, too. That's why me and Mom are out here. Jimmy and George must be together."

"You both look a mess," Ellie said, sizing up their muddied clothes and haggard faces. "No offense, Mrs. Fowler."

"None taken, dear. We've been at it all day." Jane sounded heartbroken, but her face held strong. Her fatigue could have been mistaken for stoicism.

"You've been looking for Jimmy all day and didn't bother to get help?" Magee asked. He still held Polk's lamp. Polk stood behind Magee, almost out of view. He looked dejected, and his eyes never left the back of Magee's head. "People would'a come to help you, Jane," Magee added.

"Oh, would they?" she said, an edge to her voice.

"We could've rallied more people than this if we had more time, then maybe by now we'd know where the boys are," Bergman said.

"I don't want any help," Jane said as she shoved by Bergman. "If you don't mind, I'd like to go find my son." She gave Ellie a knowing look and patted her shoulder before exiting the circle. "Come on Jacob, time's wasting. I want both my boys home in time for breakfast." She didn't look back.

Jacob took off in a gangly trot to catch his mother. The others watched as the Fowlers walked away.

"We can't just let them go," Polk said in a small voice.

"No, we can't. I say we go with them. There's safety in numbers," Dr. Thompson said. The lamplight caught and accentuated his every wrinkle. He looked ragged after only a short while searching. "Plus, we can compare notes, see what ground they've covered so far." After a moment's hesitation and silence from the others, he grabbed Ellie's hand. She went without question as he headed in the direction Jane Fowler had gone. Polk was the next to leave.

"I'm in charge here. We can't just split up like this," Bergman said.

Magee followed Polk, taking the oil lamp with him. The ground where Cooper stood darkened with the barber's every step. Cooper wanted to head back to his rented room and sink into the deep and inviting bed. If he decided to head back at this point, he wouldn't make it back to Calder's without getting lost himself. He shrugged at Bergman, then started in the direction the others had gone.

Jane never acknowledged her growing search party. They let her lead and no one said much as they weaved through a heavily wooded area. The group moved slower than when Bergman led and would stop when Jane raised a hand for them to halt. She would strain to hear the slightest sound, her eyes closed, her neck craning. Disappointed, she would motion for them to start again. With Jane and Jacob a few paces ahead of Polk and Magee, the party climbed a steep hill. Cooper walked with Ellie and the doctor. Jane seemed to be a better leader than Bergman. She certainly had more at stake than the sheriff, and was as alert and irritable as a poked badger.

Cooper glanced over his shoulder. Bergman followed thirty paces behind. His glare made Cooper look away. The sheriff was in a foul mood, and Cooper sensed that he shouldn't be in Bergman's way if he felt like taking it out on someone.

At the top of the hill, Cooper had a feeling he knew where they were, at least in relation to the railroad tracks. The raised rail line curved west, disappearing into a thicket. He confirmed his feeling when he saw the sagging farmhouse where he'd made camp the night before. Along the side of the house would be the red water pump that spouted the coldest watered he'd ever tasted. Seeing the rise of the gabled roof, the overgrown bushes, the snarled trees, Cooper had an overwhelming feeling of déjà vu. Of course he'd seen the house before, just this morning, but the sensation didn't feel tied to earlier today. This was different.

Cooper asked, "Whose house is that atop the hill?"

"That's the Blankenship place. Or used to be," Dr. Thompson said, the only person to acknowledge Cooper's question. "Now, I guess it's left to the animals, the forest creatures and such. Too bad, too. It used to be a fine house."

"Who was Blankenship?"

"Reverend Horace Blankenship. He and his wife Eunice lived there. At one point the place was filled up with kids and grandkids, but long after the kids had moved on to other locales, the Blankenships left without a word in the middle of the night."

"Why's that Doc?"

"Not sure, really. Some say it was Harvard Square putting pressure on Horace for the mortgage. Don't know. But that was long ago. Decades."

"No one bought out the lot?"

"There was some interest after the bank took possession, but there's plenty of land out this way to build your own house. As time went on, the forest started creeping in on the property. By now, you'd have to put in some major work to re-clear the plot. And the house? A shambles."

Cooper felt drawn to the house. He kept an eye on it, nearly stumbling into Polk's feet.

Thompson was quiet, his information exhausted. The doctor looked down on Ellie, and the poor girl looked too tired to walk. She put up a good front as she trudged on. Cooper nodded his thanks, then picked up his pace to catch the Fowlers.

Jacob was taller than his mother, which made her seem even smaller. Earlier, she had said she used to watch Bergman when he was a child, and with Cooper thinking the sheriff was about thirty, that put her at least thirty-five. Even so, she looked younger than Bergman, and as she walked with Jacob, she looked too young to have two nearly grown sons.

The moon had fallen behind the trees and their only light was Polk's oil lamp still in Magee's possession. As they left the Blankenship property behind and descended the steady downhill, they entered a small valley steeped in damp fog. A surge of cool, earthy air brushed Cooper's face.

"The swamps? Why would the boys head this way?" Bergman asked.

"Because they're boys, and that'd be a boy-thing to do," Jane said.

"It's not too far from either the Fowler's place or the Banyon's," Dr. Thompson added. He moved like a man who didn't often leave his office. His arthritic movements were painful to watch, but he never complained.

"It just seems like where they'd be," Jane said.

"Why's that Miss Fowler?" Polk asked as he absently scratched his beard.

"Christ, I wish I could call it mother's intuition. At first I didn't want to search the swamp, but Jacob and I've searched just about everywhere else imaginable since last night. I want Jimmy to be anywhere else but the swamp. There's just no other place to go."

They walked on in silence and fanned out again to cover more ground. Soon, Jacob was the only person Cooper could see through the thickening fog. The others scuffled through thorny patches and cautiously hopped over marshy ground. As long as Cooper could still hear them, he wouldn't worry about becoming lost.

The ground became spongier with every downward step. Blooming flowers spilled their redolence to the nighttime sky. Stepping over snaking tree roots and small algae-covered pools, Cooper came across a level clearing. Ragged tree stumps speared skyward from the verdant water like shatter bones. The canopy enclosed the boggy glade like a ceiling.

Cooper saw the body for several seconds before his brain registered its import. Its shoes pointed toes up, the legs splayed in the mud. That was all that was visible. Green-scummed water covered the body from the waist up. The tip of its nose bobbed at the surface like an emerging island in a volcanic sea.

Cooper tried yelling for the others, but his voice caught just shy of his teeth. He cleared his throat, then tried again, letting loose a shout that sent birds angrily from their roosts.

Jacob was the first to arrive. The boy sprinted into the clearing, his wire-thin limbs flying wildly about. When he saw the body, he stopped as if struck in the chest. Cooper would've done anything to avoid seeing the look on his face.

Jane Fowler's scream stole Cooper's attention away from her son. She ran across the muddy ground all the way to the body, charging knee-deep into the water. Grabbing the shirt with both hands, she yanked up hard, as if there was still a life to save. She showed astonishing strength as she lifted the body from the water and brought it to rest in her lap as she sat on the muddy shore.

The others arrived as Jane rocked the corpse in her arms. Dr. Thompson attempted to shield Ellie from the awful sight. It didn't look like she wanted to see anyway. She pressed her face to his ribs.

Algae and moldering leaves clung to the body like a second skin. Jane muttered incomprehensible half-syllables. Her fingers trembled as she cleared the debris from the face, revealing swollen dead lips, a bloodless gash running the length of its cheek, and open eyes slathered with pond muck.

"This isn't my boy." The body dropped from her arms to the spongy ground. Standing on shaky legs, she looked at the others as if noticing them for the first time. Her eyes went from her hands to the body, then back to her hands. Realization sunk in.

"THIS IS NOT MY BOY!" Her expression slipped with oily ease from relief to utter revolt and then back again. Her flushed skin quickly blanched. Shock stole all sense from her and her eyes tilted back in her head. She fell to one knee and surprisingly, went no further. Polk went to her side and grabbed her by the armpit to steady her.

Thompson handed Ellie over to Magee, then approached the body. Cooper thought he would examine it, but he simply scowled and shook his head. The doctor didn't need to examine the body. Nothing in his power could change the fact that the boy was dead. He returned to Ellie's side, touching her shoulder.

"I'm sorry, Ellie. Someone did something terrible to George. I don't know who, but whoever did will see justice." Pain choked the strength from his voice. "I promise."

When Thompson went to embrace the child, she ran past him to the water's edge, to her brother's brutalized body. Reaching down, she touched the pallid skin of George's hand.

Unaware her nose had started to bleed again, a streak flowed from her nostril, to her lips. Letting loose a heartrending wail of misery, she fell to the muddy ground. She tugged George's damp shirtsleeve as if pleading for him to stand.

EIGHT

Considering Ellie's behavior, Cooper almost wished she'd go back to her hysterics. She stood with Dr. Thompson and Jane as the other townsfolk hoisted the boy's body from the seeping mire to a makeshift stretcher. Ellie's eyes were gummy and vacant. She sucked her thumb like a child half her age. Dr. Thompson hunched over to look into her eyes and take her pulse.

To make the stretcher, they tethered two long branches together with belts and suspenders. Polk gave up his outer shirt to cover the boy's face. When the body was ready for transport, Cooper offered to help, but they shook him away. Bergman hefted the front, while Polk and Magee handled the rear handles. They no longer fought over the oil lamp and had given up its possession to Jacob. The boy held it close to the stretcher, but kept his eyes facing his mother and Ellie.

When the sheriff nodded to Magee and Polk, the three men lifted George from the ground. Water dripped from the muddied clothes as if the body had sprung a leak. Because of his small stature, Polk's side hung lower by quite a bit. The stretcher dipped and a leg slipped off and dangled in the air, throwing the three men off balance. With the rest of the body sitting squarely on the stretcher, they couldn't do anything but stare at one another. When Cooper hurried to right the leg, his fingers skimmed across the cold exposed skin of the boy's calf. Even in the balmy night, a chill danced over his spine. The leg felt too heavy when he lifted it, as if a substance weightier than gravity held the lifeless flesh earthbound.

"Let's go," Bergman said, and the procession started back.

Jacob led, followed by the doctor and Ellie, the stretcher, with Cooper and Jane following.

"I liked George. He was a sweet kid," Jane said.

Cooper assumed she'd spoken to him, but he had nothing to say. He had no memories to share, so he remained silent as they snaked through the moonlit groundcover. Cooper had never felt so uncomfortable. These people seemed nice enough, especially Thompson, Jane and Ellie, but he wanted to leave Coal Hollow as soon as possible. Even though he was bone-weary from his long journey, he would gladly take to the rails tomorrow to escape the sadness of this town.

Ahead, Magee and Bergman lowered the stretcher to make it easier on Polk. The sky was beginning to bruise at the horizon with the coming morning. After besting a hill, they parted company with the last vestiges of the night's fog.

Jane stretched her arms over her head and couldn't help yawning. Her brown eyes were her most uncommon feature. They seemed to gleam through the darkness, especially when angered or upset. Now, nearly incoherent from exhaustion, her eyes lost their luster. She noticed Cooper looking at her as she finished her yawn. He felt ashamed for so blatantly taking in her features, as if she had caught him stealing. He looked away.

Quite unexpectedly, at least to Cooper, the group broke through a wooded ravine and were now facing the back of the buildings of downtown Coal Hollow. Just moments ago, Cooper couldn't imagine the end of their walk back. They could've continued for another hour without him beginning to wonder, but now they were nearly home. While the others had a home to return to, Cooper had his inviting mattress in his rented room to think about. He made a mental note to make provisions for paying Thea Calder before he fell asleep. The idea of having Hank Calder rouse him from sleep to kick him to the street for nonpayment didn't sound at all appealing.

Polk and Magee started to turn right, but Bergman stopped. His suddenness almost overturned the body. Bergman righted the stretcher. "Wait. We can't take the body to my office."

"Why not, you *are* the sheriff, right?" Magee said.

"Yeah, but I'm no mortician. You wouldn't want to step within a block of there come lunchtime."

"So what are you suggesting? You better suggest quickly, because if feels like my arm'as bout to fall off," Magee said.

"Calder's icehouse. We'll put the body there for the time being. How does that sound, Doc?"

"Seems the best thing to do. You don't want a body sitting out with how hot it's going to get when the sun comes up. We'll also need to track down his father to figure out burial details."

"All right then, we can take care of things from here. Why don't you get some sleep? It's been a long night," Bergman said to the Fowlers and Thompson, adjusting the stretcher from one hand to the other.

"Put the little one to bed, too," Magee said, motioning to Ellie. Her eyes were glazed. She held a blood-stained handkerchief to her nose as she clung to the doctor's arm.

"I'll let her sleep for a while before taking her back to her house. I'm guessing her father's not back now anyway." Dr. Thompson guided Ellie across the street and she went without resistance.

"When you go by the Banyon place, if Charles isn't back yet, then just drop her off at my place," Jane said, raising her voice so the doctor could hear. "Actually, if he's home, you still might want to bring her over."

"Sure thing, Janie. Go get some sleep yourself. We'll regroup tomorrow after some rest, and then track down your boy."

"I appreciate it."

The doctor nodded, and then he and Ellie were off again.

"Mom, let's go. I'm tired," Jacob said.

Jane shook her head, as if she'd just woken from sleepwalking. "Okay. Lead the way."

"Well, what about you?" Bergman asked Cooper. "Where you staying?"

"Same place you're headed. I rented a room at Calder's yesterday before dinnertime, and that bed's calling my name," Cooper said.

"Come on then," Magee said.

When they reached the icehouse door, Cooper rushed ahead to open it. He found a lantern inside and lit it with one of the stove matches sitting next to it. Cold air slapped his face, chilling the sweat still dripping from his skin. Cooper maneuvered around the others to hold open the second door ten feet from the first and waited for them to heft the body through the opening.

Gingerly, Polk and Magee stepped down a set of stairs cut into the ground itself. Bergman held the stretcher, not letting it get any farther. "Just place that lantern on the stretcher pole. We'll take it from here."

Cooper slipped the lantern's handle over the stretcher pole on Bergman's end, glad he wouldn't have to venture down the rickety-looking steps.

"Thanks for your help tonight. Just one thing--"

Polk and Magee groaned in unison.

"Since you're so accommodating, Coop, do me a favor."

"Sure, what is it?"

"Stick around in case we need to talk about the night's events."

"What?" Cooper felt sucker punched.

"I'm not accusing you of nothing. I just find it a little odd is all. A stranger comes to town and willingly joins a search party, almost as soon as he settles in. Then, he's the one who finds the body. I find it a little peculiar."

Cooper stood stunned. With how tired he felt, the thinly-veiled accusation was almost beyond his comprehension. He could do little more than nod before leaving the icehouse. He parsed Bergman's words as he walked along the side of the building to the exterior stairwell.

Does Bergman actually think I killed George?

If Cooper weren't the person in question, he supposed he would be suspicious of his arrival as well. He scaled the wooden stairs and entered the building's second floor.

He bypassed his room and the one occupied by Jasper Cartwright, the Calders' perpetual guest. He made his way to the general store and wrote a brief note on a slip of butcher paper, folding two day's rent inside. He placed it by the cash register, hoping Hank Calder would come across it early in the morning. He fought the squeaking steps as he went back upstairs. Once inside his room, he took a weary breath and removed his muddy shoes. He didn't bother changing clothes. He eased back on the mattress, his mind quickly glossing over with sleep.

He dreamed of buzzing mosquitoes swarming into thick black clouds, of scummy water reeking of freshly spilled blood. With a clarity he would remember upon waking, the boy's slashed cheek spread like an opening mouth. The skin stretched, then tore, the wound gaping wider.

NINE

The Fowlers walked along Teetering Road, the one lane dirt trap winding from one side of Summerset County to the other. Jacob's mom put her arm around him, mumbling about searching for Jimmy right after they got some rest. His mom had never been affectionate, but when she squeezed his shoulder, continuing to mumble on about how tall he was getting, he didn't shy away. He knew she didn't want him out of her sight.

The last traces of night slipped away; the somber silence and leaden air became a riot of chirping birds. Teetering Road picked up a quarter mile outside town, heading in a north-south direction. The Fowler's farmhouse was a mile south, and a couple farms farther down was the Banyon's one-room shack.

He blinked away the fatigue, trying to stay alert. He didn't want to bring up how they weren't exactly safe walking alone. Whoever killed George--probably some drunk nigger wandering in from Lewiston--was probably still around, could actually be hiding behind any of the countless tree trunks lining the road. His mom wasn't up for being careful, wasn't up for anything more than getting home and collapsing in bed. He'd be a fool not to be watchful.

Teetering Road curved east, and as it straightened again, he could see the double wheel ruts of their driveway. When they walked past the gray Ford Pickup, his mom chuckled weakly. He knew just what she was thinking. All that walking and they had a truck sitting at home, unused. The day before, they began their frantic search on foot since Jimmy had been on foot. They'd followed his trail through their pasture behind the house, but the bent grass had ended at the narrow creek just east of their property. They couldn't find his trail on either side of the creek. He could've gone just about anywhere from there. In retrospect, maybe they should've gone over to the Banyon place right away, but Jimmy was always going out at all hours, oftentimes by himself, chasing some new adventure.

"We're home." Jacob opened the front door. He walked his mom back to her bedroom at the far side of the house. Standing near the door, he made sure she safely made it to her bed.

"Thanks, Jacob. You're a good boy. You're going to be a good man. I can tell by your eyes. Just like your father's. I just need some sleep. I'll wake you with breakfast before we head out again."

"Sure, Mom. We'll find him straight away."

She gave him a brief smile that turned into a yawn. He closed the door, and didn't hear another sound from her room.

TEN

After Jacob closed her bedroom door, Jane sat on the edge of her bed. Her limbs humming with fatigue, she gave in and let herself cry silently. She didn't know what she would do. It seemed like they'd searched for Jimmy all over the county, yet he was still missing. But the worst part was finding George Banyon dead. Such a sweet boy. The boys had been best friends for so long. In some ways, Jane had wanted George to rub off some on Jimmy, calm him down a little. Get him to focus his attentions. Maybe she should have alerted the townsfolk right away about Jimmy's disappearance. At the time, it had crossed her mind, but seeking help would've reinforced the town's belief that she couldn't raise her boys on her own. Most people thought she needed a man in her life to keep her safe, to provide for her family. They had always looked at her differently than other mothers. If she weren't so goddamned foolish. And stubborn. She could only hope that whatever had gotten to George... that her Jimmy...

She felt so helpless.

She fell to her side, tears spilling across her cheek. She saw her wedding photo on the nightstand. She missed Dwight terribly. Ever since he passed, the feeling of missing him would come unbidden and unexpected. It wasn't the emotion itself that would surprise her, but the sudden strength of the emotion. She could be setting the dinner table, her mind on some mundane task, but then the empty chair would be a cruel reminder. For some reason the first snowfall brought on the worst possible heartache. The pure whiteness, gently falling, touching the autumn brown grass, melting against its diminished warmth.

Dwight returned from the war emaciated and sick, irreparably damaged from exposure to mustard gas. His mind had been left even weaker than his frail body. His blue eyes had once glimmered like jewels, but during his time crawling through those God awful trenches, ducking mortal volleys and machine gun fire, they had steeled to the somber blue of a cold winter's day. Jacob was born ten months after his return, and then Dwight was gone not long after, just that quickly. Too soon. She was too young to have two children and no husband. It would always be too soon.

ELEVEN

Jacob wanted to sleep, craved it like a starving man fantasizing a banquet spread, but his mind raced. He considered his empty bedroom, but to feel closer to his brother, he went to Jimmy's room instead. He picked up his baseball glove and slipped it on. Jimmy didn't like baseball anymore; his passion for it left him years ago, replaced by his interest in girls. It meant a lot to Jacob that his big brother still took time to play catch with him. Jacob would do anything to play catch with Jimmy again. One more time, just so he could let the big oaf tease him, pretend his palm hurt from him throwing too hard, and when they finished, having him ruffle his hair as they walked back to the house.

He took off the glove, tossed it on the bed. There wasn't much to the room. Dirty, holey socks littered the floor. The heavy coat he wore on chilly mornings in the fields hung on a bedpost. Jimmy's only indulgence was a short pile of new comics, flashy Tarzans, grim Dick Tracys, all neatly stacked on the dresser. It felt like Jimmy would never return home to wear his work coat, or finish reading those silly comic books.

Jimmy could be dead right now, his body thrown away like a sack of trash. Just like George Banyon.

Tears formed in his eyes. His mom had no one to keep her strong, no one to look out for her with Jimmy missing and possibly dead. He'd always been her rock, always there for her whenever the world was too rough and unkind to a young widow. Jacob didn't know if he could do the same. He wasn't as strong as Jimmy. He fell on the bed and buried his face in the pillow.

His mind drifted and sleep swept in. He slept dreamlessly until he woke with an aching back from the unfamiliar mattress, his eyes crusted with dried tears.

He rubbed his eyes awake as he stood. Judging the sun, he hadn't slept more than a couple hours. He felt guilty for his tears. He couldn't act this way, couldn't let his mom see him crying like a little kid.

Besides, Jimmy might not be dead. There was no sense in crying, not when he could walk through the front door at any moment.

Jacob picked up the first comic from the stack on the dresser. It was a Tarzan. Of course. Jimmy's favorite. His brother would often do stunts to show how he was as acrobatic and strong as his hero. Jumping from the top beam of the corncrib as the neighbor kids watched, landing in the scratchy-tassled corn. Climbing to the highest peak of the tallest tree in the woods near where old Greta lived. Not panicking as the branch he clung to bent to his weight, swinging to lower branches until he landed on the ground. Bowing to his awed audience. Brazenly presenting his audacity to the world.

While there were other comics, westerns and superheroes aplenty, Tarzan dominated. Reaching the bottom of the stack, he came across a thin composition notebook. Jimmy had never been studious--beyond his comics, all he ever read was the occasional sports column in the newspaper. Once school was out, he never held onto anything to remind him of the drudgery he had to endure for the better part of the year. Finding the notebook in his pile of prized possessions only heightened Jacob's curiosity.

He flipped it open and started to read, uncovering a side to his brother he didn't know existed. It was a dated journal. He skimmed the initial entry dated almost a year ago--a rambling jaunt stating his dreams of someday marrying Louise Bradshaw--and then flipped to the last entry, dated two nights ago. After finishing the entry, he shot up from the bed, rushing out to wake his mom. He thought he knew his brother, but after reading from his journal, Jimmy seemed like a complete stranger.

TWELVE

Jacob sat in the chair at the foot of his mom's bed, listening to her read aloud from Jimmy's journal:

I'm not sure what I should do. I know what I want to do. Just leave home, leave Coal Hollow and just keep walking. But Louise needs me. If we're going to have a baby, she needs me to be here for her. But what can I do to support a family? I can't think any way out of this mess besides joining the army. They don't pay much, but at least I can hope for a steady income. I guess I'll look into that right away. It's not like I can put it off, not with Louise--

A knock at the front door cut off her reading. They shared a questioning look, and then Jacob hastened to the door. Of course Jimmy wouldn't knock, but maybe someone brought news.

"Jacob?" his mom stopped him before he reached the door. "Let's keep this journal to ourselves for the time being. I don't want to jump to any conclusions until I can speak with Louise."

"Okay."

When Jacob opened the door, he saw Dr. Thomson standing on the landing, looking like he hadn't slept.

"Morning, Jacob."

"Oh, hi, Dr. Thompson. Ellie."

The girl looked worn through. She stood meekly to one side, brown bags under her eyes, acting every bit the doctor's wilted shadow. From what he saw of her lowered eyes, she'd been crying quite a bit. He supposed it was better than her glazed-over expression or hysterical cries from last night.

"Your mother awake?"

"I'm here, Dr. Thompson. Come on in." As Ellie entered, his mom put a hand on her shoulder and kissed the top of her head. "Can I get you some coffee?" she asked the doctor.

"That sounds not only good, but necessary."

They sat at the kitchen table as his mom prepared the coffee on the stove. She lit the burner and placed the pot on to boil. She took mugs from a cabinet, waiting for the water to heat up. "Have you eaten? Can I get you anything?"

"No, I served up brunch before we came over. It wasn't gourmet cuisine, but we won't starve. Ellie had pancakes and eggs. Isn't that right, Ellie?"

The girl nodded, but didn't speak.

In a hushed tone that still seemed to fill the room, his mom asked, "No word on Charles?"

"Afraid not."

Jacob felt uneasy sitting next to Ellie when he still had hope for his own brother. George had always been kind, including him in games when most older kids wouldn't give him the time of day. Jacob couldn't help imagining him packed in straw inside the Calder's icehouse, waiting to be dumped into a fresh grave. He tried avoiding Ellie's gaze, but didn't need to worry. She didn't look up from her clasped hands resting on the table.

As his mom brought out coffee, including a cup for Jacob which she normally didn't abide, Dr. Thompson explained how he'd stopped at the empty Banyon house, how nothing appeared upturned or out of place. Just empty, seeming abandoned. He asked Jacob to bring in Ellie's bag from the trunk of his car. While at the Banyon's, he'd gathered a couple night's worth of clothes and her rag doll. When Jacob returned with Ellie's bag, the adults were talking about resuming the search for Jimmy.

"I appreciate your help, Dr. Thompson, but before we go wandering all over the county again, I think we should consider going about this in a different way."

"What are you thinking, Janie?"

"First off, I'd like to go talk to Jimmy's friends. He was popular--just about everybody knew him in one way or another. First on that list, I'd like to talk to Louise Bradshaw."

"That's right," the doctor said, surprised. "They've been courting, haven't they? Would you like a lift?"

"No, that's kind of you. We were heading out when you pulled up. I'd like to talk to Louise in private. I think she might speak openly if it's on a woman to woman basis."

"Is Ellie all right staying with you?"

"Ellie can stay as long as she wants."

THIRTEEN

Thinking back to yesterday, Betty Harris realized how easily and instantly a child could change. Change not just in mood, but in a single moment become a different child down to their core.

Junior had come skipping up from the rear of the farm from parts unknown, covered in fresh scrapes and mud, a writhing garter snake slithering free from his pocket. In that snapshot moment, he looked every bit a Mark Twain character. As he came to an exaggerated halt near the garden, his teeth gleamed a white streak across his mud-speckled face. Judging his carefree temperament, it must have been quite an adventure-filled day.

Betty hefted one side of a produce-laden basket while their mother lifted the other. They brought it waist high before shifting it to the wagon bed. The sun was creeping behind the trees, a lurking pumpkin ready for slumber. The wagon would be ready for their mom to take to Calder's come morning.

Before Junior's arrival, they had worked out the details of their story. Or rather, Betty listened as her mother explained how things had to play out. After letting her in on secrets only certain adults of Coal Hollow shared, they had begun preparing for Junior's return home.

Wrangling the snake back into his pocket, even as young as he was, Junior sensed something was amiss.

Betty helped their mom cover the three produce baskets with a canvas tarp against the elements. Once the chore was finished, there was no avoiding Junior.

Before he could ask what'd got their goat, their mom had blurted, "Your dad's gone. He died in his sleep. He's gone."

In that instant, like a babe opening his eyes for the first time, Junior changed. The happy, youthful energy slid from his limbs. His eyes tensed as he searched for meaning in their mom's words. With doubtful eyes, he turned to Betty, but she looked to the ground, to Junior's bare feet. The garter snake flopped free, slithering to safety without Junior noticing.

Their dad had been sick with blacklung for so long, everyone in the family assumed it would eventually take him. Junior had never known his father to be well, to be youthful, without infirmity.

"We buried him just after sunup," Betty lied, speaking her mom's words, still unable to meet Junior's gaze.

"Daddy's gone?"

"You'll go by Gerald now, son. You're the man of the house."

Junior didn't cry, at least not in front of Betty. He walked away, dismayed, as if he'd just heard that tomorrow it'd rain buckets and he'd have to spend the day inside. He took a few steps down the trail leading to Aunt Paulette's house, but backtracked quickly when he realized his dad was buried at the end of the path. Still not saying a word, he went to the barn, to the comfort of his gray foal, Iggy. He slid the door closed behind him. The horse whinnied in greeting, and then the barn was quiet. Junior didn't come out until Betty was in bed, and then, he merely slinked into his own bed. A boy changed instantly, never to return to who he was.

Her mom had been right. Junior hadn't questioned the illogic of the swift burial. He was still too young.

Noontime was sunny and their mom had yet to return from her trip to town. She'd come home with a paltry credit slip instead of real money. Her dad always prided himself on making something of that small garden plot. Betty didn't care about the credit and didn't understand his glowing pride whenever someone lauded his green thumb. Instead, she dreamed of going to those fancy shops in Peoria and picking out a new dress and bringing it to the check out girl without even looking for a price tag. But no. All of that toil and sweat in the garden would get them store credit for ice or flour or some other trivial purchase.

Betty leaned her temple against the window frame and watched Junior sitting Indian-style next to the empty grave. It was too far away for her to see the headstone, for which she was grateful. Seeing Junior's messy blond hair shifting in the breeze, his slumped shoulders and downward gaze, she felt terribly guilty for lying to him.

He'd gone out there after breakfast, still having not said much of anything. Since then, she'd kept an eye on him, worried. His only movement was to snag a fresh blade of grass to chew on before returning his hands to his lap. He was broken. Like a shattered piece of pottery. Seeing him like that made her feel fragile herself, as if she too could shatter under the weight of an uncertain world.

Junior startled Betty by standing. His blond head popped up quick as a frog jumping from a lily pad, but his expression didn't match his energy. She still hadn't seen him shed a tear, but his eyes were bloodshot. When he reached the rear of the house, he stormed up the three steps to the door, came in and swept past Betty.

"Are you hungry?" she asked.

"No." He didn't slow down. He marched right back to their bedroom.

"I can make us some sandwiches. Tomatoes and cheese."

"I said no."

His curtness made her flash with anger. She wanted to spill the secret, let him know their dad was still alive. But she didn't. He slammed the door. In a way, she was grateful for Junior's sadness. Otherwise, she might've spilled the beans. She couldn't do such a thing to her brother.

Distraction was a powerful thing. She thought about the tomato and cheese sandwich she tried to ply Junior with, and decided to make one for herself.

Gotta keep busy. Gotta get on with things. Because nothing bad really happened.

Her daddy was nearby and alive, and by now his illness would be healed as if by magic. He would never again cough up blood, his face flushed with purple blotches from the effort. Yes, he was alive, and even if he'd never walk her down the aisle at her wedding, or bounce a grandchild on his knee, he was alive.

She sliced the tomato and bread and cheese, slapping together her sandwich. She bit into it, the tomato gushing and cold against her teeth.

If he was unharmed--better than unharmed, actually healed of his sickness--why did she feel so empty?

Her appetite disappeared. She set aside the sandwich and walked down the hall. The cellar door was off to the right, but she avoided it, ignored its very existence, instead, she pressed her ear to her bedroom door. Junior's mewling cry sounded like a smothered kitten. She imagined his head under his pillow, both seething with pain and fighting to control his emotions. She was glad he was crying. Crying meant he'd get over it and move on. All for the better. She still felt guilty.

The screen door screeched open, then slammed shut. Betty jumped away from the bedroom, embarrassed for having listened to Junior when all he wanted was to mourn in private.

"Betty, come here please." Her mom looked tired and sweaty, as if she'd just mowed the front lawn with their push mower.

"How did it go? Did you tell Hank Calder?" They'd agreed they should let the town know what had happened to Gerald Harris, doting father of two, generous and loving husband, lies and all.

"Yes, I did. I also stopped in on the doctor, and he respected our wishes for privacy. They'll help spread the word," she said. As if saying the words had taken up the last of her energy, she slumped into a chair at the kitchen table, then stared off at the floor.

"That's it?"

"We got our credit. Hank gave me too much for the lettuce, but he's a kind man underneath it all. I think he did that instead of talking to me. He understands; he's lost his wife, you know. He understands what it's like."

"But it's not the same. Not with Daddy."

"You can't let on it's not."

"It makes me sick, Momma. I don't know if I can do this."

"Someday we'll see your father again. Then it'll be worth it. Just think of that. Seeing your father again."

"I guess."

"There's something I heard in town, Betty-Mae. I'm not sure how to tell you this..."

"What?" Betty approached her mom when she saw tears in her eyes. "What is it?"

"It's George."

Sensing her bleak tone, Betty's heart thrummed forcefully in her chest. "What about George?"

"He's dead. He died last night."

Betty let out a pent-up breath. Dead? The term didn't mean much anymore, did it? She let out a sharp laugh.

"Betty, I'm serious. It's not like your dad. He was mauled. By some animal. Out in the swamps."

"George? George Banyon?"

"Yes. I'm so sorry."

Her mom stood from her chair and stepped toward Betty, her arms extended in comfort. Betty pushed by her and out the back door, the screen snapping shut.

FOURTEEN

The sun was falling from its highpoint when Cooper woke. His muscles ached, but he felt rested for the first time in many weeks. He hadn't recovered from the many months on the road, but was heading in the right direction. He washed his face in the basin on the nightstand, and then changed clothes. He headed down the narrow stairwell to the dining area, letting his nose lead him. The air was infused with different aromas. Freshly baked bread and apple cider. Cinnamon sprigs. Fried chicken and mashed potatoes. The dining room was empty. Crumbs littered the tablecloth, chairs were askew, but people weren't enjoying the food that went along with the phantom aromas.

He heard a clattering of dishes, and without thinking, he headed toward the noise, passing amateur paintings of placid Midwestern landscapes, portraits of severe-looking pioneers. A recessed curio cabinet filled a wall, so prominent it seemed as if the Calders had built the entire house around a preexisting structure. Framed family photos lined the cabinet, packed as tight as fish scales. In one photo, Henry Calder was actually smiling. He sat in a chair and held a beautiful doe-eyed baby in his arms. A woman stood beside him, her delicate hand resting on his shoulder. Thea's mom matched his seated height. Her small mouth formed a slight Mona Lisa smile. Cooper could understand Bo Tingsley's harbored feelings for her.

"What are you doing?"

Cooper nearly jumped at Thea's shrill voice. "Sorry, I was just looking." He stepped away from the curio display.

"Just looking? Without permission to come back here, you might as well be a criminal." Thea's apron was wet, as if she'd been washing dishes for hours. Even so, plates and silverware were stacked in unstable towers behind her.

"I didn't mean any harm. I came down to eat, and when I didn't see anyone... I heard a noise, so I came this way."

"You missed lunch, obviously. I could shoot you for trespassing, and no court would convict me."

"I'm sorry, Miss Calder," he said as he turned quickly. "I'll be out of your way."

"Wait a minute."

Cooper faced her as she dried her hands on her apron.

"Maybe I shouldn't be so cross, especially with you being kind enough to at least drop off your payment last night."

"I didn't think I was going to wake for breakfast--"

"I heard what happened. It was all anyone could talk about at the supper table. George Banyon used to come in to buy penny candy, he and his sister. Such a shame. What a waste of a young life."

"I know. I'd never met him and it has me shaken. We didn't get back until the sun was starting to come up."

"Technically, you signed our contract, so I should boot you for breach." In the flash, Thea's spiteful side surfaced.

"So, do you want me to leave?" Cooper wondered where he would stay if the Calders had the only housing in all of Coal Hollow. He could always hole up how he normally did. Wrapped up in his blanket, hoping the hard ground wasn't too damp.

"You know, with all that's gone on since last night, and with you just arriving, why don't we make a little compromise?"

"What did you have in mind?"

Thea stepped aside and extended a hand to the piled dirty dishes as if revealing a prize.

FIFTEEN

Gerald Harris cheated death as he crawled through the numbing darkness. His time had come, had been hovering over him like a malevolent cloud since last year. He stubbornly ignored his fate when his burning cough started dredging up blood, and in recent weeks, bloody tissue. But ignore it he did. When stubbornness could no longer mask his fear, it was too late. He could do nothing to change his fate. Except, possibly, entering the Underground.

When they first entered the kitchen to take him from his family, he thought they were a bunch of coloreds bent on some kind of misguided revenge. But after a moment's hesitation, Gerald Harris recognized them for what they were. They weren't a bunch of crazed Negroes starting up a race war. Their skin was coal-blackened. Ashy dust coated their skin, clung to their curled mustaches and bushy sideburns. The melted candles at the crest of their helmets remained unlit. When they blinked, the whites of their eyes flickered like flinty moths in a dusky backdrop. They were white men stained black by their profession. His tension eased off to a steady hum.

Gerald knew about the Underground. Most of the old-timers could sift fact from fable easily enough. The three men who he had so easily followed into the hollows of the earth weren't alive, but they weren't exactly dead, either. They were the Collectors. Miners trapped years ago--long before Gerald first doffed his miner's helmet--trapped in some perpetual cycle of escape and rescue. They should've been dead, but weren't. They should have suffocated in their mining accident, should have long ago rotted and crumbled to nothing. But they hadn't.

The Collectors. With primal desperation they forged through their freshly cut tunnels, seeking out those who they could save. Their single-minded focus drove them to chip away at bedrock, layers of limestone, veins of coal, through topsoil and the foundations of houses, to at last save lives. The Collectors were myth when the mine was still open, a myth given a wink and a nod by the local miners as their patron saints. They were guardian angels looking out for them when they were at their weakest, guaranteeing their safety and survival as they toiled in the mines. In the bars after quitting time, the miners would tip a glass to the Collectors, followed by equal parts reverential silence and rowdy good cheer. Gerald never believed the stories, but respectfully tipped his glass, just in case.

When the mine closed, the young and able-bodied either signed on with other mining companies scarring the prairies of the middle-west, or wended their way back to the Appalachians, from which many of them originally emigrated. Those who remained in Coal Hollow accepted their burdens of diminished physical capacity and the poisoned lungs that accompanied a coal miner's old age. Over the years, the myth gained credibility as the old-timers closed in on their dying days. People were disappearing. Sick people. Sick *miners.* Last night had been Gerald Harris's time. The Collectors entered the Harris household with the promise of eternal life. He wondered what ultimate price they would exact as compensation for such a gift.

He couldn't see a thing, and only the shuffling ahead prevented him from colliding with the Collector leading the way. They had yet to say word one to him. The two trailing miners dragged their shovels and pickaxes, grinding the metal against the cold stone with every stride. In their silence he felt alone, as if he were a blind mole burrowing down into its den. They were moving at a generous clip, yet he couldn't hear their gusting breath. Maybe they didn't need to breathe. Gerald considered himself, and yes, from the gentle pull of his lungs in his chest, he was still breathing, still alive. But these other three men... being stuck in a lightless tunnel with these unbreathing, *undead...* Collectors, Gerald felt a surge of panic, the tight clench of claustrophobia. Thirty-six years in the mines and he had never felt so trapped; never to such an extent had he ever felt the weight of the world above him, the gravity of the cold stone earth pressing down as if to crush him.

He then heard a grunt from behind, a discordant friable voice lost in an undead chest cavity. *Did their blood still flow?* he wondered. *Did they have any thoughts other than to dig, shovel and pick their way through this lightless Underground maze?* Again, the grunt sounded from behind him, insistent and irritated. Ahead, the shuffling sounds ceased.

The sweat clinging to his skin dried unnervingly. He realized he was no longer crawling. He had stopped in order to catch his panic-stricken breath, questioning why he had so willingly followed these monsters into their lair, knowing it was far too late at this point to change his mind. There was a scraping sound from behind as a shovel was thrown forward, followed by a cold pinging sound as the shovel slammed into his right ankle. He screamed, his voice absorbed by the surrounding tons of solid rock. White hot pain burst from the impact and up his leg. After the initial pain subsided, all he heard was the Collectors' angered grunts. He couldn't find his voice--he choked on any words forming on his lips--rubbing the barbs of pain from his ankle. He blinked in the darkness, searching for clarity or understanding to this situation, but was left wanting. A shovel prodded his calf, urging him on.

"Okay, okay." Wondering if his ankle was broken, Gerald pressed on, following at the pace of his Collectors, not wanting to further anger them.

He lost all sense of time, but hours had passed, surely, since he first entered the dark tunnel. He hadn't coughed since they reached a certain level below ground, a level at least a half mile deep by his educated guess. In fact, he didn't even feel the urge, which had rarely happened in the last decade. Hand over hand he crawled through the lightless void, his knees going numb and his calloused hands sanding down to more sensitive layers for all the friction, yet with all the motion and effort, still no coughing.

He inhaled deeply, his lungs expanding to what he thought was their physical limit, then expanded more, taking in more chilly air. With every fraction of an ounce of additional air, his energy was building, and he could have sworn he felt a tingling in his chest. A good tingling. Warm and... healing. Yes, healing. A wood fire was close, and also, the warm doughy sweetness of... apple pie? In the darkness, Gerald Harris, though tentative and beyond confused, felt a smile crease his lips.

SIXTEEN

Cooper finished the last of the dishes and was wiping down a water spill around the sink's edge. *How did she do that?* he wondered. Thea Calder was beautiful, but he'd encountered beautiful women before. She hadn't blinded him by batting her eyelashes or offering him a charming smile. He couldn't pinpoint it beyond an unnatural ability for manipulation.

A heady swirl of pipe smoke let Cooper know he wasn't alone.

"She got you pretty good, didn't she?" Henry Calder stood against the doorframe, his thick arms folded across his chest. He offered a knowing smirk. His cob pipe bobbed as he gnawed on its tip, his teeth clicking along its well-chewed surface.

"I suppose she did, Mr. Calder." Cooper worked the dishrag around, chasing spilled water. "I'm sure if I stay for any length of time, I'll wind up cooking for everyone, too." He tossed the dishrag in the sink, finished with his end of the "deal."

Henry Calder laughed, the gruff tenor sounding uncommon for him, as if his voice had long ago forgotten that facility. "I think my daughter could convince a beggar to give up his last penny, and feel good about it, too. Thea's got a good heart, it's just sometimes hard to see." His expression hardened back to what Cooper expected of him. All scowl and jowl.

"I better get going."

"Before you do, can I ask you something?"

"Sure." Cooper had a suspicious feeling. Whenever someone from Coal Hollow asked him a question, it always seemed to lead him to regret.

"If you're going to stay a while, I was curious if you had any leads on what you're going to do?"

"Actually, I was hoping to find out today."

"Well, I might help you with that. It's not much, but it's something."

"You've piqued my interest." Cooper was relieved at Calder's innocuous line of questioning.

"Then follow me."

Cooper followed Henry through the general store and out the front door. He just now noticed the man's limp, how he favored his right leg, shortening his left stride to compensate.

Henry surprised him by heading toward the icehouse. Inside the first door, Calder noticed his pipe had died, so he tapped it empty against his shoe, stowing the pipe in a pocket. Shy of opening the second door, he grabbed a coat from a hook in the corner. He threw it to Cooper. "It's not the greatest, but once inside, you'll be glad for it."

He smelled sour sweat and sawdust as he pulled it on.

Donning a jacket and leather gloves, Calder opened the inner door. After the outside heat, the cold air felt harsh against his face. Cooper couldn't imagine working in the icehouse or for Henry Calder for that matter. He couldn't stop thinking about last night. They'd taken George Banyon's body into the icehouse.

Henry grabbed a lamp from a hook, lighting it with a long stick match. He waved the match like a magician's wand, extinguishing the flame. "Watch your step. Granddad cut those steps himself. It doesn't embarrass me admitting he was a better businessman than stonemason." Henry took an unsteady downward step, gripping the wall as he went.

Cooper thought back to the sight of George Banyon's face after Jane Fowler pulled him from the swamp. Cooper had touched the boy's skin when righting his leg after it had fallen from the makeshift stretcher. The skin had felt impossibly cold in the muggy July night. The boy's gashed cheek had spread wide like a second set of lips. The dead eyes flickered open--

His eyes never flickered, he corrected. *He was dead when I found him. Mud filled his eyes. I never saw them.*

They climbed down more stairs than he thought possible. The steps weren't close to level, each one beveling at a different angle, as if they climbed the spine of dead and buried monster.

"It's getting harder for me to move around, you see plainly, and I can't expect Thea to lift all these supplies. We store perishables and block ice down here. If I can't get down these steps, there's no way my business can stay afloat. I'd need you to move stock to the storeroom as needed, and on an odd day, help around the store. Also, the ice needs cutting."

It felt colder as they descended. Cooper never imagined seeing his breath in July, but it gushed from his nostrils, quite visible in the lantern glow. Behind them, a crack at the closed door let in a pencil-thin band of sunlight, but it was getting narrower, weaker. The hand-hewn stone and mortar walls disappeared. Bedrock cold as frozen February surrounded them as they left the stairs and entered a subterranean room.

"Granddad might've cut the stairs, but for the most part, the dimensions of this icehouse are God's work," Calder said with a flourish. The room's ceiling hardly allowed for Cooper to stand upright. Henry's lamp illuminated the room. Rows of rough wooden shelves held boxes and crates. The floor was bare and nearly as smooth as a man-made surface.

"How come it's so cold down here?" Cooper's teeth verged on clattering.

Henry limped down an aisle and appeared to be taking note of the stock levels of certain perishables. Without looking, he ducked a low stretch of ceiling. "I don't know all the particulars, but Granddad was on his way from Ohio to California to make himself rich. Somehow, when he stopped here to re-supply and rest his horses, he discovered the shaft leading to this room. No one's figured out the reasoning behind the cold. I'd rather not open it up for world discussion, neither. This land's allowed my family to live comfortable for three generations now. I'm not going to let nothing spoil that."

"I don't blame you."

Calder continued his tour. Large ice blocks filled nooks in the stone walls. Ice hooks as long as Cooper's arm hung on nails driven below one of the wooden shelves. He also noticed work gloves and thick-toothed ice saws.

"Usually right after New Year's, we harvest the ice from the Illinois River. I hire on local boys, mostly. They work hard, the older ones, and you don't need to pay them much. But then again, they aren't the most responsible people on the planet."

"I know what you mean."

"Ice doesn't melt a bit once we lug it down here, only shrinks some from evaporation," Calder said, then paused. His voice dropped in pitch as he continued, "Now don't get me wrong, I can understand Sheriff Bergman thinking it was a good idea to bring George's body down here last night, but I want him buried soon as possible. This is an icehouse, not a morgue."

Cooper followed Henry down the last aisle into a small open area beyond the last wooden shelf. A waist-high workbench lined the wall.

Burlap sacks covered an oblong mound the length of the table. Cooper didn't need to ask what lay hidden beneath.

"What do you say?"

After letting the words sink in, Cooper responded. "Oh, the work, the ice cutting and stocking. Sure, I'm up for it," he said, not sure if he meant it.

"Great. Can you start tomorrow?"

"Sure. Whenever you want."

"It's a deal then." Henry Calder seemed relieved Cooper had accepted his offer. He clamped him on the shoulder with a gloved hand and let out a short laugh. "Let's get our asses out of here before we freeze them off."

They walked back the way they had come, faster now with the cold setting in. Tomorrow, when Cooper started his new job, he would be sharing his work space with a dead body. He imagined using one of the thick-toothed saws to cut a block of ice, working hard enough to break a sweat in the icehouse's frigid depths, only to glance at the back wall, at the workbench and the burlap sacks. The coarse brown burlap shifting, the dead boy silently sitting up at the waist, his eyes opening, staring at Cooper.

"Shee-ite, it's cold as hell down here. Don't know how I ever managed to do all this work myself."

Cooper checked the workbench before it was out of view. He was fairly certain the burlap didn't move.

SEVENTEEN

Sitting in front of her vanity mirror, Thea Calder ran a soft-bristled brush through her brown locks. As a child she would count the strokes, reaching one hundred on each side as well as the back. While still fretful over her hair's luster, something else concerned her more, something that would lead to her inevitable ruin. She placed the brush next to its matching comb and leaned closer to her reflection. She opened her eyes wide then scrunched them almost closed. It wasn't her eyes themselves that worried her, but the slight lines at the corners. Wrinkles. They would be her death. Wrinkles spelled out demise in the hardest irrevocable lines across a woman's face. As indelible as Hester Prin's adulterous letter A.

Yes, the crease was more distinct today. Would be more so tomorrow. She could tear the ears from that new boarder's head for making her so angry. Wandering around their living quarters as if he were a member of their family--

How could this happen to her? She was only twenty-six. With the precautions she took, she could often pass for a schoolgirl around people who didn't know her. She was reeling on the edge of some precarious cliff. Every day sent her leaning farther; soon her momentum would be too great, and she would tumble down, tumble to her ruin. Someday she would be old.

She pulled back from her reflection, knowing that fretting made it worse. Instead, she focused on her best qualities. Her flowing chocolate curls always brought her attention and praise. She pursed her full lips into a bow as if ready to kiss the mirror, dabbing at the corner of her mouth with a hanky. Perhaps it wasn't so bad. Perhaps no one had noticed the new wrinkle.

If not, then they will someday, she thought unavoidably. *Someday soon.*

That was the real reason she had only two speaking parts during her time in California. Directors would say her face was fine, but her voice was fit for silent film. She could see through their lies. They watched her aging before their eyes. She could no longer pass for demure and innocent. Her appearance was heading straight for matronly.

Looking at the mirror, just over her reflection's shoulder, she sensed movement. Startled, she turned around, modestly holding a hand across her bosom as if she weren't dressed. The window was growing pale as the sun lost its strength. But she saw nothing unusual.

But it felt like eyes were on her. Somewhere out of sight, lurking in the shadows. Still there.

She knew this feeling well. Ever since her body had started to change at the age of twelve. The lecherous glare of a man. Any man. Married or not, young or old. Eyes on her, kneading her flesh with their lustful stares.

She wouldn't stand for this indiscretion. She stood quickly, toppling the stool. The narrow ledge outside her second floor window would be just wide enough for a particularly vulgar man to clamor along to gaze through her bedroom window.

A name popped into her head, and she felt right away she'd hit the nail squarely on its proverbial head.

Bo Tingsley. That lecherous bastard. First, lusting after her mother. Hoping to pry her away from her family to make her his own. People had always said Thea bore a striking resemblance to her mother. She wouldn't put it past the little bastard to redirect his lust toward her.

Without a lick of fear in her heart, she peered out the window, her nose an inch from the glass, checking at the widest possible angles for any sign of movement. She caught sight of someone's leg as he scurried along the narrow ledge and around the corner and out of sight. Full of rage, Thea Calder headed for her bedroom door. But before she could leave the room she obeyed a compulsion that had guided her life for as long as she could remember. She hastened back to the vanity mirror, checked her face, pushed an errant curl from her eyes. Then and only then could she leave her room.

That Bo Tingsley. How long has he been spying on me?

She fumed as she stormed down the hall, down the stairway and to the backdoor leading to the alley. She clenched her fingers into coiled-rope fists. This wouldn't do. Wouldn't do at all. Once she told Bo a thing or two, she would need to relax. Relax the stress from her face.

"Dear?" her father called out as she rushed by.

She heard him perfectly, but wasn't about to foist this trouble on him. She could take care of herself. He sighed at her brusqueness--such a familiar response, she noted. Indignant, he would withdraw to his dimly lit den, smoke his noxious-smelling pipe, and disappear into the memories of when their family was whole.

Thea put her father out of mind, reaching the backdoor and throwing it open. The outside stairwell angled over the doorway, leaving her standing in shadow.

The stench of rotting flesh nearly overpowered her. How wrong could she have been? She gasped as a cold hand grasped her wrist. It forced her to turn aside, her eyes taking in the horrible sight. Slick and wretched flesh falling in clumps from rotting bones. Gray lips forming a morbid sneer. Flies buzzing in frenzied feeding. And recognizing the man's eyes. Glints of starlight hovering near the pupils. Intelligent and intense. Green irises still swimming with life. So unlike the rest of his body.

She wanted to scream, but could only close her eyes as the man pulled her close. Her stomach pitched and rolled, but she willed herself to steady. The man's decayed lips brushed against hers before she could shy away, taking a step back.

"I couldn't wait to see you." The thing's voice grumbled unnervingly from around his decomposing vocal cords.

Taking in the sight of his rotting carcass and his vile odor--a mad shiver swept through Thea's limbs. She wanted to run away, flee his touch.

But they *did* have an arrangement. Even if he wasn't supposed to come to her, they still had an arrangement.

"Let's get out of here before you're seen. You damn fool."

Thea continued to scold Ethan Cartwright long after they found sanctuary within the bowels of the earth.

PART TWO

ONE

They threw Gerald Harris into the high-walled pit for refusing sex with the colored woman. The Collectors had taken him as far as a well-lit opening in the tunnel. With tired grunts, they issued him forth, jabbing him with their shovels. At that point, the strange happenings of the last few hours took a decidedly stranger turn.

His night-blind eyes took in a vast nexus-like chamber. Tunnels led away from a central axis point like spokes on a wheel. Hands clamped onto his upper arms from either side.

One of his captors began to chuckle. Another tugged at his twisted waxed mustache, and it came away in one sticky clump, leaving an adhesive residue on his lip. The others followed suit, removing their mining gear and wiping away the coal black staining their skin with equally well-stained rags.

"Who... who are you?" Torches lined the chamber walls between each tunnel spoke. He looked back to the tunnel from which he entered. These men weren't The Collectors. All he saw were filthy men identical in appearance, with once grievous wounds now healing by the second.

"We need your expertise."

He couldn't believe he'd trusted these men to be the mythical Collectors. "Expertise?"

"You're a miner, right? Your name's Harris?"

Gerald looked at the man, found it odd hearing a voice so far below the sun's reach after spending silent hours crawling through the dark.

"Yeah. Gerald Harris. Aren't you... who *are* you?"

While two of the men started laughing, the other yanked Gerald around until their noses nearly touched. There was no trace of humor in this man's eyes. His spittle sprayed Gerald's face as he spoke. "What years?" The grip on his arm tightened.

Gerald looked around, confused, taking in the broader details of each man. Only then, with the greasy coal dust smeared halfway clean of their skin, did he see they were brothers, and triplets at that. Husky men with shit-brown tobacco juice staining their chins. Their breath smelled sickly sweet with tooth rot.

The man shook him. "What years? You deaf?"

"Years, what years?"

One of the laughers regained his composer. "My dumbass brother wants to know when you worked the mines."

"Oh gosh, '91 until closing. Thirty-six years."

"Fww hoy, that's a long'un." The man spat juice to the floor, catching a dangling ribbon of saliva with the back of his hand. One of his brothers echoed him with his own spit glob a second later.

They loosened their grip. Gerald's arms tingled as the blood rushed back.

"Let's go. Time's wasting," one triplet said, laughing as if he'd just made a joke.

After traveling through a series of tunnels winding through ever-smaller chambers, they entered an unlit nook off a narrow tunnel. The triplets stopped.

The room was rank, saturated with the co-mingling scents of sweat, shit and sex.

"That's 'Wina over on that slab. You fuck her first before you join the rest."

Gerald didn't know what he was talking about. He didn't see anyone in the small chamber, and even so, he'd never do that with anyone but his wife.

He stepped back and bumped into a wall of farm-strong muscle. A hand shoved him forward.

Adjusting to the weak light, he saw the Negro girl's eyes. Then he noticed her pointed, sleek chin. Her shaved bald head. Her nude body. His confusion multiplied by the second. The Underground was supposed to be a holding ground for worthy whites, a gathering spot for those miners deserving salvation. Yet here was a Negro woman, nude, and they were expecting him to...

She didn't attempt to cover herself. Instead, she locked eyes with him, not afraid or ashamed or showing any trace of humility. Leaning back on her elbows, she spread her long legs. She seemed indifferent.

"Gotta take that girl. Go on." Another shove to his back.

A length of chain held her to the wall, the final hasp binding her neck. "No... I can't, I didn't know anything like this. No one ever told me--"

A punch to his shoulder blade both silenced him and threw him off balance. He fell to the ground in front of the girl. Piles of shit littered the floor all around her, morbid offerings laid at the feet of a perverse goddess.

Up close, a gray river trickled from between her legs. It seeped from the slab chaise to puddle on the floor. His hands were in it, cold and sticky between his fingers. He felt sick and ashamed.

"You fuck her, I don't care how or where or if you like it one iota. You fuck her."

"No. No, nonono..." Gerald pushed to his feet. The girl laughed at him contemptuously. He should have stayed with his family. He should have let his diseased lungs worsen, let the racking coughing fits tear him to pieces until he couldn't breathe, until he drowned on his own coal-stained blood. But no. He had chosen the path of cowardice.

One of the triplets hunkered in a squat, placing a hand on Gerald's shoulder. "You ain't gonna do her?" He sounded like a father imploring a child to eat his vegetables. "You gonna have to. You can't join the others if you don't. You want to go on living don'tcha? It's the only way."

The man increased the pressure on his shoulder. Gerald tensed, but didn't move. He felt immobilized, sitting on the soiled ground, staring at the colored thighs, then higher, at the fleshy breasts. "I... I can't."

There was a momentary quiet, heavy with dread. He looked still higher, over the girl's pointed chin, to her eyes. They gleamed with glints of distant torchlight. She had been watching Gerald flounder at her feet, but now her gaze lifted over his shoulder.

One of the brothers stepped forward, grinding loose pebbles underfoot. Then a boot crashed against the back of Gerald's skull. In the blink before unconsciousness, the cavern flashed with unearthly blue light. The light touched everything, and everything it touched looked like a dead thing.

Face down, eyes closed, he knew he was alive when he woke to the lump at the base of his skull throbbing like a second heartbeat. When he moved to massage the wound, he heard an ear-piercing scream. It took him a second to realize it wasn't his own. Opening his eyes, he blinked; a solid stone wall was six inches from his nose.

The screaming intensified, multiplied. It was cheering. A crazed crowd. Elated fans? He couldn't imaging what could be so thrilling. He placed his hands palm-down on the stone floor, then worked himself up to his knees. Ten feet away, another wall. He looked in every direction. The wall enclosed him. He was in some kind of pit.

"Get to your feet, you piece of shit!" someone shouted above him, breaking through the other indistinguishable shouting. "Come on!"

A rock whipped through the air, just wide of his ear, cracking against the wall. Gerald hopped to his feet, his mind still scattered from being stomped unconscious, pain spreading from his skull down his neck and shoulders.

A ring of faces lined the top of the twelve-foot high walls. Shoulder to shoulder, men and women watched him in the pit. Then a trickle of wetness struck his shoulder.

Gerald blinked through the spray, stepping out of range.

"That'll wake you up now!" a man shouted, his fly open. He knew this man. Had worked the mines with him, had trained him. Buford Higgins. He'd been to Buford's wedding, to his funeral, too. But his eyes were different now. Intense, unhinged. The man was crazy.

Gerald wiped the piss from his face, stared at the man whom he once considered a friend. Buford shifted, was swallowed by the crowd. Another face just as mad took his place.

You want to go on living don'tcha?

He'd refused to have sex with the Negro woman.

You can't join the others if you don't.

This must be his punishment.

The crowd jostled, everyone trying to get a better look, their faces twisted with a frightening mixture of hatred and ecstasy. Backlit with torches, their shadows danced along the floor of the pit like gamboling giants.

More rocks flew, some as large as ripe peaches. One thunked against his temple and he staggered. Blood flowed into his ringing ear, down his neck. He swayed on his feet, defenseless, waiting for his end.

What's happening? His mind was nearly drowned out by the screaming throng.

Above the sound of the crowd, *below* the sound, came the tortured cry of a wounded beast. Somewhere close. Gerald pressed his back against the wall, his heart aching, beating out of control. Searching the dark reaches of the pit, he detected movement at the far side, swaddled in the dancing shadow-bodies of the people above. The beast emerged; nose, face, eyes becoming visible as it left the darkness for the center of the pit. Gray skin mottled with black bruising. Ragged hair splotched with raw bald patches, as if locks had been torn out at the roots. The nails had grown long and ridged with age. It was a dead woman, draped in blood-blackened rags, somehow moving, somehow coming for him.

Keeping his back to the wall, Gerald circled the pit, searching for an escape. A doorway, a tunnel, a handhold to pull himself higher and out of reach. Daubs of darkened blood stained the walls, but he saw no handholds. No way out.

"Stay put, you piece of shit! Fight like a man!"

"Cha-chaaa!" the dead woman grunted at him.

The woman, the thing, because she was no longer a woman so much as a monster, charged him, knife-like nails bared. He tried to lunge away, but the thing was surprisingly swift. It was on him in a second, deftly pinning him against the wall, forcing the air from his lungs. Its eyes were demented, maniacal, hungry; its drooling mouth inches away and closing.

Fighting all the gentlemanly wisdom his father had instilled in him, he lashed out with his fists. With the first meaty impact, the crowd's roar surged, became deafening. He struck the top of the thing's head, hard, repeatedly, to no avail. While it was much shorter than him, it was decidedly stronger. He couldn't get away. He kept at it, pummeling head, face, shoulders, back--he might as well have been punching a wall.

The thing pulled its head back, eyes rolling back to full whites, gray-tinged teeth exposed to the torch light.

"Cha-chaaaa!" The thing's grunts became a mantra. "Cha-cha-chaaachaaar!"

As the thing swept its mouth forward, ready to bite the meat of his throat, not only did the crowd increase in its frenzy, but he also recognized this beast for who it used to be.

Mabel Banyon. His former neighbor. A woman whose delicate skin once favored mild spring days, a woman as tranquil as a baby's contented sigh.

His mind flashed to Mabel's funeral--standing with Betty-Mae and his wife, Junior not yet born, and everyone's sadness such a weighty thing--but was quickly brought back to the present as Mabel Banyon's teeth ripped his shirtcollar and pierced his skin, bored down through his muscle, before clicking together somewhere deep inside his throat. He heard gristly chewing and a contented sigh, then all was silent.

TWO

Someone was shaking Jimmy, but he didn't want to rise from the depths of sleep. Waking brought back the pain. Brought back to life his ruined flesh. He shoved away from the needling at his shoulder, rolling to his side on the cold stone slab. He wanted to remain here, unseen, just a lump in a corner of the old mining stables, not moving until long after they had forgotten about him and moved on to torment someone else. But the person shaking him was insistent, even if gentle in consideration of his wounds.

His captors were monsters. Could they be anything else but monsters? Cowering below ground. Beating him senseless. And the horrible things he'd heard. Joyful cries punctuated by tortured cries of pain. Beast-like growls followed by zealous applause.

"Mr. Jimmy, things are stirring up. You best be up and about. They're liable to get surly, they see you sleeping."

Jimmy groaned, his eyelids opening to slits. All he could see at first were the whites of Harold Barrow's eyes. In the darkness of the caverns, his charcoal skin was hard to detect. The old Negro looked concerned, not necessarily for Jimmy's well-being, but for the repercussions if Jimmy wasn't able to work yet. "Leave me alone, Harold."

"They'll get worse on you. They want you digging with me an' Benjamin."

"Let them get worse. Let them kill me. I don't care."

"But Mr. Jimmy, don't you know you can't die here? They bring you right up to where you think you can't take no more, then when you think you're gonna die, you only open your eyes again. Open your eyes to forever."

Jimmy eased to a sitting position. The faraway torches afforded little light at this distance. He could now make out Harold's face. His cheekbones were sharp, as if honed with a whetstone. His jaw line angled to a pointed chin covered in patchy white hair. His head was a mass of wiry whiteness, the hair unkempt, filthy.

"That so, Harold?" Jimmy touched the shackle rubbing the skin of his ankle. They were chained to the wall of a former stables that acted as their quarters. This section of the Underground overlapped with the old mines. The last of the cart mules left the stable long ago, but the ground was still littered with chaff dust and bits of hay, while the air carried a barn's pungent stench. A crust had formed around the ankle iron while Jimmy slept. It didn't take much walking for blood to lubricate the shackle.

The shackles bound their ankles with six feet of slack--enough length to allow them to walk in an awkward hobble in a small circle, to find a spot to squat and shit. When needed in another section of the Underground, their short lengths of chain were unlatched from the wall, and reattached to a waist-high cable lining the walls. Once attached to the cable system, they could move throughout the caverns as far as the cables permitted. Their rattling chains announced their presence long before anyone could see them. The monsters didn't want any surprises.

"You messing with me, Harold? Looking out for me; making sure I don't push them hard enough for them to go back on me, this time with their machetes?"

Harold didn't immediately answer. The old man stared into Jimmy's eyes, a chilling, angry look. He blinked several times, his expression softening in degrees. "These chains are like an umbilicus."

"A what?"

"Ain't you a farmer?"

"Yeah. Well, that's what my family does."

"You ever seen a calf birthed?"

"Plenty times."

"The umbilicus connects the calf to the momma."

"You mean the cord."

"That's right, the cord. Same as people and pigs and such. We got these chains on us, and we can't get away. If we could, God as my witness I would go this instant. Run off like a baby calf."

"What do you mean, Harold?"

"Oh, Mr. Jimmy, you'll see soon enough. You'll see so much you wish you wasn't born seeing."

A man walked along the narrow corridor leading from the main chamber to their stall at the end of the stable. Like a cavorting jester, his shadow danced in front of him on the uneven limestone wall. Hearing the approach, Harold stood quickly, looping a hand under Jimmy's armpit.

"That's trouble walking. Get up."

The man in charge of keeping order, a brute named Arthur Scully, had told Jimmy he expected him to work a full day alongside Harold and his son-in-law, Benjamin. Jimmy despised the prospects of forced labor, but what made it worse was the fact he'd been teamed up with the only Negroes he'd seen. Jimmy had seen Benjamin only once, when he first entered the cavern after swimming through the tunnel. He didn't notice right away--he had been surprised to distraction recognizing familiar faces from Coal Hollow in the gathering crowd--but Benjamin was chained to a wall, the wide meat of his back exposed. Not until Jimmy saw the lashing whip and heard the startling whip-crack did he realize he had ventured where he shouldn't. The crowd had engulfed Jimmy, and as they began to pummel him, George swam for his life toward the tunnel. They were whipping Benjamin even as Jimmy lost consciousness from the violent beating.

There was one other Negro prisoner, Harold's daughter, Edwina. They didn't put her to work along with her husband and father. They had certain other labors for her to attend to that kept her busy.

With Harold's help, Jimmy was able to stand.

"Rise and shine." Arthur Scully appeared from around a rock outcropping. His scalp was hairless and pink. His lips always seemed to quaver, as if he were verging on having a fit. A ham-sized fist swung at his side, an axe handle gripped in his clenched fingers.

Jimmy looked to Harold to see how the old man reacted to Scully. The Negro kept his eyes lowered, and his posture became more slight. His rough knit shirt hung on his lank shoulders. Jimmy tried to imitate the old Negro.

"Boy, you bring your new bitch with you and show him the ropes." He unlocked their chains from the wall, clamping the links over the cable, then relocked it. "You been at it awhile, that won't be no problem."

Scully swung the axe handle down on Jimmy, catching him in the lower back. He gave him one wallop, then stood back, waiting for a response. Jimmy writhed on the floor, his breaths accompanied by a sharp, jagged pain.

"Yeah, that's what I thought. Mornings, now on, you get one smack if you're good. Get your nose dirty, I'll club you 'til you ain't got any face left." Scully laughed, walking away.

"That Scully, he don't like you. That's for sure." Harold helped Jimmy again to stand.

"Bastard. I'm going to get him for that."

"You go on thinking that. Let's get going. Scully won't wait a minute before coming back swinging that axe handle."

Harold tried to aid him in walking, but he shrugged him off. He didn't want to owe anyone anything, especially a colored man.

Their chains rattled as they walked. Jimmy watched Harold pick up a shank of iron and pull it by hand, taking the pressure off his ankle. They passed a rough wooden door set inside a rocky face. A bloody handprint was smeared along the wall, still wet and dripping, as if someone had fought being put behind the barred door just minutes earlier. A chill seemed to pass through Harold as he saw it, but he quickly left the door behind without comment.

After long minutes of silence and near-dark, a low hallway opened off to their left. Harold quickened his pace, keeping his eyes keened ahead. Jimmy heard an animal-like grunting coming from a small, secluded room. He then glimpsed a man's white naked ass jouncing between two thin colored legs.

"Come on now, 'Wina! That's a girl, come on now!"

The girl's legs trembled as the man thrust into her. Jimmy's stomach clenched. He averted his gaze. Harold was staring back at him, his eyes haunted by sadness. Jimmy hurried next to the old man, leaving the unsettling sight behind.

"Harold--"

"Not a word Mr. Jimmy, not a word. I can't speak on it."

Jimmy kept his mouth shut. Harold slowed a bit, his bare feet scraping against the damp ground. They entered a high-ceilinged chamber, nearly running into a couple of men passing a bottle between them, taking long swigs. Upon seeing Jimmy and Harold, they looked disappointed. Jimmy figured that's where the line to Edwina started. Farther off, other men lounged on straw-padded seats cut into the limestone walls, drinking straight from hooch bottles and smoking hand-rolled cigarettes. It smelled like a barn, but there were no animals around. Just unwashed, foul-smelling men, sharing dirty jokes and laughter.

"Those men are off-shift. They're the old miners."

"Is that why they're not chained like us?"

"Sure, sure. Me, Benjamin, Edwina, we slaves. And you? They don't know what to do with the likes of you." The old man laughed weakly. "Here, we go off this way to where the work is."

"What is this place, Harold?" Jimmy whispered, trying not to draw any attention. The limestone had been carved away and wasn't a natural formation like the chamber where he and George had been fishing for White Bane. It didn't look smooth, aged by the elements; it was raw, a picked scab, gouged and irritated.

"This is just a small meetin' area. Like a social club. They drink an' tell bawdy stories, and well… you know…" They left the men behind, entering a corridor in which Jimmy had to turn sideways in order to walk. The candlelight didn't reach far into the cleft in the rock, and they walked for a short while in near-darkness.

"Who are they? Why are they underground?"

"I remember when underground was a good word for a Negro—"

"Harold, please. I've seen people I recognize from town."

"Mr. Jimmy, many of them been here long as me. There's others, newer ones trickle in here and there. Women, children, too. Miners, miners' families. See, it gets to be when you been here so long you can't never leave. But if you come here and stay, well, you come and stay long as you like."

They exited the narrow hall, Jimmy still not understanding this place. Sitting high on a boulder, Scully noted their arrival, returning to whittling a hunk of wood with a long blade. His axe handle rested against his thighs, within easy reach.

The room dwarfed the chamber they had just seen. Benjamin was at the opposite side of the room across a clear pond, so far distant his features were hard to see. He swung a pickaxe in a smooth, measured arc, carving chips from the limestone wall he faced. Every few swings, the axe spit a shower of sparks. A group of unchained white men worked the other side of the vast space, taking their time, drinking and talking as much as laboring.

"This is the new place. They call it 'Paradise.' It's gonna replace that ol' gathering spot."

"Jesus, Harold, how long have you been working on this?" It was as big as a football field, torches lining the walls. Between the stone support columns, bonfires dotted the ground, illuminating the sprawling dimensions. Carved stone seats and tables filled the room. A trio of men harnessed to a heavy wooden cart heaved by them, carrying away the waste rock. To his surprise, Jimmy saw Dewy Piersal, the owner of the last bar in town, pulling at the lead. Dewy used to give him penny candy for sweeping out the bar on Sunday mornings. After his business closed, he'd supposedly died, some said by his own hand. That must have been eight years ago. Dewy nodded to him in recognition, then looked ahead, focused at his task.

"How long? Can't say for certain, Mr. Jimmy."

"Why not?"

"Can't say 'cause I don't know what date it is."

"It's the end of June."

"June. June, what year?"

"1934."

Harold grunted as if struck in the stomach. He picked up a pickaxe for himself and handed Jimmy a shovel. "Come with me. I'll show you what's what." Harold lifted the chain to relieve the pressure, then began walking along the cable-lined wall.

Jimmy followed, holding the shovel in one hand while carrying his chain with the other. "So how long's it been?"

"Mr. Jimmy, my arithmetic ain't too good."

"Well, when did they take you and your family?"

"Oh... 1851. August 1851. I don't recall the 'xact date."

The shovel slipped Jimmy's grip, crashing to the floor. He couldn't believe his ears. When Scully shifted his weight in his perch, Jimmy quickly picked it up again.

Eighty-three years.

The methodical hammering of Benjamin's pickaxe echoed in Jimmy's head. They had imprisoned Harold and his family for eighty-three years. Looking at the hand-carved walls--unable to fathom the time and effort to do such work--he wondered if this really was hell.

Harold's words trundled through his head as steadily as the ringing clang of Benjamin's pickaxe:

You been here so long you can't never leave.

When you think you're gonna die, you only open your eyes again.

Open your eyes to forever...

Jimmy followed Harold's instructions, shoveling away the piles of chipped limestone, loading the waste rock into a wheeled cart. His back was hurting not even an hour later, adding to his miseries. Stretching out the kinks in his spine, his eyes rested on the cavern's ceiling. He imagined desperately clawing his fingers through the rock and clay and the layer of top soil above, imagined pushing back the earth, reaching the fields where he'd grown up, a land he thought he knew like the back of his hand. He wondered if his family was worried about him.

THREE

A knowledgeable person could travel during daylight hours from one side of town to the other without once having sunlight touch their skin. Few people knew about the labyrinthine tunnels tying together certain of the town's buildings, and still fewer knew who first lent spade to earth to begin their construction. Some say Indians attuned to the functions of nature began digging with sticks and rough stone tools. In sparsely traveled tunnels the remains of ancient campfire could be found, if someone were inclined to search. In crannies of rock, sharp tools had been left where aboriginals once tread. Under layers of dust, broken bones and shattered skulls remained after a long ago hunt and feast. If someone were inclined to search--and no one in the know seemed to be the prying sort--the bones might be seen as human remains.

At the time of the town's charter, the people of Coal Hollow dedicated their lives to serve God. With their every word and action they devoted their energies to their savior. Coal Hollow soon became an abolitionist stronghold. In order to spread their word, local pamphleteers and newspapermen spun out essays to a national audience at a blurring rate. North to Chicago, east to Boston and New York, and south to whoever would listen. Their efforts fell on deaf ears. They soon found alternative methods to help those unfortunate souls forced into a servitude for someone other than their personal savior.

At the town's southernmost tip, the current owners of a deacon's former home, Mr. and Mrs. Wilbur Boynton, woke every morning at dawn and took to their beds nightly at eight o'clock sharp. They slept, ate their meals and read the Saturday Evening Post without realizing their home once served as an entryway to a secret world. The Boyntons would listen to the Amos 'n' Andy radio show at 7:15 p.m. before settling into bed, all the while ignorant that their home once played a pivotal role in the local abolitionist movement. The Boyntons, residents of Coal Hollow for thirty odd years, and soon to retire to their son's home in Kentucky, didn't know people once secretly gathered in their dirt floor cellar. Or the deacon would lead these residents in quiet prayer, everyone with their hands enjoined, their eyes dewed with love for their God. Or a runaway slave would often cower inside these prayer circles, usually marred by a master's brand or raised whip scars. After the preliminaries of prayer and food, they would lead the runaway to the safety of the tunnels, where the Underground's healing touch could work its wonder, until the time was right to continue on, farther North, to safer lands.

Beneath the cellar (where Mr. Boynton currently kept his workbench for tinkering with engines and such) a trapdoor remained hidden. From the Boyntons' cellar, a narrow passage led five hundred yards northeast to the Cloutiers' home. The Cloutiers didn't know about the secret wooden panel in their basement, or the cramped, unlit room behind it that was only big enough for someone to hide within if fearful for their life. The room had been empty of all but spider webs long before the Cloutiers emigrated from France in '02.

The hidden room in the Cloutier basement connected with the tunnel system, and somewhere in Claude Cloutier's north forty, the tunnel split in two. One shaft had collapsed farther north where the overhead traffic on Teetering Road had pummeled it for fifty years. Some people wondered why the road was in constant need of repair. Others knew the reason. They knew and they meant to keep the secret within their tightly held circle.

The surviving tunnel snaked toward downtown. The most frequently trafficked section of the labyrinth, the downtown tunnel had a spur leading away from the main tunnel. The spur--so low to the tunnel floor that most people would have to belly-crawl to traverse it-- terminated at a natural gap in a limestone wall. Once inside the gap, the air grew cold. Cold as winter, no matter what time of year.

This was where Thea Calder and Ethan Cartwright passed through to enter the Underground.

After confronting Ethan outside her house, the founder of the Southern Outfitters led her down the alleyway to the icehouse. Once inside, they passed the shelves of perishables, the chunks of ice awaiting Cooper's cutting, and finally, the workbench on the backmost wall where George Banyon's body lay in stasis before his burial.

Beneath the workbench, hidden behind sealed crates filled with rocks, the gap opened up to the spur leading to the downtown tunnel. Thea and Ethan had crawled through one after the other, carefully replacing the crates behind them.

When they left the tunnel system and entered a large cavern, a burly man in bib overalls greeted them. He held a sawed off shotgun at belt level, ready to fire on anyone not permitted in the Underground.

"Morning, Boss."

"Actually, it's much closer to night than morning, Daryl," Ethan said to the watchman.

"Well, it's morning to me. Just had my breakfast, matter of fact."

"Was it good?" Ethan asked. His decomposition had advanced to the point that his lips looked ready to fall from his face.

"Oh, sure was, Boss. The women put out a good spread."

"I'll have to agree with you there. I've never been disappointed. Good thing Miss Calder is exempt from domestic tasks, or my opinion might just change."

Thea clucked as if offended and slapped Ethan on the shoulder. He was always teasing her about her cooking; it had become a game of sorts.

Daryl, keeping his eyes to the floor, acknowledged Thea. "Miss Calder." His nod of greeting deepened to a bow. She smiled innocently, but in truth, she relished the man's subservience.

Ethan clapped the man on the back. "Keep up the good work, Daryl."

Ethan's decomposition began to heal as soon as they left the tunnel system and entered the cavern. The rotting stench of his flesh abated, and the lesions in his face were knitting themselves back to normal. His gray pallor warmed to flesh tones as sinews and muscles reformed and refitted themselves. Stark white epidermis stretched across his healing muscles.

The large cavern, which Ethan considered their town square, was lit with bonfires and oil lamps. Although on a smaller scale, the Underground resembled a town. People offered goods and services, albeit without a single token of currency exchanged. Money was useless in the Underground. Everyone shared in a communal subsistence. At the first hint of capitalistic behavior, Ethan would crush those individuals responsible.

Clusters of people, both men and women, were quietly talking or playing cards. The majority were imbibing from their network of hooch stills in order to maintain the steady drunk that allowed them to remain halfway sane in their claustrophobic existence.

"They've done it again." Thea pointed out the blood splatters along the floor leading to the pit.

"Something must bind everyone who comes here" he said, looking away from the splatters. Only Thea could illicit such a guilty look from him.

Thea stopped, crossing her arms. "Did you force me to fuck that poor girl?" She tapped her foot in the sticky redness for effect.

"No, of course not."

"Would you have thrown me into the pit when I refused?"

"Thea, please. Not now."

"It's disgusting."

"Humans *are* disgusting." Ethan tried to hold her hand, but she shrugged him away.

"You can stop this."

"I said, *not now*, Thea." The look in his eye made Thea relent. She didn't take his hand as he wanted, but continued to walk by his side.

His jaw clenched, Ethan begged off the constant approach of people wanting his private ear, or those who wanted to say hello and good day. His hand, now not so much rotting meat as warm flesh and soft skin, took hold of Thea's arm and rushed them through the rabble.

Ethan Cartwright's accommodations were by far the most extravagant in the Underground. His quarters extended far into the hills and the dimensions would measure mansion-like above ground. He had a library, three bedrooms, a dining hall, and within the privacy of his two bathrooms, he had had flushable toilets installed. At the center of his expansive living room, a slow flow of water trickled into a man-made pond. He swam laps under candlelight almost every day.

"I'm sorry about what I said. It's just... you have such command of your people. If you just told them to end it." She pressed a hand against the still-healing muscles of his chest.

"What am I to do, Thea? What can I do to change their lot?"

"It's boredom. That's all. That's why they throw people to the pit. That's why they drink hour after hour. They're bored and they have nothing to do."

"Again, I say, what am I to do?"

She said nothing, but ran her fingers through the fresh blond hair sprouting at his temples. She had no response because there was no cure for the depravity of the Underground. Could there be a more reasonable damnation? She had her reasons for coming here. Her skin became more taut and smoother upon her visits. Her hair more luxurious. When she looked in the mirror, she saw herself as young as the day she left for California.

After almost three years toiling in Hollywood, Thea reached her breaking point. A hack British director named Paul Hamilton-Hart attempted to convince her that a prominent speaking role in an upcoming movie was hers to have, if she could only find a way to persuade him into hiring her. It was a sign. Not *a* sign, but *the* sign. Directors reached for the casting couch card when an actress began showing her age. It was a sure way to sully her as she exited town, a worn hag lugging a battered suitcase.

Thea didn't consent. She had more self-worth than to demean herself to that level. She returned home jaded, weeping in her father's arms when she first saw him. He never voiced a single question about her stay in California, though she saw the words niggling at him. He didn't want to know. He was just happy to see her home and safe.

As Thea tried to get on with her life, working in her father's store, her mind would often drift to stories from her childhood. Tales of passages leading to an ageless respite. A place where time held no meaning. It took her several months to stumble across the access tunnel in the icehouse. When she found it, she felt foolish for having lived her entire life without knowing the Underground existed right below her feet. As she worked her way through the tunnels that first time, a group of watchmen captured her. They were on the verge of throwing her into the pit when Ethan stayed her execution. He took her into his life, and she accepted her role in his, even if at first her skin crawled at his touch.

Her attraction for him had grown since that day he saved her life. He hadn't pressured her as the Hollywood directors had. He always acted a gentleman; it was she who had to convince *him* to consummate their relationship. Ethan wasn't attractive in any standard sense of the word. But power transformed. It made the lame appear cunning, while the ugly became unique. It took her a long time to trust him. He could be quick-tempered and ruthless with his followers, but just as quickly he could surprise her with his tenderness. He was a man, and she had never met a man outside of her father who could be trusted, but over time, she had let her guard down around him.

"I want you to live with me. Don't return aboveground. Never leave this place," Ethan said. His lips met hers, and this time, she didn't hesitate. She returned the pressure of his lips in equal measure, holding him in her arms. She broke the embrace at just the right moment, when she had his full attention.

She paused, looking at this man who appeared to be not much older than herself, but who was in actuality the father of the oldest living person within Coal Hollow's town limits. His skin was so white the blue veins at his temples seemed to shift just below the surface--baby nightcrawlers floating in buttermilk. His eyes were pink with bloodshot.

A jagged purple scar started at his collarbone and terminated just above his groin. He never spoke of the wound other than to say he received it while fighting for the Army during the Second Seminole War. Sometimes he would cry out in his sleep. Thea would never try to wake him from his nightmare; instead, listening intently, she would try to learn more of her benefactor from the gibberish spilled from his dreaming mind. His dreams would reveal little, just snippets of barked orders, and distressing cries for mercy. He was a pitiful sight, thrashing in his sheets, batting away some unseen aggressor with his fists.

Though he convalesced long ago, the scar remained, so embedded in his flesh that even the powers of the Underground would never completely heal him.

She realized she hadn't responded; she had been staring off into the flame of an oil lamp. She looked up, Ethan waiting on her answer. "I can't do that."

"But I can't live without you. Just stay with me, Thea. It's what I want."

She ran her fingers through his hair. No one else would dare defy him. And she could, to an extent. "It's what I want, too. In time; we must be patient. You need me above. You need me to hear things, and I can't do that here."

Ethan looked at her with unguarded longing. He caressed her cheek. Judging his defeated expression, he knew she was right. "Okay. Until things die down. Until all of this business about those damn fool boys dies down."

Thea felt the warmth through Ethan's touch, and wondered for the thousandth time how such a place as the Underground could exist. A place where life and death were such flighty concepts.

Her mother's oft-spoken words caught her off guard:

Love makes you old, love blinds you and bends your will...

She kissed Ethan once more, and then left him standing by the doorway. She gave him a long-lashed wink as she crawled onto the bed. Ethan's hands were at his sides, fingers twitching, expectant. He looked so lost right now, a little boy. There was still something human looking back at her. She didn't want to admit her feelings were deepening. Becoming more than just convenience. Becoming real.

Love makes you old, love blinds you and bends your will, her mother would say, *but sometimes... sometimes that's okay.*

With deliberate slowness, she started to disrobe. She could do this now; feel comfortable with this, with Ethan. She opened her blouse and let it fall from her shoulders. She watched his eyes pan across breasts that would never sag, her slim hips and toned legs.

"I'll make certain no one will come to know this place." Ethan joined Thea in bed. "Then, I won't ever let you leave me."

Candlelight danced on his bleached-white skin as he kissed her neck. She ran her hands along his sides, then around to his shoulders, pulling him close. His skin should have decayed long ago, yet he gave off a heat that would one day consume her.

FOUR

Jacob shifted the pick-up into a lower gear, the engine grinding like a wounded animal. It lurched forward, smoothing out as they left the driveway, heading north. His mom didn't flinch when the truck caromed through an unforgiving pothole. Jimmy had taught his little brother how to drive a few years prior, thinking that another driver would come in handy around the farm. It had gotten to the point that his mom would head for the passenger side whenever they went for a drive. In his mom's eyes, he was becoming a man. Without Jimmy, she would still see him barely out of diapers.

Ellie sat between them, gripping her rag doll. His mom was scanning the road, the fields, anything within eyesight, searching for Jimmy.

The Bradshaws lived off a nameless dirt road a mile north of where Teetering Road forked from Main Street and downtown. If there was an upper crust in Coal Hollow society, the Bradshaws sat atop that crust. Louise's grandfather had been on the board of the Grendal Coal Company, and the money amassed in that capacity had stayed within Coal Hollow Township upon his retirement when the company moved away. Years ago they had allowed their surrounding fifty acres to sprout to forest. Instead of a typical farmhouse, her grandfather had built a sprawling three-story Victorian, complete with intricately styled veranda and a steepled turret. Jacob thought the house looked more like a castle, totally out of place nestled in the woods growing from the unending prairie.

"You stay here with Ellie," his mom said when he made the slight left turn into the driveway. They passed through ornate iron gates and followed the tree-lined drive to the house.

"Mom--" he said, not sure how to argue his case. He wanted to hear the conversation with Louise, but he understood it would be easier to gather information if he wasn't around.

"Were you going to say something?" Her eyes narrowed.

"No. No ma'am."

"I didn't think so. This is important, Jacob. Louise might have information on Jimmy's whereabouts."

"Okay."

He slowed the truck to a stop, the creaky brakes whining the whole way. If the Bradshaws hadn't seen the truck pull up the drive, they would've heard it approach.

"Wish me luck," his mom said as she left the truck.

His mom knocked on the door. When Mrs. Bradshaw opened the door, she paused as if unsure as to what to do. After an unbearable moment, she gave his mom a stiff hug. While not as poor as the Fowlers, Jacob's family had never gotten along well with the Bradshaws, well, except for Jimmy, he supposed. His brother got on real well with Louise, probably too well after reading his journal.

His mom looked back at the truck before following Mrs. Bradshaw inside. Checking the house for movement, he saw people through a sheer curtained window.

"What's Louise gonna know?" Ellie asked quietly. Her feet rested on the hump in the middle of the cab floor. Jacob had almost forgotten about her.

"She might know where Jimmy is." He kept his eyes on the window, hoping to see his mom or Louise. The Bradshaws were strict parents; he knew this from Jimmy's grumbling after coming home from visiting Louise. Her parents permitted them to meet on their porch. They would allow them to sit on the porch swing, but would often show up with cookies or glasses of sun tea. Her parents wouldn't let Louise get into the truck with Jimmy, and wouldn't even permit them to meet in town. Obviously, they had worked hard to get around her parents' rules.

"She don't know a thing. Jimmy came to our house, and he'n George went out alone."

"Louise might know something from earlier. We think he might've run off to the army."

"How could he run off if he came to our house? They both went missing at the same time."

"You don't know for sure if Jimmy came to your house. Do you?"

"No, I was asleep until Georgie took the gun from the wall."

Jacob looked away from the window and into Ellie's wide and watery eyes. When he had discovered Jimmy's journal, it seemed like the answer to their prayers. He hadn't taken the time to analyze the possibilities. Now, sitting with Ellie, he knew his mom was wasting her time. Even if Ellie was asleep until George woke her when he picked up the gun, it made no sense that Jimmy *wouldn't* be there.

"You know, whatever got Georgie, it got Jimmy, too."

Ellie's words cut to the bone. Jimmy wasn't safe and on his way to some boot camp. At best he was missing, at worst, dead. Jacob told his mom he would stay in the truck, but he had to hear what they were talking about. He just *had* to.

"You wait here." Jacob opened the door, hopped down, then eased it closed, not wanting to make any noise. He slinked up the dirt drive and then up the veranda steps. He got even lower, keeping under eyesight from the windows. The gauzy curtains blew in the slight breeze just above his head. He looked back to see Ellie gripping the edge of the truck's window, her watery eyes blinking with surprise.

Jacob heard his mom's voice through the open window.

"How old are you, Louise?" his mom asked.

He couldn't hear the girl's response.

"Seventeen? That's old enough. I was fifteen when I married. Had Jimmy before I was your age. It's tough, but there's worse things in the world."

"Mrs. Fowler--" a man's voice said. Jacob assumed it was Mr. Bradshaw.

"I don't know what you're trying to get at. I know you must be a nervous wreck with Jimmy missing. I just don't know what you expect from my daughter."

"I just want to know if she thinks Jimmy ran off."

"Ran off?" Mr. Bradshaw asked.

"I have reason to believe Jimmy enlisted in the army."

"You think Louise might know something about this?"

"Why, yes."

"Our children might have courted, Mrs. Fowler, but they're still children. They talked socially, sure, but *with* supervision. I would never allow--"

"Dad?"

"Louise?" Her father sounded shocked at his daughter's interruption.

The girl spoke so softly Jacob could barely hear. "Mrs. Fowler, I... I think he did. He was saying something--the last time he was over for tea--he said he might enlist." Her voice periodically broke with emotion. "He said he wanted to get away from Coal Hollow. Said there was no future in such a small town."

"Fine. Mrs. Fowler, you have your answer. I'm sorry for you and your family. I hope you hear from Jimmy soon. I wouldn't have permitted Louise to associate with him unless I thought he was reputable."

"Okay, Mr. Bradshaw, I'll let you get back to your family." Her voice was strained and on edge. Jacob was surprised she'd given up so easily.

Jacob heard bustling as people rose from their chairs. He scurried back to the truck. Ellie had the driver's side door open and waiting for him. His mom exited the house, Mrs. Bradshaw watching her leave from the open door, her fingers fretting about the lace bodice of her dress.

"Ellie--"

"Don't worry, I won't say nothing." Her lips twisted at a sly angle. "Tell me about it later."

With a sigh, his mom hopped into the cab. "That man doesn't know a thing."

"Mr. Bradshaw?" Jacob asked.

"He doesn't think his daughter could have a sinful thought in her head. He had no idea what I was talking about, and her mother, well, she just stood back and stared at me like I was speaking French."

"Did Louise say anything?"

"No, not really, but she didn't have to open her mouth. I could see it in her face. She's going to have Jimmy's baby. I'm just wondering how long it'll take for her parents to notice."

"And Jimmy?"

"It's just like I suspected. As soon as adulthood stares him in the face, he runs off. Sheriff Bergman's looking into the Peoria enlistment office for me. If he doesn't get back to me soon, I'm going to go out there myself."

Jacob was about to repeat what Ellie had mentioned, but his mom's expression stopped him short. She didn't look happy, but seemed somewhat relieved. He didn't want to hurt her or ruin what little hope she had. There wasn't much sense to Jimmy running off, even if Louise was pregnant. He had gone off somewhere with Ellie's brother, somewhere where they needed to tote around her father's over/under. Now, George was dead, Jimmy was missing. Jacob still had no answers.

FIVE

By Cooper's second day working for Henry Calder, he was relaxing into the routines of the store. For the most part, he knew where everything was kept and the job itself wasn't demanding. He could help a customer find an item, or track down a mop to clean up a mess. Only sharing his workplace with a corpse prevented him from relaxing completely. Each time he filled a wooden tote with stock to bring upstairs or when he had to cut a hunk of ice, he would make sure the folds of burlap hadn't shifted, that George Banyon was really and surely dead. Every time, at least to his own eyes, the burlap hadn't moved. Even so, it didn't get any easier.

After showing Cooper around the day before, Henry Calder had checked in on Cooper a couple times today, just to see if the place was still running and in one piece. Midmorning he had told him what a nice job he was doing, and then retreated to his study to smoke his pipe. He was surprised how quickly Calder handed over so much responsibility, but he wouldn't question his motives as long as it limited his time in the icehouse. From what Cooper could see, Thea wasn't much of a help to her father--he had seen her only briefly since he started--so Henry probably relished the idea of someone else making sure things ran smoothly.

Cooper was chasing cobwebs near the ceiling with a rag-topped broomstick. The jangling bells above the door made him turn with a start. The sun was hot, intensifying through the newly cleaned windows. A thin sheen of sweat coated his face.

"Hello, Coop." Sheriff Bergman removed his bowler cap. He wiped sweat from his brow. The thin strands of his hair belied his young face.

"Afternoon, Sheriff," Cooper said. "Can I help you?"

"Oh, just in for some browsing. Not much going on in my office.

Needed to stretch my legs."

"Need anything, just let me know."

"Sure will."

Bergman lowered his eyes to the nearest shelf. Cooper raised the broomstick, disrupting a spider from its web. He squashed the pest at the seam of the wall and ceiling. The sheriff was two rows over, eyes still trained on whatever was in front of him, not seeing whatever it was.

"You sure I can't help you find anything?"

The sheriff's face strained with indecision. He swiped a damp kerchief across his face and along the back of his neck. "Well, I'm not sure. I've been meaning, well since George..." the sheriff stopped abruptly, as if he had run out of words.

To end an uncomfortable silence, Cooper cleared his throat. "Sheriff?"

"Has Hank showed you how to place catalog orders?"

"I've placed some already. Mostly odds and ends. What can I help you with?"

"George Banyon's going to be buried tomorrow. I know it won't ship near in time, but it's got me to wondering. I don't have my own bible. Coal Hollow doesn't have a rightful preacher of any sort, hasn't in years. Dr. Thompson is the closest thing we got to a holy man, so he does most the talking graveside, but the whole ordeal... it's got me thinking is all."

"How about I show you what's available." Cooper waved Bergman over to the counter near the cash register. A yellowed catalog was open from when he placed a fabric order for Mrs. Trumount just after he opened this morning. He swiveled the catalog on its lazy-susan until it faced him. Bergman walked over, still seeming sheepish as Cooper flipped through the voluminous catalog.

"Seems like you have this place down pat."

"Mr. Calder was kind enough to offer me this position; I'll do my best not to let him down."

"That's honorable enough."

Cooper waited for Bergman to strike. He couldn't shake the feeling the sheriff didn't just come in to order a bible. Flipping too far in the catalog, to an extensive button section, he flipped back until he found the right page. A total of five bibles descending in value.

"Here we go." Cooper swiveled the lazy-susan until the catalog was facing Bergman right side up.

It took the sheriff no more than two seconds to make his selection. "This one. This is it. How long will it take to get it?" He tapped his finger at the bottom, at a cheap pulp bible bound in a faux leather cover. Cooper wondered what nature of tragedy would hasten the sheriff to dole out money for real cowhide and gilt-edged pages.

"We can get that in, let's see, two-three weeks tops."

"Fine. Let's go with that."

Cooper started filling out the order form, and even with his eyes lowered to the order pad, he could sense Bergman had something else on his mind.

"Coop?"

He looked up from the order pad.

Here it comes, he thought. The transformation from a grieving, soul-searching small town sheriff, to spiteful brow-beater with an axe to grind.

"I just wanted you to know, Dr. Thompson's concluded the boy didn't die maliciously, at least not at the hands of another person. After examining the body, Doc thinks an animal done that to his face."

"An animal?"

"He said a boar could've done something like that, could've run him down. Nothing sharp caused the gash, like a blade or nothing like that. Doc says the boy probably ran into a clearing where an animal was protecting its young. He also said a rock's hard edge could've gashed him up pretty good. If something got George spooked enough, he might've fallen while running through the swamp, and with the force of the fall, and if he hit a rock just the right way..."

"So, you've personally come to tell me this?"

"I didn't mean no harm by what I said the other night. I was wrong. I never thought you did anything to that boy. I would've locked you up if I had. It's just that--"

Cooper cut him off with a waved hand. "It's all right Sheriff Bergman. I understand. You know your townsfolk. You didn't know me from Genghis Khan."

"Gingis-Can?"

"Never mind. Here's your receipt. By the way, how's Ellie?"

"She's a tough one. She's with Jane Fowler, which I think is for the best, even if Charles turns up." Cooper thought back to the night he came to Coal Hollow. He'd learned that Jane used to look after Bergman when he was a child, when she was no more than a child herself. Ellie would be in safe hands.

"So her father just up and disappeared?"

"Charles Banyon might as well just up and disappear for good, you ask me. He done nothing for those kids. If he could just put down the bottle for a while, sober up, the man has talents like nobody I seen."

"How's that?" Cooper asked, curious.

"Well, for one," Bergman said, pointing to the storefront window. "That rocker? It came from Charles Banyon's hand. He can't read, don't know numbers to make an accurate measure. It's all hand-tooled, built by sight without a single measurement. The man has a talent."

The sheriff tucked the order receipt inside his shirt pocket and replaced his sweaty bowler to his head. He nodded Cooper his thanks and made for the door.

Before leaving, Bergman said, "Problem with men with talents... seems like they always got equal parts weakness offsetting them using it."

SIX

"I can't go," Ellie said quietly, her voice barely carrying in the humid night air. She could have been talking to herself.

Jacob's mom had set the girl up on the sofa in the living room, but during the first night under the Fowler's roof, Ellie had entered Jacob's bedroom, pulling a blanket in with her. As dawn neared, he'd tumbled over her as he got up to get a glass of water. She'd curled up in a ball on the floor, covered in the blanket despite the heat. She'd tried to apologize, but Jacob would have none of it. He drank his water, returned to his bed, and was soon back asleep.

This morning, after Jacob told his mom what had happened, she moved the mattress from Jimmy's bed to his bedroom floor. Jacob hadn't said a word about it. He wasn't crazy about Ellie sleeping in his room, but didn't see any harm in it either, at least for the short term.

"Did you say something?" Jacob asked sleepily. He wasn't tired, but didn't want to let on that he had been awake since he climbed into bed more than an hour earlier. He couldn't get his mind off things. Crazy things. Things that made him wonder about just about everyone he came across. If he didn't know his brother, then who could he know, who could he trust?

"I just can't go. The burial. I can't see them pouring dirt on Georgie."

He didn't know what to say. He couldn't see her face; only a narrow band of moonlight broke through the darkness of the room.

"I'm scared he's gonna be knocking to get out, and they'll still dump dirt on him. Or maybe he can still hear and feel everything, but can't do nothing about it. Can't even move to scratch an itch from his nose."

"Ellie--" He still didn't move, feeling helpless.

"I can't, Jacob. I can't go."

"Ellie, you do what you want," he said, hoping his words weren't a mistake. He paused to collect his thoughts before continuing, "You don't need to be there for George to know you love him. He's in heaven, and in heaven, they have a way of knowing what's in your heart."

She let out a shallow, hitching breath, as if she were about to cry. Without seeing her, he knew she gripped her rag doll desperately.

"I'll talk to my mom. I'm sure it'll be okay."

They were quiet for a while, and he could sense her relaxing. Her breathing became deeper, heading toward sleep.

Staring into the murky blackness of the ceiling, he listened to his own words still ringing through his head. If Jimmy was dead, then he was looking down on him from heaven right now, looking into Jacob's heart and seeing how much he missed him, and knowing that he loved him.

That's only If. If means jumping to conclusions. If doesn't mean a damn thing.

He shook his head, angry at himself for thinking the worst, for growing comfortable with it.

Ellie's small hand reached out from her lower mattress and squeezed his forearm, nearly startling a scream from him.

"Thanks, Jacob."

"It's okay, Ellie."

"Jacob?"

"Hmm?"

"Can you... can you be my brother?"

Emotion choked the words in his throat. "I'd be happy to."

Ellie didn't say any more, just squeezed his forearm again before pulling away. He could feel the trace heat left by her touch. Such a small hand, small as a doll's. He closed his eyes, shutting out the darkness of his bedroom, returning to the darkness of his thoughts. He flashed to the memory of George's body floating in the swamp muck and his mom clearing the debris from his face. He'd felt unexpected joy when it turned out the body hadn't been Jimmy. That momentary elation was now a pit of guilt eating away at him. Having Ellie sleep nearby sharpened his guilt. She was so young and alone. Someone had struck down the only responsible person in her life. No one deserved that. No one. He wouldn't wish that on his worst enemy. Not even a colored deserved that.

George Banyon was dead. Jimmy was missing. *Missing,* he reminded himself. *Only missing. Missing just means he's not here. He's somewhere else.*

112

Somewhere safe. He had to believe it. Had to.

As Jacob's thoughts began to twist with sleep, he resolved to do whatever he could to find his brother. And though he wasn't crazy about Ellie sharing his room, he felt better knowing she was safe. And that he wasn't alone.

SEVEN

Like every other night since entering town, Cooper retired to his bed above Calder's Mart, with a full stomach and a reassuring ceiling overhead. As he began to dream, it was as like every other night.

Running through the furrowed cornfield, his heart pounding, fearing capture, adrenaline stripping his nerves raw. Finding the house, THE house. Remembering to give the knock he didn't know he knew until his knuckles hit the door, and then waiting as whoever was playing the pipe organ stops, comes over to answer the door. The screech as it opens, and the old lady with the rheumy eyes allowing entry into her house. THE house.

She doesn't say a word, this stranger, his savior. She doesn't even look over her shoulder at him as she leads him down a narrow hall, down a flight of rickety stairs. On the landing, seeing his own reflection in a mirror, his skin uncommonly lost in shadow, slick with sweat. The old woman disappearing around a corner. His fingers touching his face, unbelieving, still staring at the reflection.

And remembering the old woman, hurrying to catch up to her farther down the hall. When he finds her, she smiles, her two remaining teeth telling of hard life and advancing age. Someone so put upon, living an inelegant life of burden, and still she offers her home to strangers.

She opens a door to a small, unlit room. Walks to the far corner. Feels along the wall, finds the hidden door, presses a fake panel, opens it. She smiles her two-toothed smile, and she gestures for him to enter the hidden room.

When he enters, only rejoice, his fear subdued, not gone, not forgotten. Simply pushed aside.

For inside this hidden room, his wife, his father-in-law, all he could ever hope for. Salvation.

Cooper woke, the sun at an odd angle, too high in the sky. He blinked, rubbed the crust from his eyes. He checked the time. Late morning. He had slept the night through. He jumped from bed, a plan corkscrewing through his brain, ending in an unwavering conclusion. That house. Horace Blankenship's old house. He couldn't remember much of his dream. Just that he had the urge to step inside the house, to take possession of it. The feeling was overwhelming, blocking all other thoughts.

Cooper cleaned up, and then left his rented room above Calder's Mart, heading straight for Harvard Square Bank.

EIGHT

Jimmy tore a strip of fabric from his shirt and bound his bloody hands. He'd known hard work. His whole life had been hard work, his dad having died when he was three. Straight away, he'd started helping his mom around the farm. Jacob couldn't even waddle yet, but somehow, Jimmy knew from the moment their mom dried her tears that he would need to look after Jacob, and that his mom needed him, too. And he worked. Small chores at first. Cleaning up after himself. Taking his dishes to the sink. Making sure he didn't leave a mess. Soon enough, he starting sweeping the floors and feeding the animals. When he was old enough for school, he worked before and after class. He'd taken over much of the farm's responsibilities by the time he was eleven. Still, since taking up a shovel and pickaxe and working next to Benjamin and Harold, Jimmy had never worked so hard in his life. Had never come close.

His palms had no skin. Swinging a pickaxe and wielding a shovel for hours on end rubbed away his skin to nothing. They felt coated in liquid fire, as if lit kerosene had been poured into his open palms, left to sear and bubble.

The thought of returning to work chipping away at the "Paradise" was maddening. Knowing his captors had imprisoned Harold and his family for so long only made it worse. For the first time since entering the Underground he was both coherent and desperate enough to flirt with the idea of escape.

"Don't bind them so tight," Benjamin said from where he slumped along the floor nearby. It was the first time the younger of the two Negro men had initiated a conversation with him. Benjamin kept to himself, occasionally speaking with his father-in-law in muted tones, always after their work was through, always with a leery eye cast in Jimmy's direction.

"I have to stop the bleeding," he said, gritting his teeth.

"But you wake tomorrow, you gonna rip off whatever skin you got left." Benjamin's shoulders were thick with muscle and his rough cotton shirt was a tatters strewn across them like seaweed. Jimmy wasn't sure if the uncertain light was playing tricks, but looking at Benjamin's hands, he saw no sign of bleeding, only a hint of callusing. "You intend on stopping the bleeding, but in the end, you just bring yourself more grief. Trust me, the air down here has a peculiar way with injuries."

Jimmy loosened his makeshift bandage, just enough to get the tingling back to his numb fingers.

"What a white boy like you doing down here, Jimmy?" Benjamin shifted his weight closer, until he could speak without fear of anyone else overhearing. Jimmy wasn't used to a colored man speaking to him so openly, especially one he had never spoken to. Just being around colored people wasn't an everyday occurrence. Their kind tended to keep to the unincorporated village of Lewiston. It was an afterthought on the map five miles away, yet their populations rarely mingled. In the aboveground world that felt so far away, if he came across a colored person, he'd feel an adrenaline surge, not from fear of danger, but more from fear of the unknown.

He tested his bandages and found the pain lessening. "It's stupid." Jimmy was ashamed, not wanting to admit risking his life to chase after an old woman's folktale.

"What am I gonna do, laugh at your plight?" He shook his ankle enough to rattle his shackle.

"White Bane," Jimmy said quietly. "Ever hear of it?"

"That big old devil fish? Sure I have. Even down here you hear tales. Most times whites ignore you like you're not there, so you hear plenty. You were trying to make something of yourself going after that legend, weren't you?"

"I guess. We saw a light, me and my friend George. We went through a small tunnel. You know the rest."

"Big mistake, boy. White Bane could've gotten you before you even made the other side that tunnel. Tell you the truth, you might've been better off." Benjamin sighed and stretched his arms over his head.

"That was you, in the tunnel when they grabbed me, wasn't it?"

"I don't recall much what happened that day."

"What were you doing so far from the stables?"

"What do you think?" Benjamin said.

Was Benjamin trying to escape when they came through from the underground lake? Jimmy tucked the little nugget of information away for later consideration. Benjamin wasn't a happy man. No one would be under the circumstances. The only men who seemed happy were the former miners brought Underground and put to work in exchange for their immortality. It seemed like Benjamin's personality had a hard enough edge that he might be a valuable asset if Jimmy ever figured out a way out of here.

After a while, Jimmy spoke up. "You seen White Bane?"

"What do you think?" he repeated.

Their conversation lagged again. Benjamin reclined and a moment later closed his eyes. Jimmy thought he had gone to sleep. Only after his ears attuned to the cavern's quiet did Jimmy realize a couple of men had stumbled close to where they rested.

"Where that nigger girl at?" one man said, slurring thickly.

"Let's just get another bottle instead."

Jimmy feigned sleep, closing his eyes to slits. He could see Benjamin wince at the mentioning of his wife, a woman Jimmy had never seen within sight of her husband. While Scully allowed for the male slaves to rest after long hours of labor, Edwina never returned.

Thinking of Louise, and just how much he had let down both her and the baby, his stomach clenched like a fist. He couldn't have just acted responsibly. He had to go on one last adventure. Now he felt certain he'd never see the sun rise or set again.

"Oh lord, it's been too long," one drunk said, laughing. "Gonna get me that girl." The voices were louder, closer. Jimmy recognized one of them, but couldn't quite place it.

"That's what you get for drinking yourself 'til your willy ain't nothing more'n a keg-tap on your bladder."

"Yeah, well she gotta be somewhere 'round here."

"Gimme that bottle."

"Fine, here 'tis."

The two men entered the stables and stood staring straight at Jimmy.

The shock of seeing the two men, and recognizing one of them clear as day, forced his eyes wide. His hand went to his ankle shackle, tracing the chain tethered to the wall. The heady odor of mule shit and hay chaff intensified. Jimmy tried backing away, but the stables were a dead end. No place to hide.

"Why you little shit," Charles Banyon said, shifting his weight from one foot to the other, coming to a drunken stasis somewhere in the middle. He gripped a bottle in his hand.

Jimmy gasped. He scrabbled back, not sure what to do, even less sure what George's father might do. Benjamin still hadn't moved. He could have been a dead man.

He found his voice. "Mr. Banyon, it's Jimmy, George's friend."

"You fucker... comin' down here..." Charles Banyon slurred, staggering forward, waving his index finger in the air. He grasped the stone wall and held on to it as he walked. His eyes glistened with anger. The bitter stench of his urine-drenched clothes filled the stable stall.

"Mr.--"

"Don't say nothin' boy." Banyon dropped the bottle and it shattered on the floor.

"But... George--"

"Goddamn bottle--"

"Mr.--"

"I ain't no mister. Shut your trap," Banyon snapped, looming over Jimmy.

Jimmy didn't say a word. He tried to plead with his eyes, tried to show Charles Banyon how much he wanted to leave this place. How much he wanted to live

He had to do something. Quickly.

"This is all your fault, boy. Now we can't let you go running 'round down here, then go back up top. Back to school. Talking. Spilling all to every open ear. This place ain't for kids, this place ain't." Charles Banyon teetered over, and for a moment, Jimmy thought the man was going to pass out. But as he leaned over, his hand came to rest on a rock the size of a summer-ripe cantaloupe. He shot a noxious breath from his nose, grimaced, and then hefted the rock. His face contorted to a sneer, slightly softened at the edges by his stupor.

"They went after George, Mr. Banyon, I don't know what happened, we were fishing, and then we came to this tunnel, and then they went after George. Please, Mr. Banyon!"

Banyon lifted the stone to shoulder-level, resting his hand near his collarbone. His expression didn't change with Jimmy's pleading. If anything, he seemed more focused, more clear-headed. "George. Why, George... he's dead."

Jimmy cowered away, his back scraping the stone wall, the shackle digging into the raw skin circling his ankle.

"No!" Jimmy flung his arms in front of his face.

"This ain't pretty. Can't have a soul speaking on this place." The melon-sized rock rolled at his finder tips. Drawing his arm forward, a bulky shadow swept through the corner of Jimmy's eye. The rock tipped from Banyon's grip, and the shadow descended on him, engulfing him, changing the rock's trajectory.

Jimmy saw the white spark of Benjamin's eyes as he held back Charles Banyon's arm. Banyon's friend leapt on Benjamin's back, pummeling him with wild, drunken swings. The rock fell through the air, glancing off the cavern's wall, ricocheting back, slamming into Jimmy's temple.

Jimmy had never known such darkness. Not even in this darkest pit of hell residing just below the surface of the town of Coal Hollow. As his brain hemorrhaged, the pressure building inside his skull, flashes of still-photo memories shimmered like stars during a summer night:

His mother's stoic profile as she gazes from her bedroom window, as always, searching for something not quite tangible.

Jacob's unabashed and goofy grin, his cheerful side guarded from watchful eyes.

The curve of Louise's breast, her peaked nipple, her brown eyes peering through her tousled blonde hair. Her cheek's warm glow, awash in expectation for their child.

His father, a fading memory nearly gone, a mere outline of angled cheekbones, waxed mustache, warm laughter.

The images were gone. In their place, only emptiness.

NINE

Two hours was all it took from the time Cooper woke from his latest dream to walk into the Harvard Square Bank, inquire with Mr. Prescott about the ownership of the old Blankenship property, and leave the bank with a property title in hand.

He couldn't explain his feelings for the house. Luckily, Mr. Prescott didn't question his motives, either. If he had, Cooper didn't think he could speak about it without sounding crazy. For his life entire, his most impulsive act had been to start this trek in the first place with little more than his grandmother's dying words to drive him. Despite never having stepped foot inside the Blankenship home, he couldn't leave Coal Hollow without inquiring about the property. Once his query began, his obsession with the place only intensified. His desire for knowledge became desire to own it.

His father's voice, gruff and tired, wasn't welcoming when he answered Cooper's call from Prescott's office. Cooper began the conversation intending to explain that he wasn't coming home until autumn, perhaps not until the holidays. His father took the reins of their conversation in his controlling manner, firing off a string of questions, more an interrogation than discussion.

In the end, however, he agreed to wire Cooper the money for the property. It was Cooper's money from his Chicago bank account. His father was reluctant to send it, but he did.

With Prescott busying himself with the pretense of searching his file cabinet, Cooper turned the conversation in his favor. He raised his voice, breaking through his father's relentless questioning with one brief, yet biting, admonition:

"You lied to me, father. My whole life, you lied to me."

His words silenced his father and solidified his own determination.

He *would* buy this house. He needed to. As the silence stretched, Cooper thought the line had gone dead, or his father had hung up on him. This was Cooper's only ammunition against his father, and he used it reluctantly. Speaking with a broken, defeated tone, he asked Cooper where he could find his pertinent banking information, and agreed to go to First Federal just as soon as he got off the phone.

Within an hour of his phone call home, he and Mr. Prescott had worked out the logistics of the title transfer. Mr. Prescott, dressed in an impeccable black suit, talked by phone with his counterpart at First Federal in Chicago. He secured the money transfer, following protocols Cooper knew little about. Cooper agreed to pay ten percent of the latent mortgage. He thought it was a great deal, a steal really, but Mr. Prescott wagered it was a beneficial deal for both parties. The property was untended, a wasteland with a nominal mortgage sitting dormant at the bank for decades. Having Cooper buy the land, even at a cut-rate deal, ensured the land would be put to use, while the bank was able to cut away a mortgage taking up dead space on its balance sheet.

"We're done here, Mr. Cooper. You've signed your papers. We'll need to file some paperwork with the county, but otherwise, the property is yours."

"Great. Thanks for your help, and so quickly, too."

"Normally it takes longer for a property transaction, but I can see you want to get in before the weekend. Plus, I'm in a hurry." Prescott looked at his watch, and noting the time, blurted, "Oh, I really need to be going."

"Sorry to have kept you."

"George Banyon's funeral is in the morning, and I have to make sure my suit is pressed."

"I should let you get going then."

"Thanks, Mr. Cooper. When you get a chance, let me know how things are going with the house."

"Sure thing."

They shook hands as Mr. Prescott led Cooper through the front door. The banker locked the door, and hurried around the side of the building. Hurrying to prepare for the burial of the dead boy Cooper had found less than a week prior.

What the hell did I just do? he wondered, looking at the property title in his hands. All he had wanted was for someone to show him the house. All he wanted was to have a look around. Sate his curiosity. But the price closed the deal.

He shook his head. The store fronts seemed sleepy and slightly sad.

What have I done? Cooper picked up his travel pack tucked under a bench outside the bank, lifting it to his shoulders. Walking past Magee's Barbershop, he glanced inside. Finding the place deserted, and continued on. He considered making an appearance at the cemetery the following morning, but thought better of it. He was a stranger, after all. Besides, other matters required his attention.

He held a brown envelope in his hand, the property title folded inside. Hopefully, he'd find answers inside the envelope as well. Answers to the yearning that had grown in him since he first saw the house, and possibly even answers to his journey as well. His yearning to be inside the old Blankenship home, now *his* home, only grew as he walked from town. He walked at a good clip down the dirt road for ten minutes until he stood at the mouth of the overgrown driveway.

His overgrown driveway.

Turning up the long driveway, fat rain drops began to pepper the brown envelope. His pack gnawing at his bones, his thoughts shifted to security, warmth, a roof over his head. He would need to speak with his boss sometime soon. He hadn't spoken to Hank about his new purchase, and he was hoping to continue with the job even though he would no longer need the room rental.

The rain didn't matter. Nothing mattered to him but entering the house. He looked up at a second story window, sensing a light from the corner of his eye. He saw a warm yellow glow, then blinked away the rain spattering his eyes. When he opened his eyes again, the pane was dark and slick with rain. The rain clouds shifted overhead. He chalked it up to a glare on the glass, a small respite in the cloudbank, the sun peeking through for a moment, nothing more.

He climbed the steps of the wrap-around porch. He wondered how he was going to get inside his new house, considering Mr. Prescott, in his haste to leave, couldn't find keys to give him. But he found the front door slightly ajar, as if someone might be expecting him, a slit of darkness at the corner of the frame. Had it warped open on its frame? He touched the door, gave it a small push. It opened smoothly, and the unmarred blanket of dust let him know there weren't any squatters around.

That's one problem down, he thought. *How many to go?*

Stepping through the door, he glimpsed a memory. Or maybe a slice of dream. The door opening slowly, *this* door, *his* door, an old lady with watery gray eyes and stooped shoulders welcoming him inside. Welcoming him in to security. Salvation.

His sense of déjà vu was strong as he closed the door. The rain intensified outside the porch's protection. Lightning flashed in the distance followed by a grumbling thunderclap. Weak sunlight cut across the floor, revealing thick dust, dangling cobwebs, and hallways splitting from the entrance room. He didn't see any furniture, only a pipe organ's profile near a window at the farthest corner of the house. Somehow the instrument didn't seem out of place tucked out here in an abandoned house in the middle of nowhere. It didn't surprise him one bit to find it exactly where it was.

Cooper inhaled deeply the long closed-in air. When he exhaled, the whole house seemed to follow suit.

Cooper had been mistaken. It hadn't been the sun peeking through the cloud canopy to glare against the window pane. He *had* seen a light. A warm halo emanating from the house's interior. Waiting for him. Waiting for him to come inside, set things in motion, set things right. The lantern extinguished itself when Cooper glanced its way. As he entered the house, it retreated from the window, into the shadows gathered at the room's corner. There its owner remained. Waiting.

TEN

The shading wasn't right. The contrasting shadow hovering at the hollows of his cheeks far too dark.

Betty sat at the edge of her bed, a dull pencil held at an acute angle a quarter inch over the paper, waiting. As it had since she learned of George Banyon's death, her hand was shaking. She almost didn't notice it anymore, but she could see it reflected in her sketching. She just couldn't get it right. It was as if her mind had lost the ability to communicate with her hand.

Junior was her muse. He slept across from her in his bed, his eyes clenched shut, an occasional whimper slipping from his parched lips. But her sketch was not of him asleep, but rather of an earlier memory, the final moment before his life instantly changed. Scrapes and mud and gleaming white teeth. Tromping back from his boyhood escapades, enthralled with the feeling of living so free; the moment before their mother told him their father had died in his sleep.

He wasn't handling this well, her brother, Junior. Junior? He'd never be Gerald. Her father was Gerald, and he was alive. There was no reason to place such responsibility on a child.

Betty flexed her hand, trying to squeeze the shaking from the digits. If anything, it worsened.

For as long as she could remember she had kept a sketch pad nearby. She enjoyed landscapes, but the scope and scale were a bit daunting. Portraits were better, but sketching figures modeling her own clothing designs was her true joy. It would be her way to escape this place, or so she hoped. The first short scratch of lead to paper would transport her to a place where all women were glamorous. A place without want or loneliness. She hoped beyond hope to live her dream, to let her sketches pave the way to living that lifestyle. Problem was, who would notice her talents in Coal Hollow?

She flexed her hand again. It was troubling. How could she ever escape this place? No one would consider hiring a clothing designer with a palsied hand.

Junior shifted from his shoulder to his back. He opened his eyes, blinking twice. He looked around in confusion, but then rolled onto his stomach, slipping back into an uneasy sleep. Betty felt guilty for using him for inspiration (and not doing a good job at that), without his consent. She hugged a pillow across her lap, covering up the sketch pad, hugged it as if it were a loved one. Clutching the pillow made the shaking travel up her arms, until her whole body trembled.

Junior started snoring. Normally annoyed by the methodical ripsaw, she felt oddly comforted by it now.

She tossed the pillow aside and considered the sketch. The shading *was* too dark. While she had accurately rendered his boundless smile, and the scale of his limbs and torso was as close as she could master, the contrasting shading made Junior look cadaverous. The harsh detail of his arm muscles made him look skinless. Frozen in an anguish beyond recourse.

She couldn't tear the page out quickly enough. She crumpled it and threw it under her bed, out of eyesight. She shivered again, shivered so long it felt like she would never stop.

She knelt on the floor, took one last look at the sketch pad, then banished it under the bed as well. She might never again toy with the idea of designing. Never dream of escape. Not as long as she couldn't hold a pencil steady.

Or perhaps her pencil revealed the truth. Junior wasn't damaged in any physical way, but he might as well be. The image she had drawn was of Junior on the cusp of an indelible emotional wounding. Below the surface of his skin, flowing through him like lifeblood itself--the last moment of his innocence. She had captured that instant, first in her memory, and just now in her sketch. Having been a party to the destruction of her brother's innocence, she abided the deception following in its wake. She couldn't cast aside her subconscious while tapping into her creative reservoirs. It wasn't possible. Sketching would often reveal what she least wanted to face.

Alone with the familiarity of his steady snoring, she could easily start to cry. But she didn't. She wouldn't let herself. What sense were tears now?

She held on to the only thoughts that seemed any comfort: *He's alive.*

I'll see him again. When I do, he won't be sick. He'll laugh without coughing himself into a fit.

He's alive.

Repeating the phrase made it real, made it true.

Daddy's alive.

But she still felt like crying. Because her father wasn't the only person she missed. In a way, Junior and her father distracted from other matters.

She couldn't wish George alive and make it so.

She remembered earlier this summer, how nervous he had been standing on the river shore, dripping wet after climbing free of the clouded water. His shoulder sported a welted raspberry from crashing into the shallow river bottom after jumping from a rope strung from an overhanging tree branch.

She'd heard the rumors for weeks--since before school let out for summer--and had hoped the rumors were true.

Then it was finally happening.

Sitting, waiting, expectant, Betty closed her sketch pad before looking down from her perch on a high boulder.

"Hi, Betty." His voice cracked. His nervousness was charming.

Her heartbeat quickened, and she couldn't help laughing, both at his stupid stunt, and with the thrill of reaching the point of actual verbal communication.

George thought she had been laughing at him. He looked toward the other guys from class for a possible escape route, then wiped a droplet of water dangling from the tip of his nose.

Before he could run away, she spoke the first coherent thought to come to mind, "You're all wet."

"Yeah, well, what can I say?" he said, letting out a pent-up breath. "You should come in. It's nice."

"I'm not really dressed for it."

He looked disappointed. Practically devastated.

"Maybe tomorrow?" she offered.

"Okay. Tomorrow." His lips slanted into a grin, looking like he would say something else, something witty. Instead, he scampered off, bare feet slapping the rocky shore, right up to the swinging rope. Grabbing it in full stride, he flung himself into the air, letting out a whoop of joy. He splashed down, then jumped up with the spraying water. When George joined his friends wading in the shallow, Jimmy Fowler glanced her way before giving him a clap on the back.

She remembered the sun warming her skin and the familiar

smoothness of the sketch pad under her fingertips, and not wanting anyone to see what she was working on. Before George had approached her, she'd been drawing the rocky shore. It had only been an excuse. Everyone knew she was artistic and wouldn't question her taking in the river's detail. The absence of certain details would be more telling than those she chose to include. To keep her longing private, George wasn't in the drawing. The landscape was just a backdrop to consider at a later time, when she could add the detail of her memory. His squinty smile, his tan shoulders.

Their first interaction had been so simple, so flighty, yet when she got home that night, while trying to sleep, she considered the possibilities: Betty Harris Banyon, Betty-Mae Banyon. It had been all so silly. So naïve. Naïve, but still somehow genuine. And tomorrow, an event as genuine as life had to offer. A funeral. George Banyon's funeral. At that moment, it seemed like the worst thing in the world was that she never donned her swimsuit, never went splashing through the river at his side.

She wiped a single falling tear from her cheek and her memory drifted away like a dream. She noticed Junior had flipped again to his stomach. His snoring had quieted.

A new sound filled the void. Muffled voices. Coming from outside. Raspy, but ordered, like the chorus of a strange form of sentient insect.

Daddy's come home, she thought immediately. *No, that's wrong,* she corrected herself. *Would never be right. Daddy's never coming home.*

In her daydreaming her leg had fallen asleep. She rubbed life back into it, and then stood, warily looking out the window.

The moon was two days shy of full, hovering along the treeline like a glowing white face. The craters could be a crude mouth, a mere smudge of frown below hollow, downcast eyes--eyes that saw, just a second before Betty, people gathered at the family graveyard.

Junior was still asleep. Setting aside the distractions of Junior and her father and her fruitless longing for George Banyon, she stepped into her houseshoes. She opened the bedroom door as quietly as possible. The house was still. Her mom wouldn't be in her bedroom. She knew where she would find her.

The screen door screeched as she pulled it open, too loud. A chilling mist swept against her legs as she descended the stairs. The ground felt damp underfoot.

The mist carried the distant voices to her, amplifying the lowest tones of speech. She couldn't make out any words, just the weight of their mournful sadness.

Her every step drained her confidence. Still, her curiosity compelled her to keep moving. A steady breeze pressed the bare skin of her arms and legs like a firm hand. Goosebumps traced her spine and she wrapped her arms in front of her. Despite the unknown ahead, the darkness, the simple fact she could no longer be certain of anything that went on in this town, she hurried on through the mist.

She crouched the last twenty yards until she reached the property's edge. The voices separated, became distinct. The moon's luminescence touched the skin of the three people gathered around the newest grave.

A scream caught in her throat like a clenched fist. She wanted to cry out, but couldn't.

Her mother was weeping on Magee's shoulder, who in turn, looked terribly uncomfortable as he patted her back. Doctor Thompson held a closed book--possibly a bible--between his elbow and ribs. He was speaking over the open pit of her father's empty grave, his tone that of a preacher. A cheap pinewood casket sat next to the empty hole. Mismatched mounds filled the open casket--she could see just the crests of them--and in the moonlight they shimmered as if coated in wet paint or mud.

Thompson yelled into the grave, "We don't have all night." Hearing his tired, frail voice, Betty realized just how close she was to the grave, a grave she assumed was empty until now.

A mere twenty feet away. Her close proximity and the effect of the whitewashing moon left everyone in stark contrast to the dark backdrop of her Aunt Paulette's cornfield. Her mom looked wrung through and heartbroken as she continued to sob.

Dirt rained up from the hole, collecting on an already substantial pile. "I'm nearly done, just gimme a minute."

A minute went by, then another. Dirt flew from the deepening hole at alarming speed. It soon stopped and a shovel came flying out, clinking against a rock.

Fingers gripped the lip of the hole. The person grunted, pulling himself up and free. Betty uttered a noise like a strangled bird, unable to gain control of herself. She slapped a hand over her mouth, but it was too late.

Eyes darted her way. Her mom's. Dr. Thompson's. Magee's. The gravedigger's horrid black pustules set deeply in his gray-skinned death mask.

The man was rot and decay. Festering wounds seeped along his face, neck and naked shoulders. Pus and maggots fell in clumps like ladled stew from the cavernous hole in his cheeks. Something else twisted in the unnatural cavity. Black and sinuous. Creeping from between his ragged lips. A vile tongue lapping at his own ooze.

"Betty!" her mom cried, pulling free from Magee.

When Betty met her gaze she verged on fainting, but instead, she fell to her hands and knees, vomiting deeply, repeatedly, painfully.

Mom's involved in this? Something so horrible. How could she?

"Oh, my God, Betty! Why can't you just… stay out of it?" Her mom came to her side and rubbed her back with soothing circles as she would a flu-ridden child. "My poor girl." Tears made her voice watery.

But Betty wasn't soothed. Not one bit. "What," she gasped as the retching trailed off. She spit to clear the taste from her mouth. "What… what's going on?"

She looked from the pine coffin to the rotting man. Shock flashed across her face as if she were seeing him for the first time, as if it were possible to forget such a hideous sight. She fell to her rump and began pushing away with her feet. "No. Nonono! This isn't right. This isn't happening. This just isn't happening!"

The rotting man shambled toward her, leaving behind a slime trail of himself like a snail's path.

"Leave her alone, Scully! Don't you touch my daughter!"

"She's seen," the thing said.

"I've told her the truth."

"She knew that's her Daddy in a bunch'a pieces in that box?"

Betty gained her feet, and she couldn't help herself. Looking again at the coffin, she saw a denim work shirt that should've been pale blue from dozens of washings. But torn a dozen times over, now stained with gore that looked like spreading pitch in the moonlight. Shreds of fabric holding together shredded human meat.

She was going to be sick again, but swallowed hard. Swallowed right past the lump gathered in her throat.

"You don't need to put it so," her mom scolded the rotting man.

Betty had to get away, as far away from this place as possible. She no longer cared about her dreams of escaping to the high class fashion world, of champagne toasts with big band music ushering in the dawn. She no longer cared because she no longer harbored such hopes. She just needed to get away. Now.

Heading back toward the house, the shoe flew from her left foot in a comical arc. She didn't give it a second glance, and didn't turn around, even as her mom's cries became shrill, so shrill her voice cracked and she began to sob once again.

Her bare foot slapped the damp ground. She sprinted up the rise, into the shadows, fear straining her body to its limits. The noise from the graveyard drifted away with distance. The moon climbed out from behind a passing cloud. The pathway became visible.

In two split seconds birthed one after the other, Betty's eyes first acknowledged the animated carcass blocking her way, then a blade's cold bite piercing the skin low on her belly. It carved through muscle, violating her internal organs. Searing pain raced up her abdomen, spreading upward like the pressure of a pulled zipper. She heard the rush of fluids hitting the grass.

Her belly was split from pubic bone to sternum, her flesh rent by a foot-long blade, the warmth of her blood and organs splashing her legs and feet.She fell to her knees in her own filth, and the world seemed to shift on its axis, shifting as if to meet her falling head and lessen the impact of her collapse.

"Ethan! My girl. No, you can't, not my Betty..."

Her mom was somewhere far away, but her voice became louder as she ran up the path, closing in. Betty's senses beat a hasty retreat. For a brief instant she could smell the tang of her own blood, but then thankfully, it was gone.

Her mother's trembling fingers brushed her cheek.

Warm, so warm...

"Don't... don't try to speak, honey. It's, it's going to be okay. I'll fetch Dr. Thompson. He's right... he's right here."

Her mom croaked as if struck. Through her failing consciousness, Betty heard more flesh ripping. Smooth cuts parting the living from the dying. A distressing, protracted sigh--either her own or her mother's--she could no longer tell. A weight hit the ground nearby and didn't stir.

Mom...

Betty's eyes dimmed. In the last of her vision she saw her murderer's pale skin, his arms veined with what looked like wriggling worms. His forearm flexed, twitching the knife at his side. A blood bead seeped from its tip to the grassy path. Her murderer turned toward her house and sleeping brother. Betty's vision shrank to a pinprick then winked out for good.

ELEVEN

Scully thought he was going to have to kill Dr. Thompson, but the old man just meekly curled up in the grass and cried. That was a good thing. His boss went up to the house to finish off the family, leaving Scully to keep an eye on things at the graveyard. He was weakening. Badly. He wasn't sure he could take down anyone, even an old man like Thompson.

Gonna fill that hole up good, he thought. *Three bodies, no make that four, counting the boy up at the house.*

Just when he was about to say a prayer of thanks for Thompson's tears, Magee took out a flask from his pocket. The old barber winced as he tipped it back and drained it, answering any doubts Scully had about Magee.

Good. No hassles from nobody.

"Why don'tcha get your sorry asses outta here?" Scully tried to sound threatening, but only succeeded in shredding something in his esophagus. It hurt like hell--the ripping and rotting and falling apart--but it couldn't be helped. Not until he returned to the Underground. That wouldn't happen until he and Ethan had this big old mess cleaned up. "Another loose end severed," his boss would say.

After long years of dormancy, Ethan was taking more risks lately. His boss would repeatedly implore that it was all for good reason--the consolidation of his power and the security of the Underground, above all things, the security of the Underground. While Scully thought those were valid reasons, he thought something else was spurring Ethan's risk taking. Thea Calder. Ethan wanted her to be with him, wanted to possess her like a golden trinket hanging about his neck. He would do anything to ensure that no one would learn about their hidden lair. No, no one could learn the secret. No one could dare threaten his immortality, his eternal happiness.

Magee grabbed the doctor's elbow and helped him to stand. Neither one took their eyes off Scully.

"You have no right doing what you do!" Thompson yelled, spittle and tears flying off him. Waving his index finger at Scully, he stepped toward him.

"That hole's deep enough for another body, another two, you keep yapping." Scully hoped his tone didn't reveal how weak he felt. He picked up his shovel, then with effort, held it high like a brandished weapon. He hoped the men couldn't see the clean white of his arm bone gleaming through his rotten flesh.

Not much holdin' me together. He tried to laugh. His chance at humor couldn't hide the fact he was getting scared. He couldn't remember it ever getting this far.

Why'd Ethan have to go after the boy anyhow?

"Come on, Doc. Let's get home."

"It can't go on. Not like this," Thompson said, but his expression held defeat, not resolve. His shoulders slumped. He wasn't going to fight, and he wasn't going to say anything to cause any more bloodshed. Scully could see it in his eyes.

"Don't speak like that. Now, you know this is how it is. Let's just git while we still can."

"Magee, you have another bottle of the clear stuff?"

"Do fishes blow bubbles?"

Magee and Thompson staggered up the path, careful not to step in the bloody mess that used to be the Harris women.

Scully waited until they were gone, then fell to the ground. He wanted to simply sit and rest while waiting for Ethan, but was starting to lose control of his motor functions.

It was getting harder to breathe. He thought how funny it was to notice such a thing. He no longer needed to breathe, not up here aboveground, but his body continued to listen to instinct. His lungs sucked in air, acting out the motion of respiration. Something beat in his chest cavity, something that pushed and pulled a viscous fluid, something very unbloodlike.

Holding his eyelids closed, Scully focused on controlling the delicate muscles holding them in place. He didn't want the rotten membranes to tear. He hated that feeling; it was worse than paper cuts dipped in vinegar.

His mind flitted back five minutes, seeing that girl's insides emptied out like a tossed bucket of piss. Dead before she hit the ground.

The image sent him further back, to when he first saw Ethan laid up in a hospice bed tucked inside a crumbling Spanish mission on the edge of the Everglades, on the edge of the civilized world. Bandages bound his entire torso. Without them his insides would have spilled like that Harris girl's. He remembered the room stinking of spoiled meat, and searching for it until he realized the stench was coming from his friend. The Seminoles routed Ethan's company, cutting three dozen soldiers to ribbons, gutted stem to stern. Their ambush lived up to the Seminoles' savage reputation; added to it even. And there were niggers amongst them. Mixing nigger blood with savage. The thought had made him nauseous. Still did.

The mission's physician had sent a letter to an address he found in a stack of letters in Ethan's rucksack: his widowed mother in Pekin, Illinois. In no condition to travel the Mississippi to collect her incapacitated son or his putrefying remains, she asked Arthur Scully, Ethan's childhood friend, to go in her stead. He agreed, knowing she wouldn't want to see her son in either condition.

Entering the makeshift hospice, Scully saw mosquito netting shrouding Ethan's sick bed. Netting meant his friend wasn't dead. They wouldn't need to protect a corpse from mosquitoes. They clouded the outside material, while flies buzzed inside the shroud, having hatched from his wounds.

Ethan had been unconscious and feverish. Blisters rimmed his mouth, seeping, crusting. But he was alive.

Scully stepped through the netting and sat in a chair at Ethan's side, swatting the flies away. Taking in the severity and extent of his friend's wounds, and afraid to do anything more, he held his hand, waiting for his eyes to open.

A week later, Ethan woke from a frightful delirium in which he had raved about setting fires to scorch crops and flesh in equal measure, and the necessity to skin the conniving redskin, skin the treacherous black skin. Rid the earth of them. The last words of his delirium haunted Scully, and from that day on, he would often wake from his own nightmares with Ethan's words conjuring up the worst possible imagery.

A distant voice niggled his brain, shaking it free from memory's pull: "Scully. Scully, come on, Arthur, wake up."

Someone slapped his face, hard. Ethan. Ethan had returned from the house. A dull thud hit the ground nearby. The Harris boy. The job was done.

"We need to get you back. In a hurry." His friend lifted him, grunting with the effort as he threw him over his shoulder. "I didn't realize it was so bad. Digging the grave must've made it go faster. I told you it needn't be so deep."

Scully tried to speak but couldn't.

"Don't worry. Here we go. We're going home."

Arthur Scully's body was falling apart. Ethan's hands kept slipping through the muck that was all that remained of his flesh. "Just close your eyes, rest up." Scully didn't know his eyes had opened of their own accord. He could no longer feel his skin, could no longer see.

"I'll get you back safe, then come back to fill that hole you dug." Something from inside his skull was pressing down with the gravity of being carried upside down. The pressure built at his brow line, then found release as something gushed through his eye sockets and into his matted hair.

"We're going home," Ethan told Scully a few weeks after waking from his delirium.

"We didn't think you'd make it."

"But I did." Ethan grimaced as he stood from the hospice bed. His wound's dressing still needed frequent changing, and he wasn't up to full strength yet, but Ethan had an urge about him; he had to leave this place behind and move on. He no longer wanted to sleep in the bed where he had been expected to die.

They bought two seats in a cramped, rickety wagon from a group of trappers and merchants traveling from the Everglades to New Orleans. Sharing the wagon bed with curing skins pulled taut over wooden frames, the oppressive air smelled worse than Ethan's recovery room. Ethan was still too weak for them to travel on their own, and Scully didn't know the lay of the land, so despite the stench, the arrangement worked for the best. Once in New Orleans, they booked a cabin on a steamer heading back to Illinois, and they were soon on their way home.

Scully remembered the moment specifically. The first mention from Ethan about a venture that would change the course of their lives. Haze rose in indolent wisps from the Mississippi. They both leaned against the railing circling the deck of the steamer, watching the sunrise over the wooded Tennessee side of the river. Ethan leaned closer and in a conspirator's whisper said one word: "Expedition."

"Expedition?"

Ethan glanced around the deck, but it was early and few people strolled by.

"Private Abrahms, he died in the final Seminole raid, he used to go on about how he was going to trap once the fighting was done. He was going to trap live gators and bring them up north, sell them to carnivals and zoos. Once up North, he'd make his return trip home with rich old coots to do some of the trapping themselves. He'd set up cabins along the 'glade's shore, make them real fancy. The best liquor, the best whores, the best hunting and trapping. He'd go on and on like it'd be a damn resort."

"We don't know nothing about gators, Ethan. Don't they bite?"

"Not gators, nitwit. That's just where the seed of my idea came from. A jumping off point."

"You lost me."

"Ain't gators we're going for."

"What then?"

"Niggers. What else? We'll set up an outfitting company for rich southern folk. Some will hire us on to catch their runaways, and we'll track them and collect the bounties. Some will want to come along to bag a prize to bring home."

"Niggers... you know that sounds, well, is that legal?"

"If the right people get a take, anything's legal."

"Sounds like poaching to me."

"Exactly! That's the point. We bring in the Borland brothers for muscle, and with you and me on the business side, we'll be rich in no time."

That's how it all started. A conversation Ethan had with an entrepreneurial private now buried in an unmarked grave somewhere south of nowhere. Over ninety years ago. Now Scully's chest still fought to glean oxygen from his inhaled breath. His muscles fought the onslaught of rapid decay.

As Ethan carried his friend down the steps to the Harris's cellar, and while he dragged him through the damp, unlit tunnel carved by the Borland brothers in the guise of The Collectors, Arthur Scully's body continued to deteriorate. His mind had receded to the farthest reaches of his memory, to his earliest recollection--stumbling and falling as he learned to walk--when his flesh felt the Underground's delicate caress.

Ethan had saved him, saved his immortality. The Underground worked its wonder, knitting new flesh over putrefied, replacing the dead with something not quite. Scully gasped for air and held it deep in his rotting chest, then let out a laugh that sent oily, putrid tissue sputtering from between his healing lips.

"Let me down, old hos'. I got it from here."

"That was close. I didn't think you'd make it."

"Well, you were wrong."

They returned to the Underground, returned to immortality, with another loose end severed and Ethan one step closer to realizing his goal.

At the outset, they weren't expecting to kill the entire family. Just bury the old man. Give him peace, even though he'd turned down their offer of salvation. They were, after all, a respectable people. The wife would've held silent over the evening's events; but then the daughter came out, and judging her reaction, she wouldn't have kept silent on her own. So Ethan helped her along with that. Then the mother and son had to follow, falling like dominos.

"I best get back and take care of the boy."

TWELVE

"Are you sure you two are okay here?" Jacob's mom pulled on her black bonnet, lifting the black veil back from her eyes. Her funeral dress was old. She had worn it twice since she buried her husband, each time after losing a parent.

"Yes, Ma'am. Georgie can see me from heaven right here," Ellie said. She seemed relieved not having to go to the service.

His mom leaned over to give her a hug. When she stood, she blinked through tears.

Jacob had woken early and explained to his mom that Ellie couldn't go, that attending her brother's burial would damage more than heal. His mom had argued that it was important for her to go to the funeral to give her a sense of closure. He refused to back down in Ellie's defense.

His mom knew what it was like burying a loved one. After briefly questioning Ellie, she relented.

"Okay. I'm leaving. Jacob, make sure you two eat, come lunchtime."

"Yes, Ma'am."

She smiled sadly to both of them, then left.

Jacob went to the window overlooking the driveway and watched his mom climb into the faded black pickup. The engine roared, then she backed away, far more smoothly than Jacob could yet accomplish. Ellie joined him at the window. He parted the curtains, allowing her a better view.

"Your mom's sweet."

"I know."

Since it felt like the right thing to do, he put his hand on Ellie's shoulder, and together they watched the pickup disappear at the end of the drive as it took off down Teetering Road. "Are you hungry yet?"

"No, not really." Ellie left the window and sat on the sofa. She picked up her rag doll, holding it in the crook of her elbow.

"What should we do?"

"We can pick flowers for your mom and have them in water for when she gets home."

Ellie surprised Jacob with how she was dealing with the loss of her brother. After the initial trauma of seeing George's body, it seemed like her tears fell for two days straight. But now she seemed more concerned about his mother than her own pain. He assumed she was hiding her feelings, keeping busy enough so she didn't have time to think. Maybe she felt like she was imposing by staying with the Fowler's. He hoped she didn't feel like a burden, because she wasn't. He thought about telling her this, but couldn't find the right words. "She'd like seeing a bunch of flowers when she walks in. Where should we go?"

"Where the flowers are, silly." Ellie hopped off the sofa, her blonde braids swaying as she moved. She was out the front door before Jacob could react.

"Hold up." Jacob hurried out the door. "Wait for me."

A stiff breeze nudged the cottony white clouds across the horizon as if they were shifting islands. In short order, Ellie gathered a bouquet of flowers from the plants surrounding the house. She made Jacob put the flowers in a vase with water, and then place the white and blue blossoms in the kitchen where the sunlight would shine on them through the window.

But she wasn't finished. When he returned, she pointed to a patch of distant wildflowers barely visible in the distance.

"We should pick flowers she doesn't get a chance to see every day. That would make it special."

They spent the next hour heading away from home, over grassy hills, through gaps in rickety fences bordering properties. Jacob tried to help, but Ellie was particular about which flowers she wanted picked. He found a cluster of yellow wildflowers in a pasture beyond their property. When he called her over, she gave the blossoms a cursory glance, and then furrowed her brow and shook her head. Obviously, he was missing something important in this chore, probably since he was a boy and would rather toss a baseball around than find the perfect flower.

He was getting hungry. Acting as Ellie's pack animal, with his arms full of flowers, he was more than ready to head back. Ellie was just ahead, keeping her eyes to the ground, but clearly no longer paying attention to the vegetation.

"Ellie, we should head back. Mom'll tan my hide if you haven't eaten by the time she gets home."

She kept walking, dropping all pretense of searching for flowers. She rushed down the next hill, momentarily out of view. As Jacob hastened to catch her, he realized where they were. Dropping the flowers, a plume of pollen tickled his nose.

"Ellie, I thought you said you didn't want to come here?"

Ellie looked over her shoulder at him. Before her, hidden away in a plateau between two grassy hills, Coal Hollow's dead slept their eternal sleep. The Edgewood Cemetery was the largest in the county. Jacob's father occupied a plot in the southern corner, a peaceful weeping willow shading his military headstone from the summer sun. As a family, they came once a month to clear brush and weeds away from the marker. They would each speak to him privately. When they would leave, Jacob always felt like his father had been listening.

"I don't wanna see him, *can't* see the box they put him in. But I also don't want people seeing *me*."

"You sure?" Jacob asked. If Ellie had schemed to get him this far from the house, he knew he wouldn't get her to go home without saying a final goodbye to her brother.

"Can't we just get a little closer?" she pleaded.

The fresh grave was close by, the newest plot in a cemetery dating back one hundred years. People dressed in black surrounded her brother's grave. A packed dirt parking area sat between them and the graves.

"Follow me. We'll use the trees for cover until we reach the parking lot, and then we'll stay behind the cars. Is that close enough?"

"Yeah. Just... Jacob, I don't wanna see."

"I'll make sure, and when we get closer, you'll hear the kind things they say about George. When we get close enough, you can close your eyes."

"Okay."

It felt wrong, as if they were doing something altogether disgraceful. Maybe his mom had been right and she just needed to have a sense of closure. They crept closer, staying low in the tall grass. The scent of newly turned earth weighed heavily in the air. The mourners graveside didn't stir, even when Jacob snapped a twig underfoot. They wouldn't be mindful of noise or aware of much of anything as long as they were burying one of their own.

They reached the parking lot, Ellie keeping close to his side. Keeping out of sight, they inched as close as they could without seeing too much or having anyone see them.

Jacob motioned for Ellie to stop where she was. He craned his neck around a truck he recognized as Sheriff Bergman's. They'd already lowered the casket into the ground and the ropes used to lower the casket were coiled next to the hole.

A crowd had gathered around Jasper Cartwright, who was reading from a worn bible. He read a passage he must've had memorized, since his vision was so poor and not getting any better. Jasper spoke about someone named Lazarus, about his death and his rising from the dead.

Imagining the dead rising from the ground, the decayed corpses aimlessly moving about, didn't lend any comfort in this trying time. Not borne to a religious family, he wondered about the significance of the story.

"Jacob?"

"Hmm?"

"Who's there?"

"Why, just about everyone. My mom, and Doc Thompson, Magee and Bo Tingsley, Mr. Prescott, the Calders, Arlen Polk, lots of people. Dozens."

"Is my dad there?"

"Sorry, no."

"Are they sad?" Though tense, the girl also seemed somewhat relieved.

"Yeah, they're all sad. They all loved George."

"Good. I mean, it's nice so many people showed up."

Jacob returned his attention to the gathering. People were shuffling their feet. Arlen Polk and Bo Tinglsey broke from the group and took up shovels from the loose dirt pile next to the hole in the ground. They waited next to the grave.

His mom was the first person to approach. She dropped a small white flower inside the grave. She paused, covered her face with a hanky and walked away. She was walking toward Jacob and Ellie's hiding spot.

"I think it's done. My mom's heading in this direction."

"Did she see us?"

"I don't think so, but our truck is just a couple rows over. We should go before someone does see us."

"Okay. Thanks for bringing me. I know George can see me from heaven, but I wasn't sure if he'd be in heaven yet, or if he doesn't take his wings and fly away until… they pour the dirt."

"I'm sorry you didn't get to hear any of the kind things they said about him."

"It's okay. I didn't come for them. I came for Georgie. I wanted to say goodbye."

The crowd dispersed, fanning out in a wide wave to their respective vehicles. "Wait, we can't just leave like this. There's no way we'd get out without being seen. That tree," he said, pointing out a burly tree at the edge of the parking lot. "We should hide over there until everyone's gone."

Ellie offered her hand and he took it. Together, they hurried to the gnarled oak tree. He held her in front of him, sandwiching her with the tree trunk. She trembled against his chest, but didn't cry.

"It's going to be okay," Jacob whispered.

"I don't want to be seen. I'd be too embarrassed."

Jacob glanced around the tree trunk. His mom was walking in their direction, rooting in her purse for her keys. Sheriff Bergman followed close behind, waving his hand as if she could possibly see out the back of her head.

"Jane? Jane Fowler? Got a second?" the sheriff called out.

Jacob shied back behind the tree. Ellie's needy, upturned gaze caught him off guard. He held his index finger against his lips and then chanced another look around the tree.

"Oh, Larry, I was hoping to talk to you," his mom said, drying the last of her tears.

"I heard back from Peoria."

"And?"

"The recruiting office has no record of a Jimmy Fowler come up that way. But that don't mean that's not where he's heading."

"He would've been there by now."

"He could've decided to go on to somewhere else. Another big town with a recruiting office. St. Louis, maybe. Or even Chicago. Might want more time to think things over before he signs up."

"I suppose. Can you keep trying, check in with Peoria again?"

"I sure will, Jane. I also wanted to thank you for starting up the collection for the headstone. The Bradshaw's came forward and footed the bill for the remaining balance. I'm not sure they would've done that without you starting it."

"At least he's next to Mabel. He was a great kid. No one deserved a nice resting spot more than him."

Bergman touched her shoulder. If he didn't look so uncomfortable with the gesture, Jacob might've said something and ruined their hiding spot. "We'll find your boy. If he run off like you think, he's probably just as scared to sign his name over to the Army as facing his family here."

"God, I hope so."

The sheriff tipped his cap, nodded grimly, and headed to his truck. His mom hopped into the pickup and quickly pulled away, kicking up a cloud of dust.

The other mourners broke up quickly, with but a few people remaining in a small circle, sharing tears and memories of George Banyon. As Louise Bradshaw cried on her mother's shoulder, her parents exchanged a puzzled look at her pronounced reaction. Watching the burial, Jacob figured, her thoughts of Jimmy's fate must've taken a darker edge.

As the last mourners filtered away, Bo Tinsley and Arlen Polk alternated throwing dirt into the hole, consigning George Banyon's body to the earth. Forever.

They waited just a while longer, allowing the cemetery to clear out completely. "We should go now. Mom's already going to have a conniption when she beats us home."

"Jacob, Jimmy's not in Peoria."

"I know, I heard."

"He's not in Peoria. No one's found his body yet, either" Ellie said, pressing against him. "Jimmy's alive. I can feel it."

"I know." It felt weird admitting aloud, but he'd been harboring those very same thoughts. It felt like admitting he still believed in Santa Claus when all the evidence said just the opposite. "I feel it too."

"We can't go home, not if he's out there somewhere."

"But we've looked everywhere. Unless someone has him trapped in their house or something like that, I don't know where else to look."

"I don't either, but I know someone who might."

"Who's that?"

"Old Greta."

"Greta Hildaberg?" He hadn't thought about the crazy old lady in so long. Of course she could help.

"She knows everything."

"If we hurry and beat her home, we can ask my mom to drive us. That way she'll never know we left."

"You know she wouldn't go for that. She wants to believe Jimmy enlisted. Nothing will change her mind. We have to do this. On our own. We might not get another chance to talk to Greta."

"We better hurry then." He knew Ellie was right. His mom would just have to be angry. He took the girl's hand and they started back up the hill. As they went, he made sure to take the quickest route, trying to save as much time as possible. Not just because him mom would be angry for them not being home, but also because Jimmy might still be alive.

Sooty black clouds rolled in from the west, rolled right over their white puffy counterparts, moving quickly, carrying along fat raindrops. A storm was forming to wash the new grave, turning George's death shroud to mud.

THIRTEEN

Cooper slept the night away curled on the floor in the shadow of the pipe organ. He dreamed his repetitive dreams--stronger now that he was inside the house--the repetitive anxiety of running for his life, the repetitive reverie of finding salvation. When he awoke, he was as calm as a lamb. He had slept late, and would've continued on if not for the driving rain rattling the windows.

Cooper spent yesterday going over the old Blankenship home with a fine-tooth comb. It was a disappointing tour. The more he explored, the more damage he discovered that he would need to address to make the home permanently livable. A roof leak in one of the bedrooms had moldered the wall plaster. The likely cause was the severe warping of the upper floor, which in turn weakened the wall structure and affected the soundness of the roof. He could trace the warping to the sinking foundation at the front of the house. Most likely, the foundation also caused the front porch to list and for its boards to weather badly. The more he explored, the more he pondered his sanity for such a hasty purchase. These repairs were not merely cosmetic, but major projects he felt incapable of tackling on his own. He might be better off simply tearing down the existing structure and starting over. But that wasn't the point, was it? He could build a new house just about anywhere. But he belonged in the old Blankenship house, warts and all. He felt it in his bones.

He didn't know what he had expected when he walked through the front door for the first time. Revelation, maybe? Perhaps nothing so grand, but he'd been hoping for some kind of change to overcome him.

145

Some little *something*. Nothing changed for him. He was still the same man tramping the countryside, searching--searching and not finding--some meaning to his life.

He yawned, stood slowly after sleeping for nearly twelve hours. Judging the unmarred expanse of dust covering every visible surface, no one had stepped foot inside the old Blankenship home in many years. Decades maybe. He ran his fingers across the organ's smooth wood. It fairly filled the small room. A framed daguerreotype sat atop the pipe organ. A stern-looking couple, still quite young, stared at him through the grime-coated glass. He picked up the frame and wiped it with his shirtsleeve. The picture and organ were his only clues that anyone had ever lived here.

"Reverend Horace and Mrs. Eunice Blankenship, I presume." His volume surprised him in the empty house. He looked around as if he might receive a stern look from an overbearing librarian, a look he doled out a dozen times a day in his former life. Reverend Blankenship wore a black woolen suit, a stiff white linen shirt beneath. His eyes were piercing and cold. Deep wrinkles creased his face, as if the passion of his convictions had weathered his skin like tidewater carving stone. Mrs. Blankenship wore a dark, simple dress, fitted down to her wrists and binding her up to her chin. She seemed both timid and subservient, yet still somehow strong. He wondered if she had started losing her teeth when the photo was taken.

It wasn't déjà vu he was feeling--he could no longer dismiss it with that mystical explanation. Everything inside the house seemed familiar, expected. That wasn't déjà vu. Déjà vu was about similarity of experience or surroundings. This was something else. Something stronger. Deeper.

He closed his eyes and could see Eunice as an old woman, as she appeared in his dreams. Her stooped and withered posture, the dark hair in the photo dulled to gray. She was there, just behind his closed eyelids, a stranger from another time he had never met. It was her. No doubt. The kind old woman was the same woman in the photo.

Adrenaline surged through him. He looked around again, expecting someone to be there. The room was empty.

"What do you want from me!" he shouted. Hearing himself call out to vacant air, Cooper felt both half-crazed and inexplicably energized. As the words left his lips, it was as if an unknown vault had opened inside himself. He was supposed to buy the Blankenship house, he knew now. They wanted him to. They *demanded* it of him.

A floorboard creaked in the front room--a small cubby area where

Cooper pictured the Reverend reading religious tracts or Eunice knitting from homespun wool. A reciprocal creak sounded, as if a weight had been placed then quickly lifted from the floorboards. A footstep.

Another step followed, and then another three in rapid succession. Someone, or something, was charging through the front room, heading for the rear of the house.

He stepped into the hallway to confront the intruder (or perhaps *host*, he thought in the back of his mind). No one was there, at least no one visible. The footfalls intensified--he could feel them reverberate through the treads of his shoes.

Almost as soon as it started, the unsettling noise disappeared. As if the noise itself could unfurl a rush of air in his direction, a frigid gust washed over him. A second wave followed on the heels of the first, dosing him a second time with air the temperature of Hank Calder's icehouse. Goosebumps broke against his skin, but the cold air was gone. Gone just as quickly as the thunderous footsteps.

It took a moment for Cooper to catch his breath, and when he did, his lungs hitched in his chest. *Okay. I'm here, and now I know you're here. But I still don't know why I'm here*, he thought. He wondered if ghosts could read thoughts, then concluded that he might be a step or two beyond half-crazed at this point.

He looked at his shaking hands and noticed he still held the Blankenship family daguerreotype. On weak legs he walked to the organ and carefully returned the frame to its rightful place. After the burst of cold, the closed-in air felt stifling. He felt compelled to run through the empty house, flinging wide the doors as he went, opening the windows to let in a fresh, rain-cleansed breeze.

"One step at a time, folks," he said, trying to keep his voice level. "I'm here now. I'm not going anywhere." His heartbeat was slowing, but the jolt of adrenaline left him nauseous. "Let's just take this one step at a time. We'll figure this whole thing out. What do you say?"

The house gave no response. He felt like his feet would never leave their rooted position. But they did. He took one tentative step away from the backroom and the Blankenships' portrait. One step followed by another.

He came to the front cubby of a room, looking for any trace of the Blankenships. He found nothing. Not even the dust looked unsettled.

He wondered if he was hearing things. How could there be any other explanation? The Blankenships didn't call him here, didn't compel him to buy their home. Did they?

The sound of breaking glass pulled him away from pondering his own lucidity.

His initial thought was that he'd been caught. Someone had caught him sneaking through a house that wasn't his. His second thought was that Horace or Eunice were trying to communicate with him. The noise had come from upstairs. He bolted up the warped risers, hoping to catch them by surprise.

A bedroom window was spider webbed with cracks. The room was empty--more importantly, the room felt *empty*. After a moment's disappointment he looked through the window and saw a blond head bobbing out of sight. The rain obscured his view, and the dirty window made it almost impossible to make out any details. He pulled up hard on the window and managed to budge it open before the left side seized up.

He heard another unsettling noise, stone shattering stone.

Cursing under his breath, he forced the window open far enough to stick his head through. Lightning lit the dark afternoon. Thunder grumbled across the prairie. He saw Jacob Fowler, obviously in a foul mood, flinging stones at Cooper's new home. The boy stood in ankle-deep mud, apparently oblivious to the rain.

As Cooper craned further out the window, he could just make out a girl's mud-streaked shoes hanging over the edge of the wrap-around porch, safely out of reach of the rain.

Another rock smashed against the foundation.

"Hey! Knock it off!"

Jacob Fowler was so shocked that when he looked up he fell onto his back, still staring at the window. Realization set in. The boy recognized Cooper.

"Jacob, you wait right there. I'm coming down."

FOURTEEN

"We gotta get outta this rain." Ellie's clothes clung to her skin, and her legs were splashed with mud. They had been walking toward Greta's for half an hour. If Jacob was uncertain of his hunger when they were picking flowers, then he was beyond certainty now. He would eat his own shoe if he didn't need it for walking.

"It was sunny when we left the house," he said defensively. The day had turned into such a mess, and not just because of the turn in weather. "We can take shelter at the Blankenship house. It's not far off."

"Not in there. It's haunted."

"It's not haunted."

"Sure it is. Ghosts walk the halls at night. The old reverend and his wife carry torches and read passages from the bible."

"If there's ghosts, which there aren't, why in the world would they do something like that?"

"Maybe it wasn't their time to die."

"There's no ghosts, 'cause they didn't die there, Ellie. They moved away, or didn't Greta tell you that part of the story? It's just abandoned. Besides, we aren't going in. We'll just duck under that big porch until this rain lets up some. We'll dry out in no time."

"Fine. As long as we don't step foot inside. But let's hurry, though. I'm getting cold." Lightning flashed across the darkening sky.

"We can head back."

"No, you're right. Let's try to wait it out under the porch. If we turn back now, your mom won't let us back out to talk to Greta. This is our only chance."

When they could see the ramshackle house, they ran up the driveway, splashing mud from the deepening puddles. Jacob's chest burned by the time they reached the house. He was surprised Ellie followed so close behind. She ran past him, all the way up the steps, only reining in her speed by grabbing the circular banister supporting the porch's roof.

"You're quick for a girl." Jacob leaned over with his hands on his knees.

"Well, you're slow for a boy."

Ellie sat at the edge of the porch, her muddy shoes dangling along its edge. The fabric of her rag doll had turned gray with wetness. It now looked cheaply made instead of merely quaint. "I'm hungry."

Bushes walled off the porch from the road. Ripe blackberries hung heavily from the leafy branches. Jacob plucked a wild berry and plopped it into his mouth. At first sour, the berry dissolved, becoming sweeter, making his stomach grumble. "Look, we've got food right here." Jacob plucked the fruit into his palm, eating half of his take. "Try some." He offered Ellie the other half.

She gobbled the berries, barely chewing. As if the proffered berries gave her a sudden burst of energy, she reached into the rain to pick her own. The rain didn't ease in the slightest as they ate all the berries within easy reach. Another wave of black clouds rolled in from the horizon and extended clear over the roof of the house.

Jacob felt helpless. He no longer wanted to ponder his brother's fate, or wonder what horrible agony he could be suffering this very instant. All he wanted was to stop thinking about anything bleak or depressing. Stepping into the mud, he came across a smooth, egg-shaped pebble. He kicked it loose with his sodden shoe and spotted a target. A large boulder peaking from a cover of tall grass. He picked up the stone and cocked his arm back past his ear, then threw with all of his tension and anger as he released the rock. It spun just high of the target, cutting through the grass, coming to a stop after colliding with a tree trunk deeper in the grass.

"She'll know we're okay," Ellie said softly.

"I'm sorry?" Jacob looked up from his search for a new throwing rock. Ellie once again sat on the top porch step. With her hunger sated, the fatigue had left her cheeks, replaced by crimson berry streaks.

"Your mom will know we're okay. We left the flowers in the kitchen. She'll see them and know we're okay."

"I hadn't thought about that." Even though his brother had disappeared without a trace, Jacob hadn't considered how his mom would feel if she came home from the funeral to find the house empty.

His only concern had been trying to stay out of trouble. Now, considering how much his mom wanted to keep their family together and strong, he felt like an inconsiderate ass. "I hope you're right."

With some effort, he pulled an oblong rock from the mud. He spotted a new target: the metal coal chute door set in the foundation of the house. The rock slipped his grip as he whipped it through the air. It tilted end over end in a rainbow arc, hitting a second floor window.

"Jacob!"

"I didn't mean it. It slipped."

"You're gonna wake the ghosts."

"Ellie, I told you, there's no such thing." Ignoring Ellie's worry, possibly even spurred on by it, he snatched another rock from the muddy ground. The rain washed over him, running freely under his clothes, over his skin. He felt cold but refreshed. He aimed and fired. This time the trajectory, while truer, still missed the coal chute door, shattering against the stone foundation.

"Jacob!"

"All right, fine."

"Hey! Knock it off!" a voice called out from above.

Jacob's heart seemed to stutter as he looked up, certain he would see Reverend Blankenship staring sternly from the window, waving his bible through the air in condemnation.

Someone leaned at the waist from the window. Getting wet and angrier each passing second. Before Jacob could realize ghosts couldn't get wet--if they did indeed exist--he fell over on his back. He recognized the man--it was the hobo from the search party. Cooper something-or-other.

"Jacob, you wait right there. I'm coming down."

GLEN R. KRISCH

FIFTEEN

Cooper was initially upset at the children when he brought them inside. Once they were out of the rain he had assured them that they were safe, and after Jacob Fowler had apologized about a dozen times for breaking the window, they began to relax. They stood shoulder to shoulder, dripping puddles onto the dusty floor. Besides being soaked through, their skin was pale and they looked strained as if from lack of sleep. With such a sorry sight standing before him, Cooper couldn't stay mad.

"Here, take these." Cooper handed them each a thin wool blanket from his pack. Rain had drenched him many times in his travels. He'd learned that even on a warm day, a heavy rain could leech the heat from a person's core.

"You know, I have some chore money saved. You can have it to fix that window."

"For the last time, Jacob, it's okay. I forgive you. The window was probably no good anyway, and I would've replaced it before winter. Now just dry up and get warm. I'll heat up some tea to chase the chill from your bones."

"Did you buy this house?" Ellie asked. Her lips were no longer blue-tinged, but purple, warming to pink. She kept looking around, as if expecting someone, or something, to jump out from hiding. He thought it might be a smart caution to bear. While he couldn't feel the Blankenships' presence, he couldn't discount his earlier encounter with them, either.

"Ellie--" Jacob touched her forearm, glaring at her.

"I sure did," Cooper said and then turned his attention to Jacob. "It's okay Jacob. I'm not a vagrant or criminal by any means. Actually, I used to be a librarian." Cooper couldn't help noticing Jacob raise his eyebrows dubiously. Cooper turned back to Ellie. "I was just passing through Coal Hollow on my way back to Chicago where my parents live, but once I saw this house, I just had to have it. Strange thing is, I was never looking to buy a house. I suppose if I hadn't seen it, I would've kept walking and would've never stopped in town."

Cooper broke open his pack and pulled out a bundle from a side pocket. Unfurling the campfire-stained fabric, he sorted the contents on the floor. He then poured water from his canteen into a coffee pot and then set up his tin can stove he had been using on the road. He flicked a match, and set the coffee pot on to boil.

Just short of nightfall a week after he took to the rails, Cooper had met an old tramp named Ju-Ju Bee. As they shared a campfire that night, Ju-Ju had sorted out Cooper's plight right away. Cooper had come down with a cold as soon as he left Chicago, and now it sat in his lungs, shortening his breath. He had lost weight and had little strength to make his own food. Nipping from a flask and laughing at some internal dialogue, Ju-Ju considered Cooper. The gray bristles of his beard had twisted as his face contorted into a smile. He didn't say anything for awhile, but he did set up the camp stove--a coffee can attached to a lantern's fuel belly--just as Cooper was now doing for these kids. That night, he made a savory chicken soup and strong tea that he shared with Cooper.

The tramp had mentioned his real name, Jerome. The other tramps called him Ju-Ju Bee, a nickname of a sort for Jew-bastard. He followed up right away in a low, defensive tone that if Cooper was uncomfortable with sharing a campfire with a Jew, then he could have it all for himself. And be lucky to wake in front of the dead embers, lucky enough to wake up at all with that flu deep in his chest.

"You can sit down, take a load off," Cooper said to the children as he prepared the tea.

They followed through as if he had given an order, sitting side by side on the floor, still not appearing altogether comfortable being alone with a stranger. Perhaps they even sensed Eunice nearby.

The night he met Ju-Ju, all Cooper had the energy to do was nod, his fatigue quickly catching up to him. Yeah, it was fine. He held no ill feelings toward Jews. None whatsoever. He remembered feeling lucky he hadn't come across a tramp with a violent bent to his personality and eyes for stealing his gear.

The coffee pot began to steam, and from his pack Cooper produced three dented tin cups. He checked them for cleanliness, handing the children the cleanest two and wiping the third with his shirttail. He dropped a tea bag in each cup and poured the steaming water. Ellie gripped the cup in her palms and brought it to her cheek, letting the steam warm her. Jacob, sipping too soon, winced at the heat. Cooper exhausted the stove flame and gathered his mess.

Ju-Ju had stayed with Cooper for a week, the whole time grumbling under his breath about not wanting to take up roots for fear of dying if he did. The old tramp nursed Cooper along until he could fend for himself, albeit with a nagging fatigue that felt like a fifty-pound burden on his shoulders.

During his recovery, Ju-Ju taught Cooper how to tramp. Starting out, Cooper knew next to nothing. Ju-Ju laughed at his naiveté, wondering aloud how Cooper had survived on his own, even for a week. The first thing Ju-Ju taught him was what to look for when choosing a freighter to catch, and the proper technique to employ as to not die a miserable death under the weight of the coal-burning beasts. He would then demonstrate next to a boulder near the campfire how to hide from the bulls. Ju-Ju had all sorts of distasteful tidbits to pass along about the bulls--the train conductors of the PN&E railway being the worst. They'd club a tramp to death with their batons before he could get a word out in defense.

Through his many stories, Cooper learned how to forage for food, how to stay as dry as possible, and how to cook on the go. After dinner one night, Cooper drifted off while staring into the campfire's hypnotic flames. As he slept, Ju-Ju snuck away, catching a freighter for parts unknown, his wanderlust compelling him to get on the go.

"Little muddy out to go for a stroll," Cooper said. The tea's warmth had pacified the children. The rain had eased in small degrees over the last few minutes.

Jacob brought the cup to his lips again, tempting a scalding of his tongue. The boy nodded. Ellie's cheeks had flushed with warmth. Cooper thought she might fall asleep if she weren't so suspicious of her surroundings. He looked at the camp stove Ju-Ju had left behind. He had used the re-made coffee can to cook numerous meals of bland mush or tasteless brown rice in the last year. His savior on that long ago night was a kind man, despite his rough exterior. He wished he could've said goodbye or at least thanked him for saving his life.

Cooper was about to ask Jacob if they had been to the funeral.

Certainly the kids had attended, but he wondered why they had wandered off. Instead, he said, "Are you going to say what you're doing out in this weather, or am I going to have to guess?"

Ellie still scanned the shadowy room. She spoke to Cooper in a whisper, "Old Greta."

"I'm sorry, I'm not familiar--"

"Ellie," Jacob cut in, hoping to quiet the girl. "He don't need to know."

"Come on, Jacob. Mr. Cooper's been nice to take us in, and you seem to like the tea just fine. There's no harm." She turned back to Cooper. "Greta knows things."

"From my experience, it's good to know things," he said and found himself smiling. Despite the circumstances, he couldn't resist Ellie's charm. She possessed an equal measure of innocence and intelligence.

"She knows things no one else knows."

Jacob set his tea aside, then stood. He walked to the window in quiet protest, his back to Ellie and Cooper.

"How so, Ellie?"

"Don't know, really, but she's got a way about her. She can tell you the weather for the day you were born, down to the color of the clouds and if the crickets started singing earlier than normal 'cause the spring rains held off for the night."

"Really?"

"Sure she can. Everyone around's seen her do it. Ain't that so, Jacob?"

The boy didn't move. Cooper saw his angular profile, his crossed arms, his solemn eyes trained out the window.

"You decided to visit Greta on a day when the whole of the summer's rainfall seems to be falling just this afternoon?"

Ellie didn't answer, but her expression darkened.

"Ellie, the rain's stopping. We catch a break, we'll make it to her house without any more trouble." Jacob removed the damp blanket from his shoulders, dropping it to his feet.

Ellie's eyes briefly held Cooper's before shying away. That half-lit second revealed the weight of her unguarded anguish, the longing for her brother.

"Let's go then." Ellie stood and handed him the empty cup. "Thanks for the tea, Mr. Cooper. It was a lifesaver."

Ellie met Jacob at the door, their wet footprints trailing across the dusty floor.

Cooper felt torn. Looking about the house, he saw all the repairs he needed to tend to, that he felt compelled to do. But more importantly, his thoughts returned to his hope that he might learn more about the Blankenships and what they wanted with him. But the children. Innocent, desperate, looking for answers from an old lady. An old lady "who knew things."

Jacob opened the door for Ellie and followed her out.

Cooper caught the door before it could close and called out as they stepped from the porch to the driveway's waiting puddles. "What's this Greta going to help you with?"

The children stopped walking. Jacob didn't turn, but Ellie did. "Someone killed Georgie. No one knows who, and no one knows where Jimmy's at, but both me and Jacob know he's still alive. If there's a person in the world who knows where Jimmy could be, it's Greta. She's gotta know." Ellie blinked through tears.

"Wait a second," Cooper said.

Jacob looked back, putting his hand on Ellie's shoulder. "Mr. Cooper, you can't stop us. What're you gonna do, carry us home?"

"No. I'm coming with you."

SIXTEEN

"He's not going to last much longer," Dr. Thompson said six hundred feet below ground. He was so tired he could hardly keep his eyes open. His sleep had been spotty at best since the death of George Banyon. With the additional stress from the slaughter at the Harris farm last night, and then George's burial this morning, Thompson felt lucky to still be standing.

Ethan Cartwright was a thin white line gliding through the dark water of his private, hand-hewn pool. With machine-like precision he pulled against the cold water, acting as though he hadn't heard the doctor.

"Ethan? I need to know how you want me to proceed." He rubbed his arms. His bones hurt whenever he came to this place.

Ethan pumped his arm through a final fluid arc and reached for the pool's edge. "What do you recommend?"

"Your son is bed-ridden. He's an old man."

"Aren't we all these days?" He stood fully, the water falling from his naked body. If he stood still, he could pass for a statue extolling the virtues of perfect health. If you could ignore the purple scar bisecting his chest.

"He's going to die. I cannot be more serious. His heart is weak, terrible arthritis twists his limbs. He can't see well enough to make his way safely through his own town. He doesn't have long."

"Hand me that towel, would you?"

As Thompson handed him the towel, their eyes met.

"What would you have me do, Doctor? He won't step foot in the Underground. I cannot force him."

"Can't you? Like the others? Can't you send the Borland brothers?"

"If I brought him here, would I also chain him to a wall?"

"Go. Talk to him. Convince him."

"I understand your concern--growing up, my son was like an older brother to you. You would never see him suffer." Ethan dried his chest with a rough towel. His scar became a more menacing purple, savage and pronounced after swimming in the cold water. "But--"

"He's going to die," Thompson cut him off.

Ethan gritted his teeth, but something in his eyes softened. "Please leave. *Now.*"

Thompson looked like he would continue arguing, but exhaustion weakened his resolve. He turned to leave. When he pulled the door shut behind him, Ethan was alone.

Soon he would be even more alone, having outlived his own son, a man lived to a ripe old age. He hadn't seen Jasper in… oh, he couldn't remember how long. Decades. But he loved him even though he never again wanted to see his own father.

After long minutes of internal conflict, Ethan called to the man guarding the door to his room. He asked him to fetch Leo Borland.

SEVENTEEN

The darkness lifted from his body. An insistent heat intensified within his heart, spreading outward, pulsing through his veins, reaching his extremities. The heat itched like the worst ever case of chiggers. Oh lord, Jimmy would rip through his skin to get at that itching. If only he could move.

That was the worst part. No feeling besides the itching. No ability to move. He concentrated, focusing his energy on his eyelids, at the thin cleft where the delicate membranes touched at the edges of his lashes, until a bundle of energy formed in the middle of his forehead like a clenched fist.

His eyelids fluttered.

"Jimmy, lie still. Don't try to move too much too soon." Close by, Harold Barrow's voice. Reassuring, yet scared.

What had happened to him?

He searched for his last memory, the last thing he remembered before...

Jimmy tried to speak, but words wouldn't form. The concentrated fist inside his forehead loosened and the energy cascaded throughout his body, sparking synapses awake. His lower lip trembled uncontrollably, letting loose a quiet whimper. He could taste his own exhaled breath floating languidly at the tip of his tongue. Stale and sour. Like a slab of steak sitting outside an icebox far too long.

All at once he took in a breath, and he realized he hadn't been breathing. The cold air caressed his lungs and the feeling was

159

exhilarating, some kind of intoxicant. The breath rushed from his lungs in warm, fitful spasms. He was reluctant to let it go, as if the air itself were a friend leaving for an unknown length of time, not certain to ever return.

Until the next breath came. And another.

His chest heaved, his arms twitched, and then with all the effort he could harness, he flipped from his stationary position on his back, coming to rest on his right side. That same damned candlelight greeted him when his eyes fluttered open. Golden wisps flickering in the cavern's constant and subtly flowing breeze.

"You sure in a hurry to go on living." Harold sat on the cave floor by his side, stroking the white whiskers on his pointed chin.

Jimmy tried once more to speak, but all that came out was garbled and weak.

Hardened pools of blood pressed against his spine, at the back of his neck, in his calves. It ran liquidly again through his blood vessels, and as it flowed, it leveled off throughout the rest of his body. Blood sought the lowest point only when it stopped flowing, when the heart no longer pumped. He knew this from his experience on the farm when he would slaughter a milk cow that was past its prime. After slicing its neck--the beast hanging limply and quite dead from a barn rafter--the blood would gush from the wound, draining into a metal trough on the straw-strewn floor. If he didn't act quickly after dispatching the animal, its blood would pool at the lowest point until the distended tissues would verge on rupture, grown purple and hard.

"It's not pleasant, Mr. Jimmy, not at all. Take it easy while you adjust." Harold patted his hand, his touch warm against his ice-cold flesh. At least now he felt something.

Jimmy stopped struggling. He closed his eyes. He remembered Charles Banyon, drunk as all get out and with a drinking friend in tow, stumbling across the old mule stables where he and Benjamin had been resting. The drinking friend repeatedly bleating, "Where that nigger girl at? Where she at? It's been too long."

He remembered feeling sorry for Benjamin. For Harold, too. Poor Edwina. And the hatred in Charles Banyon's eyes. Hatred brought on for reasons Jimmy didn't understand. Banyon coldly stating that George was dead. His best friend, Banyon's own son, was dead. Jimmy's lip trembled uncontrollably.

George is gone.

He remembered the melon-sized stone falling from Banyon's grip, knocked off course by Benjamin's foolish bravery. Ricocheting off the cave wall, but still connecting solidly with his skull. A sharp, bitter agony stabbing his skull. After that, only emptiness. Cold, cold emptiness.

Jimmy had died. Just as his best friend had died. But his friend was never coming back. Jimmy couldn't wrap his mind around what was happening to him. Was this hell? Purgatory? Was he now a ghost, a memory, a dream?

"Where's Benjamin?" he croaked painfully.

Harold spoke as if he hadn't heard Jimmy, or if he did, that it didn't matter enough for him to respond directly. "You know, I find myself thinking back on my times in the fields--"

"He saved my life. Where is he?" Jimmy cut in.

Harold continued on, "Tobacco season runs from--"

"Harold, where's Benjamin?" he said sharply. He still couldn't move much.

"I got an idea where he's at, Mr. Jimmy, an idea I just don't like at all." Harold paused, collecting his words. "After that man hurt you, they took Benjamin away. For a long time, he cried out... the things they musta done to him."

"Where, Harold?"

"Pretty sure the waste pit."

Jimmy could immediately picture what Harold meant. They dumped the waste rock from their digging into the gaping hole. It was a cold mouth that Harold opined led to Satan himself. A place where light can't live, where warmth never existed. Scully would torment Harold and Benjamin by threatening to dangle them into the pit, winched down by the slack of their own intestines. Lowered as low as their guts would allow and let Satan's breath frostbite them.

"He's not coming back. Not with the Paradise about completed. My boy's gone."

They'd tortured Benjamin for attempting to save him. Jimmy kept quiet, guilt sickening him.

"You know, when I close my eyes, I can't recall a setting sun no more. Can't remember a single thing about it."

Considering Harold's word, Jimmy thought of his father, buried when he was three. The memories best remembered were of pure emotion. Laughter and good humor. Not much more than that.

"Get's me thinking there ain't no God. No God would put any of His creatures--even the lowly--through nothing like what He done to my family.

"You wanna hear something funny? Benjamin--I never liked him too much. Didn't like him courtin' after Edwina. He had book learning and was a house slave. That Joss Parkins, some say he a bit moony in the head… he had strange ideas. Raised at Parkins's plantation, Benjamin never worked a day in them fields. He learned reading and writing. Parkins thought he was doing himself a Christian duty. I never thought highly of no nigger going off kowtowing to no… well, he just wasn't right for my girl. But Benjamin, me and Edwina met up with him at a hideaway house where they're kind enough to help get you north on up to Canada, but 'course them bounty men, they catches up to us. Chases all the three of us down some tunnel into the ground. Benjamin, they killed him right off once they cornered us down underground. He fought with them, fought harder than any man before, you ask me. And they killed him dead. Then they had their way with Edwina, all of them, all of them nigger-haters had their turn… forcing me to watch the whole while. Full of bloodlust, they slit me and 'Wina's throats. We died, Mr. Jimmy. But next morning, wit' all that blood dried in black rivers on the floor, wit' all those bounty men sprawled out, passed out, Benjamin and me an' Edwina stirs awake just like you just did, and we all come to, all awake and alive.

"Seeing us rise like that, like some almighty spirits, them bounty men, and the townsfolk kind enough to help 'em find us, they just about seized up and died. They had no idea what to think. But in the end, they comes up with a solution. They up and stayed is what they did, us doing their bidding. Just like old times.

"That was the last day that was different than any the others that followed. They put us to work. You know what, Mr. Jimmy? That boy I thought weren't no good for Edwina, he learned me reading. Sure enough, an old Nigger slave boy from Joss Parkins's tobacco plantation learned reading.

"Benjamin'd scratch letters on the floor, and I learnt them one by one, and soon I'm reading words. Now, after so long practicing, I bet I read better 'an that Scully bastard."

Jimmy couldn't say much. His body could only manage simple commands. Move a finger, bend a wrist. Finally, he braced his elbows on the cold stone floor, levering himself into a sitting position. Sweat dripped from his forehead.

Pain and sweat and struggle. Dead people didn't have any of the three. Jimmy was somehow doing all three and ever more.

"But the funny thing ain't me learning to read. Funny thing is me learning I loved that boy. I loved Benjamin like my own blood, and I would've done anything for 'em. Now it's too late. He ain't coming back."

"Harold, I have family of my own. A brother, a mother. And I'm gonna be a father soon."

"If you can, forget 'em, Mr. Jimmy, that'd be the best thing for you to do to get on with things, you ask me. With them so close by, you'd go mad otherwise."

"I have to get out of here. My family needs me. Harold, you can help me, can't you?"

"No."

"Harold, please."

"I can't do that. Mr. Jimmy, don't you know it yet? You died. You're one of us now. That means you stay here or you're just as dead as your buddy George."

EIGHTEEN

The rain-soaked grass clung to their thighs as they broke from the muddied drive to cut across the back of the old Blankenship property. The rain had eased to a humid mist and the thunder had become a weakening echo. The haggard gray sky appeared to be catching its breath after taking a beating.

"We don't need your help, Mister," Jacob said.

"Don't think of it as me helping you. Maybe I just needed to get out of the house, see what the new neighborhood looks like."

At his side, Ellie looked up at him. "It's fine, Coop, really. Don't listen to him." Then she called to Jacob, who was a couple steps ahead and getting the worst of the wet grass. "You sure this is the way, Jacob?"

"It's over there, away from the road a stretch."

Before Cooper took to the rails, before its harsh miles whittled away his city-soft body and his beard sprouted into wild bristles, he worked at the Carnegie Library a few blocks from his family's home. Every morning he woke with the sun, pulled on a fresh suit and tie, and then ate a light breakfast of jam-slathered toast while savoring a cup of black coffee. He would head out the door, at ease with the world and his role within it.

Now, as he made his way through the back stretch of his new property, accompanying children fraught with worry over missing and murdered loved ones, he couldn't help marvel at how things could change in such a short period of time. Arriving early at the library, he'd gather the newspapers collecting at the door, bringing them inside. He'd open the window blinds, and as the morning sun bled through the dusty slats, he could imagine opening the library every day until his working days ended. Those quiet moments when he had the library to himself, when he could hear the slightest creak or sigh of a floorboard as he walked, he knew those times were over. His life had taken a different course.

"So, how's your mom doing?" He wanted to speak with the children, but their shared subject matter was limited. He didn't think it appropriate to bring up Ellie's dead brother. He had thought about Jane Fowler intermittently since he had first seen her on the night he discovered George Banyon's body. There was a hard edge to her, life having worn away any smooth angles.

"She's fine. Just a peach," Jacob said sourly.

As their clothes got heavier with rainwater, Cooper came to a conclusion long in coming: Jane Fowler was an attractive lady. While usually not a difficult conclusion at which to arrive, Jane was different. She didn't possess Thea Calder's starlet beauty. Jane's face was prematurely lined and somewhat plain. Her hair was dull and disorderly, while her eyes were cold and severe. But the way she walked, while assured and almost aggressive, was still graceful; he saw grace even with her nerves stripped raw during their search for Jimmy. She was authoritative, and controlling, but circumstance had forced her into that role. Thea Calder thrived in that environment. For Jane, it was a duty.

"Don't think being kind to us will in any way open her eyes to the likes of you."

"Jacob--" Ellie said, embarrassed.

He could only guess Jane's smile would sparkle in her eyes, reflecting outward, touching everything with a gentle hand. He could only guess, considering he had never seen her smile.

"I was just trying to be polite." He glanced at the boy and then looked at the field ahead, but he still felt Jacob's glare burning through him, ferreting out Cooper's intentions for his mom. Feeling threatened. Doubly threatened. Jane was both his parents.

For a boy to grow up without a father must have been a terrible thing to experience. Since Cooper's father had always worked exhausting hours, it had often felt like his mother had raised him alone. When his father was home, their interaction was limited to barked orders and submissive compliance. He never understood the man, could never figure out what he wanted from him. Cooper had tried to please him, but his efforts never seemed enough. He didn't approve of the way he dressed, the way he spoke, the career path he had chosen.

Some of Cooper's fondest childhood memories were the uncommon moments when his father would invite him to sit on his knee. In his gruff voice he would regale him with nostalgic tales from his youth, when he ran loose through the untamed docks of New York City. His gruffness would soften with wistfulness, but in hindsight, the stories were nothing more than cautionary tales intended to keep him focused and obedient. His father would emphasize his only reason for running loose through the docks--having angered sailors or half-drunken policemen chasing him--was that he had no mother to come home to. At this point in the tale, his father's voice would inevitably lose its softness, even its gruffness, becoming a dry rasp of a thing. His eyes would sheen over with tears. He would struggle to keep his emotions in check as he would once again tell the story about his mother. The same words spoken, unchanged in all his tellings, about how she had died in 1892, crushed under the weight of a faulty tenement wall. A victim of the overcrowded, wild metropolis.

But Cooper's father had lied. All of those times, all of those tellings, his fondest memories of his father, all lies.

"Cooper?" Ellie called out.

From the age when he still sat on his father's knee, until the fateful day when Cooper arrived home from work a short year and a half ago, his father had lied.

"Hmm, yes?" he said dreamily.

"Are you okay?" Ellie asked, concerned. The sun had broken through the remnant gray cloud cover. Birds once again twittered away, happy for the storm's passing.

"Just thinking is all." He continued walking with Ellie at his shoulder, feeling a wet spider web break across his arm as they cleared a thatch of scrub trees. He wiped his arm clean against his shirt.

To this day, the memory was crystal clear. His father had been away to Philadelphia on business. After braving the snow-swept, congested street on the way home from the library, Cooper stomped the slush from his shoes on the doormat and pulled off his winter coat. He heard his father speaking in the parlor. A log snapped with moisture under a stoked fire. Quite distinctly, he remembered rubbing his palms together for warmth and thinking he would catch up with his father and enjoy the parlor's warmth. He remembered hoping he was in a good mood.

But when he entered the room, the new fire banked high behind the fireplace screen, Cooper found his father speaking quietly with an old woman seated in a wicker-backed wheelchair. Hunched over, white hair pulled back from her face, a constant tremor shook through her left side. When Cooper made eye contact with her, a smile swept over her whole countenance--not just her mouth--but in her eyes her smile gleamed, in her cheeks a healthy glow warmed her drawn cheekbones.

He was struck silent but managed to return her smile. Seeing a Negro woman in their home had thrown him for a loop.

"Father, a guest?"

"Yes, a guest. A very special guest."

Cooper approached the old woman, extending his hand. Her touch was bone-dry, her ashen skin cold against his palm. He could feel a slight tremor all the way through her right hand.

"I'm Theodore Cooper."

He could sense his father shifting anxiously from one foot to the other. It sounded foreign coming from him. Unsure and nervous.

"Velma Fortune. Nice to meet you."

"Likewise."

She held his hand firmly, almost desperately, much stronger than he expected. He was finally able to pull away, turning back to his father.

"Your trip went well, I hope."

"We finalized the new distribution contracts. The expansion should go as planned."

"I'm glad to hear it," he said, not absorbing any of it. "Well, I should get cleaned up. You know how dusty books can be. I'll let you get back to your guest."

"But son, she came to see you." His voice cracked under the weight of the last syllable.

Once again he met Velma's gaze, and for a moment, for just a fragment of a second, she looked familiar, recognizable. Then it was gone just as quickly.

"Theodore, this is your grandmother. She's come to live with us--"

"Cooper?"

"Oh, I'm sorry Ellie. Did you say something?"

"Yes. We're here," the girl said.

"Really?" Cooper asked, bemused, looking around the wooded surroundings. He didn't know where they were, but he was certain he didn't see a house. "Where might this fabled Greta be?"

Jacob laughed, not saying a word. He pointed at a sprawling tree ten feet from where they stood, hooking his finger skyward, waiting for Cooper's sightline to follow his gesture.

A spiral stairway encircled the tree trunk. A wide plank platform sat at the summit of the stairs thirty feet above the ground. The building's walls were tarpaper, and he could see the corner of a closed hinged door. All nestled neatly among the ancient tree branches as if a part of the tree itself. He caught a whiff of a familiar aroma. He couldn't quite place it, not in the strangeness of this place.

Ellie tugged on his sleeve before starting up the spiral stairway. "That's cornbread, Coop. Greta's famous for it. Come on. It smells fresh from the oven."

NINETEEN

Charles Banyon wanted to die. He had snapped like a twig when he saw the Fowler boy. Seeing him Underground had surprised him, had stoked his underlying anger into a heated rage. Before he knew what he was doing, he'd brought a rock down on the boy's head. Then the nigger landed a couple wallops with his huge fists. His buddy, Ogie McCoy, went off hollering, bringing back a group of men to pry him from his back. They pummeled the bastard, dragging him off to some dark corner Charles didn't want to know about. He'd heard the nigger screaming, but tried to block it out. He never desired to witness anything like that, or anything else that happened in the Underground, but he supposed unsavory sights were his price to pay.

His anger had gone, leaving in its wake a desperate sadness.

When he'd stumbled away from the wreckage of Jimmy Fowler's body, the boy's skull was seeping blood. A lot of blood.

Yeah, he'd snapped; Jimmy was dead. Dead and damned.

Leaving the body behind, Charles had rushed to the hooch still and its flowing silvery oblivion. He'd filled an empty wine bottle with its liquid succor, and immediately commenced in emptying it down his gullet.

He didn't know when he started crying, or how he'd scraped his knees bloody. The bottle now nearly empty, the cave wall he leaned against seemed to spin a contorted whirl.

Regret. Mindless, aimless, stupid Goddamned regret. Smashing the

Fowler boy's skull, just another regret in a lifetime of regret. He'd end it all; he lived and breathed to end it all, if only...

Mabel...

Jimmy Fowler would never leave this place, this eternal hell. He used to come over to the house all the time, even staying overnight when the boys were young. George still got along with Jimmy, *HAD gotten along with him,* he reminded himself. But his recent visits had been few and far between. George had been embarrassed of him, embarrassed of the booze-swilling bastard he had become. Elizabeth was not so much embarrassed as ashamed. Charles would see it boldly articulated in her face, unshielded by her youthful honesty. Mabel existed within Elizabeth. Whenever his daughter would cast her shamed eyes on him-- her steadfast expression altogether too old for someone her age--he felt his wife staring at him through her eyes.

Mabel, let me be. Let me end this misery. This loneliness.

He tipped the bottle, emptying the last quarter of the bottle into his waiting mouth, the far-off candlelight setting the bottle aglow. The earth seemed to pitch beneath his feet, throwing him violently into a rock wall. The bottle shattered in his fist as he crashed, the glass fragments tearing deeply through skin and ligaments. Pain lanced his palm.

He closed his eyes, hoping to black out. Even if his eyes had remained open, madness would blind him, and if not madness, then burning self-hatred would certainly do the trick. He rubbed his slurred-numb and bloodied hand across his chin and wasn't surprised to find it coated in vomit.

He was staring at the doorway when he opened his eyes. The rough log door he had constructed by his own will and labor. A new bloody handprint was smeared along the edge, as if someone fought being placed on the other side. Behind the door a small cubby of a room. No lights, no water or food or anything else a living person would need to survive.

I've ruined everything. I can't do this without you.

He pressed his bristled cheek against the door, ran his fingers down the grain. He heard a stir from the other side. A low growl muted by the door's imposing thickness.

I was a coward. Couldn't bear to live when you didn't. I've done this to you.

He slumped to the floor, splinters digging into his face. The floor beneath him seemed to steady, the earth itself with its incessant spinning having slowed. His nausea, while still present, leveled off. He was sobering.

The growl intensified, becoming a howl. Her nails dug at the rough wood, seeking escape. He had done this. This madness, this cowardice.

"Ch-cha-chaaa," Mabel moaned, trying to articulate his name through her undead lips. She slammed against the door, repeatedly, rhythmically, a mocking heartbeat. Four inches of wood separated them. For all his good intention, it could have been a mile.

He didn't save her in time. Mabel died giving birth to Elizabeth. He could vividly remember the tension leaving her grip as he stood by her bedside. Her hot skin had cooled, and as it did, something slipped away from her. Her soul, her essence? Naming the sensation was pointless. She had died, yet he still brought her to the Underground, carrying her in his arms, her head lolling lifelessly, her birthing blood soaking his clothes. He had known about the tunnels. All his life the knowledge had been there, in the periphery of everyday, spoken about by his father and uncles, all of whom had toiled in the mines. He'd never given it a second thought, had never desired to seek the root of the mystery. Not until Mabel died. He had known about the Underground's powers and had brought her here and now she was this... this monster.

"Cha-Char-CHARLESss!" She pounded the door, shaking it within its frame, the wood vibrating against his cheek.

I'm so sorry, Mabel. He whimpered silently, his tears flowing thicker as he continued to sober.

She stopped pounding the door and gave off a slight whine. For a moment, she sounded real and human and so alive. Then from the other side, only silence.

She wriggled her fingers through the small gap under the door. Gray skin, filthy fingernails splintered at the tips, overly long, still growing after death.

His hand trembled as he impulsively reached for her. He stopped short, an inch away.

He could feel his wounded hand healing, his torn skin and sliced ligaments reforming, his bloodied knees scabbing, scarring, becoming soft pink skin. The immutable persistence of the Underground.

Goddamn it. "I'm going to make this right, Mabel. I'm going to do whatever it takes."

Mabel's fingers twitched at the sound of his voice. She grunted, "CHAR!CHAR!CHAR!"

He touched her fingers. The tips of his met hers, and their coldness, their roughness, only solidified his resolve. While George was dead, his poor sweet boy, Mabel lived on in the form of Elizabeth. He concentrated on the coldness of his undead wife's fingers, and promised himself he wouldn't let anything bad happen to his daughter. This time he would follow through. He could no longer turn a blind eye toward the child Mabel died giving birth to.

Unsteadily, he gained his feet. Looking at his clothes as if for the first time--the grime and vomit stained rags--he felt the shame often reflected in his daughter's eyes. This brought on a pain sharper than anything he'd ever felt before. Even worse than witnessing his wife's existence in the Underground.

"CHARRRR-LESSS!" Mabel cried from the other side of the door. Leaning on the cave walls for support, Charles Banyon stumbled his way through the tunnels--the cries of his undead wife haunting his every step--to the waiting daylight, and hopefully, to the forgiveness of his daughter.

TWENTY

The home sat across two wide, buttressed limbs spreading parallel to the woods below. Cooper's stomach flipped as he looked down. They were nearly to Greta's door, thirty feet from the ground's safety. Cooper was afraid of heights. Ellie and Jacob were obviously not. They practically capered up the rain-wet steps encircling the tree trunk.

Ellie knocked on Greta's door. When it opened, Cooper was disappointed when old Greta turned out to be no older than his own father. His mind had drawn her from the same palette as Eunice Blankenship: bowed by gravity and brittle with age, struggling through an unseen battle, fighting to live through one more day. Seeing her in the flesh, Greta held none of these characteristics.

"Children. You've brought a friend. Come in, come in."

"I hope we're not putting you out," Ellie said.

"Nonsense," Greta said, holding the door wide. Her face was broad and welcoming, her movements crisp, precise.

Cooper was the last inside. His head nearly touched the ceiling, and the spare furniture and kitchen appliances inside the one room catchall house seemed to be on a smaller than normal scale. With a familiarity of their surroundings, Ellie and Jacob took seats at a short table with four completed place settings. Greta was taking chilled milk from an icebox, while the children looked hungrily at the steaming bricks of cornbread on the plates set in front of them. Cooper sat, his knees bumping the table's underside. A wood burning cook stove was in one corner, still warming the squat home with its radiant heat. Chunks of corn textured the bread's surface. Melting sweet butter ran through the nooks and crannies in lavish rivers.

After pouring the milk, Greta replaced the glass pitcher to the icebox. She let out a contented sigh as she sat in the lone empty chair.

"Expecting company?" Cooper asked. He found it odd to see the table set for four. It looked like she had cut the cornbread even as they mounted the steps to her home.

"You must be Cooper." Greta stared at him, as if plumbing for knowledge.

"Cooper, Greta Hildaberg, Greta, Cooper," Ellie said, making a formal introduction.

Greta squeezed Ellie's hand. "I'm sorry for your loss, dear. I wish I could've warned him."

"Did you see anything before it happened?"

"No. If I had I would have done anything possible to bring about a different end."

Ellie seemed satisfied with Greta's answer. Cooper felt bad for the children so implicitly trusting an eccentric old lady living in a tree. He didn't trust what he might say, so he took a bite of cornbread. It tasted as good as it smelled.

"And Jimmy?" Jacob asked, his voice faltering.

"He's not in the army, is he? Me and Jacob know he's not, but no one listens to us."

"Do you know what happened to my brother? Where he is? Anything, please," Jacob pleaded.

"I wish I could close my eyes and see the answers written there. It simply doesn't work that way, child."

"Greta?" Jacob wiped away a single streaking tear.

"No, he's not in the army. I wish it were true." Greta frowned at her folded hands as if they had done her wrong. "You see, my visions, if that's what the townsfolk like to call them, well, they aren't my visions of the future at all. There's a peculiar trait in my family, going back, oh, I can't count the generations… but I do remember them. Every generation before me, I remember their memories. The memories of those who came before get passed on at the time of death like an inheritance."

"So your visions are of the past?" Ellie asked, confused.

"My family's memories go back a long time. From the time my ancestors were peasants in Europe, to even earlier generations, when they lived in barbaric tribes mixing with Orientals, Africans. The newest memories are the strongest, the most fully formed, of course. They get weaker the closer you get to the base of my family tree."

"But you've predicted the future. Like how Odette Fischer would win the pie contest last year with her secret recipe, her raisin custard. Or when you warned of Claude Cloutier having his heart attack while tilling his field," Jacob said.

"Sure, I know things about the future, but you have to understand, they aren't my visions. They're my mother's. She could see the future. She was the only person in all of my family's generations who not only saw the past and past lives, but the future and the coming generations. Upon her death, I inherited my mother's visions of the future."

Cooper had heard enough. "I'm sorry, but maybe I should step outside," Cooper said while standing. "I don't feel like I'm much help here."

"Cooper, you're a part of this. You might want to stick around."

"A part of this? So you're saying that I'm somehow connected to Jimmy Fowler's disappearance?"

Jacob looked accusingly at Cooper, as if the question had solidified his own conclusions.

"No, but you will be instrumental in what is to come."

"I'm sorry, but I don't believe a word you're saying. Kids, I think we should go now. This is a big waste of time."

"Greta, please go on," Ellie said quietly, as if she didn't want to offend Cooper for speaking up at all.

Greta closed her eyes in concentration. "There are places where even God won't go. The Blankenships learned this," she said, opening her eyes. She paused, letting out a sigh, looking at Cooper. "But it was too late for them to do anything about it. They were drawn in, consumed in darkness. When they were gone, God turned His back on Coal Hollow. From that day on, no man of God would step foot inside the town limits."

"Jimmy, my brother, do you know where he is, Greta?"

"I can't see that. Mom didn't know, didn't foresee this. But she did know he's somewhere close."

"Is he... is he...?"

"He's, more than anything, wanting to escape the hell he's a subject to."

There was a quick, familiar knock on the door, then Arlen Polk entered, carrying a wooden crate laden with groceries. He seemed surprised to see others sitting with Greta.

"Momma, I got your cooking things." He kept his eyes lowered. He could've just climbed from a coal bin. Black dust coated his skin. His greasy hair stuck out in weird spikes.

"Thank you, Arlen." Her son stood staring at Cooper. "You remember Mr. Cooper, right Arlen?"

"Yeah, Mom, I told you 'bout him. We found the, uh... we... went searching together that one night." He turned to Cooper. "I'd shake hands, but after the..." he said, then stopped as he looked at Ellie, "The uh... service, I went to my gopher hole. Then, I 'membered Mamma's cooking stuff, so I went to town."

"Such a good boy, always thinking of my well-being," Greta said to Cooper, smiling. She turned back to Arlen. "Honey, we're about done here. Why don't you clean up, and by the time you get back, I'll have something on the stove for you."

"Sure, Momma." He went to his mother and kissed her cheek. She feigned a giggle at his quill-like beard, and then patted him on the head and shooed him away. Arlen moped as he went out the door and down the stairs.

"I'm sorry, but that's all I have to share. I wish I could be more precise. If I knew anything else, I would say so. There's an unpleasant undercurrent in this town. It will pull at you unexpectedly and drag you under its surface if you don't watch out. Just please be careful."

The children took this as their cue and headed for the door.

"Thanks, Greta." Ellie seemed disappointed in what Greta had told her, but still somewhat relieved.

"Cooper? Can I have a private word?"

Jacob waved goodbye to Greta and then closed the door, leaving them alone.

"I think you should be ashamed for what you're doing to those kids," Cooper said, doing his best to keep his voice from traveling too far.

"You're being unfair," she said whimsically. She seemed comfortable with someone questioning her abilities.

"You give a sense of hope when there isn't any."

"Because there *is* hope. I know it's hard to see, but the life of this town will soon shift. Daylight will swallow shadows. Shadows most people don't even see, or if they do, won't acknowledge for what they are. You, Mr. Cooper, are at the center of this change."

"You speak in riddles. People speak in riddles when they are trying to hide something."

"I speak the truth. My mother's truth."

"Why should I care what happens here?" He didn't believe his own words, because in some small way he did feel a connection with this town and the people he'd met. The kids waiting outside, Jane Fowler, Hank Calder, Magee, everyone... even the Blankenships--they were all good people.

"Because you already do. Otherwise, you wouldn't have bought that house. You wouldn't be protecting those kids when you think they might be in danger of whatever fate stole Jimmy Fowler from his family. Besides, most strangers wouldn't have waited a day to take leave after George's death. You're here, Mr. Cooper. You're invested."

"I don't want to hear any more of your runaround. You're just a lonely old lady luring people to your door with your jumbled talk. Right now, I'm going to walk those kids home. As soon as I see Jacob's mom, I'm going to let her know about everything, about how you are nothing but a snake charmer."

"What if I told you I know your secret?"

"I don't know what you're talking about."

As if Cooper hadn't voiced his dissent, Greta continued: "You discovered your father's mother was a former slave, her son, your father, was born from relations with her master, and you didn't know about this until recently."

"How the hell--"

"This knowledge has left you confused about who you are and your role in society."

"I'm not going to listen to another--"

"Cooper, it's okay." Greta raised her hand to interrupt him. "I won't tell anyone. I just wanted to prove to you..."

Cooper didn't know what to say, and couldn't meet Greta's gaze. He turned quickly, and was out the door a moment later. He nearly bowled over the kids at the top of the stairs.

"Cooper?" Ellie asked. "Everything all right?"

The color left his face. Light-headedness washed over him. He hurried down the stairs, careful not to take in the imposing height, for then he would surely faint.

He reached the wooded ground, the children close on his heels. They passed Arlen as he returned from wherever he had cleaned up. His forehead and neck were still coal-black, but the skin above his scraggly beard was white, as were his hands. They were so white they appeared to have never touched sunlight.

"Bye bye," Arlen said. He seemed happy to have his mother to himself.

TWENTY-ONE

They were quiet on the way home, each lost in their own thoughts. Most certain of the quickest route, Jacob had taken the lead. Ellie stayed by Cooper's side.

Cooper had accompanied the kids to Greta's house for one and only one reason. He feared for their safety. He never believed the story about Jimmy Fowler running off to the army, or that an animal had gored Ellie's brother to death. The pieces of the puzzle didn't fit that way. No, something terrible had happened, but he didn't know exactly what. He couldn't let the kids go off on their own with what his instincts were telling him.

He never expected to hear such things. Greta had caught him off guard, and before he could react, he felt exposed, verbally lashed. But that's not what happened. Not really. Upon reflection, the sting of her words softened. When the sting was entirely gone, he realized she hadn't attacked him at all. Greta had been right about everything she had said about his past. The sting was from the vulnerability he felt with a stranger knowing his secret.

Judging the children's reaction, they hadn't overheard the conversation. That was a relief. He didn't want to admit who he was, *what* he was. The only trouble he'd ever suffered over his appearance was when he had sprouted tall at thirteen, without the accompanying weight gain. For two years he had been scrawny and sickly looking. He eventually leveled off after the family doctor instructed his mom to make sure he got extra milk and butter in his diet. Those two years had been bad enough; he couldn't imagine the reactions and ridicule if the secret of his lineage became public knowledge.

His secret. How could Greta have known? No one knew but his own parents. His grandmother had lived at their town home until cancer sent her to her grave. Despite increasing doses of laudanum, pain taxed her frail body every minute of those three months. Little could be done for her. Cooper's mother lovingly attended to her needs during the day when he and his father were at work. At night, his father would hold vigil over her as she rapidly deteriorated, oftentimes reading the bible to her in his gruff voice. From his bedroom door, Cooper would listen for when his father took to his own bed, usually after midnight, and then he would go to Velma Fortune's bedside. He would hold her hand as they talked quietly.

"Arlen's a bastard," Jacob said matter-of-factly as they walked. He pulled back next to Cooper and Ellie. The boy didn't seem as angry after talking to Greta.

"Jacob, don't talk like that," Ellie said.

"But he is. I heard it from Jimmy. A shyster named Rubell Polk, he came to town selling potions and remedies from a beat up suitcase. He swept old Greta off her feet, and then snuck off not long after. She's never hidden it, neither."

Cooper nodded, choosing to ignore his gossip bait. "That was a brave thing for an unmarried woman to do."

"People think Arlen's a nitwit because he's a bastard."

"Jacob, please."

"I'm not making it up, Ellie. You've heard it yourself."

"Doesn't mean you gotta go off talking like that."

"Just making conversation."

They continued on in silence. After awhile Jacob's eyes darkened. Cooper could only guess where the boy's thoughts lingered. He had been through a lot lately.

They covered the next half-mile cutting across a sorghum cane field. The sun had dried the grass, all except for the twining roots. Cooper drifted back to his own thoughts. Velma Fortune's dying words haunted him:

Find yourself, child. Find out who you ought to be.

Since meeting his grandmother in his family's parlor, Cooper had been confused and conflicted. Before meeting Velma, he'd thought he knew his place in the world, but that had all changed. She'd sensed his confusion, though he'd never spoken of it. Then she used her final words in an attempt to comfort him. He couldn't imagine a more selfless gift.

In her short time at their home, they had grown close. Velma always had a story to tell or a small nugget of wisdom to pass on. His only wish would have been to meet her sooner.

After a solemn closed casket wake, they buried Velma in the family cemetery. By the end of that day, eager to be on his way, Cooper traded his funeral garb for traveling clothes. His preparations accelerated when Velma's condition took a turn for the worse. Everyone had known the end was near, but no one had spoken about it. She smiled weakly, revealing more than words ever could. The reunion of her family had given her closure.

The library board had been shocked when he announced his intentions of leaving. Without his asking, they had promised to hold a position for him, if he were ever inclined to return. Velma Fortune's grave was still fresh when he took to the road.

Jacob and Ellie seemed in more of a hurry than Cooper, so the way home went quickly. They left the sorghum field and returned to Teetering Road for the last stretch home. As they approached the Fowler's driveway, he considered what he had said to Greta, how he would tell Jane Fowler how Greta had plied the kids' innocence and insecurity with her lies. But he decided to hold his tongue. Telling Jane would undoubtedly send her over to Greta's house, and in the end, potentially expose his past. He had another reason for not telling Jane: maybe Greta hadn't fabricated a single thread to her story. With how quickly she had convinced Cooper of her abilities--and she had turned his disbelief around as easily as spinning a top--he couldn't deny the possibility. Maybe Jimmy *was* close by.

"Take care, Coop," Ellie said as they reached the driveway.

He waved to her and exchanged a nod of amiable acceptance with Jacob. When the front door closed behind them, he turned to walk to his new home. Differing thoughts fought for his complete attention:

His grandmother's dying words. The image of the Blankenships spiraling away, consumed in darkness. Wondering about his own motives for buying their abandoned home, and if they were even his motives to begin with. Most of all, he wondered about Greta's insistence that he would help solve the mystery of Jimmy's disappearance.

PART THREE

ONE

Jacob's mother didn't allow him to say a word before she started in on him. Her venom left him temporarily speechless.

"You've got a lot of explaining to do, Jacob Mitchell Fowler!" Still dressed in her funeral clothes from hours earlier, she bolted from her kitchen chair, her eyes puffy and red. She was angry. Angrier than he had ever seen.

He stammered, searching for his voice. Ellie cringed behind him. He hadn't noticed Louise Bradshaw right away, but now he saw her sitting at the kitchen table and rubbing her expanding belly. As his mom tore into him, Louise remained seated and quiet.

"Where were you two? Do you have any sense at all, running off like that? Did you ever think how scared I'd be?"

"But, Mom--"

Her slap silenced him.

His hand went to his stinging cheek. His mom's expression immediately drained. She'd never struck him before. Never once in all the times he had angered her.

"Oh, Jacob, I'm so sorry. I... I thought you were gone, too, like Jimmy. I couldn't stand the thought of not having my sons."

He still rubbed his cheek, smarting more from bewilderment than pain. His mom pulled him into a hug, and he could feel her trembling against him. She felt so fragile. While she had always seemed made of granite, her bones were now balsa wood.

"Mom, I'm sorry. We won't run off again. I wasn't thinking."
Ellie stepped forward to face his mom. "We went to Greta's."
"You did what?"

"We went to her house," Jacob said, then felt the need to explain. "We went to see if Greta knew anything about our brothers."

"She said Jimmy's close, Miss Fowler. Maybe even in town somewhere. He's somewhere close, and he wants to come home."

Louise flinched at hearing Jimmy's name. She still didn't speak, but her attention seemed more acutely focused. Her hair typically fell across her shoulders in unruly waves; now it was pulled back behind her ears. It made her brown eyes more prominent and stark.

"Of course. I should have known." His mom brushed one of Ellie's blonde braids behind her shoulder. Her emotions switched yet again, this time shifting from anger to understanding. Jacob was confused. "Are you two hungry? I can whip something up. Supper won't be for a couple hours still, but I don't mind."

"Mom, it's true. What Greta said. Jimmy's still here. Somewhere. We need to find him."

"That's not possible."

Jacob tried to decipher the meaning of his mom's words. He could only come to one conclusion. Seeing Louise sitting weepy-eyed at their kitchen table, seeing how sad, how utterly exhausted his mom was, it could only mean one thing: someone had discovered his brother's body.

"Sheriff Bergman was over not more than an hour ago with the news. Which reminds me, I'm going to have to run to town to let him know you two are back and okay."

Ellie caught his attention as she shifted from one foot to the other. Sympathy gleamed in her deep blue eyes. He could easily read her thoughts; she knew why Bergman had come, she'd been through this before. Jacob listened to his mom, but wanted to put a break on the words coming from her mouth. As long as he didn't hear the words, then they couldn't be true. His brother wasn't dead. Couldn't possibly be.

"The sheriff just heard back from Peoria. The recruiting office has a record of Jimmy signing up two days ago. Do you know what this means, Jacob? Your brother is safe. He's safe as long as he's not sent somewhere to war, but at least we know he's alive. I'm going to take a strap to that boy, just as soon as I get a chance, I'm going to whip that boy raw. Running off like that, running off scared and spineless. Just like his father."

His mom hugged him again, and her strength had returned; she squeezed so hard it felt like she would break his ribs. He didn't think she would ever let go, but when she did, he turned and noticed fresh tears on Louise's face. Looking at Ellie, he was certain she mirrored his expression: shock, dismay, disbelief.

"I'm glad to see you both home safe, but that doesn't change the fact that I'm angry with you or that what you did was wrong. You're both grounded from leaving the yard until I decide otherwise. Until you prove you've learned some sense.

"So can I get you something to eat, or can you wait until supper?"

TWO

Cooper had yet to set up bedding in any of the upstairs bedrooms. Instead, as the sun dipped below the trees, he built a nest of blankets in the entryway. He felt more comfortable here, resting in clear view of both the front door and the pipe organ in the back room. He might have bought the house, but he still felt like a stranger within its walls. Watching the shifting moonlight toying with the shadows on the ceiling, he continued to parse Greta's words from earlier today:

There's an unpleasant undercurrent in this town. It will pull at you unexpectedly, dragging you under its surface.

A mysterious and corrupt member of his new community was holding a boy against his will. For some reason, this thought didn't startle him. He knew he should react differently. With anxiety maybe, with alarm, definitely.

But he didn't.

Those other matters didn't reach him within the security of his new home. Those petty squabbles, those lost little boys of no consequence to his own life--nothing could reach him here. He closed his eyes, his mind reeling with fatigue.

He heard his own voice from far away, as if he held a paper cone pressed to his ear:

I think you should be ashamed for what you're doing to those kids... how can you look at yourself in the mirror?

Then Greta's soft, whimsical voice, as if in reply:

We all have tales we want left untold and forgotten.

Cooper opened his eyes with a start. Someone was knocking on the front door. He blinked, his mind thickly slowed from sleep. When his mind cleared, he saw a maroon entryway carpet beneath his blankets. A small table he had never noticed before was in the corner by the door. At its center, a vase held a mass of long-stemmed wildflowers slumping along its rim. He could smell the sweet pollen from the yellow petals, the tang of fresh-cut stems.

Again, the knock repeated, this time with a desperate air. Two knocks, pause, one knock.

He moved to his knees, craning forward, waiting for any other sounds coming from outside. He heard none. Maybe he had dreamt the noises, the sound leaking over to his waking mind. Perhaps the wind raked a tree branch against the house.

He wasn't aware of the sound coming from the pipe organ until its mournful dirge sighed to silence. He looked to the back room, and was startled to see an old woman. As she walked toward him, she flexed her fingers as if they pained her. She seemed oblivious of his presence as she neared.

"Um, hello?" Cooper said, his voice scratchy in his throat.

She rushed by, the maroon carpet softening her steps, unfazed. She opened the front door a crack before swinging it wide. A Negro man hesitated, but stepped inside. His shoulders were broad and there was sweat dripping down his forehead and around the curve of his chin. His taut limbs relaxed slightly when the door closed behind him, his relief evident.

Eunice Blankenship moved swiftly, the man apprehensively a step behind. It really was her, Cooper realized; the fragile frame of her face was identical to her younger self captured in the daguerreotype he'd found. They went through a side room, down a flight of stairs, to a back hallway. Cooper found himself standing in the basement hallway next to a late night visitor. Even though he was close enough to touch his shoulder, he didn't seem aware of Cooper's presence.

Eunice had disappeared around a corner. But Benjamin--*yes, His name is Benjamin*, Cooper realized, Benjamin remained behind. He was staring at a mirror on the wall, unmoving. It was hung at an angle to allow people to not only view their reflection, but also to see the stairwell without being seen. Cooper was off to the side a foot away. While he could still move, not even Benjamin's eyes twitched.

"It's time to go, Benjamin," he said aloud, his voice dry with apprehension. Then in a quieter voice to himself, "I remember now. It's like every other night. Every night since I came to Coal Hollow."

He waved his hand in front of Benjamin's eyes, but he still didn't move. "You need to follow Eunice. She's in the back room. Your family is behind a secret panel in the wall. Seeing them again is the happiest moment in your life. Seeing your wife. Your father-in-law."

Cooper could hear his own voice, could feel his muscles humming with anxiety. That was it. Benjamin could have been a statue.

"Benjamin?" He reached out to touch the Negro on the shoulder.

Before he could, the man moved. As he turned toward Cooper, he was certain Benjamin's eyes would meet his. But they panned by, unseeing, checking the direction Eunice had gone, before returning to the mirror, this time turning slightly to see up the stairwell.

This was not supposed to happen. This wasn't how it happened every night in his dreams. Benjamin always moved down the hallway, catching up to Eunice. Never hesitating, never doubting. But this once he kept his eyes trained above, his nervousness resurfacing.

A crash came from upstairs. Something slammed into the front door, and the splintering wood sounded like a crying animal. Someone was axing their way in. Benjamin thought about it--Cooper could see it in his eyes--he was going to confront whoever was so maliciously breaking into the Blankenship's home. Confront them and save his family from discovery.

A jumble of voices came from upstairs:

"You sure this is the place?"

"Of course we are. We're professionals, Mr. Parkins."

"We've got our sources."

"Your sources are niggers, Cartwright."

"Old Willy'd give up his own daughter to stay free. In fact, he had a cousin hiding not far from his house in Lewiston, awaiting instructions for the trip to Toronto, he gave him up."

"He sure did. Stupid nigger. We took his cousin, and a few more darkies, besides."

"That's enough, Leo. Let's just get this done."

"I just want what's mine," Parkins said.

"Enough. Both of you. This is the place. Now, Parkins, you'll get your niggers, we'll get paid, we'll be on our way. Simple enough.

"Now, everybody spread out. The reverend and his wife gotta be around, with it pissing rain out, they're bound to be inside."

The floor above creaked with thundering strides as they began their search. Someone ransacked the kitchen. Glasses shattered, bowls crashed into walls, cast iron pans hammered the floor.

"Kitchen's clear," someone said, chuckling.

After listening to the intruders, Benjamin hesitated. Cooper could tell the Negro was weighing his odds. He stepped toward the stairway, paused, then retreated down the hall Eunice had taken.

Cooper trailed behind him, feeling like an eavesdropper on these strangers running through his house.

But it's their house. Isn't it?

More voices came from upstairs; Cooper could no longer tell what they were saying, but the menacing tone didn't bode well for the Blankenships' fate.

When Cooper caught up, Eunice was standing next to the open panel in the wall. She was speaking with Benjamin, with the people already in the hidden room. "You need to hurry down that tunnel. It leads to another house not far from here. They'll help. It's dark, sure, but you'll have a chance."

"I don't know what to say." He loomed over her; Eunice's forehead nearly reached his armpit. "I don't even know your name."

"Call me friend." Eunice touched Benjamin's shoulder, squeezing it. She guided him down to the hidden room.

As footsteps crashed down the basement stairs, Benjamin clambered into the opening. The brief voices from inside the low opening were joyous, yet ultimately sad. Dark-skinned hands pulled at him, futilely helping him inside.

Eunice replaced the panel, and instantly the wall looked whole and unremarkable.

She then looked at Cooper.

Instead of her eyes trailing away, they lingered for a second. She blinked; in that moment he saw her life, her anguish, her understanding that, while she devoted her life to preserving life, there were people who didn't give a damn about her mission; that and so much more was evident in a single gleaming blink.

He only turned away because he heard the frantic rip of metal slicing through the air. All he saw was the machete blade coming down from its full arc.

The image froze in his mind's eye, would remain there always; rage, hatred merging with madness. The wielder's eyes pulled wide, full whites glinting like silver dollars cast carelessly to a rain puddle.

Cooper threw his hands up as if to ward off a fatal blow, but the blade rushed by his forehead, pressing cold air to his brow, before tearing with a meaty thud into Eunice's skull.

"Christ, we might've needed to speak to her," another man said, pushing into the room.

She moaned submissively, but otherwise, seemed unaware of the mortal wound. Her brow furrowed in consternation, then disappointment.

She fell to the floor, dead before her body could settle. Cooper reached out for her, but his hand seemed to float away from him like dense fog. Then he was drifting on a breeze, rising above the violence. Eunice's killer didn't notice him.

He can't see me.

Cooper tried yelling, but was voiceless, tried waving his arms, clapping his hands, but was helpless. *A person's been murdered in my house, and I can't do a thing to stop it.* He screamed in frustration.

The machete wielder's hatred was no longer present. He laughed softly as if embarrassed at hearing a dirty joke in mixed company. His eyes were twitchy, too small for his head; rain blending with sweat dripped from the brim of his hat and face. A plug of chaw strained his cheek. He did not look like a killer. Under different circumstances he would've appeared apologetic as he leaned over to wedge his knee against Eunice's cheekbone for leverage. As he worked to free the machete, her cleaved skull protested like a still-green log fighting a wood axe. Blood flowed freely, seeping into the dirt floor.

"Hey, Vic, we found the reverend," said a man hefting a fire axe as he ran into the room, almost stepping on the body. "Ho'boy, looks like you found the wife."

The momentary quiet left the basement, chaos sweeping in like a violent tide. Two more men poured through the narrow doorway. Their rain-drenched leather riding coats flapped at their knees. One man carried a long-barrel shotgun. Another had a pistol in each clenched fist and iron shackles tethered to his cowhide belt. They were identical. Brothers of Eunice's killer. They were triplets.

"She resisted," Vic Borland said, unable to hold back a wicked grin. "I swear she did."

"Conspirator, was she?"

"You know it, Leo. Just another nigger-lover. I think she was a mite unstable, too."

"Tried to gouge your eyes?" the third brother chimed in.

It's like a damn game to them! Cooper raged, his ethereal body trembling.

"Yeah, even tried kicking my balls. Had to put her down like a sick dog."

"Well, good for you," the axe-wielder said, then spit a glob of chaw into Eunice's blood-speckled face. He pulled back and kicked her hard in the ribs. "Whore."

Another two men entered the already cramped room: a hulking fair-haired man forcing the Reverend Horace Blankenship inside by a painful armlock.

Black-eyed and nose-bloodied, Blankenship cried out when he saw his wife.

A tow-head boy stood in the doorway, face blanched and rain soaked. He silently took in the bloody sight. A pink-faced man appeared behind the boy, his fingers flittering at his breast.

The employer of these monsters, Cooper thought. *Parkins.*

Removing a handkerchief from an interior pocket, Parkins mopped his brow. He refolded the elegant fabric and held it to his lips as if nauseated.

The reverend didn't look at his wife, instead keeping his eyes raised heavenward, seeking solace or rescue from his God. Eunice's blood continued to spread as her body jerked through a final spasm. Her bowels released a pocket of gas and the triplets laughed.

"Cartwright, did it have to come to this? What happened?"

Still holding his armlock on the reverend, Cartwright glared over his shoulder. "You wanted this, Parkins. We're almost done. We'll get the information from the good reverend, then we'll get your property back."

"I never agreed to murdering innocent people."

"None of us involved is innocent. *Nobody.*"

"But--"

Cartwright cut him off. "You know our reputation, know we're the best doing what we do. You knew the consequences of setting us on a trail. You hired us. *You* did this."

At hearing the exchange, the boy ran from the doorway to a corner and retched, trying his best to stifle the embarrassing sound. The other bounty hunters shook their heads, slapped each other on the shoulder and laughed at the boy's weakness.

Cartwright released the reverend, shoving him against a wall. The old man slumped to the floor, rubbing his shoulder, staring at his wife's body. Blankenship crossed himself, clasped his hands together and began to pray quietly, yet intently.

Cartwright took a single step toward the brothers, and though they each had twenty pounds on him, they became quiet and sullen, looking at the floor, unable to meet his eye.

He went to the boy, placed a hand on his shoulder. "This is how things are done, Jasper. You wanted to come along. If you're going to be a part of this, I need you to be strong."

The reverend's gaze leveled at Cartwright. "You… you bastard! He's your son? You willingly led your son into Hell's embrace?" A vein throbbed at his temple, his limbs trembled. He squeezed his hands together even tighter, his voice rising, "Dear heavenly Father, I beg of You Your forgiveness, for my own sins and the sins of these vile men!"

Cartwright took two strides and kicked the reverend in the temple, sending him groaning to the ground.

"Damn it, look what you made me do." Cartwright sounded tired, but resolute. "You don't understand, that's all. Jasper's going to be in the family business."

With blood leaking from his ear, Blankenship closed his eyes again and continued praying, his lips moving without a sound.

"Ethan, time's ticking. We better get what we came for," the axe-wielder said. He seemed less frightened of Cartwright than the bounty hunting brothers. More on his level.

"Old Lewiston Willy mentioned a hidden room somewhere."

"You trust that nigger?" Parkins asked, keeping his eyes from taking in the mess on the floor.

Cooper still hovered above the melee like cigar smoke, swirling through the room in languid circles, unable to shut his eyes of sight, unable to shut his ears of sound.

Uncomfortably, Parkins squatted next to Blankenship, moving as if his riding gear had chafed his delicate skin. "Where they at, nigger lover? Where's this hidden room? Let us know and we'll be peaceable. Just tell us where my property's at." His voice was southern-sweet. Cooper could picture him sipping lemonade while sitting on a porch swing, not a care in the world.

"You have no right!" Horace Blankenship cried, his eyes still held skyward. Cooper didn't know if he was admonishing his attackers' brutality or his savior's lack of empathy. "Cartwright, you and your heathens are going to hell, God as my witness, you will burn for eternity in Satan's fire!"

The room was quiet for several seconds, all except for an occasional splatter of spit tobacco juice and quiet whimpers from the boy in the corner.

Cooper, still circling, a fly caught in the tow of an autumn breeze, shifted about the room. He saw Parkins's bald spot, Cartwright's tight-lipped grin, the machete, the fire axe, the guns, Eunice's blood swirling on the floor as he moved, everyone ready for an escalation of violence if given cause. Cartwright placed a hand on Parkins's shoulder. The southerner backed away to stand with the others. Cartwright leaned over to whisper something into the reverend's ear.

The old man shook his head emphatically. "No. No, I can't do that."

Cartwright looked at his men, shook his head. He waved for the axe-wielder. "Scully, get what we need from him. Make it quick. Trail's going cold."

Blankenship didn't flinch, nor did he look to confront his interrogator. His lips trembled in prayer, spittle gathering on his lip.

The axe swayed low to the ground as he sized up the reverend, choosing a choice spot for his strike. The swaying increased, building momentum. Choosing Blankenship's left foot, he stomped on his ankle, holding the limb steady.

The air stilled with anticipation. Cooper's swirling stopped. He couldn't catch his breath; it built in his chest as a molten pain. Before the axe could sever the reverend's foot, a slight sound broke the loaded silence: a glass jar's hollow ping as it toppled over.

Cartwright's eyes gleamed with excitement. "Hold on, Scully. I think we've found our quarry!"

A forced quiet filled the room. The throb of blood rushed through temples. Adrenaline quivered muscles. Then they heard it. They all heard it. A scurrying sound, like animals of the night cowering through shadows and afterthoughts. Even Blankenship stopped his babbled prayer and looked at the wall with the hidden panel. He started crying afresh.

Leo Borland raised his weapon, finger twitching to pull the trigger. "They're in the wall!"

"Hold on." Cartwright grinned wide enough that the parting of his sun-weathered lips revealed straight, white teeth. "Scully, why don't you have the honors."

The axe-wielder sprang forward, the others clearing a path. He threw the axe back in a half swing and sent it crashing against the hidden panel. The wooden plank disintegrated. He went to his knees, shoved aside the debris.

"It's a damn tunnel," Parkins said, astonished. "You get after 'em before you lose them darkies again."

"They're your niggers, so that means you're coming with, Parkins," Cartwright said.

They passed a lit lantern to Leo Borland, and he and his long-barrel shotgun leapt for the hole in the wall. He almost immediately pulled out. "That was a piss jar they got back here. Aw, the fuckin' thing tipped over, now I got nigger piss all over my britches."

The riders laughed. "Leo, get your ass back in there," Cartwright said. The triplet spat, scrunched up his face, then disappeared. Without another word from Cartwright, another Borland brother fell to his knees to take up the pursuit.

"What about this piece of shit?" Scully asked, grabbing Blankenship's sleeve.

"Chop him like kindling," Cartwright said, then turned to his son. "Jasper? Son, you coming?"

Scully's axe left the tow-head boy transfixed but wary, as if the iron head was a living and temperamental thing. Cooper wanted to call out to him, or to at least shield him from this horror, but was helpless to do anything but hover.

"Jasper, you come along. You don't want to see this."

The boy scurried down into the darkness. Cartwright nodded to Scully, then grabbed Joss Parkins by the collar, not at all as would be expected of a hired man with his boss. Parkins tried to pry free, but was too weak in comparison. He gave up, stooped over, climbed into the opening, his disgust at crawling through a piss puddle expressed as a whiny, petulant sigh.

Cartwright entered, his hulking form blotting out the lamp light as their group advanced. The room filled with murk and shadow, the stench of piss and fear.

Blankenship closed his eyes, his lips moving through the desperate throes of a final prayer. If God ever heard him, Cooper would never know.

Scully crossed himself, then spit into his palms and rubbed them together. He took up his weapon and brought the honed edge down at the reverend's shoulder, his thrust held in check by his desire for accuracy. The axe still easily split flesh and bone.

Blankenship's eyes shot open.

Scully stomped a boot against his chest, pulled the axe free, striking again quickly, this time more assuredly, severing the man's arm. The limb thumped to the ground. Arterial blood sprayed from the reverend like a gushing garden hose.

Scully moved faster than the reverend could react. Horace Blankenship's words were done. He would never utter another prayer, wouldn't have the chance to start pleading for his life. Scully launched his weapon straightaway at the reverend's neck, full force, a wickedly wild swing more apt to clear a century's old oak. The axe cleaved cleanly; the reverend's head cartwheeled, hit a wall, came to rest near his wife's body.

Scully waited for Blankenship's body to slump to the floor--a long five seconds--before jumping into the hidden tunnel, his maniacal laughter echoing, chasing him into the chasm.

Alone with the reek of death wafting to the basement rafters, something tugged at Cooper's chest, at the root of his soul. A physical wrenching of his body from his ethereal drift. Scully's laughter simmered from the tunnel's opening. Cooper whirled toward the sound like a dropped leaf being sucked by the wind, unable to stop his descent as he flew into the pitch-black tunnel. Once therein, he learned everything.

THREE

Ignorance was his first key to success as a lawman. Turning a blind eye fortified his position, allowed him to command the respect of those more ignorant than himself (which was most of the town as far as he could tell), allowed him to rise from the glum squalor of his upbringing, allowed him to have gainful employment when so many good men had no chance for the same.

Yet he couldn't go on lying. Not anymore. He was done doing Thompson's bidding, and through extension, whatever dark force commanded Coal Hollow's doctor.

Sheriff Bergman was done with Coal Hollow when he spoke Thompson's words--his outright lies--to Jane Fowler. No, her son wasn't in Peoria, wasn't signed up for the army, or hadn't, for crying out loud, joined a traveling circus. Bergman wasn't even sure if Jimmy Fowler was still alive. If he was, the sheriff had a pretty good idea where he was being holed up, and if he was there, then he might as well be dead.

So, folks respected Doc Thompson, so what. So what if the doctor got Bergman elected a decade ago by his simple endorsement. So God damn what. He was no God. Coal Hollow was godless. Ignorance couldn't keep a person from that unpleasant knowledge. In a town struggling to survive, godlessness and ignorance went hand in hand. He was done with both.

He gassed his Plymouth around a bend just north of town. He was planning on heading north as fast as he could, putting as much ground as possible between himself and Coal Hollow. He had no intended destination, only a desire to get away. He humored himself by thinking he was heading to his cousin Tilley's house in Fargo. But that was just a direction to follow. He couldn't think so far ahead as to know where this would end.

How far does their influence reach?

Chicago, Milwaukee, Fargo? Could they send their shambling, rotting agents a thousand miles to slit his throat?

Dawn warmed the horizon. People were rising to milk and feed their animals. No one would know that he'd quit this town. No one would've seen his hastily written letter explaining a family emergency in St. Louis that needed his attention.

The Plymouth followed the road's bend to the long straightaway knifing northward.

Movement near the road's edge drew his bleary vision.

Deer. He slammed the brakes, the car's semi-balds sliding through loose gravel.

No. Not a deer, he realized, losing control of the car. "No!"

The old man stood stark still in the middle of the road. The last thing Bergman noticed before the impact was the wide grin on Jasper Cartwright's face.

The car crushed into his hip. The impact sent him airborne, flying backward away from the road, limbs trailing his torso as if he were being yanked by a rope tied about his waistline. He landed in a wall of thorny bushes, snapping branches, rattling leaves free to blanket the ground.

"Shit." Bergman punched the steering wheel hard enough that a bone broke near his wrist. The car's engine died, flooded. Pain grated the nerves in his broken hand like a coarse file working a suppurating wound.

"Shit-shit-SHIT!"

The sheriff shifted the dead car into park, opened the door and made his way to the wall of bushes, cradling his hand against his chest.

Jasper was hidden fairly well. It was only his liquid-wheezing breath that revealed his position.

He was in obvious pain, but as Bergman stooped to his side, the old man began to laugh. The jerking movement must have thrown his body through an incredible agony, but he couldn't help himself.

The poor man must be in shock.

He lifted Jasper's head after the old man started gagging on his own spit. "Jasper, what were you doing? Wait, don't move. We gotta get you help. What were you doing in the middle of the road so damn early in the morning?" Bergman rattled on, afraid to acknowledge to himself that his opportunity for escaping Coal Hollow had just come and gone.

Jasper blinked rapidly. Gathering his strength, he said, "They were coming for me. I heard 'em."

"Who? Who was coming for you, Jasper?" He didn't know if he should trust the old man's words. He could be delusional, raving as his mind tried to flee the painful ruins of his body.

"Collec-collectors. I heard them. From my room at the Calder place."

Bergman knew about the Collectors. They were some kind of miners' mythology that would've faded away but for the perpetuation of Greta Hildaberg's stories.

"It's okay, Jasper. No one's coming for you. No one but Dr. Thompson, that is."

Jasper's breath came in fitful spasms, a panting that punctured his words. "I'm... I'm dying. It's my... m-my time."

Bergman said the softest words to come to mind, "I'm sorry I didn't see you." What he wanted to say was a lot harsher. Words that would, in the end, forcibly reveal the real reason the old man had been in the road. He held back out of respect for the old man.

"No. Understand me." Jasper reached out and grasped Bergman's arm near his broken wrist. The sheriff gasped at the pain, wanted to strike out at him, but instead, he unhinged Jasper's fingers, placing them on his other wrist, then patted his hand. "It's my time, but the Collectors wouldn't let it be. They were coming. I-I-I heard them."

"No one's coming for you," Bergman repeated.

"I wouldn't let them take me."

"What are you talking about?" He wondered if he was just wasting time, questioning a raving man on the verge of death. Because that's what he was, right? A dying man? A man he will have killed, inadvertently, sure, but killed just the same. A thick white bone protruded through the fabric near Jasper's belt buckle. The cradle of his hip or upper thigh bone--the wound was too mangled to distinguish. Blood sopped his pants and was creeping up his cotton shirt. But the flow was slowing. His face was paling. There would be no time to reach Dr. Thompson. Even if he placed Jasper in the back seat of his Plymouth, Jasper was a dead man breathing.

Jasper's breath came as shallow pants punctuated by pain that even shock couldn't dull.

"I worked there three summers."

Bergman decided he would make Jasper as comfortable as possible in his final moments. He tried to pry some of the wiry thorns from his skin, but they were dug in, not ready to let go. He lifted Jasper's head and placed it at the crook of his elbow, trying to ease the old man's pain, knowing it was an impossibility.

"Three summers toiling gets you eternal damnation. I was just a kid. So long ago."

Bergman nodded, not understanding his words, but willing to listen to his final testament.

"I wanted him to come to me when I was down there in the mines, but he never did. He... he would never leave that place, his people. And I could never return. Not after what I saw down there when I was a boy. But I'd worked three summers in the mines and the Collectors were coming to take me to that place. I-I-I never could bring myself to go to the Underground. Not even with my family there."

Bergman understood. Even his ignorance couldn't prevent his understanding. After all, he had grown up in Coal Hollow.

Waves of pain choked off Jasper's words. His panting breath became dry heaves. "Th-tha-thank you."

Jasper Cartwright breathed his last breath, smiled, then was dead. The old man felt weightier in his arms than he should have. Bergman saw the gore on his own clothes and felt sick to his stomach. Could he drive Jasper's body to town? Could he explain his roaming north of Coal Hollow, riding the quitters' road out of this place?

The truth was, he couldn't. They would know, even if they had to prize the information from him, they would know.

Sheriff Bergman took some of the broken branches, placed them over Jasper's body.

Such a nice man. He deserves better.

He covered Jasper's unseeing eyes. He considered fetching the shovel he kept in the car's trunk for snowy days. At least bury him.

No. He did this to himself. He wanted to end his life before the Collectors could take him. Let him rot in the open air. Not down below.

His decisiveness wavered, but if Jasper Cartwright could make such a grim final decision, so could he. He stepped back to check his handiwork, inspecting the bush from different angles. He saw no trace of a body. That should last a full day, long enough for him to get beyond their reach.

Keeping an eye on Jasper's resting place, Bergman backed all the way to his car. He couldn't be happier when the Plymouth grumbled to life on the first try.

Are they real? His wrist throbbed as he pulled the car straight, once again heading north. *Do they really take dying miners moments before death?*

At first cautious, he put steady miles behind him. With untold stretches waiting, he accelerated. Road dust plumed from the tires, obscuring what remained behind. Speed blurred the vibrant green leaves skirting the road into a living wall, intermittent tree trunks and pockets of earthen farm fields the only indication he actually moved.

FOUR

At dawn, Jacob's mom roused him from a deep sleep, her smile too wide, too forced.

"Rise and shine, Jacob! Come get something to eat."

The morning air was damp and cool as he took his seat at the breakfast table. His mom brought out glasses and a milk pitcher, then placed a rasher of sizzling bacon on each plate already loaded with biscuits and scrambled eggs. She practically danced as she moved.

She was acting as if nothing happened yesterday. She hadn't slapped him in anger for leaving the house without permission. They hadn't buried Ellie's brother. Greta hadn't told them that Jimmy was alive and held against his will. None of this could have occurred judging her chipper mood. It was as if she wanted today to be like any other day. But it wasn't. After yesterday, their lives would never be the same.

The addition of the confounding news passed on by Sheriff Bergman only complicated matters. It had to be a lie. Either Bergman had lied, or Greta didn't know what she was talking about. Jacob had put too much faith into Greta's words over the years to doubt her. So the onus was all on Bergman. Most times Bergman was lucky to show up in town with his shirt pressed and his face clean of crumbs, but you could always count on him to tell you the truth. Not anymore. Any stock the sheriff once had, Jacob now deemed worthless. Jimmy wasn't off in Peoria, preparing for wherever new soldiers went. Greta's words had only confirmed their conclusions.

Ellie sat across the table from him. They exchanged a questioning look before her eyes moved to a fourth place setting Jacob had yet to notice. About to ask who would be joining them for breakfast, Louise Bradshaw came out from his mom's bedroom.

"With Louise getting far enough along, her parents were finally getting suspicious. When she admitted it, let's just say they weren't as accepting as the Fowlers. She'll be staying with us for now on. It'll be a tight fit, and it'll be a snug winter with the baby arriving sometime around the first snow, but we always have room for family."

Louise walked from the bedroom to the table. She wore a long nightgown, and her hair was sleep-mussed. Holding a hand to her stomach, her face looked as white as bleached linen.

His mom placed a hand on her shoulder. "Feeling any better now?"

"Not at all. Thanks for the chamber pot, though. I'll clean it up later."

"What's wrong?" Ellie asked.

"Some women get sick when they're going to have a baby. It's natural. Almost everyone gets it."

Louise took her seat at the table. Her eyes widened at the sight of food. Bringing a hand to her mouth, she hurried away from the table and back to his mother's bedroom. A moment after she slammed the door, she heaved up whatever was in her stomach.

"If that's the way it is, then I'm never gonna have a baby." Ellie seemed appalled that women went through such travails.

Jacob's mom chuckled. "I was lucky. With you," she said, looking at Jacob, "I never had a problem." He didn't want to hear any of this. Either about Louise and her sickness, or about when his own mom was expecting. It just wasn't natural. "Now, Jimmy, he was a whole other story. I was sick every morning for four months. Thinking back on it, it doesn't seem like much of a sacrifice, not for all the happiness he's brought me. At the time, it felt like an eternity."

"Mom, I'm trying to eat my breakfast."

"You are such a fussbucket. Fine, I'll reminisce later. When you two finish up, I want you to take a couple baskets down to the creek. Those peaches should be ripe about now. Make sure you check the ground, too. If any of them fell in the last day, they still might be good. There should be enough for some cobblers and jam."

"Sounds good," Ellie said.

"I remember, with Jimmy, I craved peach cobbler day and night. I'll make a batch with a crumb crust. I hope it settles things down a bit for poor Louise."

"Mom, speaking of Jimmy--"

"Oh, that boy... Reminds me, I'm going down to the post office today to see if he's sent us a letter yet." She sipped from her coffee mug, her eyes softening with whimsy. Jacob had been on the verge of bringing up Greta again but couldn't bear to. He didn't think he could convince her anyway.

"When you go out to the creek..." She paused until they both looked up from their plates. "Don't go venturing off where you shouldn't. We need to come together as a family. It's important now like never before. A baby's on the way. We need to mind the work around the farm and the household chores. Louise might not be much help with all that, but her job is to help that baby grow. Ellie, I want you to feel like you're a Fowler. You can stay as long as you want, and we'll treat you like family. But we also need you to work as hard as a Fowler, too.

"Jacob, you need to be the man of the family as long as Jimmy's away. We all need to work to keep this farm in order for when he comes home."

"Sure, Mom. We'll do what we can."

Ellie nodded agreement.

"Oh, and another thing, thanks for the flowers you picked. That was awful thoughtful of you two."

FIVE

Hours after his tumultuous nightmares began, a gentle breeze blew against Cooper's sweat-drenched skin, chilling him awake. He reluctantly opened his eyes, still tired from a short night's sleep and its accompanying onslaught of revelations.

His new house had been the scene of a massacre.

The sun warmed the horizon as dawn lit the grimed front room windows. Sitting up, he stumbled to standing, shaking free from his tangle of blankets. He shook his head hard enough to loosen any cobwebs lurking as carryover from sleep. His cheeks flopped like those of a bloodhound. He then slapped himself hard across each cheek.

He felt finger welts rising in his beard stubble.

His mind reverted to the fact that a breeze had woken him.

A breeze.

Inside his home.

He walked along the long tongue-like carpet to the front door and jiggled the knob.

Nope. All locked here.

He did the same with the front windows, finding the same result.

All locked. All secure. No drafts strong enough to wake him could seep through the front of the house. Yet, cold still traced the skin of his neck. Like the memory of a touch. Pressure, cold and bracing.

He felt an inexplicable fear tugging at his nerves.

He listened to the house and heard nothing but the wind (from

203

outside, where it belongs) slapping the side of the house. He felt no attenuating breeze (pressure, cold and bracing) against his skin. It had to have been the flightiness during his transition to waking. He could have carried something over from his dream.

Images hit him unprovoked and with frightening force.

Slaughter.

Rape.

Forced servitude.

He closed his eyes against their vileness, their suddenness, but the images lingered, flashes from his dreams.

Shrieks of agony.

The pleadings of a little boy.

The laughter of madmen.

He staggered to the back of the house, feeling faint, nauseated, torn between two realities. The psychic charge of the house assaulted him. The quiet solitude of his reality fought to stand next to the solid reality of the past. He reached for a wall to regain his balance. His hand landed against the framed daguerreotype of the Blankenships--young, devote, decades away from their senseless murders.

He straightened the photo, found some modicum of stability seeing their stolid faces. For a split second, the glass fronting the frame reflected the space behind Cooper. A space far from empty.

An ice cold breeze lapped at his cheek, and he realized it wasn't a breeze at all.

Pressure, cold and bracing.

When he turned, he was face to face with Eunice Blankenship.

"I-I'm so sorry," he said before he could think.

Her cold fingers left his cheek. Her facial features shifted with her movement: one moment a lithe young woman, the next, a haggard, toothless crone, her motions feeble with age.

You saw.

"Yes. I know everything."

Then you know.

"What do you mean?"

It's not over. We need your help. You need to finish what we couldn't.

SIX

Picking fruit was a common chore for Jacob. If he wasn't picking peaches or strawberries or persimmons from his own property, he was off at neighbor farms picking fruit for three cents a bushel. As long as he could remember, his mom had taught him about the value of even a single penny. She would often say that if you gathered enough pennies and stacked them together, you could eventually stand atop your copper pile and reach out to touch the moon. He had taken on the habit of collecting his pennies and rushing home to stack them as high as he could. They never came close to reaching even a foot high before toppling. By the time he realized he would never build a tower high enough to allow him to touch the moon, he still enjoyed the sight of the copper pieces growing before him.

"She acts like she believes Sheriff Bergman." Ellie stood on a stool to reach the nearest branches.

The creek trickled ten feet from the last row of trees. The bent-grass trail left by his brother skirted the peach orchard. Jacob and his mom had followed it when they began their search, losing it soon after crossing the creek. The trail was gone now, fresher grass growing over his brother's footsteps.

"It's easier for her. There's no convincing her otherwise. It'll just start an argument. Once you start an argument with my mom, you might as well just admit you were wrong. She's stubborn."

"Sounds like someone else I know." Ellie picked an overripe peach and tossed it at him.

It splattered against his shirt, but he didn't do anything more than glower at Ellie's smiling face. "Well, even if she believed us, someone still has to pick these peaches before they rot. We need to build up our stores."

They filled the baskets to brimming, finding the fruit to be both bountiful and at the peak of ripeness. Before they started back, Jacob sized up the remaining fruit hanging from the trees. They could come back two more mornings and fill more baskets and still not get all of it.

"Ready?" He took one handle of Ellie's basket while she lifted the other. They would trek back to the house, then return for the other basket.

"Let's go."

They worked their way back to the house, Jacob slowing his pace to account for Ellie's shorter strides.

"I was wondering about Cooper," Jacob said, trailing off.

"I knew he had nothing to do with it from the moment I met him."

"I'm just not as trusting a person as you."

"I suppose."

"But still, if he had nothing to do with it, then he at least has something to do with finding Jimmy."

"What's cooking in your brain, Jacob?"

"I think I ought'a follow Cooper around, see if he knows more than he lets on."

"Your mom would pitch a fit if she knew you went off like that. Besides, Greta said he doesn't know anything."

"Maybe if I follow him around, I'll see something Cooper doesn't. Maybe I can help find out where my brother is before Cooper's supposed to."

"I don't know, Jacob. Greta would'a said you had something to do with finding Jimmy if you're supposed to."

They were silent as they closed in on the house. Jacob was trying to figure out how he could get away, at least for a little while, when Ellie dropped her basket handle without warning, spilling bruised fruit in a semi-circle.

"Ellie, why didn't you tell me you were going to drop it!"

Jacob glared at her, but she seemed unconcerned about the plight of the peaches. Her eyes were trained on the road, at a solitary figure walking toward the driveway.

"I... I think that's my dad."

SEVEN

"Janie, you gotta believe me. I'm a changed man. I come for
Elizabeth, now, and we ought to get home. We got work to do at the
farm that ain't gonna get done on its own. Besides, we got fences
between us need mending." Mr. Banyon had a fresh shave and wore a
clean set of clothes, but his eyes were bleary red, as if he hadn't slept
much lately. While always a thin man, he had a mangy, raw appearance.
When he entered their house, Jacob had sniffed the air for any sign of
alcohol. To his surprise, he didn't find the slightest trace.

Jacob looked from his mom to Mr. Banyon, then back again. Ellie
peeked out from behind his mom as if she were a brick wall strong
enough to turn away a tornado's wrath. His mom furrowed her brow,
and she stared at Mr. Banyon, stared and didn't say a word for a long
time.

Ellie's dad seemed to realize he still wore his hat. He took it off,
pushed back his hair from his eyes and held the hat in front of him. His
hands were shaking. He tried to hide it, but couldn't quite get a handle
on it.

"I appreciate you looking after Elizabeth like you done. It was a kind
and Christian thing for a neighbor to do, but we must be on. Come on,
Elizabeth," Banyon said, his voice strengthening. He extended his hand,
trying to coax Ellie out from behind his mom. The girl didn't move.

"Your kind and Christian neighbors buried your son, and where were you?" Jacob said.

"Jacob, hush now."

"Janie, I can't explain how or why, but I seen the light. I know now how awful a father I been. I know this and I'm never going to walk that path again. I swear. I swear on Mabel's soul I ain't traveling that road again."

"When was your last drink, Charles? Is that why your hands are shaking? You need a drink? Want me to fix you a whiskey? Will that make everything better?"

"No more, Janie, I promise. I swear it."

"What happens when you can't stop the shaking, when your rage returns from deep inside and you need to let off steam? If you're not drinking, will Ellie take the brunt of your anger?"

"Three days, Janie, I'm sorry to say it's been three days since my last drink. God, I wish it could be ten years, or that I never took up the bottle in the first place. So much would be different. But I can't change any of that. It's all been lived. All that time is gone now. My wife is gone, my boy. All I got left is my Elizabeth standing there behind you. I need her, and I think she needs me, even though she's tough as shoe leather, that girl needs her Pa."

Mr. Banyon was weeping openly, tears falling freely down his cheeks. Jacob could see his mom's will bending. Her face softened, her eyes falling to Ellie. The girl looked so sad, as if she didn't ever want to leave. Maybe Jacob was reading his own feelings into her expression; he couldn't be sure either way.

"Elizabeth, girl, I'm sorry for letting you down." Banyon extended his hand to Ellie, and she took it cautiously, but didn't leave the security his mother provided. He hunched over until he stood eye to eye with her. "You've been so strong for so long. I promise you I won't let you down. I can't change what's past. All I can do is make sure it never happens. Tomorrow or ever again."

Banyon couldn't help it any longer. He covered his eyes with his still-shaking hands, blubbering like a child.

Jacob never thought he would see the day when Charles Banyon showed a hint of weakness, or even that he possessed the slightest bit of kindness within his soul. And here he was doing just that. He was feeling all emotional himself, as if he too would start crying. He bit his lip until the feeling subsided.

Ellie left his mother's side, and while small even for her nine years, her inner strength made her seem much older. She offered a quickly-fading smile, then once again took hold of her father's hand. Mr.

Banyon hugged Ellie, hugged her as if she had just saved his life. The man sniffled away his tears and after wiping his cheeks with his shirtsleeve, seemed ready to get on with living.

"Thank you, Miss Fowler. Jacob, take care," Ellie said. She left the house, still holding her father's hand as if he were a child. Mr. Banyon didn't say another word, just followed Ellie as if she lent him the strength to take his next step.

"Are we just going to let her go with him?"

His mom closed the door, shutting out the afternoon heat. "I don't think we've got a choice. Charles has promised to dry out before, and has always ended up backsliding. With the dry laws, he sobered for a while. But temperance was never his strong suit. Not since Mabel died. A loss like that is hard to recover from. But somehow, looking into his eyes just now, I think I want to believe him."

"Mom, he won't ever change." Jacob could understand his mom's weakness for Charles Banyon. She of all people would understand the loss of a spouse. But how long could someone use an excuse? Can an excuse forgive being a sour spirited and altogether malicious person?

"I'll keep an eye on Ellie. We won't let him go bad on her. I won't let it happen."

His mom turned away from their discussion and parted the curtains of the front window. He joined her, watching Ellie and her dad walk home.

A door opened from one of the back bedrooms, and Louise walked out, her hand gingerly rubbing her stomach. Jacob gave her a glance, and when he looked back to the road, the Banyons had gone around the bend beyond their driveway, out of sight.

"I never felt so miserable in all my life," Louise said. When they didn't respond, she came closer, speaking up, "Where's Ellie?"

EIGHT

Ethan Cartwright never aged, never felt the erosive power of the passing years. He wore his purple scar proudly, the lone physical imperfection the Underground had failed to remedy. It was a sigil representing his strength, his ability to outlive a wound that would surely kill most men. But, like all the others living here, the Underground's curative powers never reached his mind. There, in a mire of hatred, paranoia and egomaniacal self-reverence, his dreams ran rampant, inflicting damage that could never heal. And there, in his dreams, he saw one night played out methodically, one second after another unchanged from the night of its tolling. One night unembellished, a night of his reckoning, a night that informed his every waking thought.

Ethan woke with a start, the image of blood splashed across his son's cheek stained into his wakened vision. He pushed the blanket away and ran his fingers over his sweat-soaked chest. His scar burned. His fingers lingered there, as if they could smooth away the damage.

He blinked in the trembling candlelight. The image wouldn't leave him:

Jasper's cheek streaked with blood from his jaw to the fine blond hair over his ear, his eyes filled with sheer terror. Of all the details of that night, he could never remember whose blood tainted the pure white surface of his son's skin. It could've been any of the runaways. They'd all bled plenty. Or it could've been Joss Parkins, the slaves' owner. It could've been his own.

Ethan had been wounded deeply across the meat of his forearm, hacked straight to the bone. The younger runaway, Benjamin, had gotten hold of Vic's machete, and empowered and desperate, wildly swung the weapon. The first strike cut into his master's shoulder, the next struck Ethan's arm. Sinking to his knees while cradling his arm, Ethan's vision found Jasper. The boy, blood-splashed and unhinged, was cowering away, cowering not just from the rampaging runaway, but his own father, too.

"Ethan?" Thea touched his shoulder, and he was fully awake. "You can talk to me. Tell me what happened."

A minute lapsed. He finally turned to look into her eyes, but she didn't look away, even though she was obviously frightened.

He'd never spoken about that night, not even upon reflection with Arthur Scully, but now he found himself opening up. "We didn't know what would happen. After everything that happened, every one of us was exhausted and bleeding badly. We didn't go to the surface, not right away. We were too weak. Too ashamed of nearly losing everything to three slaves, a group including a skinny girl and an old man. We learned enough the following morning, when we dragged Parkins to the surface. We'd thought he'd died, everyone did. How can you not die when your head's nearly cut off? But then, as we moved through the tunnels, he started moving. Turns out he did die, just not forever."

Ethan paused, seeing the scene plain as day. The details never eroded.

"It's okay. It's over."

"But it's not. Jasper's dying."

He saw in her eyes that she didn't know what to say. But she brought him to her, pressing his cheek against her chest. She ran her fingers through his hair.

He continued: "Parkins had died, sure enough, but he was rising. We thought we should get him to daylight, see if we might find a doctor for him. How else would we get the second half of our payment if he was dead? When we got to the surface, the sunlight seemed to melt his skin. He rotted before our eyes. We didn't know what to do. When he collapsed in front of us, dead now for sure, we went back below ground."

"That's when you saw the slaves?"

"We'd killed them. I saw it with my own eyes. Their blood was dry under my nails. I could smell it in my nostrils. But when we got back to where we'd left them, all we found were blood trails leading deeper into the ground."

"And you followed?"

"Of course. We'd never let a slave escape our bonds. We weren't about to start. We found them soon enough. Never let them out of sight after that." He pulled away from her, turning his back to her. He thought she might come to him again, but she didn't. For some reason this made him respect her more than he already did. "My mother lived less than a hundred miles from here. I moved her in town to watch after Jasper while we organized things Underground. Thea, he's gonna die. It's certain. I haven't seen him in so long."

"I'm so sorry."

"It's fine. I sent for him."

There was a knock on his door. Before he could reach the door, it opened.

He was angered over the intrusion until he saw the look on Leo Borland's face.

"What is it?"

"He's gone, Ethan. We were too late."

"What do you mean? He already... he was already..."

"No. He's alive, well, as far as I know. But he left this." Leo handed Ethan a small scrap of paper.

It contained three small words written in an arthritic script: *You're too late.*

Ethan tore the paper and fed it to a candle's flame. "It's over..." He turned away from Leo and Thea. He paced the room several times, then squared his shoulders and faced Leo. "Get your brothers, Scully, and three other trusted men. When you see Scully, tell him we're gonna move on that list we put together."

Leo didn't say he knew about the list, but his wide grin spoke more than words.

NINE

Jimmy woke from a terrible dream. Woke from one nightmare right into another. He was trapped forever, a prisoner in his own town.

His dreams were getting worse, and the horrible details lingered longer after waking. In his dreams, Louise was on the verge of losing her balance at the edge of a cliff. She'd reach for him, her fingers grasping the air, and then gravity would take her, pulling her away from him. Her frightened eyes never wavered as she fell. Her screams, so heartrending, breaking apart, resounding, reforming until the wail was that of a colicky baby.

He blinked in the darkness, cold sweat slicking his face, his back. He thought he would be sick. Flat on his stomach against the cavern floor, the world spinning beneath him, bile seeped into the back of his throat, gagging him. She needed him. Louise needed him and he would do whatever it took to see her again.

But if he went to her now, she would be frightened of him, even more frightened than what his nightmares could articulate. If he could ever escape this hell, his flesh would quickly decay. Harold had told him the gruesome repercussions for leaving the confines of the Underground. The old Negro believed that God had seen such horrible

213

GLEN R. KRISCH

sights in these caves that He had turned a blind eye on this little section of the world. Once He had made His decision, time dwelled on the second He left. Jimmy didn't know if he believed Harold. Jimmy wasn't raised religious, but there had to be some explanation.

"You had that nasty dream again, Mr. Jimmy?"

He didn't say anything to Harold. Didn't even acknowledge him. Since he learned he could never leave the Underground, Jimmy's thoughts had turned increasingly inward in an ever-tightening, darkening spiral. He no longer feared a beating from his captors, no longer feared the most agonizing pain. For the first time in his life--a life pursuing exhilaration and feats of daring--Jimmy no longer valued his own life.

It made him think about how he had once fallen two stories from the roof of Magee's Barbershop after attempting to walk the precarious edge from one side to the other. A crowd had formed at street level, gasping at his nerve. As soon as he lost his balance on the crumbling brick, the sighs turned to sharp shrieks. He remembered thinking as he plummeted that the onlookers were so full of fear, even though he was the one falling to the hard-packed ground below. Once his mom knew he would be fine after his broken ankle healed, she tore in to him like she had never before or ever since. Inside Dr. Thompson's office, she had cried over Jimmy's battered body, alternating between tears and rage. She pleaded with him, demanding to know why he wanted to die so much, why he couldn't value the life she had given him.

He remembered her reaction to his response more so than her words. She was appalled by his lack of remorse, shocked by his indifference, yet all he'd said was that he did value his life, and that was his reason for doing the things he did. He had told her that nothing made you value life more than risking it. She had stormed from Thompson's office, murmuring about how he was just like his father. It seemed like that was her response to everything he did, everything he said.

"You can't just let time slip away, let your dark thoughts consume you, Mr. Jimmy."

"Darkness. That's all that's left, Harold."

"Memories, they're gifts. Even with no other hope, if you keep your dearest memories to think back on, well, you're better than dead. Ain't nobody, not Arthur Scully, or the Borland's, or Ethan Cartwright his ownself can take them memories away."

"Memories fade, you've said so yourself."

"Time drags, sure, dulls details, but--"

"Shut up, Harold. I don't want to hear it," Jimmy snapped, cutting off Harold's words. "Leave me alone."

Harold didn't respond. Though their corner of the old stables was completely dark, he could clearly hear Harold scurry along the floor until he was close enough that Jimmy thought the Negro would attack him.

Let him come at me, Jimmy thought. *I don't care.*

Harold fumbled his fingers along Jimmy's arm until he reached his hand. He pried open his fingers and placed something in his palm. Without a word or explanation, Harold went back to his resting spot and settled in. It was a while before Jimmy considered the blunt shape in his palm. He turned it over with his fingers. It was a coarse metal file no longer than his ring finger. Harold had given him a tool for escape, and also the briefest glimmer of hope.

TEN

Breaking up the bunch beans was women's work, and Jacob was at the kitchen table doing just that. With a basket of beans at his feet, he was slicing with a paring knife against a cutting board to break the beans. In Jacob's opinion, cooking was and always would be women's work. He scowled under his breath as he reached for the basket and collected another fistful of beans.

After working nonstop from sunup to sunset yesterday, his mom was off to Calder's for kitchen staples. Before she left, she declared through a stifled yawn that she would catch up on some shuteye just as soon as she returned. Louise was outside chatting away with her friend Mary, ducking the cooking duties with the excuse that she needed to finish a needlepoint doily thingamabob before the baby arrived. They sat on a wooden bench in the shade of the house just outside the kitchen, doing their needlepoints. The shade was ten degrees cooler than inside the house, and as they sipped lemonade, they buzzed about their gossip like flies in a pigpen.

With Ellie gone, and the other women occupied, breaking the beans and other unseemly chores fell on him. Before turning in last night,

Jacob and his mom went over to the Banyon place to drop off Ellie's clothes. Of course it had been just an excuse to make sure Ellie was okay and to see for themselves if Mr. Banyon's sobriety had lasted another night. Much to their surprise, the Banyon place looked like a different house when they walked in. The floors and walls were clean. There weren't any dirty dishes piled up. Mr. Banyon was sober, but still shaky and bleary eyed. Ellie looked at peace being at home. She'd even laughed when her dad pretended to steal her nose between his middle and index fingers. She was too old for such humor, but any humor shared between them seemed like the healing kind. Still, Jacob didn't trust him. Jacob wouldn't admit it aloud to anyone, but he sure missed that girl. Even though things had seemed to be fine last night, he'd promised himself to stop in now and again to keep an eye on things.

It wasn't long before the gusting wind died outside and he could hear the girls' conversation through the open kitchen window. "I think she might'a fallen off her rocker. She doesn't seem to have a care in the world." It was Louise speaking. Jacob got up from his chair and crept closer to the window. He couldn't wait to find out who was off their rocker. "I know if it was my son," Louise said, pausing, "Or my daughter that'd gone missing, I'd be a little more concerned than she's showing."

Anger welled inside Jacob. He was about to rush outside to confront Louise, when Mary broke in, "But you all know he enlisted. He told you he was leaving, and then word came up from Peoria."

"I know. I'm glad he's safe, even though I'm mad as heck with him. But Lord knows I couldn't raise a baby on my own. With him taking off'n my family turning their back on me, I just can't help feeling, I don't know, insulted? offended? that no one gives a darn. As soon as I found out Jimmy was okay, oh I knew I could forgive him when he comes home. I can't wait to kiss him again. If I close my eyes, I can imagine his lips on mine. Then I can't help feeling that... that swooning feeling."

"It has to be love," Mary said, and they laughed in their chatty way. Their laughter quieted down, replaced by the sound of needles puncturing fabric and threads pulled through chintzy mosaics.

"So, are you settled in?"

"Jane gave me her room, which was nice of her, even though I feel bad with her sleeping on the sofa. I'll be here until Jimmy gets home, whenever that is, and then we'll get a place of our own. Just the three of us," she said happily. "I know the house looks small, and compared to my parents' house, it's about the size of a tool shed, but I'm welcome here, and that's all that matters. They care for me. Me and the baby. Now, if I could just shake off this nausea."

"Can I do anything to help?"

"No, it just comes and goes. Right now, it's none too bad. Doc Thompson told me I'd just have to tough it out. He's probably just punishing me for not seeing him sooner."

"It's good he saw you."

"I know. It just makes it all too real. And a Halloween baby, to boot. It is real, isn't it?"

A contemplative silence seemed to end their conversing. Jacob went back to the table to finish the beans.

"What about Jacob, how's he been?" Mary asked.

Jacob's ear perked up again at hearing his name.

"Oh, he's a bit of a devil." Jacob came close to speaking out, but bit his tongue. "Even so, I've never had a little brother. I guess how he acts is normal."

"Sounds like a little brother to me."

"You should know, with what four now?"

They both laughed again. "Well, I think he's cute. Doesn't he have the nicest brown hair?" Mary said distantly.

"Who?"

"Well, Jacob Fowler, of course."

Jacob's face felt hot, full of fire. His pulse raced; he couldn't believe his ears. Sitting back at the kitchen table, he fidgeted with the bunch beans, already done with the pile. For some reason, he wanted to appear busy. He couldn't remember a time when he felt so embarrassed with no one else in the room.

It seemed like the girls had forgotten about discretion as the volume of their conversation increased. He could hear their conversation all the way over by the kitchen table.

"Mary, he's what, two years younger than you?"

"I know, but two years from now he won't even give me the time of day. He'll be courting girls who bat their eyelashes just so and wear the nicest clothes, and talk eloquent like."

He edged to the corner of his chair, just far enough to catch a glimpse of Mary's blonde hair through the window. It was curly, a bit too long to be stylish, but still nice. He wanted her to stand up, so he could see how tall she was. Even if she liked him, he didn't think he could ever drum up the nerve to talk to her if she were taller than him.

If Jimmy was here, he'd know what to do.

He didn't know if he liked Mary. He'd never thought about her in that way. She was just Louise's mousy friend who hovered around demurely asking Jacob what he was up to. Thinking back on it, she'd been giving off signals since visiting the day of Louise's arrival. This whole time he thought she'd just been acting polite.

The pickup truck chewed at the driveway, tearing away his attention. It was his mom, fresh home from Calder's. He gathered up the bean scraps, clearing the table clean. When she came through the door, she immediately saw his look of guilt.

"What now?" She handed him a crate of canned goods.

"Nothing. Just finished up the beans like you asked." He took the crate to a counter and began unloading it.

"You sure nothing's wrong?"

"Everything's fine. How was the market?" he asked, trying to distract her.

"Got everything on my list. When you're done there, can you get the ice from the truck?"

"In a jiffy," Jacob said, heading for the front door.

A peal of laughter came from outside. Jacob looked over his shoulder cautiously, as if someone had told him to turn around with his hands up or he was going to get it.

From the look on her face, she suspected the reason for his harried expression. She held up an authoritative hand. "Jacob, wait a minute."

He rolled his eyes impatiently, but didn't leave.

"So, how do I let him know I like him?"

"Oh, Mary, there's ways of letting him know without letting him know you're letting him know."

Once again, the girls laughed. He wondered if their neighbors could plainly hear the conversation with them being so loud. His embarrassment would kill him if he didn't leave the house right away. His mom smiled at him. His cheeks burned hotter, the blush spreading like wildfire down his neck. Before his mom could say anything, he hastened out the door to fetch the ice from the truck bed.

Every day that passed without Jimmy's return, Jacob learned new ways to miss him.

ELEVEN

After carrying the ice block inside and unwrapping it from the straw-packed butcher paper, Jacob hefted it into the icebox. His rushing adrenaline made it seem half as heavy--the only consolation coming from his earlier humiliation. They would chip off pieces from the block as needed, for iced tea or lemonade, but otherwise, the ice would cool anything perishable inside the icebox for four or five days. Some families were having such a hard time getting by that they had to eliminate ice from their market order. Instead of keeping an icebox, they would store perishables in their well bucket, lowering it to the water's cool surface. His mom insisted on having ice, even if at times it seemed like an unnecessary indulgence.

Jacob removed the drain pan from the bottom of the icebox, dumping the cool water into a tub for washing the night's supper dishes. His mom would be on him if he didn't drain the melt water and it ended up overflowing. Jimmy used to perform this task, and like every other Jimmy chore, it had fallen on Jacob to take up the slack.

His mom hadn't said a word about overhearing the girls' chatter, for which he was grateful. She was scribbling away on a writing tablet when he finished with the ice. He gathered up the bean stems from the kitchen table to toss on the mulch pile his mom used to fertilize her expansive garden. Nothing in their house went to waste.

"Jacob? Got a second?"

"Sure." He left the bean scraps where they were. He wanted to get away from the house, putting distance between him and Mary, and the paralyzing thought of seeing her face to face.

"Sit down, please." She slid the writing tablet across the table. Scribbled in her stiff-angled script was a list of names.

"I was hoping you could do me a favor. I think it's high time we pulled out of our doldrums. We should always be sad over George's passing, but Jimmy is fine. In his own convoluted way, he's trying to make a man of himself by enlisting. If he's a man, then we should respect his wishes, even if we don't necessarily agree with them. We need to stop lurking about the house like we're in mourning." She played with the nub of pencil in her hand, as if deciding if she should follow through with what she wanted to say.

With the enthusiasm in which his mom had embraced Jimmy's supposed enlistment, Jacob had almost convinced himself of it as well. Thinking that way was easier, but deep inside he knew it wasn't true. Every day that went by with no letter from Jimmy, the harder it would be for his mom to believe. But as long as she believed, Jacob could pretend to believe also.

"What's the list for?" Jacob asked when she hadn't said anything for a while.

"It's an invite list. I've been thinking we should have a good, old fashioned potluck."

"A potluck? Here?" It was the last thing he expected his mom to say. He could scarcely recall more than a handful of times when they had invited anyone over. Their family was forever accepting invites to get-togethers, but his mom had always kept their home private. Whoever came to the house was considered family and in select company.

"I wish I'd been more open with our friends after your father died. I suppose I was too cautious. As the years went by, some of the townsfolk looked down on me for not remarrying. So I cut away from them even more. They couldn't understand a widow trying to raise two young sons on her own. But I've done it, and for the most part I think I've done a fine job.

"Louise can't raise her baby like that, it's too hard. For me, it was easier to close everyone out instead of risking one more person hurting me. Louise isn't like that. You know yourself, Louise needs her friends. She would just about crumble if she was alone."

"And the list?"

"I need you to invite everyone on that list to the Saturday afternoon potluck."

"I can take the truck?" he asked, trying not to get his hopes up.

"I suppose I'll have to allow it. If you walked, the potluck would've come and gone by the time you finished."

Her words freed him from invisible bonds. Except for the one trip to the Banyon house, he hadn't left the property since his reprimand for going out to Greta's house. He wanted to hug her, but instead took the list and quickly glanced at it. "I'll get on this right away. My chores are done. I weeded the garden, milked Polly, and mended the chicken coop."

Before she could change her mind, he was out the door and in the truck. It roared to life when he turned the ignition. He had to use all of his will power to not stomp on the gas and shoot gravel across the yard from all of his excitement.

The Fowlers were listed first. Initially, Jacob wasn't enthusiastic about the idea of hosting a potluck, but after thinking about it, he understood his mom wanted to accomplish more than just surround Louise with an understanding public. She didn't need to explain her logic; it was as clear to him as if he read it in a book. Have a get together. Invite Charles Banyon into a comfortable situation. See how he's handling being sober when the others would be drinking. It was almost as if she were offering Banyon a way out. If he screwed up, then Ellie could stay at their house while he stumbled home. Or, if for some reason he didn't louse it up, the neighbors could embrace him, embrace him how Louise would be embraced. Jacob wondered if he sometimes underestimated his mother.

Kicking up dust, getting away from the house for the first time in days, escaping Louise's constant updates about her never-ending nausea, he couldn't remember a time when he felt freer.

His thoughts still often centered on Jimmy, but as long as he had Greta's promise that his brother wanted more than anything to come home, he'd have to take her word for it, and wait for the day when he'd once again see his brother. He had never doubted Greta's word; she had never been proven a liar by anyone. But the truth was, he had little else to cling to at this point. He couldn't just go on make-believing like his mom.

His mother had been hovering over him like a hawk since he'd returned from Greta's treehouse, so he hadn't had a chance to follow Cooper. He thought about pitching the list out the window and heading straight for his house, but as he scanned the names while maneuvering the truck around a bend in the road, Cooper's name appeared at the bottom, just below a cross-out of his name.

So his mom had written down Cooper's name, thought better of it, then second guessed herself and added his name again. He'd be heading out to Cooper's house eventually, but since Jacob was closer to the Banyon place, it might be best to attack the list as efficiently as possible. He didn't want to risk angering his mother, not when she seemed in a better mood lately.

He pulled into the Banyon's long driveway. Coming to a stop in front of their house, he feared his suspicions of Mr. Banyon had come true. The man was tilted back in a rocker on the front porch. His arms hung askew to the sides of the arm rests, as if he weren't aware enough to move them back into a more comfortable position. He couldn't see the man's eyes--his head was tipped back too far--but he assumed they were closed.

The truck brakes needed fixing and screeched when he stopped. Mr. Banyon didn't stir.

Jacob hopped down from the truck and approached the porch. When he was standing three feet from Ellie's dad, he still couldn't tell if he was alive or dead. He couldn't smell alcohol in the air, but that didn't mean Mr. Banyon hadn't slumped in the rocker to pass out. He hoped all he'd done was pass out.

Keeping an eye on Mr. Banyon, Jacob knocked on the front door, the pressure of his knuckles on the weatherworn wood pushing it open on its rusty hinge. With his heart stirring mightily in his chest, Jacob expected to see some kind of upheaval inside. Gouts of blood sprayed across the walls. Ellie's body face down in a twisted heap.

The room unfolded in layers, leaving an entirely different, but still quite unexpected, impression.

At first, all he saw was wood. All hues of earth tones, from white pine to rustic mahogany, in all textures and shapes. Then he noticed the menacing-looking tools spread across any available open space: sharp-pointed awls, ragged-toothed saws. Tools to gouge with, rend apart, hollow out.

And the smell. Overpowering. Vaporous. Biting.

He stepped back from the open door, catching his breath.

He heard a creaking board from behind him and spun around.

"You just walk in to any old house you choose?" Mr. Banyon's voice was sarcastic instead of biting. He sat up in the rocker, stretched his hands above his head and couldn't quite stifle a whine that could have been his muscles screaming awake. "Yeah, this one passes the mustard if I do say so myself."

"You're back to making furniture?" Jacob asked, halfway ashamed for the fear he'd felt. The other half of him still stood on suspicious feet.

"Sure am. Just taking a break when you pulled up. Testing out this new rocker, why, it put me out cold in five minutes." Mr. Banyon stood and stretched his back. He didn't look as shaky as when Jacob and his mom dropped off Ellie's clothes. His eyes were clear, even though he had just woken up. "I'm hungry, boy. Want something to eat?"

Mr. Banyon walked inside, leaving Jacob to contemplate alone on the porch. He hadn't seen Ellie yet, so he kept his guard up.

He remembered the reason for his visit and his mom's invitation list. He followed after Mr. Banyon, and when he could focus on something other than the clutter of furniture making, Mr. Banyon stood in the corner kitchen, cutting slices of bread for a sandwich. "Didn't know a boy your age should drive. Your mom know you're out driving?"

"She's the one sent me out this way."

"That so?"

Jacob didn't respond. Mr. Banyon finished making his peanut butter sandwich, and then consumed it in less time than it took to make. "I better make another. You sure you don't want any? Well fine, that's just more for me. I tell you, I haven't eaten this much since I was your age. Drying out gives a man his hunger back."

"Mr. Banyon?"

"Yes, boy?"

"Ellie around?" he asked, afraid to find out the answer.

"Out back. She got the mule hooked up to the grind mill. Most time you can just leave the beast to do his burden, but that mule is stubborn even for his namesake. She's out there prodding him along, grinding corn for meal right now."

Jacob walked through a maze of unfinished furniture pieces until he could see out the window overlooking the backyard. The glass pane shined with the midday sun. It looked clean enough to eat off of. In fact, the rest of the house was just as clean, if you discounted the small mounds of saw dust here and there. Ellie was outside at the mill Mr. Banyon had designed and built himself. She had a switch in her hand, but the mule seemed to be walking his perpetual circle just fine for the time being. As if she knew Jacob was watching, she looked over her shoulder, giving him a friendly wave.

"Boy? You just gonna stand all day looking out that winda'?"

"No, sir. Mom wanted me to invite you and Ellie to a potluck this coming Saturday. If that'd work for you."

"You know, that sounds great. Saturday?" he said, thinking out loud. He put down the butter knife coated in peanut butter and scratched his chin in thought. "Yeah, Saturday's free."

"Good. Around noon?"

"We'll be there noon sharp. That way I can drop off the hutch I'm building for your Mom." Mr. Banyon pointed to a beautiful oak hutch that looked to be about halfway to completion.

Jacob didn't know what to say. Mr. Banyon could see his surprise and laughed to himself.

"Don't say nothin', mind you, it's a gift for all the kindness she's shown my family."

Jacob nodded.

"It's like... what do you call it? Restitution? For all I've done."

The back door opened and in walked Ellie, all smiles and glowing cheeks. They exchanged pleasantries, and Jacob told her about the potluck. As they talked, she seemed about the happiest girl in the world.

Jacob had to beg off a prolonged stay. As they chit-chatted, Mr. Banyon treated him like an old friend, even though they had rarely shared a civil word before now. When Jacob was at the door, ready to leave, Ellie whispered into his ear, "He was mad when he saw that Georgie took his over/under, but that didn't last. He's really changed this time. It's gonna be fine."

"I hope so."

From inside the truck cab, Jacob waved to the Banyons as they stood on the front porch. Mr. Banyon's hand rested on his daughter's shoulder, and despite Jacob's continued concern, they looked like how a family should.

Jacob stopped in town and everyone he invited from the list accepted. Both Magee and Bo, as always tending their quiet barber shop, agreed that a potluck was just what the town needed to get on with things. Mr. and Mrs. Hauser accepted, as did the Nightingales. Both families expressed their relief at hearing the news about Jimmy's whereabouts. They said he'd come home strong and focused, ready for the challenges of providing for a family. Jacob fought off a knot forming in his stomach that tightened at hearing their words. He had to put on an agreeable expression just to get through all the well wishes.

Jacob found Sheriff Bergman's office empty, for which he was grateful. He would act as if Jacob was trying to trick him or make him look a fool. He decided he would invite the sheriff if he ran into him, but he wouldn't make much of an effort to make it happen.

Mrs. Nagy accepted for her family of eight, agreeing to bring a big platter of deviled eggs. Before he left their house on the edge of town, she let him know that word had been getting around that Jasper Cartwright had taken ill. In an ominous tone she mentioned that it didn't look good, and the oldest man in Coal Hollow would certainly be too weak to attend. While Jasper's name was on the list, Jacob agreed with Mrs. Nagy.

"I guess I won't drop by his room, then. It would be hard on him knowing he'd have to turn it down for the sake of his health." He left for the next name on the invite list.

Returning to the truck, he had to admit to himself that a stronger reason kept him from inviting Jasper Cartright. He simply couldn't bear to face a man who had always been a model of vitality relegated to a sick bed. He finished the loop through town, feeling confident in his improving driving skills, crossing off the names as he went. He didn't find Dr. Thompson in his office and assumed he was either caring for Jasper Cartwright or off on some other house call. He made a mental note to double back to Thompson's office as long as it didn't get too late.

So, only Cooper's name remained. His mom had been selective in who she invited. She had omitted Louise's parents. They wouldn't accept even if they were invited, so it was no skin off his nose. Plenty of other people from town weren't on the list, people who they didn't associate with. Hank Calder was too abrasive to have a good time at a potluck, while his daughter Thea was a complete snoot. But the absence of Greta's name bothered him the most. He checked his pocket watch. Since he was making good time, he headed to her treehouse.

"Mom sent me out to invite people to a potluck this coming Saturday."

"But you came here." Greta didn't have any of her famous cornbread awaiting his arrival. She seemed surprised to see him.

"Of course, to invite you and Arlen."

"But your mom didn't ask you to invite me, did she?"

Jacob felt panicky. Could he tell her without hurting her? "Uh, no.

I suppose not."

"I appreciate you coming here, Jacob. Most times people forget about Arlen and me, which most times is for the best. Sometimes it feels like people come over, hear whatever I have to tell them, then disappear until the next time they need to hear about my visions."

"I don't do that."

"Oh, I wasn't talking about you. You or your brother, or most the other kids in town. It's the adults who can live without me until they're desperate enough to climb those steps to knock on my door."

"Will you come?"

"I bet you thought it would be a good idea if I should just show up, maybe have your mom and me talk, is that it?"

"Well, if I talk to her about you coming, maybe she'll change her mind. I bet it was just a mistake, leaving you off the list."

"It wasn't no accident, Jacob. You're mom's no fool. Even if you asked and she changed her mind, she wouldn't want me to show. She doesn't want discussing of things when she's not ready to listen. No, it's better off. Next week you come by and we'll talk about what a nice time everyone had."

During the drive to Cooper's house, Jacob was angry with his mom. He wanted Greta at the potluck. More importantly, he wanted Greta and his mom forced in a situation where they might talk. Even Arlen could be entertaining at times, that is, for him being a nitwit bastard and all. Jacob was in such a foul mood he barely enjoyed the bumpy trip on the lightly-traveled dirt road to Cooper's.

He walked up to Cooper's wrap around porch. After repeatedly knocking on the door for more than a minute, Jacob was ready to give up. Cooper was probably just not home. But Jacob wanted him at the party. It would be his first opportunity to be around him since that day at Greta's. The first time he could observe him and figure out his role in finding Jimmy.

Jacob was halfway back to the truck, resigned to having missed out on seeing Cooper, when the front door opened.

"Yes?" Cooper said, poking his head outside. At first sight, he appeared to have aged twenty years. When he noticed Jacob, he opened the door and stepped out, closing it before a single ray of sunlight could warm the floor inside. He brushed the white plaster dust from his clothes and hair, just now realizing how dirty he was. With most of the dust shaken off, his age reverted to normal.

"Hi, Coop. I was just stopping by to invite you to a potluck at our house."

Cooper blinked, as if just opening his eyes from a long slumber. "Potluck?"

"Sure. Everyone brings a dish, kinda like a big picnic."

"Okay."

Jacob waited further questioning, but Cooper simply stared at him vaguely, and seemed distracted. He glanced over his shoulder at a front window, but for just a second.

Jacob looked to where Cooper's gaze had fallen, and he would've sworn he saw movement coming from inside. Someone stepping out of sight, maybe, behind the sheer curtain. Or it could've been a breeze billowing the lightweight material.

But those windows are painted closed, Jacob thought, curious.

Cooper put a hand to his mouth and let out a harsh cough. "Sorry, I'm replastering the hallway leading upstairs."

Jacob turned from the window, drawn away from further wondering. Once again Cooper was quiet but impatient, and Jacob remembered why he was here. "It's this coming Saturday, at noon. It'll be fun."

"Okay. I'll be there." Cooper nodded then moved to shut the door. He looked up, as if something had just crossed his mind. "Beans."

"Beans?"

"Tell your mom I'll bring a pot of baked beans. I have a family recipe." He nodded once again and closed the door, leaving Jacob standing alone.

His thoughts returned to the shifting movement from the corner of his eye and Cooper's odd behavior. The only explanation that came to mind was Ellie's fear of the ghosts wandering the halls of Cooper's house. The Reverend and Mrs. Blankenship. He gave the house one last glance, but it was as still as a photograph. Realizing how ridiculous he was for even considering the idea, he climbed inside the truck and headed home.

228

TWELVE

Dr. Thompson was the first person to arrive the day of the potluck. During the week, Jacob's mom had run into the doctor while finishing up last second errands for the get together. He had almost begged off coming--what with the health of a few of his patients a concern of his-- but his mom could be quite persuasive. By the time he pulled up in his Packard, the last of the damp morning fog had burned away, and it looked like it would be a fine day for the festivities. For his contribution to the potluck, the doctor brought along a crateful of homemade mulberry wine, his specialty.

"A little early in the day for this, I suppose," Thompson said to his mom.

"Nonsense." She stood at the cook stove stirring spices from her garden into a pot of boiling water. On the counter next to her were piles of cut vegetables and early potatoes. A freshly plucked chicken was in a baking pan on the kitchen table. "The glasses are in the cupboard next to the icebox. We're here to enjoy ourselves," his mom said, then turned to Jacob. "Can you bring in another armful of wood for the stove? I don't want to run short with everything that'll need warming."

His mom had run Jacob ragged with chores for today. He was tired, but it was his price to pay for all the wonderful food.

He went to the lean-to just outside the backdoor where they stored the stovelengths. Loading his arms with what he hoped would be more than enough fuel, he heard approaching voices. Girls' voices. He had little time to react when, quite suddenly, Louise and Mary Wilmot appeared from around the corner of the house. Just that quickly, Jacob was stuck facing Mary Wilmot. Louise didn't seem to notice him, not if her dour, preoccupied expression was any indication, but Mary's eyes seemed to brighten when she noticed Jacob standing by the door. He was trapped.

He didn't know how it happened, but the logs tumbled from his arms. There they were, at his feet, and he hadn't even moved to cause them to fall. He felt like running off to hide.

"Cripes," he grumbled, bending over to pick them up. He could feel his ears flaring red.

He expected the girls to laugh at him, but they kept quiet. But then the world seemed to shift beneath him. His stomach flipped and he felt a sudden pang of anger toward Jimmy for not being here to protect him.

Mary hurried over to his side and kneeled right alongside him. "Let me help you."

Jacob stood and placed a single log across his forearms, his palms facing the sky. Mary went about stacking the rest of the stovelengths in his arms. Louise stood nearby impatiently tapping a foot. Jacob's mind began to cloud, his reasoning cogs grinding to a halt. He didn't know what to do. As Mary bent over, her blonde braids fell forward, carrying along a clean and flowery smell. He came close to dropping the growing stack again.

Mary grabbed the last spindly log. When she stood to place it atop the pile, the stack was nearly to his chin. This older girl he hardly knew--who liked him, but who didn't know he knew--was shorter than him. The crown of her head reached the bridge of his nose, and when he looked down the slight difference in their heights, all he could do was offer a silly grin.

Louise, growing more annoyed with the passing seconds, cleared her throat.

It was like a spell was broken. Jacob, still smiling, turned to the door, but was unable to open it with his arms full.

"Uh, Mary?"

"Yes, Jacob?"

"Can you get the door for me?"

Mary stifled a giggle by pressing a hand to her lips, and then reached over and pushed the door open for him. Jacob went inside, feeling safe within the comfortable smells of the kitchen, away from this girl who made him act like he didn't have a lick of sense.

In no time, everyone else showed up. They all seemed to come in one burgeoning wave. Thompson's mulberry wine filled glass after glass. Other spirits joined the wine--harsh spirits as clear as spring water. The house was all abluster with people exchanging hellos while unwrapping dishes from wax paper or old newspapers. Dishes waited in line for the warmth of the stove or were stacked high inside the ice box. With the heat of the stove, his mom had asked him to open all of the windows. He couldn't help looking out every once in a while, searching and expectant.

For the first time since his disappearance, Jimmy seemed far away. This made Jacob feel guilty as all get out, but he couldn't help it. He also couldn't help watching Mary flit about the yard as she kept an eye on the children brought along by the neighboring adults. A dozen kids, from barely walking, to a few years younger than Mary, were chasing each other, crying out in laughter and full of merriment. He realized the oldest kids were close to his own age. If they were so carefree and as riotous as any group of kids, why was he so preoccupied with Mary, a girl he didn't even know?

Every time Mary would look toward the window--her tousled hair pulling loose from her braids by the children climbing on her--his question was answered. She was laughing and ebullient. Every time they shared a glance, his chest pulsed with heat and he would break eye contact with her. He still didn't know how to handle this situation. God, he missed Jimmy. He would put everything right.

"We're all done setting up." His mom's voice startled him. He stammered defensively, but she motioned him silent. "We just need to finish up with the food. Why don't you have some fun?"

Next, his mom would say something about Mary Wilmot, and without a doubt this something would be embarrassing. So many people were mingling in the kitchen; Mrs. Nightingale, the town's worst gossip, Miss Sinclair, his grade school teacher, the Nagys enjoying glasses of mulberry wine with their six kids out of their hair outside, and still others all becoming one blurring mass. Jacob felt like jumping through the window to safety.

Before she could get a word out, the front door opened and the

Banyon's entered. The crowd swept them in, the women doting on Ellie, commenting on what a pretty dress she wore. Mr. Banyon motioned Jacob over to him.

"Boy, can you lend me a hand out at the wagon?"

Gratefully, he escaped outside, following Mr. Banyon to his mule-drawn wagon. He half-expected to find bottles of liquor in the wagon bed. He'd forgotten about the oak hutch.

Mr. Banyon had wrapped it in old blankets to secure it for the ride over. "Careful now. That's a five-coat finish, and the best I've done so far, if I do say so myself." Mr. Banyon stepped into the bed and slid the hutch to the edge where Jacob waited. It was heavy as blazes getting it off the wagon and through the front door, but hearing the townsfolk's appreciative cries as they set the piece down made it worth the effort.

His mom didn't say anything, at least nothing Jacob could hear. Once Mr. Banyon pulled the blankets away to show off the hutch's golden finish, he explained the whats and the whys of his gift. She hugged him. As they embraced, it looked like she was crying on his shoulder, but then Jacob could tell that she was whispering into his ear, giving him her thanks. Just like that, the townsfolk accepted Charles Banyon back into their fold, and just as quickly, acted as if his years of foolishness had never happened. Cash flowed at a trickle within the town of Coal Hollow, but within an hour, half a dozen people solicited his carpentry skills.

With Ellie happy about the drastic change in her father, and the rest of Coal Hollow setting aside their previous impressions of Mr. Banyon, Jacob decided he would withhold his judgment.

THIRTEEN

Jacob lounged under the canopy of a tall shade tree a ways off from the house after finishing his second supper. The Fowler's house was modest, built for efficiency rather than large gatherings, so three makeshift tables had been set up outside to showcase the day's bounty. The white and red checked tablecloths snapped in the wind. People came, loaded plates, idling like grazing animals.

Just now feeling like he could move without bursting a gut seam, he couldn't remember a day when he'd eaten more. Fried chicken, lemony-seasoned catfish, roasted potatoes drowned in sweet butter, two slices of tart rhubarb pie, a slice of his mom's peach cobbler, cucumber salad with vinegar dressing, and more side dishes than he could count. Mrs. Nightingale brought along her cornbread, and though widely considered her best dish, Jacob didn't even give it a sniff out of deference for Greta. He had nothing against Mrs. Nightingale, and anyway, he was certain no one would notice his silent protest.

Raucous laughter shook the house. The wine had flowed since noon, and now it was getting on to evening with the sun falling from its highest point, Mr. Hauser had started to play his fiddle--his enthusiasm for the instrument far outweighing any natural ability. Even so, people were stomping their feet to the beat and clapping along. Jacob could see heads bouncing, hair lank with sweat, as people danced past the open windows.

The kids stayed outside. Some reclined while recovering from too much food, others were tumbling and stumbling their way across the yard, working off their energies chasing one another.

A group of older girls had gathered around Louise, while children under their care played at their feet. Despite her discomfort, Louise seemed to enjoy the attention. She only needed to intimate a need-- more cucumber salad, a cool cloth to place on the back of her neck--and one of her attendants would see to it. She had become a local celebrity of a sort. She was an anomaly. A young, unmarried pregnant woman not living with her family or future spouse. Even so, she had been welcomed to her neighbors' bosom. His mom had been right all along.

Three boys were playing a game of marbles in a dirt patch near the barn. Others were splashing in the creek out past their stand of peach trees. From the sound of it, they were hounding bullfrogs out from under the grassy overhang lining the steep shoreline.

Jacob was content right where he was. Everyone seemed so happy, but to him, it felt hollow. He couldn't go along with it any longer; from now on, he would stay out of it. Day in day out he had to nod and agree with his mom about Jimmy's whereabouts. It pained him to celebrate today when his brother was somewhere close. He wished he could switch places with him, no matter where he was or what was happening to him.

Slumping lower at the base of the tree, comfortable and full, drowsiness nearly overtook him. But then he saw Mary Wilmot walking in his direction. Yet a ways away, her delicate hands toyed with a blade of grass. She was alone, and no one else was near Jacob. He was her intended target, he realized. Her *intended*.

Before she could get too close, he quickly stood and returned to the house. He nodded in her direction without looking, kept walking, his heart beating faster. At the back door, Cooper was leaning against the frame, sipping iced tea.

"That was a close one." Cooper's eyes were clear and contemplative. He seemed to be one of the few sober adults.

"Yeah. I guess."

"Seems like a nice girl."

Jacob didn't say anything. Mary returned to the group of girls. Ellie and a group of the younger ones were playing tiddly winks. Mary looked disappointed at his hasty retreat, but not overly so. Louise sat on a tree stump, rubbing her belly and looking uncomfortable. Mary briefly chatted with her before they turned their attentions to the children playing in the grass.

"My advice, girls are confusing, at any age. Keep a hold of your wits, or one is liable to take possession of them."

Jacob didn't want to talk about Mary, or about girls in general. Not with Cooper. He didn't want to go inside either. As if on cue, his mom let off a loud peal of laughter, and now he certainly didn't want to go inside. He considered returning to the shade tree, but thought better of it.

Cooper took a long drink of iced tea. The melting ice chips clinked as he drained it.

Jacob saw an opportunity and went for it. Maybe he didn't need to leave home to learn about Cooper's role in Jimmy's discovery. The man was standing right in front of him. "Want another?"

Cooper nodded, handing the empty glass to the boy.

As Jacob entered the house, his mother stepped out, her cheeks flushed crimson, the remains of laughter perking the corner of her lips.

"Why, hello, Mr. Cooper."

"Oh, hi, Jane. Nice day. Great food."

"Thanks. Everyone seems to be enjoying themselves. I just needed some fresh air." She blew a stray strand of hair from her eyes. Her hands were on her hips as she scanned the children carousing across the yard. Seeing her so carefree and relaxed, Cooper could see a glimpse of the girl she was before the responsibilities of adulthood stole the last of her childhood.

A roar of laughter came from inside as the music stopped. Too-loud voices engaging in several conversations at once filled the silence.

"Yeah." Cooper laughed. "Everyone seems to be having a fine time."

Certain that the children were behaving themselves, she turned back to Cooper, smirking. "That would be Dr. Thompson's mulberry wine. He brought along two cases." Jane fanned herself with her palm in an effort to cool. "I didn't have any myself."

"Didn't I see you with a wine glass?"

"You caught me. That was just a prop. I'm not much of a drinker, but I didn't think I could enjoy myself if I didn't at least appear otherwise. Besides, Mr. Cooper, the day isn't about me. It's about Louise. Family. Community."

Before an uncomfortable silence could settle on their conversation, Jacob stepped outside with a tray with three glasses of tea. He gave one apiece to his mom and Cooper, and then took the last for himself.

"Thanks, dear. I was getting parched. Why don't you go off with the other boys. Me and Mr. Cooper are talking."

Jacob looked upset having so quickly been cast aside. Cooper was surprised at Jane's forwardness. He had planned on staying just as long as it took to have his drink, and then take off for home. He was beginning to feel the familiar pull of the Blankenship home. They wanted him home.

The boy gulped some tea before returning it to the tray. He slinked away toward the splashing sounds coming from the creek. They watched him leave before continuing. "Now, Mr. Cooper--"

"Jane, please call me Ted, or Coop. My dad is Mr. Cooper."

"Fine, Ted. Thanks for coming. We're not so bad, are we?"

"No, not so bad."

They both laughed, their eye contact lingering.

"Jacob's a great kid. I've seen how he is with Ellie."

"It's been tough sometimes, but you're right, he's a great kid. Both of my boys are."

"Children are a direct reflection of their parents. It's admirable, you taking on all that yourself."

"It wasn't by choice, trust me. I married Dwight a month shy of my sixteenth birthday. Jimmy came along a year later. I was so young when Dwight passed, I didn't know I was in over my head until the boys had grown and it didn't matter."

Cooper was doing the math in his head while trying to pay attention to what Jane was saying. Thirty-two. Jane Fowler was thirty-two.

A couple stepped outside, surprised at how dark it was getting. If memory served from his earlier introduction, their name was Nightingale. They were farmers. Mr. Nightingale used to also work in the Grendal mines before they shut down. He still carried a nasty miner's cough, and tended to hack away when he laughed, but he didn't seem put out by it. They seemed like a nice enough family.

"Children?" Mrs. Nightingale asked Jane. She leaned against her husband for both comfort and balance.

"I just saw the girls running around down by the barn. Ralph is probably down by the orchard with the other boys collecting lightning bugs."

"Thanks. Wonderful evening." At that, the Nightingales went to search for their kids. When they were off a ways, Mr. Nightingale growled into his wife's ear. She gave off a girlish shriek and scampered away.

Cooper, regaining the thread of their conversation, said, "Fifteen is awfully young to be marrying."

"I know, I know. One of the hardest things in life is to tell love to wait. Sometimes it hits so strong. When you're young, you just can't help it. I wouldn't do anything different, well, besides..."

After a moment's pause, Cooper chimed in, "Dwight?"

Her eyes drifted to the yard, the distant trees, seeing, but not taking anything in. "I've had years to think on it. I would've put my foot down. Not let him go." She turned to him, and her eyes were glassy, intense. "He was a few years older than me, but he seemed to know so much more. At the time, I didn't think I could convince him to stay, if push came to shove. Instead, he convinced me that the world needed him to join the fight. Since then I've realized that all he was was a scared boy. He ran instead of facing a life working in the mines."

"Sometimes it's hard to change a person's mind."

"Oh, I know. You can't change the past. I just sometimes wonder if Dwight would've stayed the same happy-go-lucky man I married if he wouldn't have gone. He was a changed man when he came home. Not just physically. He was weak and prone to pneumonia--that's what eventually took him from this world--but his mind had changed, too. I believe to this day his mind came back more damaged than his body."

"I've met people who fought in Europe, and not a one has much good to say about it. If they're willing to talk about it at all."

"When Dwight came home, I expected all sorts of heroic stories, but all was mum. His stories played out through his eyes. They darkened somehow. He didn't have to say a word." She stared off at the circle around Louise. There were fewer children playing in the yard. A couple here and there. Adults had filtered away to their homes, their kids in tow, waving goodbye to Jane, nodding to acknowledge Cooper. Nightfall was quickly descending.

He wanted to apologize for speaking about the war at all. He should've steered the conversation away from the sensitive subject, but he couldn't help wanting to hear more.

Then Jane blinked several times, and then turned to him, almost smiling. "You bought the old Blankenship place, right?"

"I'm about as surprised as anyone."

"Now, don't take this wrong, I don't mean any offense, but no one who seen you come into town would've thought you were in any position to buy a house like that."

"I'm not a wealthy man by any means. Mr. Prescott offered the property as a foreclosure. He just wanted it clear from the bank's balance sheet."

"So how do you come strolling into Coal Hollow, looking like a man who hasn't been settled for quite a while, and all of the sudden buy a house?"

Cooper was surprised at her candor, and it must have shown.

"I'm sorry, that's a bit personal isn't it? Can you tell I don't interact much with anyone but family? When you're the mother, it's always a matter of telling the children when to wipe their feet and when to sit up straight. The more direct you are the faster the results."

"Oh, it's all right, Jane, it's just a long story is all. I'm not from a wealthy family, just comfortable, and until a year ago I worked quite happily as a librarian in Chicago."

"A librarian?"

"We all have our secrets," he said and chuckled.

The sun had gone; all that remained was its weakening echo, and soon it would be full on dark. A concentrated soft yellow glow bound through the yard, accompanied by the giggles and whoops of children. The remaining kids were on the hunt, filling mason jars to the point they could've been used as makeshift lanterns.

"So why did you leave if you were so happy--there I go again. Don't answer that. I'm sorry," she said, patting his arm.

"Oh, I loved my job, but I just came to a point where I couldn't stand the silence."

"There would be a lot of that in the library business, wouldn't there?"

He laughed. Sure, the library had been quiet, but he had once savored the silence. Then, after meeting Velma Fortune--he still had trouble thinking of her as his grandmother--the silence had become palpably heavy. And with it came self doubt. Wondering who he was, what he was doing with his life. Wondering if he was denying who he was now that he knew his heritage. He had felt lost. A fraud. The silence became maddening.

"I once loved the quiet of the library and the occasional rasp of pages being turned… knowing people were seeking knowledge and enriching their lives." He finished the tea that Jacob had brought him, now watered down from the melted ice.

He suddenly wanted to leave, but couldn't find a way to break off the conversation. Jane seemed too close.

When he looked into her eyes, she seemed close enough to see the thoughts inside his head. He looked away.

"That changed?"

"Oh, yes, definitely changed."

The library patrons sought knowledge, and he missed joining them in the pursuit, but he'd made the right decision. His journey of discovery couldn't take place in the insular world of the library; that would've been impossible. Finding his rightful path could only happen in the real world with people made up of flesh and blood instead of ink and paper.

"Tell me about it." She leaned closer to him, he assumed so she could see him better in the dark. But the look on her face. Was Jane Fowler leaning in to kiss him?

Before he could find out either way, he started talking, "You see, my grandmother, I thought she had died when my father was young. That's what I was always told. But last year she came to live with us."

"That must have been exciting. A new family member coming out of the woodwork, so to speak."

"I suppose." He couldn't believe he was telling her any of this. But he couldn't stop talking, and she seemed so kind, and it had been so long since he had been so close to a woman.

"You see," he paused, looking at her face so close to his. Her eyes glimmered, her lips forming a brief smile. "Velma was weak when she came to live with us. She was dying."

"Oh, how horrible. Just meeting her, too!" Her smile tensed with sadness, then with understanding. After all, her Dwight had been so sick when he returned from the war.

"We made the most of her months with us. I got to know about a part of my family I never knew about."

"At least you had that time together." She placed her hand over his and squeezed. He expected her to pull away, but she didn't.

The last guests came by, a young couple with arms loaded with leftovers and a newborn set of twins, ready for home.

What was their name? Webster? Brewster? That was it, Cooper realized. Mr. and Mrs. Brewster. They seemed so young, but still somehow fully realized adults. They were set on their rightful path, a path they would follow unwaveringly and in its entirety. He wondered if they knew how lucky they were to be in such a position so early in life.

"Good night all," Mrs. Brewster said, the baby starting to squawk in her arms.

"Get those little ones to bed," Jane said, smiling.

"Thanks, Mrs. Fowler. You've set the standard for future potlucks," Mr. Brewster said. With arms burdened with a basket of cooling leftovers and an irritated baby, he leaned over, extended his hand to

Cooper.

"Kent. Nice to meet you."

"You too, Coop. We'll be seeing you around town."

His treatment from the guests surprised Cooper. All with welcomes, well wishes and pleasant good byes. As if he were Jane's equal in the community's eyes; an accepted and respected neighbor. It surprised him even more how good this felt.

The Brewsters reached their truck. Kent revved the engine, and they were gone. They were once again alone. This time truly alone. Louise had retired when her gaggle of girls had dwindled. Jacob was probably in the barn, or still by the creek. All was quiet.

Sitting so close in the near-dark, Cooper could only make out Jane's profile, her delicate nose, her soft lips, a gentle crease at the corner of her eye.

"Family is the most important thing in the world. The only part worth mentioning, if you ask me." She turned to him. "I can't wait to have my family together again. But maybe I'll make due with news on Monday."

"Monday?" he asked, happy about the change of subject.

"A letter should be waiting for me. From Jimmy. It better be, or I'll raise a stink when I see him. I'd at least like to have a return address so I can send him the bundle of letters waiting for him. I'm afraid I'm not such a nice mom in some of them. I thought about pulling the harsher ones from the pile, but decided against it. I held my tongue with Dwight; I'm not about to do that with my son."

He watched her smile broaden, and it nearly broke his heart.

His pulse stopped racing, as if all at once his adrenaline had frozen solid between heartbeats, leaving a gnawing pain in its wake.

"Jane... Jane look at me. The kids were right."

"What do you mean?" she asked, her voice traced with anger.

"Jimmy's not in the army." His words erased any trace of her happiness.

"Not you too. He's in Peoria, in training--"

"No, he's not."

"How can you say such a thing?" she said, pulling away, standing, her hands on her hips.

"He's somewhere in Coal Hollow." He reached for her hand, and reluctantly, she let him hold her limp fingers. "Greta was right. I don't know how Bergman came across that information about Jimmy's enlistment--if he made it up himself or someone pressured him to lie-- but that's what it is. A lie."

She pulled away from him, stepping from the back porch, striding across the grass. She started speaking--she would've even if he wasn't following: "I've never trusted that old witch. Never. And you--I obviously can't trust you either. Here I was thinking we were making some kind of connection, and then this."

Cooper closed the distance between them, continuing, "Jane, it's true. You can trust me."

"Don't use that word with me. You make it sound obscene. Trust."

"I have proof."

She stopped, her back still to him. After a long moment, the croaking of bullfrogs broke the silence. "Fine, show me this proof."

"We'll have to leave. Visit Greta."

"I told you I don't trust her."

"The things she told me, Jane, there's no other possible way she could've known any of it unless her visions have merit. As crazy as it sounds, I believe in her abilities, and I was beyond skeptical before I met her."

He reached for her, touching her lightly on the elbow, but she shrugged him away, hugging her arms in front of her.

She stared into his eyes, boldly, unflinchingly. He didn't look away. Perhaps she sensed his sincerity; perhaps her concern for Jimmy overrode all other matters. He didn't know either way, but in the end she squeezed his hand.

"Fine. Show me this proof. I couldn't live with myself if I didn't try to learn the whole truth."

PART FOUR

ONE

Crouched low in the back of Dr. Thompson's Packard, Jacob and Ellie hid beneath a tattered blanket they'd found draped over the floorboard. She hadn't told him much, yet, just enough to convince him to follow Dr. Thompson when he left the potluck.

It had stung when his mom dismissed him in order to talk privately with Mr. Cooper. But maybe it would be for the best. Maybe he would finally learn something of Jimmy's whereabouts.

He'd left the other remaining boys down at the creek when their moods turned torturous. Archie Beaumont was the ring leader, shoving gravel into the mouth of a thrashing bullfrog. After weighting it down the boy tossed it back in the creek, waiting for it to resurface, if it would at all, laughing uproariously.

Disgusted with Archie's behavior and the other boys' willing complicity, he left, walking aimlessly from creek to barn, then back up to the house again. He'd kept a wide berth, hooking wide of the back porch to avoid his mom and Cooper's conversation. He entered the house through the front door. That's when Ellie found him.

Someone approached the parked Packard. They'd been waiting a solid five minutes, too worried about being spotted or heard to make a peep. The person opened the trunk and slid something heavy inside. Jacob assumed it was the doctor's leftover wine. He was surprised there was any remaining with how the neighbors were putting it away all day long.

They held their breath, but their worries were unfounded. Dr. Thompson walked by the rear door without so much as a glance, then opened the driver's side door, groaning as the seat took his weight. Ellie's head was against the door directly behind Thompson, but Jacob could see into the front seat from his hiding spot. A slice of dusky light washed across the doctor's face, and he looked tired, sober but tired.

Jacob would've bet the doctor had polished off two bottles of mulberry wine by himself just this afternoon. But he seemed steady and aware, ready for home. The doctor started up the car, took a turn nearly too wide for the narrow turn-about, then thundered the engine down the double wheel ruts. They'd made it so far, stowed away, hidden and leery.

He still couldn't believe that a person as respected as Dr. Thompson would conceal knowledge concerning Jimmy. Ellie had been keeping her ears perked during the potluck, panning for any useful information. She was a sly one, moving from one crowd to the next, as noticed as a shadow on a cloudy day. Few held their tongues around the girl, and after hours of wine and rich food, their tongues only loosened.

As dusk settled over their farm, Ellie struck pay dirt. The doctor and Magee the barber were speaking in quiet tones, quiet enough not to draw a further crowd, but loud enough for Ellie to get the gist of it. After hearing the conversation, Ellie had pulled Jacob aside, whispering a transcript while cupping his ear.

Magee had spoken to Thompson about a man named Ethan. Ellie could hear the fear in Magee's voice. Ethan was consolidating his power, severing loose ends. When Jacob asked what that meant, she told him the names Magee mentioned. Jimmy, George, Greta, Cooper.

As the Packard jounced down the road toward town, Jacob analyzed the brief interplay.

How much did either man know?

Who else knew?

Quite abruptly, the doctor stomped the brake pedal, the tires ripping coarse grit from the ground.

"You can't stop this." Thompson slammed a fist against the steering column.

Ellie stirred, as did Jacob, but after checking on Thompson, Jacob caught Ellie before she could blurt out or startle the doctor.

Thompson continued to talk to himself. "You're too old. No, age doesn't matter in any of this, does it? Not with that damnable healing. Age doesn't matter, but courage does. And you don't have an ounce in you, old man."

Thompson rubbed his eyes roughly, as if trying to erase some horrible indelible image from his sight. The doctor laughed to himself. At first a chuckle, the laughter grew in intensity and timbre, flooding with a volatile mixture of madness and relief. He laughed and rubbed his eyes some more, then took a deep, quavering breath. He let it out and opened the door.

"Well, let's see what can be done. Sure wish Jasper was well enough to have a part in this foolishness. This should've happened decades ago. Me and Jasper, going in full-bore, guns blazing…" Thompson spoke, as if the words were no longer his own, or that perhaps he was not even aware that they were issuing from his mouth. Jacob made eye contact with Ellie, and as Dr. Thompson closed the door behind him, she placed a hand on his calf and squeezed. Even though they didn't know what the doctor had been rambling on about, she looked terrified. Her look mirrored how Jacob felt.

"Should I look?"

"Yes. Just be careful."

Jacob peered out the rear window. It took a few seconds to orient himself, but he quickly put two and two together. It was the scrubby patch of gravel that hooked behind Dr. Thompson's house. The driveway ended at a disused barn that had weeds grown tall before it, green tendrils extended to reclaim the land for the wild. A small shed leaned against the barn's listing southern side. If Thompson ever did any maintenance of his own property (with advancing age and his position in the community, he'd been hiring on boys to do those simple jobs for years), the hoes, rakes and saws would be found inside that shed. Some years before, Jacob and Jimmy had found a pair of coal shovels inside when the doctor hired them on to clear the three foot snow fall from his drive and front steps. It was a small shed, a shallow path between piled tools and equipment.

Of all the things Dr. Thompson could do on such a night, after drinking and sharing in his community's good spirits, he went inside the shed.

"It's his place."

"What's he doing?"

"He just went inside his old shed."

"What's he getting?"

"No idea. But he just lit a lantern."

Ellie joined him looking out the window.

"That sure is weird."

"Isn't it?"

"Maybe he's still drunk."

"I don't think so."

Jacob conceded to her experience; Ellie would know a drunk when she saw one.

"What was all that laughter and crazy talk about?"

"I don't know, Ellie. I don't know any more than you."

"What should we do now?"

"Wait for him to come out."

"We can sneak into his house, so we're there first, before he comes in."

He could think of no better option. "Fine. We better move, though."

"Wait. What just happened? The lantern went out."

"No. Not snuffed out."

"Maybe he ran out of kerosene."

"No. I don't think so. Looks to me like that light faded, like a light going down a hallway would."

"But there's no hallway in that tiny shed."

Jacob waited, thinking. Making a run for the house had been a good idea. But wouldn't the doctor have gone inside, if that's where he intended to go in the first place?

No, something strange was going on with how that light just faded like that. "I want you to wait here."

"No, Jacob, you can't leave me."

"It'll be okay. Just stay out of sight."

"But it's not safe without you here."

He waited for a reasonable argument to surface, but none did. "Fine, but you better be as quiet as a church mouse."

Ellie found a relieved smile, and though they were venturing into an even deeper unknown, they felt safer than they should have, knowing they had the other. It was a feeling of trust Jacob hadn't felt since Jimmy's disappearance.

TWO

The night had turned quiet, mere murmurs of bullfrogs hunkered at the distant creek, a lone cricket's unanswered chirp. His welcoming neighbors had gone, by now settling their energy-sapped and surly kids into bed. They would have moved on to thoughts of tomorrow's chores and errands, the minutiae of the manual hardships of farming.

Alone, Charles Banyon fixated on his unrelenting failure as a father and husband.

What a row I've hoed. He sat slouched over on the outhouse bench. The stench held in by the closed door was an appropriate bombardment to his senses. He deserved nothing better.

But his neighbors had been so kind. So forgiving. Not to mention the furniture orders that would keep him busy through the winter. They'd accepted him once again.

And once again he'd slapped the hand of kindness away as if it were a buzzing mosquito. But he had his reasons.

Acceptance and kindness begot expectation, which in turn begot pressure and anxiety, which in the end, brought on a maddening panic that left him reeling, trying to hold together the broken fragments of control. The only way to gain control of the panic was by giving himself over to the harsh touch of the gentle hand of his beguiling mistress.

He tipped the bottle, hating the numbing burn as it surged down his throat and spread through his chest, reveling in the coming darkness. He sobbed silently, trying to hide from the world that he had failed once again.

With his head swimming and self hatred buzzing about his ears, he still noticed how silent the night had become. They were all gone and turned in for the night. His neighbors, the doctor, that kind lady, Jane Fowler, and…

And Elizabeth.

Hellfire.

His poor Elizabeth. All alone. No mother to calm her fears, no brother to turn to. A father pissing his life away.

"God damn it!" He lurched to his feet.

Gotta find my girl. He thought it again, then again, like a mantra. He dropped the empty liquor bottle down the outhouse seat and then opened the door. The air was cool, weightless, too pure. Too pure for him to breathe.

A single light shone from inside the Fowler's home. He walked what approximated a straight line toward the light. His Elizabeth would be up there with Jane. What would he have done without Jane Fowler's kindness?

The three makeshift banquet tables stood empty. Almost empty. Faint moonlight caught the curve of a wine bottle, as enticing as the swell of a woman's breast. His mouth watered as he approached. Flush with adrenaline and anguish and pain, his senses became more alert: his eyes peered through the shadowy yard for onlookers, watched the lighted window to make sure he was left alone. Alone to sin, alone to indulge, alone to quench the fire of craving, of loneliness.

He reached for the bottle, but stopped. Gave himself a mental slap.

Elizabeth. Gotta find my girl. My girl, my girl, my girl.

He righted his path, leaving the table and the wine bottle's magnetic pull.

Dusk had weakened, giving way to full-on night. *Where did everybody go?* He stopped dead still. *How long was I in the shitter?* It felt like he had lost time, as he often had while on a bender. Hell, he was on a bender, wasn't he? A new bender. The bender to end all benders.

"Elizabeth!" Instead of a shout, his daughter's name issued from his liquored lips like fingernails rasping on sandpaper.

He unsteadily climbed the porch steps. It felt wrong knocking on someone's door so late at night. But hadn't he been invited? This was a potluck and Jane Fowler had invited him and Elizabeth over. None of that changed, even after he went off to the shitter with that bottle.

Managing to quell his anxieties for the moment, he knocked on the door. A silhouetted figure walked through the kitchen to answer the door. He swatted the air in front of his face, trying to clear the alcohol vapors. He exhaled into his palm and smelled it, but couldn't tell how hard he would need to work to fool Jane. She could be a tough nut.

When the door opened, Charles was relieved to see Louise Bradshaw. Louise he could fool. Jane on the other hand...

"Yes?" Behind Louise, he saw the clutter left in the wake of the potluck. Piles of dirty dishes. Furniture pushed to the room's corners. But no sign of Elizabeth. No sign of anyone.

"My girl, Elizabeth, I've come for her."

Louise didn't say anything for quite awhile, simply stared into him with a shameful look. Nightsounds seeped into the silence. The whisper of branches bending to a gentle wind. Frogs croaking, a fox's baleful cry.

"Everyone's cleared out. The party's over."

"Please, you gotta tell me: where's Elizabeth?"

Louise continued to scrutinize him with her unflinching gaze. The lamplight glowed behind her. Inside it seemed so warm, inviting. But quiet. Empty.

"Where is she?"

Louise folded her arms across the top of her expanding belly. She winced, then rubbed it. She was so forthcoming he could strangle her. It'd feel good to get his hands around her judgmental neck and wring it like a chicken's. Oh, how it would feel, and then he'd find another bottle and disappear for awhile into oblivion.

"I don't know where she is."

"How so? She was at the potluck."

"Which has ended. Potlucks end. People go home."

"So that's where she went, back home?"

"I told you I don't know. If I *did* know, I don't think I'd tell you anyway." She reached for the doorknob behind her.

He shoved it open. Exasperated, Louise stepped back, allowing his entry inside. The odors of the feast and spilled wine and sweat permeated the house.

"Where is she?" He snatched a solid grip of her upper arm.

She cried out, tried to pull free, but her efforts only angered him.

"Please. Don't. I don't know where she is."

Her simpering plea made his fingers constrict, made him grind his fingers into her flesh and deeper, into her bones.

She cried out again, this time troubled by her unborn child. Her free hand went to her belly while her eyes fluttered, unable to focus.

"Feisty one, is it?" He placed his hand on her belly, and sure enough, felt a resounding kick. It was a feeling he hadn't felt in so long. Since just before Elizabeth's birth.

Disgusted, she swatted at him to remove his hand.

He raised his hands, dirty as they were, palms out, to show his harmless intent. "How far along are you?"

Louise stepped away and breathed deeply.

"Not much for talkin', huh? Well, by the looks of you, I'd say you're five months tops."

He inched farther inside.

She said nothing, but her eyes spoke of her growing fear.

"You shouldn't shame a child, especially one not yet born. But you hid it. Shamed it. Hid a miracle as if it were a blight." Rage built at his temples, blurring his eyes. The last few days he'd fought so hard, the sweats and cravings, feeling like a marionette pulling against his strings. He fought the newfound clarity of his thoughts, the brightness of the day. But most of all, he fought the guilt for all of the troubles he'd caused, and everything he'd done that no matter how long he remained sober, he'd never be able to repair.

He could never have a fresh start. Not after tonight. Not after he so easily grabbed that bottle when no one was looking, grabbed it guiltily, but with lust also. He no longer had Mabel, not the Mabel he'd fallen in love with. With his own selfish actions he'd turned her into a monster. His boy, George was gone, too. As for Elizabeth, she would never see him as anything other than a vile, sticky thing clinging to the bottom of her shoe. Someday she would scrape him off, toss him away, and move on. Maybe today was that day.

Louise's unborn child kicked the hardest yet, making the girl catch her breath. Tears fell down her cheeks as she gritted against the stabbing pain.

He felt bad for her with no husband to calm her anxieties, no one to hold her hand through these baby pains. Jane Fowler was no where to be seen, either.

"Baby coming?"

"No, just doesn't like," she said, cut off by another kick. "Baby... doesn't like potato salad." She somehow smiled when she looked at him.

He closed his eyes and saw his beloved Mabel as young as Louise. So lovely, so humble and pure. The image blurred and distorted to the horrid thing she'd become. Undead, mindless, soulless. He heard the scraping of her nails against the door, wanting to get out, to ravage and tear him apart.

When he opened his eyes, Louise had drifted to the kitchen table, within reaching distance of a dirty carving knife.

"You know that Jimmy a' yours?"

Her hand stalled inches from the blade.

"He's dead."

"No. You don't know that."

"A' course I do. I brained him dead myownself."

Louise reached for the blade.

"And here you are, shaming a miracle."

He took two steps, grabbed her wrist with one hand, taking hold of the carving knife with the other. She screamed, but no one was near enough to hear.

THREE

It was a rough go trying to find Greta Hildaberg's treehouse in the dark. Cooper had only been there once and was still unfamiliar with the wooded surroundings. Jane hadn't visited since she was a girl, on the eve of her marriage to Dwight Fowler. As they searched for signs they were in the right area, Jane told Cooper that she had gone (with a fair amount of skepticism, she emphasized) to ask Greta how her marriage would play out. Greta had told her during that long ago visit that her marriage would be loving and fruitful. If Jane would've only thought to ask if it would also be long-lived, she could've saved herself years of heartache. When you're fifteen, you never think you or a loved one is anywhere close to death. Death doesn't come near you. It is but a rumored condition afflicting others.

An amber glow warmed a wide tree canopy in the distance. They covered the remaining quarter mile quickly, kicking through a waist-high field that transitioned to a rough undergrowth of brush. The tree was the tallest around, with gnarled branches, roots grown grasping through the soil's surface below, a mantle of leaves blotting out the moon above. They mounted the spiral steps. Cooper found the nighttime effort considerably more amenable than his earlier attempt while accompanying the children in the bright sunshine. By the time Jane tapped on the door, he'd nearly forgotten his fear of heights and that they were now thirty or more feet in the air.

Greta answered the knock almost before it was finished.

"Good, good. Come on in. Cider's at the table. Have some if you will."

Jane looked at Cooper, but neither said anything. They entered, each taking a seat at the low table. Two cider filled wooden mugs were at the table. When Cooper touched the wood, steam poured over its rim. Neither drank.

"Time's almost gone. You know that, don't you?" Greta said directly to Jane. "You wouldn't be here otherwise."

There was no need to explain the reason for their late night visit. "I just need to know. I can't leave a stone unturned."

"I suppose, since I haven't seen you since you were a girl, I must be the last stone for you to consider." Greta turned away, peering through the wooden slates of the small kitchen window. She appeared to be gathering herself, while at the same time, checking the neighboring vale. "Your boy, he's in trouble."

Jane was going to say something, but held her tongue.

"There are dark forces at play--"

Jane cut in, "Greta, please. If you know anything, you have to tell me. He's my son. What if Arlen were in danger? You'd want to know, wouldn't you?"

Greta joined them at the table. Her eyes glistened with emotion. "Why of course I'd want to know. But we're all in trouble, not just your boy. There are reasons I live like this, in this damnable tree like some mad monkey. But I'm not crazy. No, no, I'm trapped here. Trapped by fate. I wanted to leave Coal Hollow and be done with it when Arlen was born. But I couldn't do that, even with my son's best interests at heart. I had to stay--we both did. Because we all play a part in this. If I had left, evil would have continued unabated."

"What evil, Greta?"

"First off, Janie-girl, you know what I'm telling you. You can't live in Coal Hollow a lifetime and not know. It's the Underground. The evil is underground. But it strays. Sometimes it strays to the surface; sometimes the evil of above drifts below, too. But when it does surface, it will at times take along innocence when it returns to its lair."

"They took my boy?"

"In Jimmy's case, he stumbled upon it. It was an accident, but sometimes accidents have unforgiving consequences."

Seeing pain etched in Jane's face, Cooper chimed in, "I know we've come unannounced, Greta, but if you know anything about Jimmy's whereabouts and how we can bring him home, you need to tell us, straightaway. In plain and simple language. Drop the hyperbole; no more talk of 'evil and dark forces.' That doesn't help the situation."

Greta didn't look at him, didn't even acknowledge him. Instead, she gazed at Jane with mounting intensity.

At long last, Jane broke under her glare. "I know. Well, I've heard stories. The Underground is a place where men venture who soon become beasts. That's what my grandma once said." Her voice was soft, but thick in her throat. "Less human than animal."

"Depraved, yes. Indeed." Greta nodded, knowing she'd finally gotten through.

"Why didn't you tell me?" Jane looked miserable, as if she'd just gone through a physical trauma that began without certainty of her survival. Her face was gaunt, and she appeared a decade older than her thirty-two years.

"Oh, dear, I would've if it would've done any good. I had a right mind to follow those kids home after their recent visit and try to get through to you as well. I could've told you the day before Jimmy went missing. Or when you came asking about your marriage prospects all those years ago. I could have been done with it by whispering to your newborn ear. At no other time would you have listened. Not with open ears and understanding. Not until now."

A crash from outside halted their conversation, a slight pounding against the clapboards. Cooper thought a bird might have made an unwise flight path directly into the wall of Greta's home, perhaps a crow or barn owl, but an accompanying sound did away with that notion: the lively rush of rapidly expanding flame.

"We need to go now." Greta's voice trembled. "If it's not too late already."

Flames burned just outside the kitchen window. Greta stepped back. Heat pulsed from the window as the fire fed on the treehouse. Cooper went to the far side of the little home and looked out the small window by the kitchen table. A single row of torches marched through the tall brush toward the treehouse.

"What is it? Who's doing this?" Jane shouted, grabbing Greta's arm as the three of them rushed for the door.

Greta didn't answer right away, but Cooper knew.

Sometimes evil strays to the surface to steal away innocence.

Greta shrugged away from Jane's grip. "You can't leave this woman's side, Mr. Cooper," she said, then turned back to Jane. "You need to stay with Mr. Cooper. You will find your answers if you don't stray from his side. You'll be safe; that's as clear as day in my visions. You hurry down those steps, make your way North through my field. There's good covering ground in that direction, which will give you time. I need to take care of this, end it now. They want to scare me off. But I won't let them hurt you two. Now go. Off with you." Greta patted Jane's hand, squeezed Cooper's shoulder, then ushered them out the door.

"Greta, you're coming with us. The fire. It's spreading."

"Don't you worry. They won't let anything happen to me. They just want to scare me is all," Greta repeated. Her tired expression belied her words.

"Who are they?"

"The undead."

Greta closed the door on them, terminating the conversation. Fire spread across a third of the home, licking along the ancient tree branches, wilting the moisture from its leaves before they also caught fire. Smoke twirled along a gust of wind, enveloping Cooper and Jane as they nearly tumbled down the spiral steps.

"She's not going to make it out," Jane said.

Cooper didn't respond. The row of torches was closing in on the house. They didn't have a second to dawdle. He took Jane's hand and pulled hard as they made a break for the nearest gap in the surrounding brush. Together, they bound through the undergrowth as it tore at their clothes and skin.

They ran. Blood pulsed through their ears, but it seemed the sounds of the destruction they left behind only intensified--the flames overtaking the treehouse, timbers crumpling, upending, crashing to the forest floor. And voices, none-too-distant, closing in on the ruins, reveling in the destruction, basking in the warm glow of their hapless victim.

After a tense ten minutes, Cooper eased their pace. They caught their breath, tasting smoke on their tongues, smelling it in their hair. "They killed her. There's no way she got out in time. Why didn't she come with us. Why, Ted?"

"They--whoever 'they' is--didn't kill Greta. She *let* them kill her."

Behind them, the fire glowed over the treetops. Cooper saw how recklessly they'd trampled the grass during their escape. They might as well have painted a line of arrows in the bent blades to indicate their direction.

"Did they see us?" Jane asked the question before Cooper could.

"I don't know, but I'm guessing they were coming if we were there or not."

"Who are they? What did Greta mean, undead? The dead can't do that. The dead can't start fires and destroy, because, damn it, they're dead!" Their slow progress screeched to a halt. "Ted, what aren't you telling me?"

"Greta knew what she was talking about. About Jimmy and the Underground. She knew we could escape safely if we headed north through her field."

"How can you be so sure?"

"Well, first of all, just over the next ridge is a meek runnel of a creek, and at the top of the next hill past the creek sits my house. She knew what she was talking about. We just need to figure out how that helps us find Jimmy."

They stepped across the meek runnel of a creek, the grass lining the shore lush and green, becoming sparse not more than twenty feet beyond. Cooper realized they were still holding hands long after it was practical for them to do so. It was a comfortable thing, a warm reassurance during such an disturbing night.

"You must be a wealthier man than you let on earlier tonight."

"What do you mean?"

"Your houselights are on."

The house was indeed alight, the two facing windows on the ground floor bright and wide-eyed, the upper floors awash in an umber of flame. It appeared as if the grand celebration of the day had assembled at Cooper's house instead of Jane's. But the house was empty. Essentially.

"Let me explain." He guided her by hand up the porch steps. He opened the front door, but when they stepped inside, the lights warming the house all went out. The entryway was dark and cold. No hint of a lantern's lingering warmth.

"That's odd," Jane said, looking around.

"Not from what I've seen." He closed the door behind them.

"You must have some draft," she said, chuckling nervously.

"No, I have guests. Or more precisely, I'm a guest in this house."

"Are you going to buy furnishings, or just sleep on the floor?" she said, pointing at his nest of blankets. He felt exposed having her see his bedding, as if she would instantly know the dreams he experienced while sleeping there.

"Eventually, I hope to restore the house to its original state. Period furniture, fresh paint, and the like."

He felt strangely at ease considering what they had just been through. The burning tree, the marching row of torch-bearers cutting across the open field. He felt like he should be hospitable, perhaps offer a cup of tea as he had to Jacob and Ellie. Relax a bit. Maybe continue on with the general flow of their earlier conversation.

But then Jane jerked her head aside as if a fat spider had plopped down on her shoulder. She jerked her head the other way, and Cooper could see the fear in her eyes.

He felt it too. A cold caress against his cheek. An invisible fingernail rasping through his five o'clock shadow.

Pressure, cold and bracing.

"Back to what I said earlier, I'm a guest in this house, regardless if the property title says otherwise."

With a jarring abruptness, Eunice Blankenship appeared between them. She looked like the young, righteous and vibrant woman of her youth.

You need to hurry.

Cooper heard Eunice's voice in his head, and from her reaction, so had Jane. She was backing away from the apparition, reaching behind her for the doorknob.

NO, the reverend said, also inside their heads, a heady timbre that was nearly a shout. He appeared behind Jane, and he placed a hand on her shoulder. She jumped away, as if the spirit had inappropriately goosed her.

"Ted... what's going on?"

"As I said, a guest."

As was his penchant, the reverend's ethereal body diminished to nothing. A cold wisp of air rushed by as he whipped through the entryway. A lacy curtain pulled aside, held there by an invisible hand.

There's not much time, the reverend said, looking out the window Cooper had just checked for security.

"What do you mean?" Cooper asked the open air, then turned to Eunice. "What's happening?"

Eunice's body took on a more corporeal form, as if a dial had turned, sending additional energy surging through her body. She aged rapidly as the details of her face became more clear. Wrinkles creased her face, her skin sagged, her eyes dimmed, dirtying with cataracts. She extended her hand, touching Cooper's forearm. Her touch was as cold as the frigid reaches of Hank Calder's icehouse. Her lips moved, and a sound came from her throat, and it was a real voice. *"NOW,"* she said. Quavering, and ancient, but real nonetheless. *"Come with me!"*

The lacy curtain fell and settled as Horace Blankenship abandoned his lookout position. Once again, an icy wind whipped by. Jane, while as frightened as ever, no longer seemed set on rushing out the front door and away from these unsettled spirits. The reverend threw the basement door open. Cooper assumed his spirit then went down the steps, but then a coercive hand pressed between his shoulder blades. His feet began to move, and standing next to him, so did Jane's.

"They're here," Eunice said.

A moment later something heavy slammed into the front door, while both front windows crumbled at once, leaving jagged shards clinging to weathered frames. Arms darted through the gaps, flailing, reaching, limbs slick with dark blood and something more vile. Another crash snapped Cooper's attention back to the door. The impact nearly forced it from its hinges. Time was fleeting; the door wouldn't hold much longer.

Something wriggled partway through one of the broken windows. It was a horrible sight, this creature with its pus-flesh seeping with decay, its maniacal eyes panning the entryway. Its eyes found Cooper's. It struggled through the opening, shredding its skin, losing a finger that was sheared off by a long, bladelike shard of glass. It didn't seem to notice.

The remains of the man wore overalls. His torso was tree trunk thick. A rancid odor swept over Cooper. One last push from the spirit of Reverend Blankenship ushered him down the steps. Side by side with Jane, they took the steps two at a time.

The tumult of crazed activity upstairs shook the basement's ceiling. Dust and flakes of mortar rained down from above.

"What are those things?" Jane held his hand.

Cooper had never seen such unfettered fear so close before. For some reason, he thought of Jane's husband, Dwight. The trenches changed him. He'd come home fragile, fractured inside.

Can fear stain a person's soul?

"Cooper, come on. Snap out of it."

Dazed, he heard voices, could *feel* the destruction reverberating from above, but somehow he couldn't move from the spot at the bottom of the stairs. He looked around, saw Jane's face welling with tears, overflowing, tracing jagged streaks down her cheeks. His eyes drifted past, to the mirror hanging on the wall at the bottom of the stairs. The mirror angled so you could see upstairs as well as your own reflection.

He saw the white-illumined spirits of the Blankenships, just over his shoulder. The impatience in their faces was considerable. Then Eunice stepped away from her husband's side. In the reflection, Eunice gripped his cheeks with both hands. Her icy touch quaked through his facial muscles and down the nape of his neck. The ghost's body became entirely corporeal, appearing as it had in her final state--ancient and stooped, kindness still warming her eyes. Then a rift appeared at the crest of her forehead just below her hairline. It widened, spreading as wide as a machete's blade. Thick blood flowed from the opening, down her face, and as Eunice revisited the final moments before her last breath, she gained an immortal strength that rippled through her flesh. Her grip on his face tightened. She reeled back with her left hand, then let loose with a teeth-jangling slap across his cheek.

Cooper came close to falling to the dirt floor. But he didn't. Instead, he snapped out of it. Eunice began to fade, her energies sapped, the resilience he normally saw in her face flagging along with it. She looked defeated.

"Cooper, please? What do we do?"

For some reason, he smiled. "Come with me."

He took her hand and they went down the hallway, around a corner, and into a small room.

"Now where? That window's too small for us to get through." A wedge of wan moonlight cut across the floor. Its glow found their faces, casting them in somber blue.

"Here." He left her side, went to the far wall, rapped it with his knuckles. He ran his fingers along the surface until he found the right spot, pulled out and to the side, and the secret panel opened up.

"What's that?"

"A hiding place. Created for the Underground. The real Underground."

He crawled into the opening, reaching out in the near dark, searching. Just as he had figured, the bricked up wall five feet into the opening was a hastily constructed thing. He felt around until he found a gap at the top of the wall, a small rift where the ground had shifted and the stones had sunk over the years. He jammed his fingers through the opening, then pressed as hard as he could against the wall. Stones scraped one another, and then the topmost one fell into the tunnel.

The sounds from upstairs came in ever-increasing volume and intensity. The monsters (that's what they are, right? Cooper thought, monsters?) had gathered in the entryway. Stomping feet clomped in every direction as they searched the house.

One of their pursuers had seen their escape into the basement. It didn't take them long to find the stairway and trundle down in a wild clamor.

Cooper had succeeded in prying away a number of stones, pushing some ahead, pulling some toward himself.

"Quick," he called out to Jane. "Get in here and pull that panel closed behind you."

She did as he requested, and after a moment of panic as she fought to fit the panel square in its opening, they were alone in the lightless tunnel, the sound of the approaching undead momentarily quieted.

"I can't... I can't do this. I just can't go on. I need to get out of here, I need to see my family. They need me."

The undead filing into the basement quickly deduced that their quarry would not go quietly. Growls of rage came from the small room they had just exited.

"Jane, we need to move. There's no other choice. They'll tear us apart if we don't get moving now. It won't take them long to realize we're in this tunnel. They know about this tunnel. They've been through this tunnel, and I'm pretty sure they are the ones who tried to wall it up so no one would find the entry point to their lair."

"I can't. I can't do it anymore."

He reached out in the dark, found her hand, squeezed it. Speaking with his lips an inch from her ear, "This is a tunnel that served a purpose during the Underground Railroad, but it also leads to the Underground, the corrupt Underground. Greta gave her life to send us on this path. She sent us to my house. She was trying to help us; for whatever reason she didn't or couldn't outright tell us what to do. But, Jane, Jimmy is in the Underground. They have him, and if we take this tunnel, we'll find him. We can set him free."

His words struck to her core. He couldn't see her, but could feel a change go through her. She took a deep breath and pushed him on the shoulder. "Let's go then. Let's get my boy."

FOUR

Arlen Polk's gopher hole resembled more a trash heap than a furry animal's living space. Trash was strewn alongside mounds of broken rock where Arlen sorted the precious coal from the worthless slag. He'd staked a canvas tent near the gopher hole where he could rest and eat meals packed by his mom. But now, forty feet below, Arlen toiled as he always had, sweating a mindless salty lather, humming to fill the empty space.

He'd been at work all day, and close to quitting time, the vein he was chasing opened in a wide berth of rich ore that alluded to an even deeper source. Every swing he took he hoped would lead to prosperity. He kept at it, long hours after simple fatigue ceded to exhaustion. He alternated swinging his pick axe and shoveling crumbled stone into a rickety cart.

His humming died off. Spittle flew from his lips.

Greta's death hit Arlen like a physical blow, fully a quarter mile from their treehouse, burrowed at the deepest point of his gopher hole.

"Mom," he called out in a whimper, as if she could soothe him. Pain seared across his forehead, making him drop his pick axe in mid-swing. He fell to his knees, grinding his palms against his temples. In the yellow kerosene light, the rough tunnel walls quaked, the floor rumbled, sending him in a rumpled heap stomach-flat against the coal dirty floor.

The hot fist of pain bloomed throughout his brain, triggering synapses that had never been alighted with intelligence. Nerve endings jangled, snapped, sparked. The pain quelled, fell apart, became bits of words. Words crystallizing into a single, distinct voice.

"We'll always be together. You will always carry me in your heart." They were his mom's oft-repeated words. Words he never truly understood until now. He'd spoken them with his own voice--his flat, masculine voice merging with her lyrical speech patterns. Hearing her through him in the enclosed air of his gopher hole scared him. Scared him nearly senseless.

The worst part was finally understanding. After all these years, understanding the depth of her unflagging love for him, feeling its warmth filling him. Knowing fully how blind he had been to the world.

He also understood the generations of children's leers and laughter, the men folk's crude humor, the women's condescending tone and dismissive behavior. He had been an unwitting outcast; his whole life he had smiled agreeably, lent a helping hand and gladly labored at tasks others would have considered a menial tedium. But now he understood. Completely.

His mother's knowledge was flooding him. *She* was flooding him. Her stories and secrets, everything, hit him boldly, his vision swimming in the torrent of information. Others' knowledge--Grandma Nina was there, too--Nina, whom he'd never met but knew through his mom's stories, she was there with her photographic memory for numbers and their patterns. Also, a man named Rubell, another named Quint, they swept in too, deposited their lifetimes' knowledge into his brain.

Rubell... he knew now. His mom's lover. The shyster of patent medicines. Arlen's father. And Quint, his great uncle, a man from whom his mom had to fight off advances, an engineer who dabbled in steam locomotion in his youth. Ranging from disturbing to ingenious, his knowledge was now Arlen's.

Earlier voices, ancestral voices, guttural and thickening with accents (their words morphing into languages he didn't know, didn't know until now) they coursed through him as well, and he understood. Every word, he understood.

"Oh, Mom," he said, crying from the burden. "Mom, why?" It was his voice subsuming hers, for a brief moment.

"People I love are going to suffer," he once again spoke his mom's words as if they were his own. "No, Momma. Please." He was pleading, alone in the dark, hoping she would hear him, and in the back of his mind, hoping she was safe.

"Good people will suffer, oh God in heaven, will they suffer. If I walked the streets of Coal Hollow, I could point to certain people, say, 'You will be dead by the first frost.'" His voice was regaining strength, fortified by the generations that had preceded him. His words filled the tunnel, guttered the lamp's flame as he grabbed it from a hasp embedded in the soft rock wall.

With his understanding, he learned the role he was destined to fulfill. Such a responsibility placed in his care after a lifetime of being treated like a child--he felt such a warmth of pride. He could do this.

"But it has to be. Has to be, or nothing will change." His mother's voice filled him. He no longer fought it; he embraced it, found comfort in the familiarity. He gathered the supplies he would need. Well, nearly all of the supplies. The rest he would have to get from the locked trunk in his canvas tent.

"Sometimes death leads to life. Sometimes there's a greater good." Arlen's shadow ebbed and flowed as he trudged up the incline to the entrance of his gopher hole. "I know, Momma, and I know now... you're gone. I know they took you from me. You'll always be in my heart. Always."

He made his way into the encompassing night. Unlocking the trunk he kept hidden in the back of his tent, Arlen Polk smiled.

"Found it, Momma." He could feel her pride, as soothing a balm as ice cream in July, though she no longer lived on this plane. "But you always knew it was here, didn't you, Momma?"

He would need to be sly. Slyer than he had ever been. Fulfilling his destiny, he would honor his mother's memories and the memories of past generations.

Now, he just needed to find one wall, find and breach one wall.

FIVE

Dr. Thompson's lantern sputtered and exhausted itself minutes after Jacob and Ellie decided to follow him into the tunnel under his tool shed. The old man sighed, exasperated, swore an oath, but continued on in the dark.

Their need for secrecy as well as the pitch black of the tunnel kept the children quiet. Otherwise, Jacob would have laughed a good stretch over the doctor's vulgarity, repeating it to himself to hear it issued in his own voice. But nothing seemed funny right now.

With the sudden darkness, Ellie held fast to Jacob's shirtsleeve. He could feel her quavering as she fought the urge to call out. But they remained silent, confounded by circumstance to follow the doctor through the low-ceilinged, downward-twisting tunnel.

In the absence of light, sound guided their way. Keeping a safe distance, they listened for Thompson's shuffled, unsure strides, his occasional grunts when he bumped into a wall or low passage, his labored, throaty breathing. They also listened when he picked up his mumbled train of thought concerning Jasper Cartwright. The crazed, one-sided conversation he'd begun in his car started again and halted, running in fits and starts, as he made his way deeper into the earth. The doctor chastised himself (ostensibly spoken to his dear friend) for decades of cowardice made immeasurably worse by its accompanying guilt and shame; he rambled (is he still drunk? Jacob wondered more than once) about his need to rectify the situation, at least make an effort, no matter how feeble, after all these years of silence. Sometimes he would ask Jasper questions directly, as if the doctor's oldest friend walked at his side, and after a momentary lapse, Thompson would grunt, as if hearing just the right answer.

Jacob could guess what Ellie was thinking as they walked through this narrow vein of emptiness into an ever cooler unknown, for they would be the same thoughts as his: Who is this man they're following? How could you *not* know someone could be so... so *strange*? How could you not know about a seemingly endless tunnel burrowing in to the ground of your own hometown? Who else knows about the existence of such a tunnel?

And then suddenly, Jacob realized, there was no sound ahead. No aural beacon to hone in on.

He must have tensed at Ellie's side, because she broke their silence: "Where is he, Jacob? It's so dark down here."

"Shh."

"We should turn back. I think I can find our way. It's not too difficult. Only that one place where the tunnel split, otherwise, it's a straight shot to the tool shed." She would've said more if Jacob hadn't squeezed her arm.

In a voice no louder than an exhaled breath, he spoke with his lips brushing her ear, "Just because we can't hear him, doesn't mean he's not ten feet from us. Keep your voice down."

"I think we lost him," Ellie said, ignoring him. "Besides, it's Dr. Thompson. He's the nicest man I've ever met. So what if he hears us? He's our friend."

"Besides talking crazy, why's he ducking into hidden tunnels in the middle of the night? Remember, he mentioned Jimmy to Magee."

"I don't know, but we can't see a thing." Her voice rose in pitch, verging on panic. "It's cold and I'm scared. So are you, Jacob Fowler."

"An even better reason for keeping your voice low. Wait--feel that?" Jacob held her left hand with his right, while extending his other hand to feel their way down the tunnel. He lifted her hand, tracing it along the wall.

"What? What is it?" she said, this time barely audible. "Oh, another split. Which way? Which way did the doctor take?"

"I don't know, just give me a second--" he looked in each direction, but didn't find a clue to make their decision any easier. Turn left, turn right, go back the way they had come, no direction felt like the correct answer.

"Let's go right."

"Why right?"

He didn't say anything for a while.

Ellie nudged him. "Jacob, did you see something, hear something?"

"No. Just a gut feeling is all. Let's go right."

"Okay."

"Let's just be quiet about it."

She didn't say anything, merely took up her latch on his shirtsleeve. They started down the tunnel, ears and eyes alert, fighting phantom light and the sound of dripping water.

They stayed in that formation for a long, straight stretch of tunnel, softly shifting their feet along the damp cold floor, fingers flailing ahead, touching the walls as if searching for directional signs written in Braille.

A groan came from somewhere ahead; a raspy sigh swimming with pain, abruptly stifled. Or it could have been from another direction--the cavern walls distorted and so recklessly tossed about sounds that a person familiar with the tunnels would have been left confused. They couldn't turn around, not now. They had come too far. What if that sound was coming from Jimmy? Could they turn their back on him when they were on the verge of reaching him?

They heard the groan again, and this time they were ready for it. Without a doubt the sound was coming from in front of them. "Let's check it out," Jacob said.

"I don't want to."

"Have a better suggestion?"

Though reluctant, Ellie went along as they inched forward. The groan became louder. It was a man; he could hear it in the muscular quality of the voice. It was deep, wounded, irrevocably broken. Not Jimmy. No, Jimmy didn't sound like that. Jacob hoped he didn't sound like that. If he did he was in a world of pain, and he didn't know if he could see his brother in such a state.

Around a zigzag in the tunnel, they came across an area where a weak light washed over the walls, defining the craggy surfaces, revealing bottlenecks and small cubbyhole rooms.

Another bend in the tunnel revealed the light's source. A dying torch hanging in an iron ring. The flame had marred the wall with a black halo, and on the yellowish floor, an expansive depression nearly filled the small room, appearing like an embedded, unblinking eye.

Ellie screamed, her fingers clawing Jacob's arm. A second later, when he saw what had frightened her, he hoped his eyes were deceiving him.

A Negro man writhed on the floor, or rather, a mere torso straining to pull himself toward the dilated emptiness in the floor. His insides were no longer inside; guts trailed behind him, shredded flaps of flesh slimed with blood and mucus. His face and neck were a mass of scabs, some old some fresh, while his grimace was a testament to his effort to simply move.

He groaned, pulled his arm forward, slapped his palm down, found purchase and pulled again. He gained an inch, maybe two along the floor. But still, he started again, this effort just as vigilant as the last, his motions the final struggles of a dying swimmer.

Jacob felt like screaming too, but wouldn't. He couldn't let himself lose it, no matter how he felt. Ellie was counting on him, Jimmy was counting on him. His mother would never recover if he didn't keep a level head and get out of this predicament unscathed.

Ellie couldn't take the sight. She released her grip on his arm, and not taking her eyes from the man struggling on the floor, bolted down the tunnel. She would have made a good clip, putting distance behind her, but she slammed into the twisting tunnel wall, stunning herself. She slumped to the floor, blinked a few times, but didn't lose consciousness.

Jacob approached the man, careful to avoid the puddle of blood flowing down a slight dip in the floor.

As he got closer, he could see the man was naked, and that below his ruined entrails, there was nothing. No hips, no legs or feet. Yet, he was alive.

"Hello?" Jacob said, not sure what to say.

The man kept at it, fighting to move, his eyes blinking through sweat cooling into a pasty sheen on his skin.

Jacob stepped closer and touched the man on his meaty shoulder. The man jerked his head aside, crying out. He radiated fear like a cookstove's heat.

"I, uh, my name's Jacob." The man looked at him, as if not comprehending. But Jacob could see his mind at work, trying to understand something. The man wouldn't stop blinking, his lids fluttering like a butterfly's wings, shedding tears or sweat or both to stream down his cheeks to meet at the point of his chin.

"I know you." The man reached for Jacob. "I know you."

Jacob ignored the man's ravings. There was no way he could know this Negro. He didn't know a single one, was proud of the fact he didn't. His kind didn't belong in a Fowler's life. He inched away from the Negro's grasping fingers. "What is this place?"

"Hell, boy. You're in hell. Help me up now. We gotta get to digging."

Jacob glanced at Ellie. She was staring at the last bit of the torch's flame as it struggled to stay alight. She seemed unaware of their exchange. For the first time since they found her brother's body, he saw her sucking her thumb.

The Negro caught Jacob's pant cuff, and he instinctively smacked him away. He felt bad as soon as he did. "Hey, what is this place, this room? That pit?"

The man groaned again, whirled his arm in front of him, pulled himself another meager inch. Toward the pit. Biting cold wind blew from the void. Jacob was shivering. Ellie's lips were turning blue. The man reached the lip of the precipice. "It's the end, boy. It better be. Better be." Exhausted, he rested his head against his forearm, his gaze longing for the black emptiness of the abyss.

Such a pathetic sight, Jacob had never seen.

The man twitched, then quite silently, began to cry. He couldn't do it, couldn't reach the pit in order to end his life. Couldn't just die. Some unnatural force kept him breathing and alert with full understanding of his awful predicament.

Jacob couldn't stand it any longer. Something inside him snapped. If the man had been an injured dog, he would have stomped his skull, but instead, he reached into the muck remaining at the man's waist, grabbed two fistfuls of something slithering and rope-like, then manhandled the Negro the final six inches. Instantly, the man was gone. His descent didn't make a sound. He never cried out. He was simply no longer there.

Jacob peered over the edge, and though he couldn't see into the pit, his stomach swirled with vertigo. The harsh wind stung his cheeks. When he stepped away, his feet slipped in the cold sludge of spilled blood.

He took the dying torch from its mount, then helped Ellie to stand. She went willingly, letting him guide her as if she were a blind person negotiating a busy street. Before the light could wink out for good, he ripped a strip of cloth from his shirt, and wrapped it around the torch, careful not to snuff it out. Luckily, the flame caught hold of the fabric, fed off it, brightening the tunnel. His footprints looked like long brushstrokes in the trail of blood. He could feel it still on the soles of his shoes. It sickened him knowing where it had come from. And worst of all, knowing what he had done.

"You found a light." Ellie perked up at his side. "We can leave now." She sounded relieved, reminding him of when they saw Cooper's porch and knowing they would be able to ride out the storm there.

"Let's just keep quiet. Please?"

She was, and they made their way.

SIX

"Did we lose them?"

Cooper didn't give Jane an answer. He wanted to say yes, but that would've only been a guess. At first, they'd seen flickering light trailing them and heard the unnerving growl of their pursuers. After moving at a breakneck pace for several minutes, the light dimmed, then was gone. The sound, Cooper had never heard anything more strident and hateful, soon seemed to scatter, at moments sounding behind them, while at other times seemed to echo from branching shafts ahead of them.

"Ted?"

"I... I don't know."

"Who are they?"

"I can't say who they are now."

"Damn it, Ted, talk to me!" Since they entered the dark tunnel he had kept track of her by listening to her steps, but now she'd stopped. He couldn't remember a time he felt more alone. "Did Greta tell you who they are?"

"No, not Greta. Horace and Eunice Blankenship."

"They're dead, Ted. This is crazy. This is so unbelievably crazy."

"I know what you're thinking, but you have to--" he was going to ask her to trust him. He seemed to ask that of her a lot. But why did she have to trust him? Why would she?

"Okay. This is going to sound crazy, and no matter how crazy this sounds, don't stop me, because if you cut me off, I don't know if I could start again."

"Okay. Fine."

He waited, listening for any signs of pursuit. All seemed clear. He fumbled for Jane's hand, and it gave him a feeling of calm when her hand found his first.

"Okay, here goes--" he said, then proceeded to tell Jane about the strange pull he felt toward the Blankenship home, and about how after he bought the place he started to hear noises, then to see things. "You saw for yourself. The spirits, they're real."

"I never thought... well, I guess..." Jane stammered, but let him continue.

He told her about his onslaught of dreams, the most telling dream revealing the details of the murder of Horace and Eunice Blankenship.

"The men chasing us were bounty hunters?"

"Yes. Ethan Cartwright, his toady Arthur Scully, and a set of triplet brothers."

"They're the men chasing us?"

"Yes. And no, I have no idea how this is possible."

"If I didn't see what I saw at your house, I would never believe--wait, did you say Cartwright?"

"I know. Jasper. It's his father, Jane."

"Why didn't you tell me any of this sooner?"

"Because it's just like you said, you wouldn't have believed unless you'd seen it. It's crazy--the whole damned story. I could have told you after I met with Greta--that's when things started making sense to me. But I didn't want you to learn a family secret of mine. I think it's my family secret that's caused me to feel such a connection with the Blankenships. Why they might have chosen me to help them."

"Don't tell me, you're a son of one of those sons'a bitches?"

"No, nothing like that. Do you remember when I said my grandmother came to stay with my family?"

"How could I forget?"

"Well." He paused, but before he could have second thoughts, he blurted it out, "It turns out she was colored."

Three feet away, there was a scratching noise and a small flash of sparks. The flame danced from the cigarette lighter, shedding light on a face beset with quickly healing lesions and gaping wounds. It was one of the overall-clad triplets. He was laughing to himself, apparently proud to have gotten so close without them knowing.

"This whole time we been chasing you, I never did know you was a nigger. But then again, only a nigger would run away like you did." The man's laughter sprayed tobacco juice from his grizzled maw.

Jane glanced at Cooper before returning her frightened gaze to the undead bounty hunter. In that brief glance he saw such unabated disappointment. As if he had just revealed that he'd spent the day of the potluck (was that really today? it seemed so long ago) pissing in her iced tea.

When he looked back at the bounty hunter, Cooper had just enough time to duck under a swiping blow from the hunter's machete. It whirred an inch from his scalp and crashed into the wall behind him.

Jane screamed, no longer caring to hide their location. He took Jane's hand once again (did he feel reluctance in her touch?) and they took off down the tunnel as the bounty hunter worked to free the machete. Cooper glanced over his shoulder. Having placed the cigarette lighter in a nook in the wall, the bounty hunter's anger welled-- his mouth sputtered oaths and spit as he worked the blade free--just as his brethren closed in bearing torches.

Several long minutes passed with their hearts racing madly. The other bounty hunters joined the machete-wielding triplet as they took up the pursuit. Their healing bodies moved more swiftly than aboveground and they quickly gained ground. A sense of hopelessness grew within Cooper, but after turning down a branch in the tunnel, light was shining ahead, bright light that could only signal a large gathering of people.

"Gonna get you, nigger!"

SEVEN

Almost to Charles's disappointment, the Bradshaw girl hadn't fought him. Oh sure, at first she cried a bit, tried prying her arm away from him, but he made sure she didn't get any disagreeable ideas. He raised the carving knife at her. At first she'd shied away, shielding her face with a flung hand, but then he lowered the blade to her belly. When that notion settled in, the starch fell off her convictions. She became timid as a lamb. From the time he shoved her into his wagon, and even as they entered the Underground from a hidden tunnel entrance near the town dump, she didn't try anything.

Torchlight reflected the hatred simmering in the girl's eyes. Five feet away and draped in shadow, she crossed her arms and shifted on the coarse limestone floor. She didn't look away, not for a moment, as if her scathing stare alone could scar him. He paid her no mind; in fact, he would accept whatever vengeance her mind toyed with. He deserved no less.

He mirrored her positioning on the floor, but with his back to the wooden door he so often visited when dark moods swept over him. "You look sweet as a peach."

She spit in his face, quick as a snake strike. He didn't bother to wipe it away as he chuckled to himself.

With the knife pressed against her belly, she'd barely made a peep the whole way. Probably trying to think of a way to outmaneuver a drunk man getting drunker by the minute.

But, oh, that would never happen.

His thoughts were never so clear as when he could scarcely stand and his words were all a jumble. His inebriated actions might not mirror his thoughts, but drink allowed him time to think, to ponder, to self pity.

As if she could read his mind, Mabel scraped her claws on her side of the rough door. She whimpered, a gruff choke of corrupted flesh.

At hearing Mabel for the first time, the girl jumped as if she'd sat on a pushpin.

"Cha-chaaa."

"I'm here, love. Always here for you." He touched the door, longing to touch his wife's cheek and the delicate line of her neck, yearned to pull her to him. He swigged from a new bottle he'd taken from under the seat of his wagon. The cheap 'shine was still high in the bottle, just below the level of the narrow neck. He was never so happy or miserable as when he had a full bottle, and in the Underground he had time enough to ponder, time enough for eternity to come and go.

"Sorry for my rudeness. Wanna pull?" He offered the girl the bottle. For the first time since he knocked on the door of the Fowler home, she looked terrified. Her eyes were wide and she reflexively placed her hand over the swell of her belly. He waited for her response, and she eventually shook her head no.

She cried softly. Her hatred bled away and she didn't seem so confident now in her chances of escaping.

"Char-char-char!" Mabel cried out, and as always, he heard a meek remnant of her former voice. "Charrrr-les!"

He unsteadily closed with the girl until he loomed over her, looking down the angle of his nose. "You ready for this?" he asked the girl.

He hadn't told her his intentions, but she wasn't waiting to find out. She took a stumbling stride, but only one. It was easy. He reached for a long lock of blonde hair, grabbed it like a horse's reins, and heeled her to the floor.

She screamed so loud it popped his ears.

"Char-Char-Charles!" Mabel echoed the girl's scream. She began pummeling herself against the door, but when he had constructed it he had used the finest timbers. She would pulp herself before breaking through.

Charles shook his head, trying to clear the swimming numbness. He tightened his grip on the girl's hair, wrapping it around his fist a couple times. Using one arm, he pulled her over to the door.

Fearing he would rip out her hair at the roots, she half walked along with him.

He reluctantly set down his bottle and used his free hand to reach inside his shirt for the key hanging on its twine necklace. He ripped it off, and never thinking he'd willingly remove it from his body, an odd despair settled over him. Neither the girl struggling at his feet, nor his shrieking undead wife behind the door, would let him dwell on any thought or emotion for more than a split second.

"Please, please, stop! Whatever you're doing, please, don't." Snot dribbled down the girl's lip, mixing with tears.

"Charles!" Oh, his poor Mabel. Sounding so normal, so alive. Hearing her voice reassured him that this was the right thing to do. It made everything all right.

As he worked the key into the lock, Mabel slammed into the door. He nearly dropped the key, but he squeezed it, stabbed it into the lock, turned.

How easily everything could have fallen apart if he would have dropped the key.

"*Please!* I'm begging you, I won't tell anyone."

The key engaged with a click he felt but couldn't hear over all the hysterics.

The door flew open and a shadow seemed to fall in its wake. Then he saw her sharp nails flailing, her ashen skin, eyes wild and seeking.

He shielded himself with the girl's body. She screamed and writhed in his arms, trying to get away. Mabel was shredding and tearing into the girl as if she were a plaything thrown into the pit. But he held fast, more out of a sense of preserving his own safety than anything. The girl screamed once more, more shrill and maddening than any of the others, but it was her last. Mabel swiped her claws across the girl's throat, and her voice was silenced.

Maybe it was instinct. Maternal instinct. Or perhaps some small part of her brain still functioned on a human level, but Mabel halted her assault, stepping away from the girl, apprising her as an artist would a canvas.

As the girl's body fell to the floor, Mabel looked at Charles.

He extended a trembling hand to touch his wife's cheek when she stepped closer. She flinched at his warmth, appeared ready to snap at him with her vicious teeth. But she didn't. Her eyes held his, and she *did* understand. In that moment, it felt like all those years ago, when she could look into his eyes, knowing exactly his intentions.

EIGHT

None of the knowledge passed on to Arlen gave him any forewarning that he would see Ellie Banyon and Jacob Fowler lurking in the shadows of the Underground. They seemed raw with fear as they bumbled their way down the tunnel. When he heard their approach, he didn't know who it was. Not wanting his destiny so easily derailed, he pressed flat into a vertical crevasse. A handful of uncertain strides and they were upon him, walking side by side, inches from his hiding spot. At first he didn't know who they were, but his vision was well adjusted to limited light. To conserve fuel he would often work his gopher hole in little or no light once he found a ripe vein to tap, digging at it by feel. He thought about calling out to them--they had both been nice to him, and now more than ever he valued those who had acted so graciously-- but decided against it the last second. He didn't want to have to explain his reason for being Underground or what he was carrying. His rucksack was heavy with dynamite. If they got hurt, which he thought was more likely than not, he would feel bad, but that couldn't be helped.

He listened, waited. When he figured they were gone, he waited five minutes more. Then he left his hiding place, listened again, then went on his way. He was close, he felt it in his bones. They ached from the damp. The air was laden with the smell of it, earthy, moldy. Cleansing. He needed to find a single wall, but it had to be the correct wall. Otherwise, it would just be a tremor rumbling through the tunnels. Maybe there would be smoke or a collapsed stretch of tunnel, but little more. Once he found the right place to stash his bundle, there would be a lot more than just a little trembler.

He'd found the six sticks of dynamite in a damp crate in an abandoned shaft of the Grendal mines the previous spring. He almost didn't bother opening the crate; it was oily and sodden, but when he unwrapped the oil-clothed bundle inside, the sticks were dry as bone. They must have been there a considerable amount of time since they had a timing wick instead of a plunger detonator. Those sort of things hadn't been used since…

…the mines opened in the 1840s, and even then, those wicks were quickly abandoned for more modern, safer detonators…

He knew this information as if he'd been there wearing his helmet with its candle flaring on its brim, crawling through the deplorable murk of the early mine.

Recalling whose knowledge he just accessed would be easy if he tried, but he didn't have time to waste. His fingers fluttered against the uneven rock walls, ten independent divining rods searching for a sweet spot. He closed his eyes despite the darkness, concentrating, calculating, understanding.

He never told his mom about his find. At the time, he didn't think she'd let him keep the explosives, but maybe she knew all along. She always seemed to know what was on his mind. So he'd locked the dynamite away for the most opportune time to use it. There wasn't a lot of it; he'd figured if he'd ever come across a large vein in his gopher hole, he'd use the sticks to blow it wide and get to its root. Strike enough coal to keep his mom comfortable in her waning years. Now that she was gone (I miss you already, Mom) would there be a more opportune time?

A spreading numbness in his fingertips quickly became a thrumming vibration. He could sense it in his fingers, his arms, the sound of it seemed to fill his ears. His memories. His family's memories. Rushing water, violent, kinetic. He pressed his hands flat to the wall, the tips of his index fingers meeting, his thumbs also, as if he were about to push the wall in and let loose the stored energy hidden behind it all these many millennia.

Behind this wall, the underground lake. Waiting.

NINE

"Ellie, you won't tell anyone what I did, will you?" The guilt had
gotten to him, enough so that he broke their silence. He didn't know
how much time had elapsed since they saw the living remains of that
colored man, but he couldn't stop thinking about the total lack of sound
after he pushed him into the lightless abyss.

"I didn't see nothing, Jacob." For once Ellie sounded younger than
her age. Normally, talking to her was like talking to someone from his
own class at school, but now he was reminded of the fact that she was
five years younger than him.

School. Class. He couldn't imagine rejoining his schoolmates when
the school year started in a month. "Whatever happened, you wouldn't
have done nothing wrong. You always do the right thing."

He felt better for a few seconds then realized that wasn't true. If he
always did the right thing, he would've done something, anything, to
prevent what happened to George (and possibly his brother), and he
wouldn't worry his mother so often. She didn't deserve it; she'd been
through too much trauma in her life and had withstood every wave of it.
Just as soon as they got out of this, he would hug her, ask her to forgive
him for all he'd done, and do his best not to bother her nerves another
day of her life.

The torch's flame was once again dying, and there was little for him
to do. The fabric trick worked for a few minutes, then the light would
quickly peter out. They would soon again have to walk in complete
darkness.

Fretting over the dying torch, he heard noises coming from branches
in the tunnel. It didn't appear that Ellie noticed it. She was just a
walking, blinking, scared little girl, not ready or willing to take on any
more of the unknown. He tried to steer their path to avoid the sound.

They were voices, he could tell now. Rising and falling in volume and intensity. It sounded like an animal articulating with a human voice. Then came the sound of metal impacting stone, followed by a high pitched scream. A familiar scream. His mom.

"Miss Fowler!"

"Shh! Quiet. I have to hear... wait, there it is. It's this way. Let's go!"

"What's she doing down here?"

"How would I know? Be quiet."

"Maybe she followed us down here."

They followed a sharp-turning left bend, then a less severe right. There was light ahead. Rich, warm and golden. At the same time, his torch gave up its flame. He tossed it aside.

"There's people ahead. I bet Dr. Thompson's there. We're saved, Jacob!"

He didn't respond, but he did feel a rush of relief knowing they weren't just drifting farther into the earth with no end in sight.

There was a soft noise behind them as if someone had kicked a rock. Before Jacob could turn around to investigate, a hand reached around from behind him, slapping over his mouth. From the choked scream next to him, the same thing happened to Ellie. He felt instant rage. They had come so far, had done so well to stay hidden.

His mom was in trouble. Somewhere close. And someone was keeping him from helping her. He started to struggle, jerking from side to side, searching for a weak point in his captor's hold.

Jacob's shoulder knocked into Ellie's as the person pulled them against his chest. Both filth and a trace of dread emanated from their attacker.

"Shh," a quavering voice spoke as the person leaned over their shoulders. "Don't say nothing, knucklehead."

The hand eased from Jacob's mouth and it was all he could do to stifle the volume of his voice. "Jimmy? Is that you?"

His brother answered by hugging them both.

"Jimmy? Hey, Jimmy?" Jacob said after several moments.

"What is it?"

"You stink worse than a pig sty."

"Sorry 'bout that. Been awhile since my last bath."

"Mom's in trouble. She's up ahead."

"I know, that's why we can't go that way."

"What do you mean? We can't just leave her."

"We're not. We can't just storm down the tunnel like that. Not this tunnel. There's a better way that's quieter and more roundabout."

"But, Jimmy--"

"Jacob, you listen to me. You don't understand what you've gotten yourself into. They will kill you without batting an eye. They don't care that you're a kid, or Ellie, either. They'd kill you like--"

"Like they did George," Ellie said, and it wasn't a question at all, but confirmation of what she'd been thinking for a while.

"Yeah, like George."

They all embraced, no hint of embarrassment ruining the moment for Jacob. He had longed to see his brother again, more than anything, and now here he was.

"I missed you, Jimmy."

"I missed you, too. We better get going. We'll find Mom, then get you out of here."

TEN

Cooper held Jane as they cowered in the middle of the high-walled pit. Blood stains patched the rough ground and walls. The group of men who captured them (and killed Greta, and oh God, George and possibly Jimmy, too) gathered at the pit's mouth, animatedly discussing their fate. Their appearances were returning to normal; rot receded, wounds healed, but Cooper thought they sure were an ugly lot just the same. When they were at their most degraded, he couldn't distinguish one man from another, but now he could easily size them up. Two of the men were identical, he realized, the same as they appeared in his dreams. Two of three identical brothers who stormed the Blankenship home in search of runaway slaves. They looked like misplaced farmers. These two were the most vehement of the bunch. They raised their fists in anger as they vented their wrath. They spit into the pit, disgusted with intruders in what they termed their "Paradise."

Every time they mentioned his "nigger blood," Jane winced at his side. Trembling as she looked above, her eyes caught firelight. She had yet to react to his pronouncement. He feared he might have misjudged her. They wouldn't be in this whole mess if he hadn't opened his big mouth. Jane wouldn't be shying away from looking at him if he would have kept his secret to himself.

But her clammy hand fell into his, and he clutched it, and for the briefest moment, it was like none of this was happening.

"They're going to kill us," she said angrily.

"If we let them." He tried to sound more courageous than he felt. A rock blurred by his shoulder, cracked against the wall behind them. The man who threw the rock wore an unabashed grin. Cooper's courage was swiftly fleeting. There was no place to hide, no way to scurry up the walls without being attacked and thrown back down to break their necks.

Jane inhaled sharply. He followed her line of sight to the gathering people, now standing three deep all around them. Of all the people, one person focused Jane's attention.

The woman stood out as she had when Cooper saw her in the normal aboveground world. Luscious lips painted red, flowing hair catching and holding the dim surrounding light. An alluring figure, yet one glinting with barely controlled anger.

Thea Calder.

She saw that they had taken note of her, and it seemed as if the crowd did also. There was a temporary ebb in the volume of the throng, broken when Thea bunched up her fists and stormed off, the crowd parting before her like a split seam in fabric. The crowd roared as if making up for the momentary quiet, before finding a steady static hum.

Slurs and spit and more rocks hurled into the pit. Cooper and Jane huddled low, covering their heads with their hands and forearms. This caused another roar to ripple through the crowd, this one tinged with laughter.

Yes, yes you *are* getting to us, Cooper thought.

A voice cut through the rest. Confident, somehow mirthful, Cooper recognized the voice from his dreams, and just recently, as the leader of the bounty hunters. Ethan Cartwright. "You two make a wonderful couple, I've gotta give you that. Ted Cooper. That's a white man's name. You have your white skin, your greasy white man's hair. You have white man's money, yet, you're a nigger. How about that, friends? Vic Borland heard it from his own mouth. That'll show you what they'll do, what they'll try to get away with. But it never works out the way they want, taking and taking and taking some more, taking right from the white man for his own. It never works.

"And you, Jane Fowler, cowering in filth with your arms draped over a nigger, when all these years you wouldn't let a white man come within an arm's length. Toiling along at your pathetic farm since your husband's demise, all these years acting more a man than not, not even attempting to keep your place. Makes you question things, folks. It surely does. What really happened to Dwight Fowler? How convenient a death he had! You, taking up his plow, his sweat and toil, taking up the burden of your land as if you were a man. Makes you wonder if Jane Fowler would rather take up with someone of the fairer sex, doesn't it?"

A grumble flowed through the crowd, agreeing with their leader. She no longer looked at the crowd. She dipped her face to her palms, sobbing.

"These two are vermin. Deserving of each other, deserving the same fate--" His speech became a garbled scream. Cooper looked up and saw someone attacking Ethan. A long knife handle protruded from Ethan's neck, and a group of angered men were prying the attacker away from their leader.

"This must end!" the attacker shouted, his voice drowned by the shocked clamor of Ethan's followers. Cooper saw clearly the gray wispy hair cut in a blunt Magee haircut, and the angular frame of an old man unfamiliar with manual labor. But he'd never seen such rage in the man or the vigor in which he moved. Dr. Thompson lunged with a blood-soaked hand for the knife sticking from Cartwright's neck. His fingers closed on the slick handle and held. The doctor's eyes lit up in triumph as he twisted the blade and tugged the wound wider.

"I will end this, Ethan. Even if I have to cut your head from your shoulders!"

Ethan's eyes boggled as his blood poured down his front. Thompson yanked back on the knife and a crimson spray arched down into the pit. He struck again near the original wound, driving the blade to the hilt. The room was strangely quiet. Ethan's followers stood back, unsure what to do, or perhaps even glad for the attack. Many in the crowd stepped away, as if it were possible for them to be sickened by the sight of blood.

"This must end! You--"

Ethan mustered his strength and punched the doctor in the Adam's apple, silencing him. Thompson went over in a heap, grasping his crushed throat. Two of the Borland brothers rushed over and grabbed the doctor by either arm, securing him long after any practical need. The old man's face was creased with veins, his skin darkening to purple as his air flow ceased.

Ethan took hold of the knife handle and pried it from his neck. Blood dripped steadily from his drenched shirt, but his strength never appeared to ebb.

"Foolish old man." Ethan kicked the doctor under the jaw, sending him tumbling back.

The doctor struggled to his knees at the lip of the pit, grasping at Ethan's pant cuffs.

Ethan squatted to the doctor's level and took hold of his chin, staring into his eyes as he suffocated.

"Do me a favor," Ethan said between gritted teeth. "Say hello to my son." Cartwright slapped Thompson and he cartwheeled into the pit, crashing a short distance from Cooper and Jane, dead on impact. Jane flinched next to Cooper and backed away from the body.

A nervous hiss passed through the crowd, but Ethan barely missed a beat. Blood flooded through his fingers as he held a hand to his neck. He cleared his throat and spit into the pit. The crowd's energy began to rise again. Ethan's voice was weaker, but still vehement: "So be done with it. The world, our Paradise, will be a better place without them. All three of them, in fact. And anyone else who chooses to stand against me will follow suit."

The words were barely out of his mouth when a renewed barrage of stones flew.

They pounded Cooper's flesh and fell dully to the floor of the pit. A large rock smashed into Jane's forehead. Her eyes rolled and she fell backward as if flung down by a rubberband. Her head bounced on the pit floor. She shuddered, then lay still. Pelting rocks stung his skin, but he still managed to crawl to her. He tried shielding her from the worst of it, hoping she hadn't received a mortal wound.

ELEVEN

They skirted around the area where Jacob and Jimmy's mother had screamed, drifting farther from the light. Jacob would have simply sprinted blindly into the fray, but Jimmy seemed to know the tunnels and the importance of stealth in such a place. He was also acting strange. Jacob couldn't put a finger on it right away. But as they moved cautiously, walking with deliberate vigilance, pausing to listen, walking another ten feet before stopping yet again, it became obvious. His brother was uncharacteristically skittish with fear. He jumped at the slightest sound, waved for their little group to lean against the wall, melting into deeper shadows. It didn't matter how he was acting, Jacob would still follow Jimmy. This was Jimmy, after all. His brother. His hero.

A pungent odor wafted through the tunnel that assaulted his senses and made him more reluctant to move. It was decay, not old and desiccated, but new, fresh and wet with rot. Ellie scrunched her face and held her nose. Jimmy seemed unfazed.

"This tunnel follows directly around to what they call their Paradise. I'm pretty sure that's where they're keeping Mom. Once we free Mom and get you guys aboveground, I'll go back and free the others," Jimmy said.

That word piqued Jacob's ear. Paradise. Down here. In the gloom, in the damp, with screams echoing down mysterious corridors. "Paradise, what's that?"

"That's what they call it. It'll be their main gathering place. Kinda like a town square."

Ellie stopped dead in her tracks. "There's others down here? Other prisoners?"

"Harold and Edwina. They're imprisoned too. I can't leave without them. Harold helped me escape from my chains."

"Let's find Mom first," Jacob said, trying to keep focus on what was most important.

"Of course," Jimmy said, then held up a hand yet again to quiet them so he could listen. When he was satisfied, he waved them on. Periodically, lighted tunnels branched away from the one they were keeping to, dimly lighting their way.

"Who are they, the others?" Ellie asked. Still swooning from the cloying stench, she spoke with her hand covering her nose and mouth.

"A family. There's Harold and his daughter, Edwina. Benjamin, Edwina's husband, he was here too, until recently. I haven't seen him, not since they took him away when he tried to save me from being attacked. Harold thinks they did something to him. Something terrible," Jimmy paused, as if recalling the gruesome details. Jacob thought about the man/torso, the living person he had shoved into the pit, perhaps as much to rid his sight of him as to ease his suffering. He was going to ask his brother if the other prisoners were coloreds, but decided against it.

"But maybe he's free now," Jimmy continued. "Free or dead, either option is better than what happens down here. They've been enslaved for a long time. Too long."

"Any amount of time would be too long," Ellie said.

Jimmy looked down at her with unwavering affection. He put his hand on her head, softly, as if he didn't want to muss her hair. Jacob knew how easy it was to love Ellie's innocence and strength. She really was the sister he never had.

"Who attacked you, Jimmy?" he asked. He wondered who could have done that to Benjamin, if the man/torso had been Benjamin.

The tunnel curved even more sharply back toward where their mother had screamed. He hoped it was the right direction. He already understood how easy it was to become lost down here.

His brother, still looking at Ellie, grimaced as he turned to face him. "Just two men. Two really bad men."

Thinking Jacob was satisfied with such a vague answer, he returned his attention to the girl. "What's wrong, Ellie? Do I need a bath that bad?"

Jacob saw a glimpse of Jimmy's old silliness.

"Don't you smell that?"

Before he could answer, a voice issued from the darkness ahead, little more than a whisper: "He took it. He took it, Jimmy. Took it from me."

Jimmy held up his arms to halt their progress.

Strides scraped across the floor, a slow grating of bone on sandpaper. "Jimmyyyy..."

A wash of light was at their feet, a distant torch's farthest reach.

The girl stepped into the light, her face pasty white--not just pale, *bloodless*. Blood stained her lower half, from just below the swell of her breast to nearly touching her feet. A rent traveled the same distance through the fabric of her dress. Jacob didn't want to acknowledge this girl. That would make it all too real. Next to him, Ellie yelped as if slapped, then slumped to the floor, having fainted.

Jimmy. Poor Jimmy. He just stood and stared at Louise--Jacob could deny it no longer, it was Louise, and she was in sorry shape, and her belly was no longer taut and rounded--then his brother started trembling, finally stepping forward, catching the girl in his arms.

"Thank, God. I found you, Jimmy... He took the baby. It hurt so... s-so bad, but... but..." She shook free of his embrace, stared into his eyes. She placed her hands where they used to rest at the crest of her pregnancy, but they encountered empty air. "It was a boy, just like you wanted. A little boy, oh he's so small, and he's screaming and squalling and afraid. He needs me, Jimmy. He's going to starve, and it's so cold down here--it's *freezing*."

"Who, Louise, who did this to you?" His voice was quiet, yet firm, trying to console while still cutting through her shock. Jacob didn't know how Jimmy could be so rational when he himself had trouble staying upright and cognizant. "Who took our baby, Louise?"

"Banyon," she said finally. Her eyes fell to Ellie's slumped form. Jacob didn't think Louise was aware of where she was, or that she was looking at the daughter of a killer. Her eyes rolled back and it was like an invisible hand swiped her soul from her flesh. She was a thing now, an object--no longer living--merely blood and bones and wasted youth. Jimmy caught her under the arms, eased her to the floor. He kissed her closed eyelids, one after the other. When he stood, the rage in his eyes made Jacob take a step back. Rational thought was gone, caution thrown out along with it. Hands clenched into tight white fists, he headed in the direction from which Louise had emerged. Before Jacob could call out, his brother was lost in the darkness, consumed with still darker intent.

TWELVE

Arlen snugged the dynamite bundle at the wall's base. He lit a wooden match, transferring the flame to the timing wick. Once certain it caught, he snuffed the match, then turned to walk away. The sour sulfur odor of the match trailed after him. The wick sparked and spit as it ran its length, the duration of its life a matter of a few short minutes.

THIRTEEN

Jacob felt torn. Should he follow his brother? He didn't want to let him out of sight, not after fearing he would never see him again, but Ellie was groggily murmuring to herself as she recovered on the floor. He couldn't leave her, either.

"Wha... what happened?" She sat up, still woozy.

He went to her side and put a hand at her elbow to help her stand. "Are you okay? You didn't hit your head, did you?"

"No. No, I think I'm fine." Ellie saw Louise. Thankfully, when she died she fell forward at an angle that hid the worst of her wounds. Her awkward position was the only outward sign that she wasn't simply sleeping. No one would choose to sleep like that. "Oh, Louise. Who could do something like that?"

He recalled Louise's final words, but didn't repeat them. "I don't know. Jimmy went to find out."

"What do we do now, Jacob?" she asked as tears flowed down her dirt-smudged face. Jacob was tiring of seeing her cry. He didn't see it as a character flaw by any means; he simply wished she wouldn't be thrust into situations that compelled her to cry.

"I... I just don't know."

Sitting close for warmth, they were as lost and tentative as two kids could ever be. Water dripped nearby, methodically, maddeningly. Next to them, Louise began to stir.

FOURTEEN

Jimmy charged down the tunnel, angry at himself for destroying his life, his future with Louise, their baby. Their baby boy. A fragment of him wanted to feel proud, but the feeling was buried by the rage compelling him through the twists burrowing into the earth.

When he came to the Banyon home in the middle of the night to share one last boyhood adventure with George, he knew that Louise was pregnant. But he couldn't face reality, not just yet. He just had to go searching for the mythical White Bane.

How could I be so stupid?

He wasn't sure how long he had been hearing the sound; rage thrummed through his ears, an all-encompassing claustrophobia that made him feel submerged inside a heart's chamber, with blood flowing over his skin instead of air.

But then he heard it. A cooing sound. Cutting through the morass.

Ahead, a feeble light outlined figures with foul luminescence. A torch wavered on the cave floor, cast off and dying. A wooden door was open wide leading to an unseen chamber. He'd found the source of the stench Ellie had complained about. Living rot and corrupted flesh, she huddled on the floor cupping something in her scabrous pale arms.

She was cooing.

The incongruous nature of an inhuman beast attempting such soothing sounds halted Jimmy.

An amorphous shape next to the undead woman shifted, stepping toward Jimmy and the sallow light. The light articulated his features. Scrubby salt and pepper beard, bleary eyes, paunchy stomach, skinny limbs. Charles Banyon raised a hand to stop Jimmy, and for some reason, Jimmy stopped in his tracks. Charles looked back at the cooing form, his lips flirting with a grim smile that quickly disappeared.

The woman rocked the bundle in her arms, too quickly, too *ungently*. She didn't know what she was doing. Even if she wanted to, she would be incapable of giving maternal care. That particular trait was reserved for the living.

The bundle twitched in her arms, squawked pathetically, then fell silent. Eventually, the cooing stopped, too. The cold air, laden with anticipation, became still weightier with the passing seconds.

"CHRRR!" the thing grunted and stood. The bundle fell to the floor, tumbled away, forgotten. Its contents unrolled partway from the blood sodden rag, but didn't move. A tiny arm fell out, hanging at an impossible angle. "CHRRR!" she grunted again, rising to her full height.

Jimmy saw her eyes (how could someone lacking a soul have such emotion, such fury?), and vaguely recalled a similar face. A face imbued with warmth and hope and tranquility. It was Charles Banyon's wife, Mabel. Long dead. No details from his recollection existed in the woman standing before him. But it was her, no doubt, and somehow she still moved. Somehow she had held his baby boy as he died. She had taken what little time his child had in this world, had looked on his face with those crazed eyes as he took his last breath.

Mabel grabbed her husband's shirt collar, pulling him close to her, as if to embrace him. She pinned him to the wall, forcing the breath from his lungs. She went at him with her long, razor-like nails, ripping fabric, flesh, burrowing rails of muscle and bone. Blood pulsed from his wounds, falling in a wash, forming a growing puddle at his feet.

He never put up a fight. His expression, while pained, never wavered as he gazed with ill-fitting affection at his wife. His life was draining as quickly as his blood.

Jimmy didn't have long. Crouched low, keeping to the shadows, he reached the rag-draped boy and rewrapped him, as if his actions could stave off the cold. He hefted the form to his body, and oh God was he a light thing! Not much more a burden than the rags themselves. Before he was seen, he turned away from the Banyons. The baby felt like bones in a sack against his chest. Hollow bird bones, undeveloped, fragile, and... dead.

He was crying. He couldn't help it. He never thought he would ever want this baby. He was too young, not sure yet what he would do with his life, but now he wanted his boy to be alive and sighing in his arms like a contented, thriving bundle of joy.

Eyes blurred with tears, he didn't want to look back. Seeing any more just might break something inside him.

But then a brief explosion flashed behind him. Loud enough to ring his ears even at a distance. It *had* been brief, and he *did* look back, and he was astonished that a shotgun blast could be so earth shaking.

One of those Borland brothers wore a wicked grin, the barrel of his weapon threading smoke through the air. The blast had catapulted Mabel Banyon into a wall. She slid to the floor, painting the wall with a crimson streak like a misplaced shadow.

Charles was still alive. Barely. Flayed bands of flesh trembled on the floor next to Mabel. It disgusted Jimmy to see him still trying to get at that Borland brother. His loyalty to his wife remained even though she had effectively killed him.

Borland laughed and launched a shit-brown gob of spit in Charles's face. He waited until that hopeless mess on the floor got real close, then placed the gun barrel against his forehead and pulled the trigger. The concussion of the blast and barrel flash assaulted Jimmy's senses.

Charles no longer moved. When the ringing in Jimmy's ears dissipated, he could hear Borland laughing even harder.

Mabel's knife-sharp fingernails stopped his laughter. At once, the sound seized inside him as if he were choking on a hambone. Mabel had circled around to his side so he couldn't see her movement in the shadows (how a beast can be so cunning but can't properly rock a baby, Jimmy thought), then jammed her nails into his chest, wriggled them with a twisting motion, impaling him to the third knuckle. She coiled her wrist as if searching for something, and Borland let out a bewildered shriek of pain. Mabel probed some more, each movement punctuated by a more perplexed yet fading cry from Borland.

Jimmy didn't wait for Mabel to notice him. He turned back, heading toward Jacob, Ellie and… Louise. He had almost forgotten about Louise. How could he forget about Louise? His love, his child's mother. She had died in his arms. Only minutes ago.

Now she could never leave.

What had he done to deserve this? He was damned to never leave this place as well, to never walk under the warm sun, never enjoy the fragrance of spring carried by the wind. And his family, stunted before it could find its roots.

Sprinting through the near-dark, he resolved to not spend his damnation alone. Louise was dead, but would she have yet risen? The thought gave him the briefest, dimmest spark of hope. But he clung to it as if it were a blazing nova. It was all he had.

FIFTEEN

Within seconds Cooper would lose consciousness, and once that empty black wall descended on him, he would never wake.

Pinned beneath him, Jane moaned. Through the murk, he reached out to touch her face. The rock that had hit her above the right eye had left a nasty welt. His fingers came away bloody, but she was twitching below him. Remarkably, her eyes flickered open.

"Don't move," he said, the dark veil of unconsciousness thrown aside.

"I don't think I could if I tried."

"If we don't move, they'll think we're dead."

"My skin--"

"It's tingling?"

"Yes. What is it?"

"I think, somehow, it's healing. I feel it, too."

"What is this place?"

Cooper didn't have a chance to respond. A concussive blast trembled through the cave floor, through the walls, shook the ceiling until still more rocks and still larger boulders, collapsed in on them. The air itself vibrated with violent energy. A blanketing wind throttled down the tunnel, came crashing full-tilt into the people gathered at the lip of the pit, sending a handful over the edge. Screams rose from above; rocks fell; people flailed against each other to get away. The world was chaos. The ground trembled, then again with less force, and then a final time a faded echo of the first.

"What happened?" Jane huddle against Cooper's chest. While the ground no longer quaked, boulders still dislodged from above, thudding to the floor nearby.

Many of the torches had gone out. He could barely see. "Some kind of explosion. The walls are coming in." He grabbed her as he stood,

293

pulling them both flat against the wall, trying to make themselves as small a target as possible for falling debris.

The crowd was recovering. Dust showered down now with only intermittent stones. Whatever caused the explosion, it seemed to be behind them.

Four others were in the pit. Two women stood together, crying. An old man cupped his hands around his mouth, shouting for help from above. The women held one another, scurrying away when they noticed Cooper and Jane on the far side of the pit. They looked like they expected to be attacked or bludgeoned.

The fourth person was one of the bounty hunters who chased them from Greta's house. Blood flowed over his face from his gashed scalp, coating him in a red mask. His wicked grin was made more wicked by debris that had shattered most of his front teeth. He spit out the remains of teeth, and oblivious to the surrounding chaos, he advanced on them, flicking a machete at his side as if testing its weight.

Cooper stepped in front of Jane. They circled the pit as the bounty hunter stalked them with deliberate slowness.

Having heard the old man's screams for assistance, a kind soul tossed a thick rope down into the pit. Immediately, the two women began shoving each other to gain an advantage in reaching the rope first. They were soon scratching and clawing each other over who would first receive a lift to freedom. It was a catty thing, more bluster than anger, until a fingernail of the shorter of the two dug a furrow in the cheek of the other. This ended any possibility for a civil ending. Fists were thrown and landed with meaty thuds, hair was pulled and came loose at the bloody roots. The two ignored the saving rope, scourging one another during the time it would take to hoist both to safety one after the other.

After staring at the fight for a moment, the old man looped the rope around his waist, and with the help of those above, he crab-walked up the wall. As his spindly legs disappeared from view, a sound with the sudden ferocity of a dozen locomotives nearly deafened Cooper.

He covered his ears instinctively, but his eardrums popped as the tunnel's air pressure abruptly changed. Jane cried out, and though she stood just behind him, the sound came as a whisper through a paper cone.

The bounty hunter was ten feet away when the uproarious sound ripped through the tunnel. After briefly hesitating, he quickened his advance.

There was no place to go. No hiding place. This is the last second of my life, Cooper thought morbidly. The machete glinted through an upward arc, leaving Cooper with only enough time to meet the blade with an upraised forearm. He waited the inevitable bite.

It didn't come.

What did come was water. A raging flood as mighty as Neptune's thrown fist, it hurtled down from the tunnel above, pouring into the pit, catching the bounty hunter squarely in the chest. The force bent him in half backwards, and if not for the water's beast-like roar, Cooper would hear a dozen bones snapping. The man disappeared in a flume of white water that crashed into the far wall. The curve of the pit redirected the water's energy, swirling it around to scour the edges, flooding higher.

The water had lost some of its punch, but it still upended Cooper when it reached him. He lost contact with Jane, and as he struggled to keep his head above water, she went under, her face falling forward as if she had simply fallen asleep. The water lapped over her, still higher, rising to fill the pit. If Cooper didn't find her within seconds, she would never survive this.

SIXTEEN

Jimmy carried his dead son wrapped in the soiled rag. He heard their voices--bewildered and frightened and escalating in volume--long before he came upon them.

So Louise *had* risen.

He had hoped to reach them before it happened, if for no other reason than to prepare his brother and Ellie. But he was too late. Too late to save his son (his son... his son, would the boy ever have a name?), too late to shield Jacob and Ellie from the awful sight of Louise rising from the dead. His mother, she was down here too, and she'd been screaming in pain. Would he be too late to save her as well?

"Jimmy?" Louise's voice was stronger now than during her life's final moments.

There was a hesitation, but then Jacob said, "He's... he's not here. He left."

"Where? Where's Jimmy? I need him. Our boy, he was taken... taken by Banyon." Louise spoke the words Jimmy was hoping to never hear again, words he hoped Ellie would never have to hear.

"No, not Daddy. He would never. No! NO!"

Jimmy sprinted into the tunnel, the trio awash in meager light. All at once their gazes fell on him. Pinning him in place. Those stares seeking knowledge, truth, coherency. And then, as one, their eyes fell to the bundle in his arms.

"Jimmy!" Louise shouted and ran to him. He held her against his chest, the dead thing held between them.

She felt the bundle between them, understanding what it was. "Jimmy! You found him!"

"No. No, babe, I was too late. He's gone."

Ellie stepped toward them. "It's a lie, Jimmy. Why would she say something like that? Daddy would never do something so..." her own choked sob cut her off. Because she knew. No matter how hard the man had tried to live the straight and narrow, the gravid pull of darkness had an even stronger magnetism. Simple enough: she alone was not enough to keep him good.

Louise was still trying to pull away, stunned by knowing what he held in his arms. But he didn't let go. If anything, he held her more vehemently. He didn't want Ellie to see any more. Didn't want to let go of his first and only love. He wanted to never leave her side, he realized. He would never let her go.

"Ellie, please, don't." Jacob took hold of her arm.

She regained her voice. She trembled and stepped closer to him, "Say it, Jimmy. Say he didn't do it!" she screamed through streaming tears. Her wounded voice quaked. She was daring him to lie to her. As if lying to protect her feelings would confirm that her father was an evil man more so than the outward truth. She was challenging him, waiting his answer.

Jimmy didn't have a chance to speak. The explosion hammered through the tunnel, sending everyone sprawling.

Jacob fell atop Ellie and covered both their heads. Jimmy held fast to the unmoving bundle, Louise also still in his grasp. He didn't know what was happening, but if this was a final judgment sent down by some higher power, he didn't want to lose contact with his family. Jimmy leaned over--rocks peppering down in a violent hail--and pressed his lips against Louise's. She kissed him back, and her lips were still death-cold, stealing the warmth from him. A trail of blood had dried across her mouth, and he tasted the coppery tang, but he didn't care.

The explosion grumbled and growled, losing its strength. A nearby wall had partially collapsed, but for the most part, the area was clear of debris. Dust billowed from one far end of the tunnel, sweeping across them in a cool wash. It passed by and continued on, as if compelled to escape some further calamity.

"Is everyone okay?" Jimmy called out.

Jacob answered, walking from the settling dust toward Jimmy's voice. He had his arm around Ellie. Their faces were powdery white, like actors painted as ghosts for a stage play.

A thundering noise shook the walls; it was the violent rush of water, undoubtedly, as loud as Jimmy imagined it would sound going over Niagara Falls. Jimmy had always considered it the most daring feat to attempt, and he'd often dreamed about surviving the foolhardy plunge, but now with the sound so close, the idea seemed absurd.

He handed the baby to Louise, who held it close to her bosom. The walls themselves were shaking. He touched the rough surface, and he could feel the water rushing just on the other side of a thin rock wall, pounding, gouging, seeking further avenues to drown and scourge.

"This wall is gonna come in. Get moving!" Everyone followed him down a tunnel he knew would take them to higher ground. The wall wouldn't last long assaulted by the force of that water.

He reached out, held Louise's hand. "I thought I lost you."

"Never. Everyone said you ran away. That's what everyone was trying to tell me. That you went off to the army. But I didn't believe it."

"I'd never leave. Just wanted one last adventure. I'm sorry I was so stupid. I've ruined everything."

Every ten seconds or so Jacob looked back to make sure their group was intact. The way his little brother was handling things, Jimmy knew he could lead their family once aboveground. He was growing up. Maturing into a man. Much faster and less reluctantly than he had managed. It was a small comfort.

Jimmy nodded to him, urging him on. Jacob kept his arm around Ellie. She was holding up as good as could be imagined. Her family was gone now, too. And she'd just learned her father was a killer. Whatever came of this, he'd never let her know he'd also killed him, despite Benjamin's best effort to thwart his attack. Some things were better left unsaid.

He was damned to stay in this hell forever. But Louise, he still had Louise--

With distance, the roaring water diminished, but now the sound was intensifying again, increasing rapidly. It was so loud Jimmy didn't realize Louise was trying to speak to him. She yanked on his arm to get his attention.

He leaned over so she could yell into his ear. Even at such close proximity, it was hard to make out her words.

"What!"

"The baby's moving!"

No, no, I can't let this happen. To me yes, if it has to be anyone, let it be me, and Louise, if that's the only way I can be with her, let it be so. But not the baby. Not my boy!

His mind was jumbled with conflicting thoughts. He had to sort through the clutter, figure out how to handle this. All of this. It was nearly too much to take in at once.

The tunnel was splitting ahead. Jimmy knew where they were. There was a way to the surface in either direction.

Frightened by the coming violent wave, the group pulled tighter. "What's happened?" Jacob asked.

"The wall is gone, the tunnels are flooding."

"Oh no," Ellie said in a deflated voice.

Jimmy shouted to be heard, "You have to go. I couldn't live with myself if you didn't make it out of here."

"What do you mean? You're coming with, right?"

"Not yet. I want you two safe, but I still need to get Mom, not to mention Harold and Edwina. You get Ellie to the surface, get help, whoever will listen. Let them know what's happened."

Jacob looked like a child who was just told Santa didn't exist. His lip trembled. "But..."

Jimmy shook his head. Louise cried out at his side, and Jacob looked at the writhing bundle in her arms.

He understood immediately, even if he didn't comprehend the nature of the Underground. "Okay, Jimmy, but you better be right behind us," he said nervously, trying to be brave.

"We'll catch up to you."

"We can't leave you," Ellie said.

"We'll be fine. I know these tunnels and what paths to take to be safe. All you two have to do is stay left, stay left and keep climbing through to higher tunnels. You'll reach the surface in no time. Now go. I'll see you topside."

Before Jacob could be dismissed, he hugged Jimmy. He said something into his ear, but the rushing water was too loud for him to understand.

Long after Jacob and Ellie had turned away and were swallowed by the shadows, Jimmy wondered what those final words had been.

SEVENTEEN

Jacob labored climbing the tunnel's steep incline, and while rosy-cheeked and panting for breath, Ellie seemed to be holding up fine. Looking at her, you'd never think someone so young and frail-looking would be so resilient.

But she was pushing him to keep up with her. Surging water roared behind them, still gaining ground with the passing seconds. The prospects for escaping seemed so remote; if Ellie weren't here with him, he might have given up by now.

Remembering Jimmy's advice, they stayed on a leftward path, even when the direction seemed misguided. They reached an alcove that contained a pond lapping at a steep stone shore. Jacob searched the room, but could find no other way out. The raging water was once again nearly deafening.

He expected to see fear or possibly resignation in Ellie's eyes. Instead, the girl left his side, making her way to the water's edge.

"Ellie, what are you doing?"

"This is the way," she said, stepping into the water. Her face bunched up at the cold, but she took another step. She was thigh deep, and not turning back.

"There has to be another way."

"This is the direction Jimmy told us. Besides, those waves in the pond have to be coming from somewhere. They come right from that wall. There's a hole there, and since the waves are coming from inside it, it must be a tunnel. A way out." She kicked into a fluid swimming motion, not waiting for his response. In a few quick strokes, she was halfway to the tunnel.

He was unsure what to do. He wasn't the best swimmer, and they weren't certain that this was the right way to the surface. The sound of the approaching water made it hard to think.

"Will you look at what I've found," a voice said from behind him as a hand gripped his shoulder. Jacob didn't recognize the beady-eyed pudgy man. While the man smiled innocently enough, an axe handle swayed in his hand, while his grip tightened on his arm. He was no friend. "I thought I was the only one making a run for it."

The stranger raised the weapon and smashed it across Jacob's chest before he could react. The wind left him, and he curled up on his side on the floor. Ellie disappeared into the tunnel, unaware of the attack. If he had the breath to shout a warning to her, she probably wouldn't hear him over the raging water.

The water.

It was coming, finally flooding the lower tunnels (Oh, Jimmy, Mom, please, be okay), rising higher, ready to sweep them into its roiling slurry. He had to act. Now.

Fear chased away the clenching pain in his chest. If he didn't get away from this maniacal stranger, the water would certainly kill him. He had to move.

He stumbled from his stomach to his hands and knees, scuttling along as fast as he could toward the water.

Behind him, the man laughed. A couple strides and he lunged for Jacob, easily grasping his foot.

Jacob fell flat on his face. The man wrenched his ankle as if they were wrestlers performing at a carnival. Pain twisted him until he flipped to his back. Blood flowed down Jacob's lips, and his nose throbbed, possibly broken. He didn't feel it.

He looked up, seeing the man reel back with his axe handle.

Who is this guy? Doesn't he know the water'll snap him in two?

He obviously didn't, because he flung the axe handle down with full force, connecting with the meat of Jacob's thigh.

He screamed, screamed so hard and forcefully that he was instantly hoarse, but he subdued his reaction as best he could. He had to. The man was wheeling back for another blow.

With his arms at their highpoint, he was also at his most defenseless. Jacob struck, ignoring the shooting pain in his thigh. He managed a side kick that landed against the man's kneecap, crumpling him to the ground.

It wasn't much of a kick. He couldn't gather much leverage from his position on the floor and the pain in his leg seemed to be getting worse. The kick only stoked the man's rage. He retrieved his dropped weapon, and then crawled toward Jacob, wincing at his damaged knee.

Jacob didn't think twice. Despite the pain in his thigh, he stood, then half-ran, half-stumbled his way to the water's edge. Losing his balance, in the process of falling once again on his face, he pushed off the best he could, transforming the fall into a dive for the water. He splashed awkwardly on the flat of his stomach. His chest hurt where the axe handle had connected, but adrenaline was coating everything in a thrumming numbness. He barely felt the pain as he started swimming.

"God damn you, boy! I'm gonna hurt you for that. Gonna hurt you real bad." Jacob glanced back to see the man at the shore, gingerly stepping into the water.

Jacob reached the tunnel's mouth just as the stranger let out a startled, blood-curdling cry. A tremendous splash disrupted the water near the man's kicking legs, then he was pulled underwater.

What the hell?

Jacob had never seen anything like it. At first he didn't know what he was seeing, but then the man surfaced--just his flailing arm, one shoulder, half his face--before getting pulled under again. Something wide and translucent curled above the water, then a massive fishtail slapped the water's surface. The stranger surfaced just once more, but the fish's mouth, with its sharp, bladelike teeth, its snaking white whiskers flapping--had clamped onto his torso. The jaws closed off all remaining sound from the man. The fish went under, taking its prey with it.

White Bane? Jacob thought. The beast from Greta's stories? No one believed that story. Even the youngest children understood that the myth was intended to tingle the spine and caution against the perilous nature of the unknown.

But it was real. White Bane. Real.

It was gone. He never caught sight of the crazed man, nor the giant fish. Not a single white scale. The flooding waters reached the tiny alcove, a rioting wall of white water, and Jacob turned away for the tunnel, futilely trying to escape the inevitable. The water crashed into him less than a second later.

EIGHTEEN

"What are we gonna do, Jimmy?" Louise asked.

He had to look away; she would see the answer in his eyes.

They could stay down here with the baby, and God knows what would happen when the boy fully wakened. Or, they could reach the surface, leave this place behind, get their boy as far away from the Underground's cursed touch as possible.

"You know what would happen if we went to the surface?"

"I... I think so. It doesn't matter. We need to get him out of here."

She gave the answer he felt in his heart was the only path for them to take. They would take their son with them, escape the flooding water.

They would bury him. Give him a resting place that would never become unsettled.

The flood water was close, dangerously so. They would have to hurry.

"Let's go."

They held hands, winding their way through a narrow tunnel, heading to higher ground.

NINETEEN

Arlen thought he'd be dead by now. That would've been okay with him. He'd done his job by setting free the underground lake. The waves would purify the blighted depths. His mom would be proud of him. She *was* proud of him. He could feel it.

After lighting the timing wick, he'd aimlessly ambled away. Sometimes veering up inclines, sometimes descending, sometimes following curving spines in the tunnel that seemed to wrap around themselves. All the while he traveled in darkness, letting his mind wander, his only thoughts centering on his contentment.

Mom is so proud of me!

But as he walked--in the back of his mind awaiting the explosion--the air became cooler, downright cold. He soon entered a small chamber with a single candle burning low; though dim, the stark contrast to the previous impenetrable darkness stung his eyes. He blinked away the pain as his vision expanded to fill the room.

A hole covered most of the small room's floor, and from this hole, a bitter updraft gusted.

The panting, frigid breath of the devil, he thought, not sure where the notion originated, one of his ancestors obviously, but that wasn't important. He peered into the open maw, the wind frosting the sweat on his brow.

He first felt the blast through his feet.

Then a rock hit his shoulder, sending him to the ground. The earth quaked as if trying to purge itself of a violent sickness. Rocks tumbled all around him. The ones that fell into the open pit never made a sound.

He sat on his backside, resting his head on his arms propped on his knees. He waited for the explosion to weaken, and when it did, he waited in expectation of the coming flood.

Will it wash me away, down this endless frigid pit? he wondered. The thought didn't scare him. Nothing did anymore.

The water came sooner than he expected. He stood to face the curling waves, their constant collapse and rebirth.

The wave drained into the pit, inches from his feet.

Bodies bobbed in the water, mere debris taken into the plummeting maw. While he didn't care to save his own life, seeing his neighbors' bodies thrown about made him want to scream. He leaned into the flowing wave and timed a reckless swipe for one of the bodies, snagging it by the collar. Though a slim woman, her sodden clothes and momentum nearly sent him over. He yanked hard, and the body fell into his lap. The water continued to rush by, falling into the pit. Arlen was exhausted. He couldn't summon the strength to make another saving effort.

Warmth flowed through the woman's abraded cheek. Not only was she alive, but she had a caring, pure soul. He could see his grandmother's visions of this woman's future. She would accomplish great things, would be the bedrock for her family's coming generations.

When the flow eased, and he had room to maneuver from the small room, he hefted Jane Fowler onto his shoulder and started for the surface.

TWENTY

Jacob coughed. Flood water burned his lungs as his body tried to expel it. The sun was drying his clothes.

How am I alive? he wondered, yet again. Was it a miracle? He thought perhaps it was.

The water had hit him full-on in the back, and had carried him along, higher through twists and dips in the tunnel, then still higher, until the earth vomited him through a grass-veiled crevasse. The water spewed from the opening for a short while, then slowed to a trickle, before stopping completely. The flood had lost its punch.

He was alive.

And so was Ellie.

She sat on a mossy felled log, staring at him with a bemused expression. "I told you to follow me. I knew it'd lead to a way out."

Once the coughing fit subsided, he tested his bruised thigh. The leg took his weight. A gash bled across his nose, and each of his limbs felt blanketed with bruises. But nothing seemed broken. He gave her a half-hearted glare. "What now?"

"I don't know. Jimmy should be coming, right?"

"I don't think so. I think he's never coming out. I don't think anyone else is. Not even..." he couldn't say it, but it felt like a certainty that he would never see his mom again.

Ellie didn't respond right away, but he knew what she was thinking. Her dad was down there, too. He was never coming out, either. She turned away to walk down a narrow game trail. He hurried to catch up.

"I'm sorry, Jacob."

"Stop saying that. I don't want you to ever say that again."

"We need dry clothes."

"True."

"We can come back later, maybe bring along some food. We'll see who comes out."

He didn't like the idea, but it was something for them to do, something to keep them busy. Jimmy had told him to tell anyone who would listen about what had happened Underground. But if someone would listen long enough to hear the story and not think him crazy, would they be the trusting sort, the kind of person would didn't know about the evil happenings below their hometown?

No. They wouldn't tell their story to anyone. Not right away. Not right now. His emotions were simply too raw.

"Jacob! Look! Come quick!" Ellie cried out from around the next bend.

He skirted an impenetrable stand of underbrush and saw Ellie cradling his mom in her lap. Ellie looked deceptively like his mom when they found the body of her brother George. Was that only weeks ago?

But one detail was different in this setting. His mother was moving. She appeared to be gulping for air, as if she had just surfaced after a long time underwater. But no, she was simply overcome with emotion. Her chest hitched, her tears fell.

"Mom!" He ran to her, calling her again and again.

He hadn't seen Arlen Polk right away, but he was standing close by. His arms were folded, and he looked apprehensive, but he also wore a smile. He looked different, as if he was the only person in on a joke that he hoped to share with all. Arlen gave Jacob a nod, and Jacob returned it, finding a smile of his own forming.

When his mom saw him, her crying stopped. She struggled to stand, slumping in his arms as they embraced. She finally stepped back and looked at him. "Look at you, in those wet clothes. You're shivering!"

He didn't want to admit that he wasn't shivering from the cold. When the wave crashed into him, he thought his life was over. But it wasn't. Somehow he'd survived the riotous waves and the jutting rocks and other debris without drowning. And so had his mom and Ellie and Arlen Polk. If so many people he cared about could survive the flooded mine, maybe he could still hold on to hope of seeing others. He promised himself he would never give up on the idea of seeing his brother again. No matter how much time went by.

EPILOGUE

I

At the very moment Cooper gave into the ceaseless bombardment of water, when he resigned himself to death and possible interminable damnation, a set of strong, calloused hands grabbed him at the armpits and yanked him above the surface of the water. He choked and vomited and choked some more, his eyes blurred and unfocused. The water continued to rage at his side, carrying bobbing victims off like driftwood after a spring storm.

"You'll be fine, now. Better move, though, before that water gets worse."

Cooper felt too weak to stand. He remained on his hands and knees as he looked up at his savior. He recognized the man. At first his heart leapt with joy, as if this sudden meeting hadn't been a simple coincidence, but a long-awaited reunion. But these people didn't know him. And he only knew of them from his dreams.

"Come on, Papa. Let's go." The girl's voice was insistent, edged with desperation.

He remembered the surging water and how it carried Jane away from him, too fast for him to ever hope to catch up. "I couldn't save her. She's gone."

"No one's saved in the Underground."

"Papa--"

"But you saved me." He looked from Harold to his daughter, draped in a thin blanket and naked beneath, then back again. "Where's Benjamin?"

"How do you know about him?" Harold Barrow stepped in front of his daughter to shield her from Cooper.

Close by but out of sight, people screamed in pain, wounded mortally but fated to never succumb to their wounds.

"You're Harold. That's your daughter, Edwina. I've dreamed about you. The Blankenships wanted me to help you. Their spirits linger inside their house, unable to move on knowing they couldn't help you. They showed me--their spirits--showed me everything."

Harold looked at him sharply and took up a defensive stance.

"I know this sounds crazy--"

"You know the preacher?"

"I bought their house. My name's Ted Cooper. I've dreamed of your family coming to the Blankenships' house, how you listened for the sound of Eunice's organ and saw the water dipper sign. You gave the secret knock. They took you in and you waited for Benjamin to arrive."

The flowing water rose higher to breech the banks. Cooper stood and for a moment he thought he might black out. Harold grabbed him by the arm to steady him.

Harold leaned in as if for clarification, his posture relaxing. "You really knew them?"

"Papa, I don't trust him." Edwina looked at Cooper with disdain. Since the night of their capture, her hair had been shaved. Her eyes were cold and unwavering.

Cooper felt his eyes well with tears. "I've seen what you've had to endure. I'm so sorry."

"Oh, Mr. Cooper, it's not your fault," Harold said.

"I can help you. I know the way to the surface," Cooper said, certain that everything the Blankenships had revealed to him had led to this moment. "Where's Benjamin? We have to get moving."

"That's a story too long even for this place. We'd be happy though, if you know the way to daylight."

"Papa!"

"Hush, girl. We need all the help we can get. I haven't been this far from the stables in fifty years or more."

"It's this way." Cooper shouted into the old man's ear to be heard over the sound of the raging water.

Edwina was reluctant, her father less so, but they followed as Cooper navigated to higher tunnels, twisting away from their nightmare.

Cooper knew they were close when he came across the stones set at the corners of the low tunnel to mark the distance leading to his home. The Blankenships never intended for the markers to be used to travel back toward their house, but they served a vital and reaffirming role just the same as they came across one after another.

"This is it. Mr. Cooper, we're close, aren't we?"

Cooper pushed aside a few large boulders, exposing the hidden entryway to his basement. He climbed through the opening, helping the Barrow's one after the other.

"I haven't seen this place in so long. But it feels like yesterday." Harold held his daughter's hand as they shared a heartbreaking look.

"Oh, Papa--" The coldness left Edwina's face, and the transformation revealed the true depths of her beauty. She embraced her father, looking at Cooper over Harold's shoulder.

The skin of her cheek had begun to sag, showing blood and pus beneath. When her face creased into a smile, the skin began to separate along those lines.

"It's coming on. Oh, how I've prayed for this moment."

"We better go, Papa."

His embrace lingered several more seconds, then he held his daughter at arm's length. "I wish Benjamin were here, Sweets. He was a good man."

Edwina's happiness dimmed for a moment, but she blinked it back to full gleam. Decay flowed from her eyes in the wake of her tears, trailing gray runnels down her face like melted wax.

When Cooper turned to lead the way upstairs, a bitter gust of air slammed into him. In the stagnant basement heat, he nearly staggered, but the sensation quickly passed.

He whispered as he climbed the stairs, the Barrows a step behind, "You said I would help save them, but they saved me. I bet you knew all along, didn't you?"

A fading cold caress brushed his cheek, then was gone. He never felt the Blankenships' presence again. His deed was done. The Blankenships could finally rest.

"Sunlight, sweet Jesus, sunlight!" Harold cried out as they reached the ground floor landing. Cooper's home was in shambles after Ethan and his men tore through it, but no place had ever seemed more inviting. He guided them upstairs and through the hallway leading to the front door. Broken glass littered the floor. Dust billowed in the sunlight streaming through the windows.

"Papa, it's beautiful!"

Cooper turned to face the Barrows, but they didn't take note of him. Their failing faculties were focused on the warm glorious sunlight--a sight they'd been deprived of for over seventy years. Cooper rushed ahead and opened the front door, stepping aside to let them walk by.

By the time they reached the outside porch, Harold and his daughter could barely move. They were rotting. But their vigilance never flagged. Cooper sat on the edge of the porch and rested. Harold and Edwina walked down the steps, up the drive and around the bend near the street. He thought they wouldn't have lasted much farther, but Cooper never found any evidence that they hadn't made the end of the drive, and just kept walking.

Whenever he reflected back on that moment, that's how he pictured it. Father and daughter walking hand in hand down the road, occasionally exchanging smiles, every moment free.

II

The grave was small, but so was the boy. Jimmy just hoped it was deep enough. Louise had collapsed ten minutes ago, too weak in her advancing decay to lift her head. But Jimmy wouldn't rest until the job was finished. The boy had to be buried.

They had reached the surface in reasonably good shape, exiting from a tunnel hidden beneath a shed. They didn't know the property owner. Just as well.

They reached a side lot, and under a large oak, they began digging with large sticks. The ground was rocky and laced with knobby tree roots. It was hard, slow digging, but the surroundings would make a serene resting place. Once the hole was deep enough, Louise handed him the bundle, then collapsed.

Her eyes were still open and blinking. She gasped when he placed the wrapped blanket in the hole. He shoved in the loose soil, and though he felt the tremors as he cried, he didn't feel any tears. He could no longer cry, too far gone now. He could barely stand as he finished the burial.

His skin was dissolving and pus slicked what remained. His lungs tugged in his raspy chest. It was coming. He had to hurry.

They'd planned on returning Underground once the burial was complete, but they would never make it.

Jimmy fell to his knees next to Louise, then stretched out next to her. He placed an arm over her. Her skin was cold.

Either the sun was dimming with the coming night, or his vision was failing. Either way, he would never see it again. Each time he blinked he was surprised when his eyes opened again.

"Dwight."

"Hmm?"

"Your father. We should name him after your father."

"I like that. Thanks."

"I love you."

"Love you--"

III

Maybe it wasn't so bad. Wounds heal in time, don't they?

Thea Calder fell to her knees inches from a glass-still pond with clear water that revealed her face.

Sure she felt the sharp rocks crashing into her as she attempted to escape, but certainly it couldn't be this bad.

Blood flowed from her flowing locks across her forehead, drying in a morbid inverted crown. She touched the wounds on top of her head and pain shot through her eyes and her vision dimmed. She leaned closer to the water and wished she had her fancy brush and its matching comb.

She closed her eyes and tried to remember her escape. All she saw in her mind's eye were falling rocks, and brash sparks flashing across her vision when she was struck, and the walls, the very walls were coming in. And then she was running. Running blind and scared and with no hope of escaping. But then somehow she did. Somehow, she'd found a pathway to the living world, a world where people aged and wore down and eventually died.

She opened her eyes and her reflection had somehow worsened. The fugue of shock was lifting. Left exposed in its place was a lightning bolt gash in her right cheek. Her nose was also shattered, both flattened and swelling at the same time. And when she opened her mouth to scream, she discovered the splintered remains of her front teeth glaring back at her.

She shoved away from the pond. Her hand encountered a good sized rock. Hefting it as she stood, she threw it at the water and shattered the image. She turned, retracing her steps from where she'd emerged from the earth minutes earlier.

Ethan. Ethan will help me. No. Don't count on him. You can never trust a man to help.

But the Underground. She craved its curative touch with a growing intensity that bordered on lust.

Gray dust still billowed from the small hole in the ground when she crawled inside. It choked her, clinging to her lungs and clogging her sinuses. She closed her eyes and pushed deeper inside. Her heart was beating crazily and she tasted blood as she moved. But she was moving. And soon the healing would begin. And then she would never age again. Would never suffer the indecency of wounds or scars or pronounced leers from nosey neighbors. Because once she was Underground, she would never leave ever again. With or without Ethan.

After several minutes, her grasping fingers encountered a solid wall of tumbled in stone. She began to panic as she searched for an opening.

There wasn't one.

No. No, not now.

She couldn't go this way.

She knew of other tunnels.

But she could never face the world above.

What if someone sees me?

She fell to the floor and begged the Underground to stretch its powers to reach her. She sat like that for a long time. Waiting, feeling phantom healing tingles that she quickly dismissed. Her tears flowed. Long after the dust settled, her tears flowed.

IV

It felt like Ethan was back in the Everglades, slipping in and out of consciousness. The weight bearing down on his chest was reminiscent of the pressure from his wounds inflicted by those damnable Seminoles. The poisonous infection running riot throughout his system had swollen his tissue, making him nearly choke on his own blood and phlegm; that's how he felt now, but in this case, the weight on his chest was countless tons of rock.

He inventoried his senses. He couldn't see, but his years belowground accustomed him to the heft of this sensation. The sounds of rocks grating, falling, finding a place to settle for the coming millennia came from all directions.

Otherwise, he could blink, wiggle his nose, lower his bottom lip. His left index finger budged a fraction of an inch when he tried with all his might to move... anything. Boulders sandwiched his body practically flat. His limbs ached dully, but he was helpless to do anything about it.

This was hell. No doubt. He closed his eyes, let his mind drift. It didn't take long for his thoughts to coalesce, and as they did, they found a focal point. Thea.

Thea, Thea, my lovely Thea. He would never see her again.

The stones pinning him shifted, crying like a lonesome animal searching for one of its kind. His bones crumbled under the weight, compression fractures networking through his limbs, his chest. He'd never felt a more intense pain. In all the world, there had never been a deeper wound. Never in existence had such a hapless soul been less able to simply let go of the mortal coil.

The damned Underground.

Tears formed at the corners of his eyes, but they didn't fall. Instead, they were absorbed into the crusted rock and dust pressed into his skin.

If I cry long enough, will my tears dissolve these stones, freeing me?

He opened his eyes to blink, but he never finished the task. What he saw kept his eyes open and once open, they remained.

The shifting stones revealed a two inch shaft through the innumerable layers above him. Two inches opened to sunny daylight. Motes of fine debris filtered down into the hole, but he didn't blink. He couldn't take his eyes off the sight of the sun above him. He could never look away. Never was going to be a long time, indeed.

Twelve Years Later

"Hold still."

Jacob frowned as his mom fussed with his collar.

"It's fine, Mom. Straight as an arrow."

A whirl of gray streaked the hair over her left brow. Her face was tan from working around the farm. She smiled up at him.

"I can't have you looking disheveled. It's a big day, you know."

Through the kitchen window he could see their guests dressed in the their finest Sunday attire. It seemed like everyone in Coal Hollow was in attendance, and certainly most of the town had been invited. They stood on either side of an aisle leading to the edge of the peach orchard.

Ellie stood under a white lattice archway, holding a bouquet of flowers. He remembered that day so many years ago, the day of her brother's funeral. Her biggest concern had been trying to find the most beautiful wild flowers to pick for his mom.

Ellie's father never surfaced after the incidents in the Underground. On a larger scale, an official story was created to explain the loss of twenty-two residents of Coal Hollow. Since Jimmy's body was never recovered (at least in the official story), the devastating loss was easily explained away as a tragic accident. The story described a search party valiantly combing the abandoned mines for any trace of one of their own. How inopportune for a cave wall to collapse during their searching and an underground lake to sweep them away.

After escaping the Underground, and with no evidence that her father survived, the Fowler's had taken Ellie in for good.

"Are you ready?"

"Just a minute, Mom."

He took a deep breath, trying to gather himself. The last time he could remember such stress was on the beaches of Guadalcanal. The white sands washed red with American blood, the air thick with smoke from weeks of artillery bombardment. He'd seen bloodshed before, but this battle had changed his friends. Their vengeance had turned them into something unrecognizable, but still somehow all too familiar. Once the momentum turned in their favor, they scourged one tunnel after another with flame throwers at close range, and when their enemies still wouldn't submit, they would enter the dark burrows with bared bayonets, killing anything that moved. They'd become monsters. Jacob had already seen too many monsters. He would never again raise his weapon.

"Where's Cooper?"

"He's by the orchard, right where we should be, I might add."

Even as Jacob became a man and soldier, even later when his life took a decidedly unexpected turn, he missed Jimmy. He wished he was here by his side, jabbing him with funny barbs, but ultimately putting everything in perspective. Simply thinking about his brother tended to put his mind at ease, and right now was no exception.

He could do this. When he exhaled a deep breath, it came as a long, calm gust of air.

"Okay. So everything's ready?"

"Absolutely." She offered her arm. They hooked arms and walked out the back door.

Jacob leaned over and whispered, "So, you don't think it's weird, us walking the aisle together?"

"I wouldn't have it any other way."

He reminded himself to walk as slow as reasonably possible. He took in the guests as they walked, trying to smile and make eye contact. People sighed and a polite round of applause greeted them.

"See, everything's perfect."

Many of the faces in the crowd were new to Jacob--spouses of Coal Hollow residents he had never met, or people with whom he had grown up but no longer recognized after being away for so long. A few faces never changed, though.

Arlen Polk stood at the end of an aisle. Now an old man, a spark lit his eye that showed his wits only grew stronger with the years. Shortly after surfacing from the Underground, he opened the grain elevator just outside of town. After his elevator enterprise took off like gangbusters, he imported stone masons from Chicago and opened a school to teach select local boys their skills. Though still in its infancy, the school was gaining a national reputation, while keeping quality jobs in town. Arlen had an uncanny knack for business. Some people claimed his higher functioning resulted from injuries he received during the search party accident. Some people claimed he had been touched by God. Some other's knew the reason, and they kept his secret.

At the end of the aisle a small gathering: Ellie, Hank Calder leaning on his walking cane, Cooper.

Everyone counted Cooper as one of the victims of the mine disaster. Jacob's mother only learned of his survival when he showed up at her door a year ago, his beard now mostly gray, but his eyes warm and inviting. At the time, Jacob was finishing up his studies and only learned of the reunion through his mother's weekly letters. Through the weeks, Jacob saw their relationship evolve.

"Nervous?" his mom asked in a whisper.

"A little. You?"

"No. Not when I'm this happy."

Jacob handed his mother over to Cooper and he took his place under the arching flowers, facing the crowd. His collar felt tight on his neck, but he didn't allow it to choke back his words as he began the wedding ceremony.

NEWSLETTER

I have many projects that will come to fruition over the next year. To keep up to date on my release dates, and other exciting news, sign up for my newsletter.

Send me an email at glenkrisch@gmail.com. Use "newsletter" for a subject line, and indicate your preferred ebook format. I love to give away free books, including previews for unreleased works.

GLEN R. KRISCH

BOOKS BY GLEN KRISCH

NOVELS:

The Nightmare Within
Where Darkness Dwells
Nothing Lasting (forthcoming)
Arkadium Rising: Brother's Keeper, Book 1 (forthcoming)

2-IN-1 NOVELS:

Twice as Dark, Two Novels of Horror
(omnibus edition containing *Where Darkness Dwells* and *The Nightmare Within*)

NOVELLAS

Loss, a paranormal thriller
Brother's Keeper, a post-apocalyptic novella

COLLECTIONS

Commitment and Other Tales of Madness
Through the Eyes of Strays (from Dog Horn Publishing)

ABOUT THE AUTHOR

Glen Krisch has written three novels: *The Nightmare Within*, *Where Darkness Dwells*, and *Nothing Lasting*, as well as the novellas *Brother's Keeper* and *Loss*. His short fiction has appeared in publications across three continents for the last decade.

He is also an editor for Morrigan Books. As a freelance editor, he has worked on books by Tim Lebbon and Lawrence Block, among others.

Besides writing and reading, his interests include his family, simple living, and ultra running.

He enjoys talking to his readers. Feel free to stop by his website to see what he's up to: **www.glenkrisch.wordpress.com**

Made in the USA
San Bernardino, CA
03 August 2013